SILENCE
OF THE
SOLERI

ALSO BY MICHAEL JOHNSTON

Soleri

SILENCE
OF THE
SOLERI

MICHAEL
JOHNSTON

TOR

A TOM DOHERTY ASSOCIATES BOOK
NEW YORK

SILENCE OF THE SOLERI

Copyright © 2021 by Michael Johnston

Map by Michael Johnston

A Tor Book
Published by Tom Doherty Associates
120 Broadway
New York, NY 10271

www.tor-forge.com

Tor® is a registered trademark of Macmillan Publishing Group, LLC.

The Library of Congress Cataloging-in-Publication Data is available upon request.

ISBN 978-0-7653-8775-2 (hardcover)
ISBN 978-0-7653-8776-9 (ebook)

Our books may be purchased in bulk for promotional, educational, or business use. Please contact your local bookseller or the Macmillan Corporate and Premium Sales Department at 1-800-221-7945, extension 5442, or by email at MacmillanSpecialMarkets@macmillan.com.

First Edition: February 2021

Printed in the United States of America

0 9 8 7 6 5 4 3 2 1

For Mel and Mattie

THE
SOLERI
EMPIRE

Rifka

Kingdom of
Rachis

Kingdom of
Feren

THE FEREN RIFT VALLEY

Catal

THE SHAMBLES

THE
DROMUS

Kingdom of
Harkana

Solus

Harwen

Kingdom of
Sola

Blackrock

THE WYRRE

Gate of
Coronel

Desouk

THE
CRESSEL
SEA

Scargill

You reach a moment in life when, among the people you have known, the dead outnumber the living.

And the mind refuses to accept more faces, more expressions: on every new face you encounter, it prints the old forms, for each one it finds the suitable mask.

—Italo Calvino, *Invisible Cities*

SILENCE
OF THE
SOLERI

≩ LIFELESS THINGS ≦

They were statues, but the darkness gave them life. The shadows lent movement to their black eyes, and the gloom made their stone lips grimace.

Nollin Odine half expected to feel the warmth of human flesh when he touched one of the charred figures, but the surface was cold and lifeless. Yet there *was* life within it. A moment ago, he'd heard a voice cry out to him from within the burnt effigy.

It was a statue, yet somehow it was *not* a statue.

"What are you?" he asked. "And what do you want from me?"

See what has not yet been seen. The words echoed in his thoughts.

A dim light shone from somewhere high above, but it did little to illuminate the chamber. Still, he searched, looking for this thing he had not seen, uncertain of what he might find. When Noll first came upon the hidden palace, he arrived with Sarra Amunet and they discovered the twelve burnt figures. The Soleri were assumed dead. Sarra had thought that was the end of it. Hence, her scribe had uncorked a drink. He produced a cup and offered it to Noll. The wine held poison and he drank it.

Secrets are power.

Sarra Amunet whispered those words as the venom took hold of Noll. He died but he *was not* dead, and there *was* something in the chamber, some new mystery that had yet to be unearthed.

He found it in the dust or, rather, he found a place where there was no dust. In fact, there were twelve such places. In the grand solar, he stumbled upon twelve patches of stone where the rock was scorched black and even the dust did not settle. Twelve voids, the shadows of the ones who'd stood against the Soleri. Noll knew what stood before him. These were the creatures who pursued the twelve, the ones who wielded a flame as hot as the sun, or so he guessed. This was all just speculation. He had no way to know the truth. Hence, he turned once more to the statues.

"Who were these creatures and where did they go?"

The mouths of stone did not move, but the words of the twelve echoed in his thoughts.

Return us to Solus.

"Why?"

To witness the end.

THE SHATTERED VISAGE

1

Shot like an arrow, Rennon Hark-Wadi bolted from the darkness. He stumbled out of the Hollows and onto the streets of Solus. The flames were behind him, or so he thought. Ren had expected to see the sun when he left the underground passages of the city, but smoke filled the sky. It was everywhere, in the air and in his nose. The wide boulevards and sprawling plazas of the city were choked with it, and there were men and women charging in every direction. Something was amiss. There was panic in the streets, but Ren had other concerns. They were coming up the stairs at that very moment. "Are we all here?" he called to the others.

There were seven of them. Seven former ransoms of the empire. A few grunted in reply.

Twelve escaped the burnt ruins of the priory, their former home, their prison. *Twelve.*

Or was it more? He didn't know. They'd stumbled through fire, met bandits, and soldiers too. *I saved more lives than I lost,* he thought, if only to reassure himself that he'd done some good—that all of this had in fact been worth it. Ren had gone looking for Tye Sirra, and he'd found her in the flaming ruins of the priory and led her and the others out of the Hollows and into the crowded boulevards of the empire's capital.

"Ren," said Tye, interrupting his thoughts as she came running up the stairs. "Give me your hand."

He offered it, absently. He was still thinking about the priory, and the cell where he'd spent his youth.

"You're squeezing my bones apart." Tye shook loose his grip almost as quickly as she'd taken it.

Ren hadn't noticed what his fingers were doing, but his hand felt empty when she pushed it away. His palm was checkered with soot and grease. Dried blood drew circles around the tips of his fingers. "I hadn't meant—"

"To mash my fingers?"

"Something like that," he said, too tired to think of any other reply, too out of breath to even form a sentence. "Seven," he said. "We've got seven—is that the number?"

"How in Mithra's name should I know?" Tye asked, frank as always. Even in their exhaustion, she hadn't lost an ounce of her fire. Ren was glad to hear it, happy to have his friend back at his side.

They were the first ones out of the Hollows, but not the last.

Kollen Pisk emerged from the shadows. Like some beast born out of darkness, he staggered toward them, hair singed, skin caked in ash, clothes blackened with soot.

"Where in Horu's eight hells am I?" Kollen asked. "I thought I'd left the fires."

"There's no leaving them," said Tye, "so just get yourself out of the way."

Adin Fahran was coming up behind Kollen and he looked to be in worse shape. His hands were burned, the skin black and blistering. He waved them in the air, trying in vain to soothe the hurt.

"C'mon, old friend. We're almost there," said Ren, glancing warily at the crowds, the city guard. *Are they looking for us?* he wondered. *Do they even know we're alive?*

Lazlo Dank blundered into Ren and Adin, nearly toppling all three of them. Laz was lost, confused, and out of breath. The boy had no shirt. The flames had taken it from him. They'd stolen his hair as well. He was in shock, lost, too baffled to even speak. He was only a child after all. Laz had not yet reached his tenth year, or maybe even his ninth. Ren held Adin with one arm and Laz with the other. He cupped Tye's shoulder as Carr Bergen lurched over the threshold. He carried Curst Falkirk, the youngest among them. Only six or seven, Curst had the look of death upon him, but when Carr set him down the young boy ran to Adin. They were both Ferens. Perhaps that was why Curst clung to Adin's leg, huddling there, immovable, as if he'd holed himself up in some tower and planned on never leaving it.

"Seven," said Ren. "That's it. Seven." They were the last survivors of the Priory of Tolemy.

An arrow whistled through the air and Ren's attention was drawn once more to the crowds. "There're soldiers," said Ren. "We need to move." There was good reason for them to get out of the soldiers' path. The ransoms were the property of the empire. Only Ren and Adin were freemen. The rest were tributes. They were the emperor's possessions and those soldiers might be coming for them. If captured, they would be punished, a foot cut off or maybe even a hand. Either way, they'd end up back in a cell, minus a limb or two.

"Go!" Ren cried, but his call was met only with confusion.

"Which way?" Tye asked.

"Away . . . from the flames," Ren said, still a little shaken, not yet focused. "Oren said the blaze started in the Antechamber of the Ray, which is at the city's core."

"Away from the flames?" Kollen asked. "How"—he waved his hand in a circle—"do we know which *way* that is?"

"The smoke's everywhere and the soldiers too," said Carr, stating the obvious and taking a knock on the head from Kollen for doing it.

Curst remained at Adin's side, Laz paced, pinching his nose to keep out the smoke. "I want to go home," he chanted, but Ren didn't know which home he meant. The priory was destroyed and the boy was a long way from his father's keep in Rachis.

A man in black leather brushed past Ren.

The soldiers had arrived.

"So much for our escape," said Kollen. "What now?"

Everyone looked to Ren. He was the one who'd fathered this endeavor. Although he had not claimed leadership, the ransoms looked to him for it. Their eyes begged. They pleaded for answers he didn't have. He was not their leader, but he *had* led them. It was too late to shirk that duty. He had assumed some tacit responsibility for the group when he led them out of the priory. It was time to see things to their end and find a way out of this city.

A pair of fighting men bolted past them. *Who's at war?* Ren studied the approaching soldiers. *Who's doing the chasing and who is the chased?* He pulled Tye close to him, taking her out of one soldier's path just as he sidestepped another. In the priory, he'd always been the one who protected Tye. He knew her secret. She was a young girl hidden among the priory boys. Protecting her was a hard habit to lose.

"I can take care of myself," she said, pushing him away and nearly stumbling into another soldier. A fourth man appeared. This one wore pale-red armor and there were others at his side, all of them similarly clad.

"What is this?" asked Tye.

"Armies," said Kollen. "We need to fly."

"He's right," said Ren, "we should—"

A spear tore through Laz's chest. The boy hit the cobblestones and his body split open like a crumpled gourd, ribs and viscera tangled about the wooden shaft. At the sight of it, at the sheer terror of what stood before them, Tye screwed her eyes shut. Curst buried his face in Adin's belly, but Ren did not flinch. *This is the price of my indecision.*

There were six of them now.

Ren wondered if there would soon be five.

The soldiers had arrived, but this time he got a good look at them. Their armor was boiled and black and each chest piece bore the eld-horn symbol. He saw the burnt skin, the long hair, and grizzled beards.

"You're Harkan." Ren nearly choked on the words.

A flood of soldiers surrounded him.

"Harkan," Ren said it again, louder this time.

"We're not *just* Harkan," said one man. "We're the god's damned kingsguard."

The soldier leapt past Ren, pulled the spear from Laz's chest, and launched it into the smoke. Laz's whole body stiffened. Mercifully, those were his last movements.

"What are you doing?" Ren asked, but the soldier was already gone. The men in black were forming lines, lifting shields.

Why is the Harkan kingsguard in Solus? Did my father summon them before his death? That was the most likely answer. They'd come to aid one Hark-Wadi, but had instead found the other, the son instead of the father. They just didn't know it yet. The men paid him no notice, but he knew these soldiers. They called themselves the black shields, the king's chosen men. *My men,* thought Ren.

"These are Harkan soldiers," he said, shaking Tye, tugging at Kollen's sleeve. "They can help us."

"Then make them," said Tye, "before they cut us to pieces."

"Or stomp us to death," Kollen said as he dashed out of one soldier's path and nearly ran into another.

Ren reached for the eld horn. Perhaps, if he held it up, the soldiers would recognize it. The horn was a symbol of the king of the Harkans, but he hadn't carved it into a proper ceremonial blade. It looked like nothing more than a mud-slathered stick. Ren knew as much, so he un-sheathed his father's dagger. Every king wielded the sacred blade, and he wore the silver ring of his father. He hoped the soldiers would take notice, but the smoke made it difficult for Ren to see his own hand, let alone the ring that sat upon it.

"How do I get their attention?" Ren asked, eyes darting from Tye to Carr to Kollen and back.

No one answered, but they did act. Tye shouted in one man's face. Carr tried it and the soldier jabbed him with an elbow, knocking the boy to his knees. The Harkans were engaged in some sort of retreat.

"In a moment they'll be gone," Tye cried, frantic.

"Some of you must know me!" Ren poured the last of his strength into his voice. "Were any of you in the Shambles or on the road to Harwen?" On that same road, Arko, the former king, named Ren the heir of Harkana and gave him the knife. A number of soldiers in the kingsguard saw him do it, so Ren raised the blade a bit higher. "Do any of you know the king's iron? Do you recognize me?" He said it again, but no one stopped.

"For fuck's sake, you fools," cried Kollen, "don't any of you know your king's son?" Kollen planted his shoulder squarely in the center of a Harkan soldier's chest plate. Ren followed suit, throwing himself at one of the men, forcing him to stop. Tye tried it out, but was knocked to the ground. Her head hit the stones, but her eyes were still open, lips curled into a blood-soaked grin.

"I'm the son of Arko," Ren said.

The soldiers were at last forced to listen to him. The black shields had nothing else to do. Ren and the other ransoms had blocked half the street. In a moment, he guessed the soldiers would either lop off his head or raise him up on their shoulders—either seemed likely.

"Out of our way," said the man who'd ripped the spear from Laz's chest. His sword teetered a hair's width from Ren's chin.

Perhaps I will lose my head.

But Ren was defiant, he would not budge and neither would Kollen. Tye had gotten to her feet and was bustling about, taking the younger ransoms and making certain they weren't lost among the soldiers.

"Look at his face," Kollen shouted. "Some of you must know it!"

"I am the son of Arko," Ren cried out. "I met him in the Shambles and on the road to Harwen!"

There were more men, swarming all around them and more soldiers in the distance, but none of them recognized him. Honestly, he feared only a handful could see his face. He pushed the sword aside and delved into the crowd, the dagger held high. "Does anyone know this blade? Was anyone there when I met the king?"

A scuffle emerged, one man pushing his way through the others, moving toward Ren at a furious pace. He ripped the dagger from Ren's grip.

"Where did you get this?" he asked.

"My father, he—"

"He what? He gave you this?" the man asked, but he did not wait for an answer. "Does anyone know this boy?" he shouted in the stentorian tones of a captain. "Has anyone seen him? Were you there with our king?" Clearly the man had heard Ren's words and was testing them.

There were a few shrugs. More than one man stood on his toes to get a better look at Ren, but there was smoke in the air and the views were all cut through with spearheads and the tips of shields. The men simply could not see him, not enough of him at least. Perhaps, given a moment, one of them might have recognized him, but time was in short supply.

"I know this blade," said the man who'd taken the dagger from Ren, "but I don't know you. None of my men know you. I'm Gneuss, the king's second and the highest-ranking captain in the company. We're the black shields, and you're either the heir of Harkana or some damned thief."

The captain had only one eye. A mound of scar tissue sheathed the other one, and he wore no patch to conceal the injury. *Curious,* Ren thought. *This is a hard man.* A bit of iron would not convince him that Ren was heir to the kingdom of Harkana. He opened his mouth to speak, but a pair of arrows fluttered past Gneuss's helm, truncating their conversation. The captain shouted orders to the men, urging them to march. They formed ranks, but their escape was once more arrested.

"I'm Edric. You all know me." A young man blocked the way. "I saw that boy in the Shambles. I kneeled to him. Yes, and I was there when the king slipped that dagger in his hand." Edric was tall and his armor was torn. He was a bit thin for a fighting man, but he still had the look of a Harkan, his skin burnt like leather, teeth ground smooth, eyes glistening.

His words drew others.

"Are you certain?" Gneuss asked, his one eye looking askance. For him, this was all a distraction, a hiccup in his escape plan, or so Ren guessed. He could see the distrust in Gneuss's eye, hear the irritation in his voice.

Edric took Ren by the chin, turning his head right and left, lifting it. "It's the same damned boy. Floppy hair and big dumb eyes, built just like the father. He's the one."

Gneuss swallowed, clearly disappointed at the man's conclusion. "Too bad."

"Why?" Ren asked.

"Look," said Gneuss.

Soldiers emerged from the smoke, thousands upon thousands of them.

Men with tall shields brandished spears of improbable length. On rooftops, archers nocked arrows. Everywhere, men readied themselves for the attack.

Gneuss patted Ren's shoulder. "See what I mean, son of Arko? You've found your men and now you're going to die with them."

≡2≡

The walls of the Soleri throne room were as thick as they were tall, impenetrable to attack, yet somehow vulnerable to the crack of iron breaking upon armor.

"What's that?" Sarra Amunet asked. She'd spent the better part of an hour bandaging Ott's wounds, making a splint for her son's injured leg and wrapping his damaged hand with cloth torn from her dress. A broken spear would serve as his crutch.

"A battle," Ott answered. "There's no mistaking the sound."

"There isn't," said Sarra, the disappointment clear in her voice. She'd thought the fight was done. After all, the Protector, Amen Saad, was dead, as were most of his generals. And Arko Hark-Wadi—the man who had been both the Ray of the Sun and her husband—was equally lifeless.

"Can you walk?" she asked.

"Well enough."

She helped Ott to his feet, but he stumbled and nearly fell when he took his first step.

"I think not," she said, "but I'll take you with me anyway. There're only ghosts here and I can't stand the idea of leaving you alone with them." Admittedly, the dead did outnumber the living in the throne room of the Soleri. The corpses of a dozen priests littered the floor, the blood still fresh, the eyes open. The Protector's body had not yet gone cold. The whole room stunk of blood and the dank odor of perspiration, and just to make things worse, Suten Anu's remains were gray and bloated and stinking wildly of decay. The throne was burned, as were many of the furnishings. Soot covered everything and the wind howled through the chamber like some phantom determined to give life to a place that was utterly devoid of it.

Only the dust stirred. Gray motes spiraled about their sandals as the pair made their way toward a slender door Sarra had spied while she was bandaging Ott's leg. This was not the ceremonial entryway of the throne room, the gate through which Amen Saad had come with Sarra to see the emperor and instead found his death. No, this was a smaller door, unexceptional save for the dim slivers of light that limned its edges. That pale glow could mean only one thing: This door led to the sun. In all likelihood, it would take them to gardens of the Empyreal Domain. Sarra had no interest in taking the long way out of the throne room. That one led through the ritual corridor and the Hall of Histories. She'd lose an hour or more if she followed that passage, but there was no need to retrace the sacred way. Sarra hit the small door and it gave way. She had no idea where she was going, not really. She hoped to see the sun, but clouds blocked it. Smoke rose in the distance, and shouts bounded over the Shroud Wall.

"The battle must be close," she said. "But who's fighting it? What battle rages in my city?"

Ott gave no reply.

The two of them walked, Sarra half carrying him as they stumbled onto a well-trimmed sward. Soft grass caressed her feet, tickling at her toes as it gathered around the tongs of her sandals. She stopped. There was no grass in Sola—none that lived.

Abruptly, Sarra noticed that she was not alone. Around her, the humble servants of the Kiltet went about their work. With slender blades, they nipped at each piece of grass, shaped each flower petal. They did not look up. Not one of them attempted to meet Sarra's gaze. She'd come from the domain of the gods, which meant they were her servants. The men and women of the Kiltet went back to their garden work and Sarra stopped to take note of what surrounded them.

Beauty accosted her from every direction. Sinuous paths meandered into shadowy grottos. Statues of gold and silver poked unexpectedly from leafy vales. There were wonders here. She glimpsed the faint outlines of what she guessed were the Shadow Gardens. The sun itself drew this maze of changing paths. It gave her pause. Sarra was moving slowly, taking it all in. Up ahead, there were strange fountains where figures emerged from the water, their bronze limbs animated by some unseen mechanism, arms and legs lifting and falling in elaborately choreographed motions. She'd read of this place on countless occasions. Somewhere, there was said to be a grotto where the statues were made of light and nothing more, their forms materializing out of the reflections of the grotto's polished walls. The beauty of these gardens could tease the eyes for eternity. This was the domain of the Soleri.

If only I had time to look at it.

War had come to the city of the gods.

Amen Saad's bloody handprint still clung to her robe, and the boy's last breath had barely escaped his lips. She'd thought the fight was over when she defeated the Protector and claimed the mantle of the First Ray, but unrest echoed in the city. War rattled the city streets and Sarra needed to see it, so she hurried through the gardens, heedless of what she crushed or bent. Her sandals mashed clusters of autumn sage, and she trampled the delicate nibs of blue flax and red hyssop. She paid them little or no notice. Sarra had nearly lost her life that morning. She'd risked everything to put Amen Saad to rest and the city to heel. Her work was done.

So why is there turmoil in Solus?

She stumbled onto a pebbled trail, scattering stones as she hurried sidelong across the curving path. Up ahead, smoke gathered at the rim of the Shroud Wall.

The blaze was Amen's doing. He'd sealed the doors of the Antechamber and set fire to the former Ray of the Sun, putting Arko Hark-Wadi to the old test, Mithra's Flame. Unfortunately, Amen Saad had lit a torch he could not snuff. The fires consumed half the Waset, and the smoke from the blaze still lingered at the wall, hanging there like some great cloud trapped upon a mountain's summit.

"Is it the fires?" asked Ott. "Maybe they've caused the commotion?"

Sarra wrinkled her lip. "No, this isn't about Arko or the fire that followed his death. I doubt a single tear was shed for the man." Sarra had wanted to shed one and perhaps she had, but she doubted any citizen of Solus had done the same. "No," she said. "This is no protest. The people wanted him dead; they cheered at the flames."

Sarra stumbled backward when the smoke came tumbling over the wall like some great gray waterfall.

"I see a stair," said Ott. He motioned to it with his good arm, his broken finger raised to indicate a spiraling set of stones.

Sarra choked down an apology when she saw him tremble, when he screwed his eyes shut in pain. She wanted to explain why she had not been able to beg for Ott's release when he was a captive of the former Protector, but the words died on her lips. She'd played a delicate game and won, but her son had been caught somewhere in the middle of it all.

The fingers on his right hand were broken, jumbled together like sticks tossed haphazardly in a pile.

"Stay here," she said. "You can't climb and I need to have a look at the city."

Ott shook his head, his teeth clenched in pain. "You're not leaving me, Mother."

Sarra didn't bother to argue. He was her son; he shared her curiosity.

They scaled the winding stair, and when Sarra reached the first wall walk she braced Ott against the stones with as much care as was possible.

"Are you all right?" she asked, fearful of the answer.

"I'm fine."

"You are anything but fine, but I need to get a look at the city. Give me a moment," she said, pacing, looking for a window. "Where're the arrow loops?" she murmured. "There must be some hole in this wall."

As Sarra circled the wall walk, Ott fell to his ass with an uneasy thump.

"I don't think I can stay here for very long," he said. The smoke had covered a good portion of the wall and was starting to settle on the path.

"Where are the windows?" she asked, circling the walkway, her eyes at last alighting upon a square of amber no larger than her head. Sarra pushed her fist through it and the panel flew from its moorings, opening up a window onto the city.

Outside, in the streets, two armies clashed. One was small but still formidable, their armor black. She knew them well enough, but the second she did not recognize, not fully. She'd seen them in the past, in a parade of one sort or another. They were clad in bronze mail, but much of it was painted red. It was a pale color, a shade the military houses often favored.

"Tell me what you see," said Ott as he tore a bit of cloth from his robe and covered his mouth.

She described the soldiers and their livery.

"The red armor," Ott said, "tell me about it."

"It's madder or carmine, and there's a symbol on the shields, a serpent coiled into a labyrinth of some sort."

Ott was uncharacteristically quiet, the gray smoke gathering about him.

"What is it?" she asked. "What do you know?"

"I can't be certain, but I saw that symbol once before, on some guards."

"Dressed in red?"

"All of them."

"Where?"

Ott heaved a bitter sigh, eyes fixed on his broken hand. "I saw them in the tower of the Protector, the great Citadel of Solus," he said, his tone full of mockery. "In that damned cell where they held me."

"I thought as much," Sarra said. Then she too was quiet. Once more, Sarra was sorry she'd allowed her foes to take and torture him, sorry her plans had overshadowed the needs of her son. "I . . ." Sarra came up short for the second time. "Who were these men, did they say their names?"

"No names. There was one who came frequently, an elderly man . . . I think. He wore a veil. I could not see his face, but he questioned me often enough. He asked about you and about my true father. He knew I was Arko's son. He asked how I was kept hidden all these years. He wanted to know everything. I'm sorry . . ." Ott stuttered a bit, his broken fingers twitching. "My secret is revealed."

Sarra knew as much. Amen Saad had already boasted of the discovery. The house of Saad knew that Ott was the trueborn son of Sarra and Arko, the heir to Harkana's throne. Arko's bastard, Ren, had gone to the priory in Ott's place without even knowing that he was not the king's legitimate son. To this day, he was ignorant of the truth, or so she guessed.

"These were not Amen's men?" she asked.

"No," said Ott, "but they were acquaintances. The elderly man was in command of the soldiers. In fact, it seemed as if he were in charge of Amen, as if *he* were the one controlling the whole thing."

At that, Sarra's head jerked around. She'd thought that Amen Saad had acted alone, that his ambitions belonged to no one else, that he alone had been her foe.

I was wrong.

Amen Saad had a master. This veiled man. Sarra had already guessed at his identity, but she needed to be certain of it.

"I must go into the city, Ott. I have to know what is happening in those streets. The Protector's Army is stationed well outside of Solus; this is not their fight. These men in red belong to a private army and they've taken it upon themselves to wage a war within my city, usurping my power as well as my position." She needed to take charge of the situation. She was the First Ray of the Sun, the mouth of the god. She was the voice of an emperor that did not even exist, which meant that she was in fact the emperor and this was in fact *her* city.

The smoke engulfed the walk as Sarra lifted Ott to his feet. They blundered down the winding stair. "I must go," she said as they stumbled past the stair and back through the gardens. "I'll exit through the ceremonial arch. I am Ray and I must announce myself to the city."

"And me?" Ott asked.

"Stay here until we can find a way to disguise you. The House of Saad took you from me once. I won't let it happen again. We must be cautious, circumspect in every fashion," she said, though she knew that was not the whole truth. *Stay here,* she thought, *so I know you are out of harm's way.* Sarra did not want to worry over Ott. She wanted to file him away somewhere safe where no one could reach him.

"There are things you can do in the archives of the Soleri," she continued. "We still don't know the whole truth about how we found those statues in the Shambles. That boy—the young priest, Nollin—led us there. I'm certain of it. He had some agenda, and it had something to do with the twelve. In the archives of the Soleri, there must be some account of the children of Mithra-Sol, the sons of Re and Pyras. Learn what you can. Stay here, Ott. Worry over these matters."

She gave him no chance to respond. Sarra simply plowed through the fields of delicate blossoms, trying to wipe Amen Saad's blood from her robe. It would look terribly suspicious were she to emerge from the domain with a bloody handprint on her sleeve. She hid it as best she could, but some hint of the mark remained and it made her recall the boy's last moments. When she'd stood above Amen and told him she was emperor, she'd thought that was the end of it. Sarra had won, but the fighting in the streets told a new and different story.

Her struggles had just begun.

₹3₹

In the narrow streets of Solus, the soldiers in red made their assault on the Harkan kingsguard, hurling spears, pressing forward, arrows raining down from every direction. The soldiers in black did their best to arrest the charge of the red army. Shield pressed shield. Shoulders butted. Iron screamed against bronze. The kingsguard fought back against their attackers, but there were simply too many soldiers in red and not enough in black. Hands flailed and shields crumpled.

"We're digging in our heels," said Gneuss. He huddled alongside Ren, keeping his head low. "But we can't hold out for long. Sooner or later these sons of bitches are going to break through our wall. So when the boys in red make their push, we're going to give them a surprise. They'll expect us to hit back. Instead, we'll retreat into that open space, the one up there," he said, pointing to the place where the street emptied out into a wide plaza. "It'll look like chaos when we hit the clearing." Gneuss wrapped his fingers around the neckline of Ren's tunic. "They'll expect us to fan out like a bunch of fools, but we're going to do the opposite. The men'll draw in close and form a wedge. That second part'll happen quickly, stay near."

"I wasn't thinking of running," said Ren. He'd found his men, but he'd lost sight of the ransoms. "Have you seen my friends?"

Gneuss set his jaw. "They're safe with the kingsguard."

Ren didn't think any of them were safe. They'd never be safe in this city. The streets were a jumble of men and armor and the fighting was all around him.

The soldiers in red thrust out their spears and pushed forward. They wedged one shield against the next, forming a makeshift wall of red and bronze, and they used it to drive back the Harkans. The red army advanced, beating some terrible drum. From the sound of it, Ren guessed the thing must be as wide around as a man was tall. And worse still, at intervals, a clarion call punctuated the drumbeat. The two sounded in patterns, part of a system, he presumed, one that directed the soldiers to attack or pause, to loose arrows or toss spears.

An ill feeling formed in Ren's stomach, or maybe it had never left him. He'd thought the underground was congested, but the streets here were packed even more tightly. He could barely breathe, barely move. He did not walk but was carried by the retreat.

"Tye!" Ren cried. He was still worried about his friends, concerned about them getting lost in this crowd or taking a spear through the chest. He put his hands on a pair of shoulders and lifted himself above the bustle. He struggled to catch sight of Tye or one of the others, but the streets were a blur of men and metal, smoke and ash. An arrow nearly pierced Ren's neck. He'd made a target of himself and it was all for nothing. In the commotion, he couldn't tell a soldier from a ransom, and Tye was shorter than most of the fighting men.

"Stop wiggling around," said Gneuss. "I've lost one king today and I don't intend to lose another."

So they know, thought Ren. *They know my father is dead.* Arko Hark-Wadi had perished in the fire set by Amen Saad.

"Stay back, and for Mithra's sake, stay down," said Gneuss, concern overwhelming his voice. It was clear that he wanted to protect the heir to the throne, but Ren heard something else in his words. They were tinged with regret, and he guessed it was because Gneuss had failed to save Ren's father. Perhaps he was a friend of the king. Ren didn't know. He understood almost nothing about his kingdom. He didn't even know why the black shields were in Solus, not for certain.

"Now!" Gneuss cried, his voice growing distant. In the flurry of motion that followed his command, Ren and the captain were separated. There was simply too much pushing and shoving for any one person to stand in place for much longer than the span of a heartbeat. One moment they were all packed into a long and narrow street, the men pressed shoulder to shoulder, and the next they were in a wide-open clearing, everyone jostling for position. The Harkans did as Gneuss said. Men dashed in all directions before settling back into orderly ranks, each one finding his spot in the formation. All seemed well as the Harkans readied themselves for the charge. They were headed toward the city walls, away from the fires, which were once more visible in the distance.

Hooves beat like thunder upon the stones. Mounted cavalry, men dressed in blue, charged the Harkan lines. They came out of nowhere, striking from the far side of the clearing, where their presence was concealed by a high wall. *They planned this,* thought Ren. *They were waiting for us to enter the plaza.* He guessed a whole army or maybe two of them had stood in waiting while the soldiers in red drove the Harkans into the open.

It was a trap, plain and simple.

Gneuss had made his plan, but his foes had made one as well. Theirs appeared to be the better one, or in any case the more successful one. They had the advantage of superior numbers. For every soldier who wore black, there were easily ten who did not. The Harkans were walled in on three sides, and archers lined the rooftops of the plaza. *It's a box,* thought Ren, *and they've forced us into it.* All it would take was a little time and this would be the end of them.

As if to prove the point, the blue riders smashed into the Harkan formation, shattering the heavy shields of the kingsguard and trampling the men. Iron hooves crushed metal and bone, crushed whole men beneath their weight. The Harkan lines exploded and the men were driven outward in a hundred different directions, split apart not just by the riders in blue who had come at the black shields from the Harkans' left flank, but by the men in red who had charged the black shields head-on, and a third army, soldiers in yellow livery, who had come from the right.

The field was a loose patchwork of red and black and yellow and blue, a weave with no pattern to it. There was no order and nowhere to hide. Ren was unarmored, largely weaponless, and standing among soldiers who bore not just mail but shields as well. Even the horses were clad in metal. And the soldiers in red bore spears that were easily twice his height. Ren held only a dagger, so he fled when the soldiers approached, taking a crooked path through the field, eyes trained on the crowd and searching for the ransoms. Everyone else was wearing blue or red or yellow or black. Only the ransoms wore their linens, so it was no surprise when Ren caught sight of them. Five soot-stained tunics fled toward a garden of statues. He guessed the place held cover, from the archers above and the cavalry too.

Ren sped toward the statues, calling out to his fellow ransoms, shouting their names. His voice was loud, overeager, and he immediately regretted his enthusiasm. He'd wanted to find his companions, but he'd only drawn attention to himself. Instead of finding Tye or Adin, he found soldiers, well armed and well armored. A pair of fighting men chased after him. *I ought to be able to outpace a man wearing bronze,* he told himself, but the soldiers pursued him with frightening speed, moving as if they themselves wore no armor. The men darted between the statues, their agility as surprising as it was unsettling.

One approached from the front while the other edged around to Ren's side, drawing his attention in two directions. A blade kissed Ren's thigh, but missed doing any real damage. Ren crouched low and tumbled to avoid a second attack. He rolled past a tall statue, and the soldiers followed, pivoting, coming around for another attack. Ren drew the barbed horn he'd cut from the eld. He could not fight with his father's dagger. It was too short to wield against swords, but the horn was long and as sturdy as iron, its barbs as deadly as any spear. He raised it just in time to arrest the next blow. The red sword might have cleaved Ren in two had he not blocked the attack. Still, the sound of the blade striking the bone made an unexpected din, a kind of ringing, like the chiming of a bell in some tall and distant cathedral, and to make matters worse the sword caught on one of the horn's curling tusks, momentarily binding the blade to one of the barbs. Ren tussled with the soldier, the sword grinding against the horn. The fighting man was stronger than Ren and better trained. He dug his heels into the stony path and threw his weight against the eld horn, hurling

Ren back toward the granite pedestal of a tall statue. Ren's head hit the stone and his vision went white.

He lost sight of the battle as a sudden darkness closed in around him. He was lost. Alone.

Then voices rent the silence, men talking.

Ren's eyes blinked open.

He was no longer wedged against a pedestal, and the statues were gone. Living and breathing men, women, and children stood in their place. There were at least a dozen of them, and they regarded him with a warm familiarity. One offered Ren what seemed like the heartfelt grin of a friend he'd not seen in some time, or perhaps it was the glint of recognition found in the eyes of a distant relative he'd only just met after years of separation.

His head parted with the granite pedestal and the vision shattered. The dream was gone, and he had no time to contemplate it. Ren stood face-to-face with the sweat-soaked grimace of his attacker, their noses just inches apart. The stink of the man was horrendous, as was the grinding of his teeth. Worse yet, the soldier was slowly pressing on the horn, forcing the crooked barbs into the soft flesh of Ren's forehead and cheek. Soon the points would dig deeper, and in a moment, more would prick his skin. Ren twisted his body left and right, shuffled his feet, and tried to push back against the blade, but the soldier was simply too strong, the blade too heavy. Ren had only his desperation, the sheer desire to live. With a cry, he pushed down on the horn, threw his head forward, and struck the bridge of his attacker's nose. A terrible crunch rang out and the soldier fell backward, stumbling momentarily as a great gush of blood flooded down his chin.

"You little bastard. I'm going to stick this blade so far up your ass it'll cut your tongue in two," he said, and Ren did not doubt the truth of his words. The man had freed his sword from the eld horn. He raised it up, his lips parting to reveal an eager grin, blood dribbling from his upper lip. He swept the blade downward, a killing blow, but halfway through the act his whole body went limp as a sword sprung from his chest. The blade was red, but the color was not born of the man's blood, though there was plenty of that. The iron was sealed in paint. The weapon belonged to the red army, but the one who held it did not. Tye, drenched in sweat, gripped the sword in her still-trembling hands.

"Don't just stand there," she said. "Help me pull this god-awful blade out of him."

Shocked that he was still alive, Ren stared at the sword for a moment. Then he went over to Tye, put two hands on the red-leather grip, and gave it a tug. It took their combined strength to pull the sword free, and even then the two of them toppled backward and hit the ground.

Head resting uncomfortably against the cobblestones, that vision of the statues flashed once more through his thoughts. He saw the stone figures moving about, looking as if they were alive. *I'm losing it,* he thought, *having visions of statues walking the earth.* Surely that blow had knocked him senseless. His head ached and there was an odd buzzing in his ears. *I must've really knocked myself out,* thought Ren. He knew no other explanation for what he'd seen and heard.

"I suppose we're even now," Tye said, her smile brighter than it ought to be.

Ren guessed they *were* even. He'd come to Solus to save her and she'd returned the favor. "Where're the others?"

"Behind me. We tried to stick together when the whole thing went to shit, but I think we lost Carr. Adin!" she cried, and the boy appeared. He was holding Curst with one hand and a stolen sword with the other. Ren was the only one without a weapon, so he nabbed the fallen soldier's blade and slung the eld horn over his shoulder and into his makeshift sack.

"Adin, I thought I'd lost you," said Ren. He slapped the Feren boy on the shoulder. "Where's Carr and Kollen?"

"With the kingsguard, not far," he said. "We should find them, it's not—"

"Safe," said Ren. "I know. Let's go."

"We're already doing that," said Adin.

"Where're the Harkans?" Tye asked. "I saw them just a moment ago."

"Did we lose them?" asked Ren.

"Lose them?" asked Adin, his voice turning contemplative, eyes glancing at the distant streets. "Maybe we should lose them," he said. "Forget the kingsguard. Let's grab some beggars' cloaks and slip out of here. You did it once, Ren. You escaped the city, and the two of us made our way into Solus."

"He's right," Tye echoed. "We should slip out of here. There may be hundreds in the guard, but there are thousands of soldiers in the city, maybe tens of thousands."

Ren nodded his understanding, but something held him back—some urge within him would not allow him to leave his father's men. "No," he said. "I can't. It's—"

A red blade struck Adin's shoulder, parting the flesh, blood saturating the air. Ren half-arrested the sword with his own, stopping the edge before it cut Adin in two. Still, the boy dropped to his knees, eyes rolling backward, vomit escaping his lips. Worse yet, the sword of his attacker was wedged between Ren's blade and Adin's skin. The soldier put his foot to Adin's back and pulled hard on the iron.

Adin uttered an almost inhuman moan.

Quick to act, Ren struck the man on the jaw. He hit him with as much strength as he could summon, but the blow did little to distract the soldier. Ren, however, was awash in distractions. Adin whimpered and blood emptied from his chest. Somewhere, Curst screamed. Ren prayed the boy didn't run. They'd never find him in all this chaos. Tye simply cursed.

The soldier gave his sword a second tug, freeing it for another strike. He was too late. Ren drove his blade straight into the man's gut. He pierced the skin just below the soldier's shirt of mail and drove the sword upward until it would go no further. The blow was fatal, but the soldier in red did not seem to realize it. The pain must have frozen out his senses. He was lost, disoriented. He let go of his sword and stumbled backward, collapsing awkwardly to the ground and heaving one last breath before falling still.

Ren watched it out of the corner of his eye while he knelt beside Adin to inspect the wound. He pressed his hands to the cut, but the blood welled up between his slender fingers.

"Bandages!" Ren kept one hand on the wound and used the other to rip a piece of cloth from his already-torn tunic. Tye offered a wad of cloth ripped from her sleeve. As Ren pressed it to the cut, Curst came running out from the gap between the statues. Apparently, he'd been hiding, but he screamed when he saw the wound.

"Do anything," Ren said, "crumple yourself into a ball, but do not cry out." They'd already drawn the attention of the soldiers once. If more arrived, they'd be finished. "Give me something else, more cloth." Ren put out his hand and Tye produced a second wad of linen, but Ren needed more bandages. He saw more blood than he thought a body could hold.

Adin shivered, his body convulsing as Ren cinched the fabric around the cut.

"Is it bad?" Adin asked, his voice weak, face pale, lips turning to blue. Ren was not certain if he was joking or merely hallucinating. It was worse than bad, worse than any wound Ren had seen.

"It's just a little nip, nothing to worry about," Ren lied. He feared the wound was mortal or soon would be if Adin did not receive better attention.

"That's good. I'll be all right," said Adin, who was possibly delirious, most likely in shock. "I told you we should have run." He was still muttering, talking about hiding, stealing cloaks, and making their way out of the city. Ren didn't listen. Adin could not be moved. He needed a physician and only the kingsguard had one of those, or at least they *did* have one when Ren rode with them all those weeks ago. The man had bound a wound on the king's arm, tending to some injury he'd incurred during his hunt. Ren prayed the physician yet lived and traveled with the kingsguard. Without his attention, Adin was a dead man.

That much must've been clear to all of them. Curst wept openly. He knelt at Adin's side, tears streaming down his face. Ren feared the child's crying would draw more soldiers, and it did, but this time it caught the attention of the men in black, not red. One after another the black shields surrounded the ransoms. They must have all fled into the garden, but had only now caught up with Ren. Gneuss plowed through the bunch. "I told you to stay—" The words sat idle on his lips when he caught sight of Adin's wound.

"Physician!" Gneuss called out. He gripped Ren's shoulder. "We'll do what we can. Now keep close to me, all of you."

"Why, what's happening?" asked Ren.

In the distance, the soldiers in red gathered at the edge of the garden. Curiously, none chose to enter it.

"What're they doing?" asked Tye.

Ren understood, "They're going to—"

"Surround us?" asked Gneuss. "They've already done that."

"What then?" asked Tye. She looked to Ren and Gneuss too.

Both were silent.

It was the soldiers in red who gave the answer. Jars of clay arched through the sky, striking the edges of the field, bursting into flames as they struck the ground. One by one the fires sparked to life, encircling the field of statues.

"They're trapping us here," Ren said, the ring of fire moving closer.

"Hell," said Tye, "they're going to roast us."

I'll die like my father, thought Ren, *burned by Mithra's Flame.* His hand left Adin's chest. There was no point in saving him, no point in saving any of them. With each explosion, the fires rose higher, feeding off one another, growing taller and hotter, the ring of flame encircling them.

⋛ 4 ⋚

A man cloaked in a robe of pale-red linen barred Sarra's exit from the Empyreal Domain. Behind him, smoke filled the sky, billowing upward from the Statuary Garden of Den. The clash of swords had ceased, but the fires had intensified. The battle had entered some new phase, but the man in red just stood there, silent, as a cadre of well-armed soldiers, men with tall spears, gathered about him. A cowl hid the upper half of the cloaked man's face and a veil wrapped his nose and mouth. Only the man's eyes were visible, but they were enough to unnerve Sarra. They did not blink, nor did they move from side to side. Rather, they bored into her as if the man were probing her soul and plucking out her secrets while he was at it.

"I am Mered Saad," he said. Through the veil, his voice sounded odd, distant—as if no one had spoken at all, as if the words had simply materialized out of the air.

This is the man who held Ott, the torturer who commanded Amen Saad to hold my son captive. The veiled man was about to get a terrible a surprise.

"Where is Amen?" he asked quietly, patiently. "Where is my nephew? I am here to witness his ascension to the high seat. Is he not Ray? Did he not enter the Empyreal Domain with you as his guide?" Despite the fires that raged in the distance, Mered was utterly calm.

His cool will be gone in a moment, thought Sarra. *Too bad that damn veil masks his face. I'd like to see some bit of it when he learns the truth.*

"Amen's dead." She saw no need for obfuscation. A little might not have hurt, but it was too late for that. Sarra was tired, exhausted, her limbs still aching from her confrontation with Amen, and she wanted desperately to give Mered the bad news.

"When Amen approached the veil of Tolemy," she said, "when he went and stood in the immortal light of our god emperor, the flame consumed him. He was not—" She wanted to say that he was not fit to survive the god's light. He was a murderous pig who had tortured her only son and laid a dead priest at her doorstop. She wanted to spit every curse she could recall, but she traded her hatred for something that resembled Mered's cool composure. "He was not chosen to be Ray." She completed her sentence. "It was an unfortunate end, in my opinion, because I myself was eager to see Amen wear the Eye of the Sun upon his brow. Sadly, the task did not fall to him," she said, her face revealing the faintest of grins.

"You then," asked Mered. A puff of air escaped his lips, rumpling the veil. "You are the First Ray of the Sun, the right hand of Tolemy the immortal, the intangible vessel of the sun? *You*," he said, his tone turning the word into an accusation, or maybe even a question.

Sarra ignored it.

She had walked into the domain of the gods and lived.

She was Ray, but he looked at Sarra as if her presence here, as if her being the First Ray of the Sun was not even a possibility. After all, Sarra was just a priestess. She was the highest and most holy, but behind all that she wasn't much more than a peasant girl, the daughter of a bankrupt and disgraced Wyrren house. When Sarra first traveled to Harkana, when she was named Arko's bride, she'd barely had enough royal blood to fill a thimble. Women had held the post, but no one of her breeding had ever sat in the Ray's seat. The Anu clan controlled the Antechamber for two hundred years and their family was once the wealthiest in Solus. The house of Saad had since claimed that honor, so it was only natural that they should covet her seat. They felt entitled to it, and Mered, as the eldest of the clan, thought himself the beneficiary of that entitlement, or so she assumed.

Sarra met his blank gaze, trying to peer back at the man, to see what lay beyond the veil. *It was you all along—wasn't it? You were the one pulling Amen's strings, making him dance.* In retrospect, it was a smart move. If Mered had walked into the Empyreal Domain, he would be the one lying dead on the floor of the emperor's throne room, but he did not strike her as the sort of man who made such mistakes. Everything about him spoke of circumspection. He did not even show his face, and he hid behind Amen, putting the boy in harm's way, making him fight for the Ray's seat. Mered had taken no such chances.

Sarra let a glimmer of triumph creep into her face. She raised her lip, trying on a bit of a smile. Her eyes widened. Yes, she was a woman, and yes, she was born of meager blood. And yes again, she had once been wed to the great king of Harkana—a thorn in Solus's ass if there ever was one. The warm grin that was slowly unfolding across her lips revealed all of that, and it no doubt angered Mered. In all likelihood, it was driving him mad at that very moment.

"These are my soldiers," Mered said, indicating the fighting men. "You were indisposed, as was my nephew, when the Harkan kingsguard entered our city. They said it was the Ray himself who summoned them. However, as we both know, that man is dead and discredited, as are all of his edicts. When he died, Arko's order was dismissed and the city guard took the Harkans for enemies. The yellow cloaks sought to remove this foreign army from our city, but the Harkan force was considerable, too large for the guard to overcome, or perhaps too fierce. They called on our humble citizens for aid. Along with the red army of House Saad, you see the yellow of House Entefe, and the azurite of House Ini." Indeed, there were more armies hurrying to the fight. A clarion sounded in the distance, a drumbeat, announcing what she guessed was some maneuver.

The flames rose in the distance.

"You see that?" he asked. "That is the end of the Harkans. I've saved our fair city from the rough hand of Harkana, sparing the city guard and our citizens from whatever ravages these barbarians had planned."

"You've done all this?" Sarra asked. She questioned not his actions, but the extent of his authority. She was probing to see just how much power he'd seized. "You lead these armies. They follow your command?"

"These are my men, my war," said Mered. Clearly the man had no notion of modesty. "The need for action was immediate, so I took charge of not simply the city guard but the armies of the wellborn too. We've done well. We outmaneuvered the Harkans in the Plaza of Miracles. Then we trapped them in the statuary garden, where they will be burned alive—just like their king."

"How noble of you," said Sarra, "to come to the aid of our holy city. But I think I can take charge of the matter from this moment onward. It is my task to ensure that the *emperor's* will is enacted." She gave him a moment to comprehend her challenge. It was a hollow one, she realized. This man controlled an army that looked to be at least the size of the Protector's, and he had the city guard in hand. She commanded no one.

There truly had been an absence of leadership and he'd filled it. While she'd fought Amen in the throne room, this man had taken charge of the city. He was in command and there was little Sarra could do about it. The highborn were granted special privileges to operate within the city. There were limits to their power, but she didn't know them. The city guard served under the Protector, but she didn't have a Protector and she did not know if the private armies were sworn to the emperor or simply to their masters. Sarra was unaware of the hierarchy. There were too many machinations, many of which she did not even understand. The speed of events, Arko's passing and Saad's, too, had become an unexpected disadvantage—to her at least. Mered appeared to savor it.

"No," he answered the question that had long since passed, "do not concern yourself with this quarrel. You are Ray. You must let your light shine upon the Denna Hills. And we must all feast in the Cenotaph. We shall bedeck every street with golden banners. There are preparations that must be made, feasts to plan, and ceremonies to attend. There is much glory for you to enjoy. I look forward to seeing my name carved into your tree. You are Ray and you must do as every Ray has done. Even the Harkan sat through the great feast. I was there."

Sarra bit her lip, betraying her displeasure.

The bastard has me, or at least he thinks he does.

He was leading her into the same trap Arko had fallen into, drowning her in customs, stuffing her full of banquets.

"I am sponsoring the Opening of the Mundus," he said, "a two-day feast. I must admit that when I agreed to underwrite the festival, I did it for Amen's sake. It was to be *his* feast, but the preparations are made. I see no reason why the holiday should not celebrate you. I intended to honor the new Ray. A different one, perhaps, but one nonetheless. I will contain the Harkans. You have no duty here. Go. Return to the domain. Prepare for your glorious ascent. I will see you at one of the many feasts."

He's trying to banish me, to send me away like some dutiful child, she thought.

Sarra would not have it.

"I am the first Ray to hail from the Wyrre. I've already broken with one tradition, so I see no reason why I shouldn't break with a few more. There'll be no light on the mountain and no feasting in the halls. I've escaped the Empyreal Domain, seen the light of the immortal god, and lived. The people need no other sign. My presence here, at the mouth of the domain, standing beneath the Shadow Gate, alive and untarnished by the light of Mithra, ought to be enough for them. I am Ray." Sarra spoke so quickly her words blurred into one long, unsteady sentence.

She heaved a tired breath when she was done with it, waiting for Mered's reaction, but all she got was a shrug. A long, painful silence. Then he muttered something to his soldiers. For a moment, she was uncertain just what he was doing, then she realized he was leaving, going off to tend to the fight. His soldiers withdrew, but Mered lingered at the gate, stepping toward Sarra unexpectedly and whispering in her ear before he departed.

"You survived nothing," he said. "There are no gods in the Empyreal Domain."

⇒5⇐

The flames danced about the edge of the statuary garden, coming closer to the kingsguard with each passing heartbeat. Already, Ren's skin felt as if it were on fire and the blaze was still a good way off.

"It's just flame and more flame," said Kollen. "All I can see are the damned flames."

It was true enough; the fires climbed the wrinkled vines of the statuary garden, they scaled the arbors, and they wound about the ancient pergolas. They eclipsed the sky, blotting out everything, churning out great clouds of black smoke that came tumbling toward them.

"Down," said Gneuss. "Put your head to the stones if you plan on taking another breath."

Ren had already planted *his* head on the ground. He'd been holding his breath to keep out the smoldering air, but he could only do that for so long. He quickly inhaled, choking on the first breath, but he took a second one anyway. While he drew it in, his eyes fixed on something in the distance. A gap had opened in the flames. In it, Ren spied the black gates of the Hollows. The path to the underground was clear.

Ducking beneath flaming arrows and pots that threatened to explode upon contact, he crawled to where Gneuss kneeled. A dozen or so men gathered around their captain, discussing some plan.

"What now?" Gneuss asked Ren. "Do you want to hold hands while we roast in the fire?"

"No. I was thinking about getting out of here."

"Out of here?" asked Gneuss. "And into what? The path of three armies, or is it four? I lost track of the colors. Maybe I saw five." The black smoke swirled, momentarily concealing the man's face from Ren's view. "What'll it be?" Gneuss asked when it cleared. "Roasted or skewered?"

Ren ignored the jibe. Instead, he pointed to the open gates of the Hollows, which had once more come into view as the smoke briefly thinned and the fires moved out of the way. "It's not far," said Ren.

Gneuss scoffed, but he did not dismiss the idea—not outright, at least.

"It suicide," he said. "If you haven't forgotten, there's a wall of fire out there and we're going to have to pass through it to reach those gates. Butting heads with a churning heap of flame isn't like striking a line of shields. Those fires are hot enough to roast the lot of us. I'll need volunteers," he said quietly, as if he were already weighing the consequences of their escape, the men who would die.

"It's the only sensible way out," said Ren.

"Sense?" asked Gneuss. "There's no sense in war." The captain glanced at his troops, and for a moment Ren saw his resolve start to waver, so he pressed his case.

"These armies own the streets," Ren said. "That much is plain. But down there, in the dark and narrow tunnels, their numbers won't matter and there are paths, smugglers' routes—"

"Yes, I've heard the stories. They say Solus has three gates and a thousand doors. A smuggler's route might be the way out, or it might not."

"It's my call," said Ren, humble but firm. If he were going to assert himself, now was the time. Though he had not stepped into the King's Hall and he wore no crown, he was as good as king, the son of Arko and the heir to the throne. These men were his kingsguard, but there hadn't been time for oaths. Still, Ren gave the command and offered no indication that it was anything but a command.

Gneuss weighed it. "King without a crown—is that what you are, boy? I hold five hundred souls in my care. Five hundred men with five hundred wives and thousands of fucking children. You ready to lead them—to take that responsibility? You're Arko's heir, but you don't have a crown. We've sworn oaths to the king of Harkana, but are *you* the king? Remember, Arko named your sister regent. When he threw down his crown, she picked it up. Are you ready to claim it? Right here, right now?"

It was a challenge. Ren was not yet crowned, but his father had named him heir. When they reached Harwen, he'd take the throne and the kingsguard would be sworn to his service. They would be subject to his absolute authority. Gneuss weighed this, Ren knew. He contemplated his prospects and the consequences he might suffer if he disobeyed a future king.

"It's your decision," Gneuss said after a considerable silence. His smile was flat, eye fixed on Ren. "I won't stand in your way, but if you do this, if you take charge of my men, their lives will rest in your hands. That's the burden. Can you carry it?"

Ren gave no reply, not at first. He did, however, catch hold of the gravity of the moment. This was his coronation. He'd thought he would take his crown on a bright and sunny day in Harwen, in a hall festooned with banners, every warlord standing at his side. Instead, it was happening here, in the thick of the fight.

Take charge or cower behind some soldier's shield.

That was his choice.

With this order, he left behind his old identity: a boy, a ransom, a child who thought of nothing more than the safety of his friends. He allowed himself the luxury of a single breath. Then he narrowed his eyes at Gneuss and spoke.

"The Hollows are the way out," he said.

Ren had made his decision.

It had been an impulsive one. He'd chosen what seemed like madness. He was thirteen years old and a onetime ransom who had never even set foot in the King's Hall of Harkana, but with those words he claimed his crown.

"Your command, your choice," said Gneuss, "and it'll be our asses if you're wrong."

"I'm not," said Ren, feigning certainty, trying more than anything to exhibit a king's confidence. "And even if I'm wrong, we're out of time."

Indeed, the flames were drawing closer, the heat coming at them in waves, searing Ren's hands, his face. Soon the smoke would overcome the men, and Ren knew it. Gneuss knew it too. The captain was tugging at his beard, his eye fixed on the gates. He tore off his helmet and the sweat poured down from his already-sodden hair.

He called out names, "Edric, Butcher!" Then he murmured, "My captains and yours." He pointed at a gap in the flames. "We're going through that gate—see it?" asked Gneuss as the captains gathered around him. "Tight as a foxhole and only Mithra knows where it will take us."

"There are passages that lead to the surface, secret pathways in and out of the city, smugglers' routes," said Ren, seeking to assert himself, to explain his intentions.

"And you can find these tunnels?" asked the man called Butcher. He was a strong but portly fellow who carried a war hammer in place of a sword.

"I can," Ren said. He'd heard countless tales about the smugglers' routes, but he had no notion of how to locate one or where to start looking.

"You'll find them," said Gneuss, "or we're dead men. We're nearly out of food, out of amber, too, and it's a day's march to Harwen. These armies will pursue us wherever we go, and this is their city. They are no doubt aware of these same smugglers' routes and for all we know they've posted guards at each of them and at every gate in the underground."

Ren nodded his understanding, but the time for talk had come and gone. For better or worse they needed to move. Gneuss was already handing out orders, calling for volunteers, arranging some strategy that would allow them to pass through the flames.

Though he had not spoken, Kollen stood at Ren's side. "Sure you don't want to ditch these soldiers and make a run for it?" he asked.

"And leave Adin?" Ren had once risked his life to save his friend from Feren slavers and Adin had returned the favor when he took that blow to the shoulder. Ren could not imagine abandoning Adin, leaving him with soldiers they hardly knew.

"Are you utterly unaware of what's just transpired," Ren asked, "what's happening at this very moment? We've made our decision. We're heading back down into the Hollows. I'm not going to slip away like some coward. Even if I wanted to sneak off, I don't think we'd have much luck slipping out of here as we carried Adin along on a litter. No doubt that would draw much attention." Ren shot Kollen a sideways glance. "We'll need two men to lift the thing and the physician just to keep him alive. The time to steal our way out of this city has come and gone. As for you, Kollen, you were always an ass, but when you joined us, when you helped us free the others, I thought I'd found some shred of decency in you. Maybe I was wrong. Perhaps you're just a coward, some bully who's lost his gang and his nerve along with it. That's not my path. I'm not abandoning the guard or anyone else," Ren said. The ransoms had all gathered around him to listen. Ren looked to each of them for reassurance, for agreement. He was not their master. Each of them was the son of some other lord or king. They need not follow his dictates, but Carr nodded his assent and so did Tye. They all looked to Adin, but the boy was too weak to speak. His condition was clearly deteriorating, but somehow, amid all that pain, he managed a nod. Curst went to his side, "I'll go wherever Adin goes," he said meekly, as if not wanting to assert himself.

"Then it's all of us," said Ren.

"All of us?" asked Kollen. "King of Harkana and now you're the emperor as well? Maybe you'll be Mithra, too, by the time the day's done."

"Kollen, if we live through this day, I'll name you the god's damned emperor. Until then, shut your mouth and follow along with the rest of us—is that fair enough for you?"

Kollen spat. "You better be right. There better be more doors than rats in that sewer . . ." he said, his words swallowed by the shouts of men. Not far from where they stood, the kingsguard had begun their charge. They were clearing a path through the flames. With shields, they wiped away the tar, but the fire had a mind of its own—one that would not be easily tamed. Tongues of flame lapped at the men's armor, turning their oilskins into ash. The air stunk of burnt leather. It was an almost impossible task, but somebody had to beat back the blaze and these men had offered to do it. Their heroism shocked Ren. *I did this,* he thought. *I asked for this charge and these men offered their lives to make it happen.*

The kingsguard rushed into the breach and the ransoms followed, but they had no armor of any kind. With bare arms and unshod feet, they could not pass through the flames with the kingsguard, so men with tall shields marched on either side of them, making a second wall to shield them from the heat. Still, as he passed through the wall of fire Ren felt nothing but searing heat and saw a light so white and hot it made the naked sun seem like yesterday's campfire. He shut his eyes lest they be burned like the skin on his arms. He nearly stumbled too. However, there were three or four litters coming fast behind him, shoving him forward, so Ren pushed past the conflagration.

Outside, the soldiers in red and blue appeared to have been caught off guard by the Harkans' sudden advance. Perhaps they thought the kingsguard dead. By the time their foes drew blades and formed up ranks the black shields had already fashioned a corridor made of shields, a path that led straight into the Hollows, and they were hurrying through it by the dozens.

The soldiers pelted the black shields with stones; arrows shattered against the Harkan wall. Those among the kingsguard who held shields raised them above their heads and Ren tried to steal a bit of cover. Everyone did, but there simply wasn't enough of it. One man fell, then another, and soon Ren was leaping over bodies and he still hadn't reached the gates. The ransoms moved in a pack. Even Kollen joined them. But the closeness of the men slowed their progress. Ren slammed into a soldier, stumbled, and struck another. An arrow whizzed past his nose. He looked for Tye and caught hold of her hand, tugging her along. He grabbed Kollen by the belt. Adin followed on the litter, accompanied by Curst, who'd been tossed hastily beside the injured boy. That was how they came upon the gates of the Hollows. The yawning chasm looked more sinister than it had when he first entered it. Ren sought shelter from the armies in red and blue and yellow, but he wasn't sure if he'd find it down there. Passing through the gates, he felt as if he were being swallowed whole, as if some beast had engulfed the kingsguard and the ransoms too. An ill feeling overcame him, and he lingered at the gates. The last of the kingsguard rushed past him, fleeing down the long flight of stairs.

Gneuss and a few of his men brought up the rear, fighting their way back toward the place where Ren stood. The captain gave some muffled cry and the men formed a semicircle around the gates. They split off, one by one, moving with the precision of highly trained soldiers, of men who had drilled for such things, for guarding exits and making hasty departures. The last of the black shields pulled the gates closed, wedging a sword between the bars and bending it to hold them closed. Ren stood beside Gneuss. They were the last ones at the gates, the only two who had not yet fled down into the Hollows.

"Look," said Gneuss, his lips curled downward into a terrible grimace, the tip of his blade indicating the distant armies.

Ren had won the day. He'd escaped the ambush these armies had set for the kingsguard, but he could not help but feel that the fight was not yet over—that perhaps he'd wriggled out of one trap only to find himself ensnarled in another, more elaborate, one.

The soldiers made no effort to pursue the kingsguard. Not one of the men, be he a red or a blue or any other color, chased after them. Their foes ought to be nipping at their heels, but they simply stood there, waiting.

6

The clash of swords had ceased, as had the constant patter of arrows striking the cobblestones. The battle was over, but the city was not quiet. Rather, it had returned to its usual clamor, the daily bustle of the empire's capital. Soldiers abounded. Men donning house colors hurried in every direction. The yellow cloaks of the city guard dotted the crowd. The red soldiers appeared here and there among the masses, but there were fewer of them. In fact, most of the fighting men were gone, and the sounds of the city had replaced those of the battle. The familiar tapping of sandals reverberated throughout the streets. Hawkers cried in the distance. Heralds announced the day's tidings. The conflict was ended. The Harkans had fled into the Hollows, or so it was said. The talk was everywhere. Some cheered when they heard it, while others simply went about their business as if nothing had happened at all. Soothsayers plied their trade while the spice traders cried out lots, screaming to be heard over the perfume makers and silk traders. Moneylenders stood on corners, shoving the chickpea vendors aside, fighting for space to do business. Men sold bushels of dates, tossing them into the air to tantalize the eye while all around them the buskers sang from lonely alcoves, already inventing tales about the battle that had only just passed.

This was the city Sarra knew, wrought by violence and contradiction. The discards of war were everywhere. Ash and broken arrows blanketed the stones. Tar soiled the plazas. The Statuary Garden of Den smoldered. The statues there, however, were untarnished, which was not entirely surprising. Those golden figures depicted the family of Den, the last true line of the Soleri. Suten Anu had once said they were blessed with the light of the Soleri, and for all she knew it was true. There was something decidedly unnatural about the way they glimmered amid the ashen remains of the garden.

As she passed beneath them, Sarra came upon a great number of priests. The men and women of the cult had apparently gone looking for her when they heard news of her exit from the domain. They were all whispering about it. She silenced them with a wave of her hand, but she did not send them away. Their arrival was well timed. Sarra was eager to see the city and she wanted all of Solus to see *her*, the Ray, but she could not walk these streets unaccompanied. Hence, she went with her children, protected on all sides by twenty or so white-robed priests. She was headed to the Antechamber, which was the Ray's formal office and one of only a handful of places where she could easily access the Empyreal Domain. Amen Saad had set fire to the thing. The floors had likely burned, but the rest was made of stone. She hoped it could be salvaged. She wanted to put the Antechamber back into working condition as soon as was possible. Sarra needed to assume the trappings of the Ray, to show the people that she was the chosen vessel of the gods. A restored Antechamber would offer all that and more, so she set off toward it.

The walk was short, but the crowds forced her to move at a snail's pace, which she did not mind. Sarra was here to take the city's temperature and to be seen. She walked at the considered pace of a leader, of one who held absolute power. She did not hurry, nor did she glance to either side to acknowledge the people who gawked at the red-haired priestess who had gone into the domain of the gods and lived. She was Ray and everyone knew it, or soon would. The whispers were everywhere and her presence—here, on the streets—made them double. She even raised her chin a hair's width. It's what Suten had always done. He'd once told her that a Ray should never hurry when he walked, lest the people think some crisis was at hand. The Ray and his concerns were above the rabble, or so he'd claimed.

Soldiers hurried through the street, their armor clanking, all of them gathering around one of the many gates that led down into the Hollows. *Is that where the Harkans fled?* Sarra sent one of her priests to make an inquiry. A moment later he returned with his report. "They're down there," he said. "The Harkans escaped through that very gate, but they'll never come out of it. The exits are watched."

"Perhaps," said Sarra. Nothing was ever certain. Mered had contained the Harkans, or they'd gone down there and contained themselves. There was no way to divine the truth of the matter, but it did appear as if Mered had trapped the kingsguard in the Hollows just as he'd tried to confine Sarra within walls of the Empyreal Domain. At least *she* had stood her ground, but she had not quarreled with the man. Sarra was not yet ready to confront the father of House Saad. For the immediate future, the most powerful gesture she could make was to simply walk through the streets of Solus. If the Ray died without naming a successor, the post fell to the Mother Priestess, and Arko had named no successor. The criers were already singing her song, telling of the priestess who met her god and lived. For no man, save for the First Ray of the Sun, can stand at the foot of the sun god and live. Her presence in the street was all the proof the people needed of her legitimacy. She was Ray and would soon be celebrated as such. The evidence was everywhere.

Men stood atop ladders, stringing golden bunting between posts. They wrapped the poles with heather and jasmine. It was an odd sight, but not entirely out of place in the city of light. Sarra had once joked that Solus had more festivals than the calendar had days, which was no exaggeration. It was not uncommon to celebrate the blessing of a temple at morning meal, the anniversary of a minor deity at midday, and the rebuilding of some monument at sundown. Half the time, the attendants at such feasts had no idea what they were even celebrating, but Mered's high holiday would be an entirely different affair. His feast would draw every man, woman, and child in Solus, and when he'd plied them with bread and drink he would boast of his victory over the Harkans. He would claim the ear of every person in Solus, but she didn't know what he'd say or how he would attempt to expand his enterprise.

Hence, she walked, contemplating her newfound adversary as the workers in red gathered at the statuary garden, sweeping away the shattered arrows and broken spears. There were servants with clay vessels full of water and others with wide, fanlike brushes made of twigs bound by rope. They'd come to douse the last of the flames or to wipe away the tar and ash. Each man bore the pale red of House Saad. Some were soldiers. They lingered at the gates of the Hollows while others milled about, dispersing the crowds and assisting the city guard in the general labor that was required to prepare the city for the festival.

We are at war, she thought. *A Ray is dead and a Protector too.* The Harkan Army fled, but they could not have gone far. Solus was in chaos, but Mered readied the city for its next feast. In a day, or maybe less, his men would wipe away every trace of the fight. They would cover the charred pergolas with wreaths of laurel and drape boughs of heather over the half-burnt arbors. Soon, there would be nothing but bright, golden flowers wound over posts or strung between towers. The people begged for pageantry, they always did, they lusted for their spectacles.

The city welcomed its fantasies.

Reality, on the other hand, had never been a welcome guest in the city of the gods.

Mered knew this all too well. *He's coming for me,* Sarra thought. *He comes for my head and my robe. He desires the Ray's seat and the cowl of the Mother too.* Amen, his nephew, had failed to take either from Sarra, but none of that mattered. Amen was a tool with a chipped edge, discarded when its usefulness was ended. She guessed Mered had a whole box full of tools: chisels and knives, axes and other pointy things.

The thought made Sarra anxious, her head filling up with questions and finding few answers. What did Mered truly know of the Soleri? He'd said there were no gods in the Empyreal Domain, but he didn't elaborate. He did not say the Soleri were dead. He had simply stated that they were absent. In fact, as she recalled his words, she realized Mered had said very little on the matter, which made her think he was testing her knowledge.

"The Soleri are everywhere. They are with us right now," she'd said. "They listen to our every word." That was her response. Mered had not replied. He'd only retreated, claiming that some duty required his attention, that he was personally supervising the campaign against the Harkans and had only come, briefly, to greet his nephew.

His silence had again revealed much.

He knew little about the Soleri, and maybe that was all anyone understood. Perhaps he guessed the Soleri had fled the domain, that they'd left the management of the empire to the Ray and her servants. Such an assumption was easy enough to derive. The two-hundred-year absence of the Soleri had raised more than one rumor. Everyone—every peasant or nobleman who'd ever walked these city streets in the last two centuries— had guessed at their gods' whereabouts. Some thought the Soleri had deemed Solus unworthy of their gods' attention, that they were a cursed people who must earn back their gods' love. Others assumed the opposite, that the gods were apathetic. They had no interest in this world. They simply feasted and fucked one another without a care for what happened beyond their garden walls. Others—the peasants and pilgrims—believed the word of Mithra. They imagined noble gods who spoke through their holy vessel, the First Ray of the Sun. They trusted every passage in the *Book of the Last Day of the Year.* In their hearts, Tolemy's every utterance was poetry, ripe with meaning and folly for endless interpretation. The Ray carried her subjects' words and wants to the gods. She was prayer incarnate.

Heavens, thought Sarra. *Just what in Horu's eight hells have I gotten myself into? Maybe there is no truth in Solus—maybe too much time has passed since the Soleri perished.* She knew that twelve statuelike bodies rested in the Shambles. Sarra had found those stony effigies, but she did not know who had reduced the gods to stone. And she was ignorant of how this truth was kept secret for two centuries. She hoped Ott would piece together the story. Perhaps Suten Anu, the former Ray, had access to some secret knowledge. Surely his predecessors had kept some record of how it all began, how the first Ray was named and the system was devised. Like Mered, she lusted for answers.

Truth was power.

Mered's brief insinuation, his suggestion that she had lied about Amen and what went on in the domain, had all but disarmed Sarra. *There are no gods in the Empyreal Domain.* That was what he'd said. Maybe it was all he knew, but it was enough. This sliver of truth had emboldened the man. He understood that some bit of the story was false, so he was testing the whole thing, pushing Sarra to see how she would respond. Would the Soleri reduce him to ash if claimed power in their holy city? No. He'd already done it and had suffered no consequence, so she guessed he would advance his agenda. He would test the sun god and His servant, probing for some new morsel of truth.

Mered was more of a threat than his nephew had ever been. She did not even know his face. She recalled only those dark eyes and his skin— too soft for a desert man. She knew that he was wealthy beyond all reckoning and a menace, one that wore a veil and spoke little of his true intentions. She guessed he was already mulling over her every word and gesture, trying to glean some truth from their conversation. She hoped he'd find none.

"Stay close," a priest whispered, interrupting her thoughts. The streets were more crowded near the Antechamber. Men and women hurried past her procession, stealing glances but never stopping.

Where are they all going? she wondered as they entered the plaza that stood before the Antechamber. She saw no reason for the crowds. In fact, she was a bit confused. She'd thought the site would be abandoned. Arko died here, and they all thought he was a traitor, a rebel king, and a usurper, but the plaza was packed. There were so many people in it that her procession came to an abrupt stop and Sarra stumbled into one of her priests. The people were everywhere, all of them gawking at some inferno. *What in Mithra's name is going on?*

A fire was a simple thing to douse, and this was the office of the most important person in Solus. "What is this?" she asked aloud to her priests. "If it's just a fire, why haven't they drowned the thing and gotten it over with?"

No one replied, but a moment of observation provided an answer.

The Antechamber fire burned with a life of its own. It was no candle. It could not be smothered with the pinch of a finger or even a bucketful of water. No, this fire was something else entirely. A hundred or more guardsmen toiled at the blaze, but every time they choked some part of it with sand or water, the flames would simply reappear or sprout up at some other location. The guards heaved great barrels of water upon the fire, turning the liquid to steam, sending columns of white soaring into the heavens, but none of it did any good. The flames burned, undeterred and undiminished. They shimmered with an almost golden hue, flickering and dancing, teasing the men who strove to extinguish them.

Gods, what did Saad do? This is not fire.

She edged closer to the ruins, her priests clearing the path ahead as best they could.

Sarra had always counted herself a nonbeliever. She'd seen no miracles in her lifetime. If there were gods, they were either deaf or inept. She was once the Mother Priestess, the mistress of the faith, but she had not once witnessed the gods' blessings. The priesthood had done its share of good, but all of it had been hard labor, nothing more. They fed the poor and ministered to the weak, ushering the underprivileged into their ranks. Boys like Ott. Women like Sarra. Beggars and cast-outs. All of them were welcomed into the faith. There was no *magic* in these things.

Sarra's thoughts on the matter changed when she saw those statues in the Shambles. Those things were not of this Earth. The Soleri were not people, not like Sarra. Her body would turn to ash if it burned. It would not transform into starry stone. Those statues had glistened as if the heavens themselves were trapped within them. *And perhaps they are,* she thought. In the Shambles, she saw things that were not of this world. In the great conflagration, she witnessed another of these things, these creatures of the unknown. A miracle, maybe. Or maybe *miracle* was just a word that described something that was not easily understood. A fire that never guttered out and died. Somewhere beneath that pyre was the Eye of the Sun, the glistening citrine worn by the Ray, a crystal that was said to hold the light of the gods. Was that the source of the fire? Had Amen Saad offended Mithra Himself and was this His response? Sarra shrugged. She held no faith in such things, but she could not deny her eyes. This was no ordinary flame and the people sensed it. They felt their gods' power. They saw a miracle in those golden flames.

Sarra saw something different.

It was not her hand that lit the blaze, but surely it was her will that set it. She had all but commanded Amen Saad to murder the Ray of the Sun. This was her doing. Without her influence, none of this would have come about. The realization hit her like a hammer blow, and a brief panic fell over her.

Is this a curse? Am I damned for killing the mouthpiece of the gods? And damned again for killing my husband? Does this flame burn for me? Does the sun god rage against the one who threatened Him, who set fire to these holy grounds? Sarra didn't know. Perhaps Mered could be blamed for the strange fire, but she doubted it. This flame burned for Sarra. The constant churning of the smoke, the clouds of steam, the bright sparks and hungry fires reminded her of what she'd done. And they stirred something among the people.

Everywhere, all through the gathering crowds, there was strange talk. A woman held aloft a dead baby. "Born with two heads!" she cried. "It died the moment it left my daughter's womb!" She was indeed holding something dead, but it was blackened and Sarra could not see how many heads the thing had. For all she knew it had three. The woman was frantic, almost hysterical, and she was not alone.

"I saw the temple of Mithra struck by lightning last night," cried an old man. No lightning had struck the temple. That claim, at least, was false, but the man went on. "Surely it was an ill omen!" he cried. "We are cursed. That's why the sun did not dim."

The others cheered him on and the woman threw the dead child on the blaze as yet another came forward to speak. A black-robed woman pushed her way through the crowd. "I am a flamine of the cult of Horu," the woman claimed, though the black bands on her arms had already made that clear. "And this morning, the god took none of our offerings. The ripe fruit lay there rotting, and when it began to stink, spiders and rats came out of nowhere to feed upon it."

This last one didn't seem like much of an omen. Insects were always pecking at the offerings.

"It's happening at all the temples," she cried. "The gods will not accept our offerings!"

Or the priests forgot to remove them as they did at the end of each day, thought Sarra.

Clearly this had all gotten out of hand. Each person encouraged the next, and the tales became wilder by the moment. "I saw a goat give birth to a human boy, but he died upon taking his first breath," said a young girl, one who smelled of manure and no doubt worked the stables. Others echoed her cries. A middle-aged man said he'd seen no stars in the sky the previous night, that the lights had fled, but Sarra guessed it was just the smoke that hid the stars. A woman cried out that all the birds in the city had died that morning and another said that every child would be born deformed. There were rumors everywhere, ill portents, talk of unexplained deaths.

"Show yourselves!" cried one man, shaking his fist at the great Shroud Wall of the Soleri. This time it was no beggar, but a well-dressed man, his caftan woven from fine muslin, the neckline dotted with studs of azurite. He was not alone.

"Come to us," begged a woman with two babes. She too was well-born.

"Let us see your light," said another and another.

In some small way, the power of the gods had returned, and the people wanted more of it. They begged for the Soleri to speak.

Solus would no longer tolerate the silence of the gods.

⋽7⋿

Ren hurried through the lightless corridors of the underground city, the darkness of the passages enveloping him, blocking out his senses. In the gloom of the Hollows, the faces of the golden statues flashed in his thoughts. The vision in the garden returned to him, and although it seemed like madness, like pure insanity, he could not stop thinking about it. He'd seen statues come to life, seen them talking and moving about, and they'd seen him too. They'd looked right at Ren, grinned, and gestured to him like some long-lost friend. The whole thing was unnerving and no doubt the product of having his head slammed against a slab of granite. In fact, there was still a faint buzzing in his ear and in the back of his head. As before, he guessed he'd simply given himself a good knock on the head. He knew that vision had been pure nonsense, but he could not get it out of his head. It came to him unbidden, haunting him as he plunged through the darkness and out into what seemed like a great chamber, the biggest he'd seen.

Ren slowed to catch his breath, to stop and survey the place. "Seems like a good spot to rest," he said, chest heaving. His skin burned, and the smoke had only just left his lungs. He'd been running for what felt like hours, maybe longer. He could not recall stopping, not even for a moment. He'd wanted to put himself and his men as far from that garden and those flames as was physically possible, but he could only run for so long.

"Anyplace is fine with me. I'll vomit my guts out if I take another step," said Kollen.

"I need amber," Tye croaked, her mouth as dry as her voice.

"And I need a place for five hundred men to have a rest or a drink of amber, to sit or to loose their bowels," said Gneuss.

"Adin could use some help," Curst said, his voice as small as the boy himself. Gneuss called to the physician, who went and found Adin. He inspected the injury, pulling away the blood-soaked layers of linen, an even grimmer look passing over his already-grim face.

Ren looked away. "Where are we?" he asked, not really expecting an answer. When they'd entered the Hollows, they hadn't known which way to go. They'd searched for a route that led away from the gate. Unfortunately, they'd found little more than darkness, accented by the occasional beggar's fire. Ren had stumbled into more walls than he dared admit, but they had at last found a place to stop and rest. The kingsguard lit torches.

They were in what looked like a great cistern, Ren guessed, or at least it had once been a great vessel of some sort. It was a wide, round space, large in volume and dotted with circular openings, places where pipes had once fed water into the vessel but had long since been abandoned or removed. There were a dozen openings, though a few were covered over with stones. A string of archways ran along one wall. Trying to get a better look at the chamber, the kingsguard lit torches and lashed oil lamps to spears, holding them up and illuminating what appeared to be a black river of sewage that ran beyond the arches. It smelled as foul as it looked, but the stench did little to deter the starveling dogs that drank from the black water or the rats that scurried at its banks. There were people too, the clay-eaters. That's what they'd called them in Ren's lessons. He'd heard of these folk, but never guessed he'd come across one, let alone a whole clan of them. Mud slathered their lips and chins. It dribbled down their arms as they dredged the clay from the riverbank. Ren saw them feeding it to their children or drinking from the ancient sewer.

"We can hide here," said Ren. "I doubt the clay-eaters will report us to anyone."

"I couldn't care less about the starvelings. It's the cistern I like. It's a defensible position," said Gneuss. He eyed the many openings. "If the red soldiers come for us, we can hold them back and there's more than one way to escape if we should need to mount a retreat."

"But they haven't come for us," said Ren.

"They will. If I'm not mistaken, the red armor belongs to the house of Saad. It's a wealthy house. They have resources and time."

Kollen shook his head. "This thing feels like a great big bottle. What if they plug all those holes? What'll we do then? Drown in our own shit?"

"It won't come to that," said Gneuss. "I've placed guards at the entrances and we left scouts as we fled, each within earshot of another. This isn't the first time we've mounted a retreat. Or were you too busy spouting off to think of that?" Gneuss made a small motion with his hand, swatting Kollen away like some pesky fly.

The older boy came up short and, after a moment of what seemed like silent deliberation, he actually did shut his mouth and sit his ass down on the riverbank. Ren joined him, Tye too, settling down at his side while all around them the kingsguard decamped. More than one man needed a long draft of amber, a bit of rest, or a good piss. They stopped to catch their breath, to regroup.

"How long do you think we've been down here?" Ren asked.

"Got me," said Tye. "It's all a blur. I can't tell up from down or left from right in this place."

Ren thought she'd gotten it correct for the most part. They'd hurried through tunnels, darted around corners, ducked through shafts, and trudged through heaps of moldering filth. They truly were lost, but they were not alone in the Hollows.

"There are people here," said Ren. "There must be ways of coming and going. There's got to be some door that doesn't have a guard standing beside it."

Tye opened her mouth to reply, but something caught her attention and she stood. Gneuss had returned after what seemed like only a moment. He hastened toward them, soldiers at his side, but he allowed Ren a moment to stand. Perhaps it was a token of respect, or maybe they were all just trying to catch their breath.

"My forward scouts, the ones who ran out ahead of us, returned," Gneuss said. "They spied more tunnels. We'll scout them. There are markets too.

The men'll procure rations and try to ferret out the smugglers' routes. They'll ask for maps or men who can guide us to the surface. We'll know soon enough if you were right about those passages," he said, looking at Ren, reminding him again of the promise he'd made.

Ren *had* promised they'd find a way out of Solus. Those were hasty words, but he owned them. "There are routes," said Ren, not wishing to sound weak or uncertain. In truth, he wanted to sound like a king, but he'd never commanded anyone, never stood at the head of a line of soldiers. The only queue he'd ever stood in was the soup line in the priory. In that case, he'd been pushed aside more often than not, but that memory felt distant.

In a few short weeks, his whole life had been turned on end. He was changed, a different man with different responsibilities, or at least that was what he told himself. He'd made a choice, made himself king, and he would not back down from that decision.

"What about the red army?" Ren asked. "Have we seen them?"

"They're out there," Gneuss said. "They've doffed their armor, traded their leathers for beggars' rags, but we spotted them. The soldiers are too well fed, their shoulders too broad, faces too clean. Everyone down here looks like they've been living off mud and stepping in it too. Let's hold tight until the next round of scouts return. If anyone'll have answers it's them." Gneuss turned. Something had caught his attention. Sandals tapped in the distance. A man in black leather approached, motioning to Gneuss, whispering something in his ear. Gneuss turned back to Ren, his right arm extended, finger indicating a blotch of red moving in the distance.

"They're coming," said Gneuss.

A man approached.

No, there were two of them and their armor was pale red. They approached the cistern. One held his shield flat above his head.

Ren thought it an odd gesture. "What's that?" he asked.

"A sign of truce," Gneuss replied. "They haven't come to fight."

They want to talk, thought Ren. *But what is there to discuss? Our surrender?* The thought of it made his guts twist into a terrible knot. His brow went cold and his chest dampened. He looked for Tye and found her standing nearby, among the ransoms. She was probably thinking the same thoughts as him. He saw it in the contortions of her jaw, her fidgeting hands.

The two men settled on the far side of the river. One of them, the man who'd taken up the rear, fumbled with an oilskin sack while the other spoke. "I'm Admentus and this is my scribe, Demenouk, and we speak for Mered Saad, father of the house of Saad, high priest of Horu, commander of the Army in Red." Admentus spoke slowly, his words calm. He still held the shield above his head. Gneuss nodded at it, and the men exchanged glances, a silent agreement passing between them.

For his part, Ren could only watch. He hadn't known what the gesture meant until Gneuss explained it, and he certainly hadn't known how to respond to it. *Some king,* he thought as Demenouk wrestled a slip of parchment from his oilskin, held it up for everyone to see, then handed it to the other man.

"I've got a parchment to read, from Mered Saad, just like I said." Admentus unrolled the scroll then read it aloud in a voice that every man could hear. "May it be known that the ransoms who escaped the Priory of Tolemy—emperor of the Soleri, the Bright Star of the Desert—shall be pardoned for the crime of fleeing their lawful imprisonment. Any who wish to come forward will be returned, without recompense, to proper captivity, where they will serve out their time as was previously negotiated and agreed upon by their respective kingdoms."

They'll send them back to the cells, thought Ren, *to sit and wait for their fathers to die.*

"As I said, the ransoms need only step forward and they will be returned *safely* to the care of Tolemy."

"And the kingsguard?" asked Ren. "What of the Harkans? Can they leave the city? It's only fair."

That one made Admentus chuckle a bit. "Can they leave?" He repeated Ren's question as if he had not heard it or believed it either. "Of course, they can all leave right now. Just line the fuckers up and they can walk right out of here. Of course, their heads will have to stay. We'll hack those off and toss 'em in the river."

As if to emphasize his point, he spat into the channel of filth that ran between them. "The Harkans trespass in the holy city of the Soleri. Mered Saad commands that every last one of them pay for this insult with their life. Does that sound fair to you, boy?"

Ren said nothing.

"It'll be a fight then?" said Gneuss.

"It will be," said the man in red. "You the one in charge?" he asked, looking to Gneuss, but eyeing Ren.

Ignoring the question, Gneuss pressed his case. "The kingsguard were called here lawfully by the First Ray of the Sun. We will leave peacefully if you allow it, but I've heard no such offer."

"Nor will you," said Admentus. "Ever. The little ones will come with us. They are the sons of kings and other highborn men. They are useful to our patron, but the rest of you, well, you're just a bunch of dead men who don't know it yet. We surrounded you and killed your scouts. We took twelve of your men in the markets, another fifteen in the passages beyond. That makes twenty-seven. Did I catch them all?" The man's face twisted into a terrible grin. "Or did I miss one?"

Gneuss said nothing; his face was stone.

"I reckon I'm right then. I got 'em all. We'll send you their heads, but not just yet. Maybe later, when you're starving we'll return them. See, I've blocked every passage out of here. There'll be no provisions for your men and no way out. You've got a place to piss, I'll give you that, but not much else." He took a step back, indicating that the conversation was nearly at an end.

"We'll give the ransoms a moment to make up their minds," he said, raising his voice again so that even those in the distance could hear him. "They may come forward, and if they want to say their farewells they can do that too. The ransoms will leave with us and the rest of you will go to whatever miserable fate awaits you. Starvation maybe, the spear in all likelihood."

With that, Admentus scrunched up the parchment, twisting it into a clumsy little roll. The two men backed away, but they did not leave. Admentus flashed an odd grin, a kind of twisted smile—like the smirk of a torturer who'd just brought out his most vile implement.

"Mered asked that I relay a last piece of news," Admentus said. "It's a little thing, but he thought it might be of interest to the kingsguard. A boy called Ren is rumored to be among your men. He is not the true heir of Harkana. He is the bastard son of Arko, and his mother is just some peasant girl named Serena—some wench the king took into his bed each night while the queen fiddled in her bedchamber. Mered recently came upon this news, so he thought you should know it. Your king-in-waiting is nothing but a bastard, but we'll take him too if he wants to flee with the rest of the ransoms." The man looked to Ren. "That you, boy? The bastard of Harkana?"

Ren made something like a grunt. The shock was too much to fathom, too much to even acknowledge. His heart hammered in his ears and his skin prickled. He worried he was shaking.

"Stings like a bitch, doesn't it," said Admentus. "Sorry to be the one to bring you the news, but it shouldn't bother you, not too much. I was born a bastard. Half of us hired men are bastards. You'll get used to being one," he said, and this time the two men finally did retreat.

Behind them, spears glinted in the lamplight. The red army was moving, hurrying down stairs, taking up positions, and stealing cover wherever they could find it. Then, when the soldiers had reached their positions, one after another they extinguished their lights. They snuffed out their lamps and ground their torches into the earth, darkening the already gloomy caverns. The shadows gathered and the soldiers of Mered advanced.

THE BARTERED QUEEN

8

Merit Hark-Wadi had been away from the kingdom for too long. She felt it as the wheels of her carriage rumbled over the spindly bridge, crossing the Rift valley and leaving the woodland kingdom. War was afoot. An army massed at Harkana's doorstep, but the Horned Throne sat empty in the King's Hall. As queen regent, she'd left it in the care of one of her father's best generals—Tomen Cannet, a good warrior and decent politician—but he was no king, or queen for that matter. The kingdom was in decent hands, but they were not *her* hands. She'd spent a good portion of her life pursuing that throne. Yet, when she'd finally attained it, she had not even taken a moment to warm the age-old seat. Instead, she'd gone off to Feren on a fool's errand, chasing a husband that was not hers.

All of that was in the past. A mistake, perhaps, but at least it was over and done with, or so she told herself. The hurt still throbbed in her veins, coming and going with each passing moment. She'd loved a good number of men, but not one of them had ever caught and held her eye like Dagrun Finner, the king of the Ferens. Only in hindsight could she see it. She'd loved the man, loved him with such force that she'd been afraid to admit to it. She'd feared it. Merit had dreaded the helplessness that accompanied such unbridled feeling. That dread had forced her to keep him at arm's length. Merit had forestalled their passions, teasing the man mercilessly. She'd enjoyed that part. She liked when men wanted her. The fact that she wanted him was a more unfamiliar feeling, or perhaps even an unwanted one. She guessed that was why she had kept him out of her bed. *We must first join our kingdoms and unite our armies.* That's what she'd told Dagrun. She'd sought perfection in an imperfect world.

That was an error.

Her whole plan was riddled with errors and innocence.

Her desires would never be sated. The king had his queen and it was not Merit. The matter was settled. Over and done.

If only *she* could settle the pounding in her chest. *That will take time,* she told herself. Yes, time would dull the ache. Her duty, perhaps, would do the same. Maybe there, in her work, she could find solace. After all, she had attained that which she most desired. She was queen regent of Harkana, but not all was as she'd imagined. Her throne was contested. In Feren, Dagrun said the boy—Arko's heir, Ren—had completed the Elden Hunt. He'd slain the eld and taken his trophy. For all she knew, the little ransom was sitting on the throne, awaiting his coronation, so she rode with uncertainty in her heart.

They left behind the lumbering hills that sheltered the woodland kingdom, striking out into the barren lands beyond, the first traces of the desert sand passing beneath their horses' hooves.

A half-day's ride from the rift, they came upon a spindly tower. It was the last Feren outpost. Framed between the crenellations of the wall walk, a man stood, flag raised, giving some sort of signal that they ought to stop. Catching sight of it, Merit lifted a hand and her caravan halted. The procession was large, a hundred Harkan soldiers, all mounted on destriers barded in black leather. And they rode with another fifty men from Feren, so it took a good amount of time for the caravan to slow to a stop. There were a dozen carts. Most held their supplies, but one carried her husband, Shenn, who was injured and weak, and thus unable to ride. Her captain, Sevin, was at her side and her father's man, Asher Hacal, First Captain of the Kingsguard, accompanied her on the ride.

The whole caravan clustered about the lonely tower, and the Feren guard must have felt intimidated by the sheer size of the force because he took his time on the steps. They waited as he made his way down some stairs, the wood groaning beneath his weight, locks clanking softly, then they heard the screech of what must have been an old iron hasp that refused to be loosed. Finally, the door flung open and a young soldier appeared, bright eyes and long hair. He cast about for a moment before catching sight of Merit and her characteristic blue dress. He must have recognized the garb because he went and addressed her directly. "You're the queen regent—am I right?" he asked. "I was told to expect you. I have news if you've time to hear it."

"I do," said Merit, mild irritation in her voice. Her fingers drummed on the saddle of her horse, but the man hesitated to speak, stumbling over his words.

"Out with it," said Merit.

The guard swallowed, still reluctant, but she shot him a terrible glance

main. Carters from Solus said fire had claimed half the Waset,
soldiers he'd encountered thought it was simply the Antecham-
he Ray that had burned. In fact, there were all sorts of rumors
e Mother Priestess.

y say she has a son," the soldier said. "I suppose he'd be your
then."

last one stopped Merit dead in her tracks. "A son?" she asked.
om? Who is the father? The Mother Priestess takes no husband.
rbidden any such congress."

. I know as much, my queen. The boy is older, a man really,
father is the same as yours—if the rumors are to be believed.
y he's the trueborn son of the king and the other one—Ren's the
is just some bastard boy. We heard this news from the fighting
Solus, the patrolmen at the Dromus. It might just be soldiers' talk.
ade in all sorts of gossip," he said, perhaps trying to console her.
eyes twitched, her fingers trembled. Her father was dead and she
rother she had not yet met. No. An heir. There were two of them
ne held the horns and the other the parentage.

hat's all, we'll take our leave," said Asher, speaking for the queen.
hanked him with a nod, backing away from the tower guard, the
of the moment still overpowering her thoughts. She needed time.
k. To mourn. To somehow grieve amid all this uncertainty. That
would no doubt prove the most challenging.

it gave the destrier a good kick, her mind clearing as the horse's
brought cool air to her face. With this much confusion at hand,
y safe course of action was to return to Harkana, and to do it as
as possible. Her father was dead, so there was no sense in going to
he could not be certain of Ren's location, and there was no point
ing after the boy. In fact, this news about Ren raised more ques-
an it answered. Why had he gone to Solus and not Harwen? Had
alled his bastard son to the capital? Had he wanted Ren to serve
Did Ren know the empire's secret? Merit certainly did. Her father
t it to her in a letter, but as far as she knew he'd told it to no one
t there was no knowing what had transpired in Solus. The notion
ustrated and relieved Merit. She had devoted an undue amount
to keeping that boy away from the Harkan throne, but it had all
r naught. Ren was nothing more than the love child of her father
ne whore. The news might have consoled Merit were it not for
k of a second heir, a trueborn son of Harkana. She shook her head

so he spoke at last. "In Solus, in the city of lig[...]
bit, "the Ray of the Sun, your father . . ."

"What about my father?"

"He . . . was put to the flame, forced to end[...]

"A trial by fire," Merit repeated. It was no[...]
had been no trial. No man survived Mithra's Fl[...]
that matter. Fire was fire and it burned every[...]
he's dead then," she said, the words coming slo[...]
Her eyes stung. "A moment." Merit had not s[...]
last meeting at the Battered Wall.

How long had it been? Three weeks? Four? S[...]
on the morning when they last spoke: half-dru[...]
orders while the whole of Harwen gathered a[...]
been a hard end for a hard man. A bitter and[...]
awful than his death, of course. She did not w[...]
and how he might have passed, burned alive in[...]

She drew down her cowl and readied to lea[...]
tapped his spear, indicating that he had other ne[...]

"It's all just rumor," the soldier said, a dro[...]
brow. "They say the heir of Harkana—your bro[...]
of the gods and the kingsguard is there as wel[...]
king. Arko was his name. The one who was ma[...]
got to him, not before the flames took their k[...]
terrible mess, a foreign army trapped in the ho[...]
no one knows what happened to the boy. Some[...]
guard, while others swear he fled to Harkana."

Merit gave no response. She'd hardly had ti[...]
her father's death, and now there was this new b[...]
painful moment for her to wrap her head around[...]
did this happen?" she asked, her words again con[...]
ing. "And why have I not heard this news?"

"It's all just happened in the last few days. You'[...]
anyone else. You've been on the road—right? Fou[...]

"Yes, of course," she said, quietly, chastened b[...]
She had been on the road, deep within the for[...]
that the desert, held hostage by Hykso traders.[...]
Any other news?" she begged, and the guard said[...]
He'd heard the Protector had gone into the domai[...]
returned. Others said it was the Mother Priestess [...]

at that. There were too many unknowns here and too few answers. She did not know the state of her kingdom, nor that of the empire.

She sent out scouts to scale the hill, too see if the way ahead was clear. They reported little. The route to Harkana appeared safe. Barca had not yet encircled her kingdom. There was still time to reach the Harkan throne in advance of a possible siege, so they rode out, moving at a scout's pace, stopping as little as possible, pushing the horses to their limit.

The men chafed at the pace of their ride, but Merit turned a deaf ear to their gripes. There was too much at stake. She wanted to be the first to reach the King's Hall. If she were able to sit herself upon the Horned Throne and claim her place as the queen regent, Merit was certain she could block the bastard's claim to the throne. If the trueborn heir of Harkana returned, she guessed she could do the same. From her father's seat, she could maintain the power and authority of the throne, or so she told herself. It was a child's hope, perhaps, but it was buoyed by this most recent news. If Ren had gone to Solus, he might still be there. He might, in fact, find himself in unwelcome company. If her father was dead and her mother had an heir of her own, Ren would find no friends in the city of the Soleri. Moreover, he might just find himself surrounded by foes. She tried to imagine what he was doing there in the first place, but quickly realized she hadn't a clue. She hadn't a care either. She thought only of Harwen. The Horned Throne was hers, after all. If neither heir had returned to Harwen, she was still regent. The seat belonged to her and she would not allow it to be taken by some dirt-faced boy from the priory or a priest who had never set foot in the kingdom. Arko was dead. He could hardly confirm the identity of this new heir, and news of this king-in-waiting had appeared just after her father's death. The whole thing stunk of lies or some other form of subterfuge.

"We've come upon the first Harkan outpost," said Sevin, momentarily forcing her thoughts to return to the present. Perhaps the Harkan soldiers would have the answers she desired. Eager for news, Merit rode up to the tower, charging ahead of the others, her heart beating so loud she feared the men might hear it. To her dismay, she saw no guard upon the tower.

"Where are the sentries?" she asked.

"Damned if I know," Sevin said as he slipped off his horse. He prodded the tower door with his spear, moving slowly, carefully, prying open the wood then ducking inside to have a look.

"The bastards better not be sleeping," Sevin said, his voice sounding distant as he crept deeper into the tower. Through the partially open door she saw him reach a stair. "I suppose I'll have to climb," he grumbled.

"I suppose you will," Merit shouted.

Sevin returned a moment later, face grim, head shaking. "No one's home," he said. "And no scrolls, either, no messages of any kind, but a chair was broken and the lock on the door was cracked, the hinges bent."

"An attack?" she ventured.

"Perhaps," said Sevin. "But these towers are old. Half the locks are broken and I ain't seen one door that didn't have a busted hinge or two. Could be the boys got drunk and one smashed the other over the head. Could be bandits too."

"No." Merit sensed something was wrong. "That's not it. We need to ride." She gave no voice to her suspicions. She did not want to worry the men, nor did she want to guess at their foe's identity, not aloud at least. It was one more mystery—one more reason to return to Harwen.

Her caravan left with as much haste as it had arrived, sprinting over the low desert basin that stretched between the kingdoms. They made good time. The roads were empty, which made it relatively easy to move her caravan across the sometimes-narrow path, but the emptiness of the desert way raised yet another suspicion, at least to Merit's eye. Where were the carters? Why hadn't she seen the desert caravans or the waste traders, the multitude of men and women that walked or rode the trails between the kingdoms? It was as if Feren had vanished and taken Harkana along with it.

An uneasy feeling crept through her bones, making her all the more eager to return home. Consequently, they stopped as little as was possible, watering the horses only as needed, skirting the most desolate stretches of the desert, straddling the low hills of Harkana, drawing ever closer to Harwen. *I was gone for too long,* she thought, chastising herself again for leaving, wondering about the tower and its absent guard as they caught sight of another of the many outposts that flanked the desert trail.

Merit had wanted to ride right up to it, but Sevin insisted she remain at the rear of the company. He led the men, Asher at his side, the Harkans close behind, the Feren entourage galloping around to the back of the tower should they need to outflank some attack. It was a war stance. Asher was a cautious man; it's why she'd chosen him to lead her guard. Merit allowed the men to do their work. She waited a good distance from the tower, her back straight, hand resting sternly on the pommel of her short sword. If she looked the least bit tired or pained in any way,

Sevin would only use her exhaustion as an excuse to halt their march, and she had no intention of allowing that to happen.

She rode up to him as soon as he emerged from the tower. She was hopeful at first, but when she caught his eye, his head shook twice and she knew the outpost was abandoned. No soldiers and no horses. "We ride out then," said Merit. She did not even bother to question the man. "To Harwen," she said, though the men hardly needed any instruction. The sight of a second abandoned outpost unnerved even the footmen. Something was amiss in Harkana and these men had wives and children in the kingdom.

"Are my suspicions unwarranted?" Merit spoke to her commanders, testing her logic against theirs. "After all," she went on, "the army *is* in the south, defending the kingdom against Barca and his army. Perhaps the outposts were poorly manned. If they held only a single guard, he might have gone ill or been robbed. Maybe the posts were abandoned."

"Could be," said Sevin. "Maybe the towers were overrun by robbers or sand-dwellers. The big fight is in the south, but the outlanders have made a mess of the north end of the basin. If I had to guess at our adversary, I'd put my coin on the sand folk."

"I'm unconvinced," said Merit, still uncertain, unnerved.

Again, they stopped only to water the horses, and twice they ran afoul of a small group of marauders, Hykso mostly, packs of a dozen or so, which were easily and ruthlessly bested by her soldiers. Their presence made her think the sand-dwellers *had* attacked the outposts, but she could not be certain. She sent out soldiers to man the abandoned outposts. In doing so, she chipped away at her own force, but she guessed she had enough men, and Harwen was near. They meant to arrive before nightfall, so they rode out one last time.

When they crested the last of the low hills that stood before the city, her heart quickened at the sight of Harwen's walls, at the *badgir* swaying in the wind. At last, this was home.

And unlike its outposts, the Hornring *was* intact and well defended. Even from a distance she saw men moving here and there along the walls, as tiny as ants, their spears looking no larger than the hairs on her arm.

"At least Harwen's safe," she said to Sevin, and to herself as well. Her time away had cost her a potential husband and a sister's love. Briefly she'd feared it had cost her Harkana as well. Barca might have stormed the walls before she returned, but there were no signs of battle, just a well-armed fortress. At this point, her only potential foe was that thirteen-year-old boy her father named heir before riding off to Solus, or his brother if that one dare lay claim to her throne.

Merit rode once more to the head of the column, ignoring Sevin's objections. *This is my kingdom,* she thought. *I need no protection, no chaperone.* Heedless of danger, she galloped across the Blackwood Bridge, right up to the great gate, turning her horse this way and that while she waited for the sally port to swing wide so she could enter. She guessed the men on the wall walk would recognize her upon approach or while she circled. Merit listened for the familiar whine of the ancient hinges, the creak she'd heard each time the port opened at her return, but the door remained steadfastly closed.

Another mystery, thought Merit as her sandals hit the Blackwood Bridge with a thud. She eyed the familiar door, the eld-horn ornament staring back at her, the hinges unmoving. From this spot, she caught sight of the Battered Wall, that homage to all the humiliations her kingdom had suffered at the hands of the empire. It gave her an unexpected chill. *Am I about to suffer one more of those indignities?* The door had not opened for a reason.

"The queen regent returns!" she cried out. That announcement ought to have elicited a quick response. The men should be hurrying about, opening the door, and readying themselves for her arrival, but the soldiers on the wall walk paid her no attention. Merit had made a point of knowing the names and faces of the Hornring's guards. She did not recognize the man who peered down at her, nor any of the others who joined him. They wore the proper livery, black leather and an iron helm, but the armor fit loosely.

Asher rode to her side. "Do we have an issue?" he asked the man on the wall, and when the sentry did not reply Asher asked for the man's name. Her captain swallowed bitterly when the sentry again refused to answer. Sevin eyed the wall, the gates. She knew his thoughts. Did they have enough men to storm the Hornring? Who occupied Harwen? The army was in the south, the kingsguard in Solus. And the rest of the men were with Merit. Harwen had been ill defended in her absence. An easy target.

"What happened here?" she asked.

"Nothing good, my queen. We should regroup, and we ought to do it somewhere far from these walls."

"No," said Merit. "I demand entry into *my* city. I was regent when I left it, and since I do not recall passing the crown to anyone else, this is still my kingdom!" she announced, her tone bright, her words confident, her chin raised. Sand caked her blue dress, but she looked like a queen, a dusty one, but a queen nonetheless.

Again, the guards gave no reply.

Behind her, the soldiers in her company tapped their spears and the horses beat their hooves. The air was tense, the frustration palpable. It had been an arduous ride, and this was hardly the welcome her soldiers had expected. Merit guessed her men were eager to return to their wives or to their children or to whatever whore they'd been dreaming about for the last few weeks. The Ferens, who had been readying themselves for the ride home, stopped to watch what was happening. Even the birds seemed to pause and listen, for she could no longer hear their chirping. Only the desert wind was audible, but it gave her no comfort. Sevin had asked her to retreat, but Merit would not move. *This is my city,* she thought, *and I'm not going anywhere.*

Some of the men retreated. A few went off in search of dry grass for their mounts. Asher whispered in Sevin's ear, and the Feren captain conferred with his men. All were anxious, and the silence on the wall did little to ease their tension.

Merit was implacable. She would stand at the gate until acknowledged. She knew the game. They were making her wait, humiliating her in front of her company. Her shame would only double if she gave up ground, so she held her place until a soldier poked his head out from between the crenellations. The man was hunched low, his face half concealed behind the stones.

"Make your camp," he said. "Go, set your tents outside the city walls." He eyed her bitterly. "The king'll send riders when he's ready to see you."

9

The House of Ministers was the largest administrative complex in Solus, and thus the largest in the empire. It sat dead center along the Rellian Way, the House of Viziers on one side and the Forum of Re on the other. It was an august address, and regal to behold. Three tiers of lotus-topped columns led to a magnificent barrel vault whose buttery-yellow stones curved elegantly upward, disappearing from the eye as they followed the gentle slope of the vault.

Sarra needed a place of office, and since this was the largest and most prominent workplace in the empire, she guessed she could make do with it. Hence, she had arrived there at first bell. Ott waited for her at the gates. She cocked an eyebrow when she caught sight of him. "You don't look like yourself," she said, appraising the false arm he wore to conceal his identity.

"I thought that was the point," he said, gesturing to the place where his withered arm had for the better part of his life hung loosely within the sleeve of his robe. It was gone now. An arm fashioned from layers of wool and mastic covered the stumplike appendage. With this false arm in place, Ott carried the appearance of a boy with two strong shoulders and two equally broad forearms. He wore gloves, of course, with one of them stuffed just like his sleeve and the other fit tightly over his bandaged fingers. The costume made him look common enough, and he was growing out his hair, trading his shaved pate for a bit of scruff.

Her true son was a one-armed boy who concealed his honey-colored hair, or so the stories claimed. Some alleged he had two heads and an extra finger, while others asserted he was an albino, white-skinned and hairless. Ott had spent the better part of his life in the Repository at Desouk. His pale complexion had no doubt given rise to the albino rumor, but the rest was pure whimsy. In truth, Sarra herself had started half the stories. They helped hide what was now a rather handsome but average-looking boy. Renott Hark-Wadi—Ott, the true heir of Harkana—had spent his entire life hiding in plain sight and now he did so again, albeit in a different fashion.

"This arm's as heavy as a log," Ott grumbled. "And the robe itches. It's wool and I don't like it, not in Solus." There was perspiration on his brow, but a little sweat was a fair price to pay for the safety these new robes granted to him. In truth, the costume had been a compromise. Ott had wanted his freedom, and she had insisted that he disguise his appearance.

"You wanted to leave the domain, so be a dear and suffer a little—won't you?" she asked.

"It's all I do." Ott held up the glove that hid his bandaged fingers. The physician had set the broken digits, but the pain no doubt lingered. "I'm not even myself—am I?"

"No. You're Geta, my new scribe, fresh from the Wyrre and eager to learn the ways of Solus. That's why you're here with me at the House of Ministers. I have no son, and if I ever did have one I certainly wouldn't keep him in Solus." Her priests had busily traded stories not simply about Ott's appearance but about his location as well. Most said he was spirited out of Solus and that he was safe in the city of priests or sheltering in the high towers of Rachis, where his father's two sisters, Eilina and Atourin, lived with their mountain-lord husbands and the snow fell so deep that no man, not even the Alehkar, dare tread. Each hour there were new rumors; they appeared as often as Sarra could invent them.

"Do you think Wat is ever going to open these gates?" she asked. The bell had rung. The time for their congress had come and gone.

Ott's mouth twisted in pain. "Remember, Wat *was* Suten's man and Arko's too. Can we trust him?"

"Trust?" she asked. "No. Never. We trust only each other. Everyone else is—"

"A foe?"

"Potentially. Do you doubt it?"

"No. I've learned plenty about our foes. They multiply by the day, but surely there is someone we can trust?"

"I wouldn't hold my breath," said Sarra. She was a bit surprised by his last comment. "I hope you're not going weak on me, *Geta*." She grinned when the false name left her lips. "Not long ago, we were simple priests. I was once a landless queen, and don't forget that I started my life as a Wyrren girl from a bankrupt house. Today, we preside over the city of the gods. True friends will be hard to come by, and any ally we make will be nothing more than an opportunist." She rattled the gate. "I wonder if the second bell will ring before these doors open."

Bronze gates sheltered the entry to Wat's complex. A curious set of oculi graced each panel, the openings varying in size and aperture. Some sort of map, she thought, of the moon's phases, perhaps. The Soleri were obsessed with such things, and they were the ones who had built this place. Through the various waning and waxing crescents, she saw snippets of what lay beyond: a garden, a columned hall, and a fair number of guards, all clad in the bright yellow of the city of Solus.

Unexpectedly, the gate parted. A man appeared in a robe of fine muslin, the sleeves trimmed with gold. He motioned and they followed him into a courtyard packed with guards.

"Wat isn't taking any chances," she said.

"None of us should, what with the fires," said Ott, "and those pilgrims at the Antechamber. The city is . . ." He hesitated.

He did not often question Sarra. In fact, she could not recall the last time he'd done it. "A mess," she said. "I know the state of the city, and I'm equally aware that I've done little to correct the situation, but all of that is about to change," she said, her voice clear and strong. *Even Ott mustn't doubt me,* she thought, though she feared he might already question one aspect of her leadership: her ability to protect him. The days he'd spent in the Protector's Tower had changed him somehow.

She looked him up and down as they waited, Sarra in her finest whites, Ott looking corpse-white in his woolen robe. They were sheltered from the sun, but not the heat and the noise. The cries of the pilgrims, though distant, drummed in her ear. Sandbags held back the flames, but the smoke was not so easily subdued. It was everywhere in the Waset. The fire beneath the Antechamber showed no sign of retreating. It was an angry, stubborn thing, as unrelenting as the man it consumed.

"They're calling it Mithra's Flame, the Light of the First Ray," said Sarra, who had only just heard the name on their short journey from the Ata'Sol to the House of Ministers.

"I've heard it called Harkana's Revenge, though it's hardly a name I'd repeat," said Khalden Wat. Suten's old servant had at last appeared.

"I wouldn't repeat it either, though I fear it's closer to the truth," said Sarra. "Khalden." Sarra used his first name because she had, as of yet, bestowed no title upon the man. He would have to earn back whatever power he once held, and she wanted him to know it.

Wat looked only slightly injured by her greeting. "Mother Priestess, they say you have been elevated to the position of First Ray, the eyes and mouth of our lord, Tolemy. Is this so?" he asked, which was perhaps his own way of putting Sarra in her place—making her announce the role she had already acquired.

"It is," said Sarra. "My exit from the Empyreal Domain was witnessed by many, including one of our more prominent citizens."

"I know as much," said Wat, "and your predecessor's death *is* well known." He inclined his head toward the Antechamber.

"Yes, the fire," said Sarra. "I wouldn't worry about it. The Antechamber blaze is just the mob's latest entertainment. I'm sure they'll find another one or they'll go home when their stomachs start to growl."

"Let us hope. We haven't slept well in this house, not with the chanting and the smoke."

"No one sleeps well in Solus these days. Don't start thinking yourself a victim, Wat. There's work to be done, which is why I am here."

"As am I." Wat bowed. "I offer you Mithra's greatest blessing and wish that your reign is both long and distinguished."

Sarra grinned slightly, the smile never reaching her eyes. She hoped her reign would be a long one. Her predecessor's had been rather brief and anything but distinguished.

"Shall we go somewhere more private? Your offices?" asked Sarra.

"Oh, of course," said Wat. "Follow me." He ushered her forward, then glanced toward Ott. "Shall *all* of us go?"

"Yes, I always travel with a scribe. This is Geta," said Sarra, and she gave no further explanation for Ott's presence or his physical condition, which must have looked absurd. Wat said nothing about it. He was a keen man and had likely guessed at Ott's identity.

He led them up a grand flight of steps, through a marvelous hall, windowless, but lit by tiny pinpricks in the walls and ceiling. "The Hall of Stars," he announced. It was the first of several great chambers. Wat had apparently arranged a tour of some sort. He led Sarra through the Hall of Rushes, where the ceiling was hung with a thousand dangling rushlights, all of them swaying this way and that. He guided them into the Chamber of Spheres, pointing out a row of globes that illustrated the various known landforms, as well as a few mythical ones. It was all a lavish affair, but she hurried through the room with the spheres and the libraries that followed, hastening past tapestries of improbable height and carvings both large and small. Wonders surrounded Sarra, but she did not lift her head to acknowledge them. Wat tried to point out one or two. "This statue was carved by Rehnet the Tenth himself," he said, but she brushed aside the comment. She did it again when he paused to point out the detailing in a frescoed ceiling and once more when he attempted to describe the quality of the workmanship in some glassware.

"Your offices," she said to Wat.

"What about them?"

"Where are they? I thought we were going straight to them."

"We are. I just thought you might like—" Wat bit down on his lip. He turned and led her in an altogether different direction, through a smaller corridor, one meant for workers, she guessed. It led to a large hall, a place without grandeur. There were no statues or ornamented vaults, but there were a great number of trestle tables—hundreds, actually. On them, ministers copied notes and proclamations. They scribbled on wax tablets or sheets of parchment. Men with careful eyes affixed seals or contemplated the legitimacy of ones that had only just arrived. This was the great machine that kept the empire churning.

"It'll do," said Sarra.

"For what?" Wat asked.

"For my place of office. The Antechamber is destroyed. I cannot rule the empire from that smoldering ruin, and if the Ray held office in the Ata'Sol it would only confuse the people. I am no longer the Mother. I am Ray, nothing more or less, and this is surely a suitable office for the emperor's first servant. The place is big enough for a dozen Rays. I'm sure there's sufficient space for the two of us."

Wat stumbled a bit with his words, or perhaps he was only pretending to do so and was instead hiding a bit of frustration. "Yes, of course. In fact, these men are already in your service. I've simply been keeping them working, as I have for some time. You must have known that Suten was ill for many years before his departure, and the Harkan barely had time to comprehend the scope of his role. I've kept the messages flowing, doing the thankless work that keeps an army fed or an outpost stocked."

"Good. Change nothing, but give us a little space. The Ray needs an Antechamber. I trust there are private rooms within the hall. In fact, I've heard there is one that is adjacent to the Shroud Wall itself?"

"Yes, we can visit it if you'd like."

"Posthaste."

When they arrived at the chamber, servants closed the doors behind them, sealing them into the room. Sarra gave it a good look. The ceiling was high, and a clerestory ran along one wall, providing a bit of light. Frescoes of gold and lapis shimmered in the afternoon sun. Wat indicated a slender door.

"It leads to the Empyreal Domain," he said, "but it's locked from the other side."

"The Kiltet will tend to the door. I'll need it," she said, still looking around the room, sizing it up. "And I'll require you to furnish this chamber in a manner that is suitable to my office."

"Of course," he replied, a hint of nervousness in his voice. "I'll have it done today."

"Good," said Sarra as she leaned her back against the wall. Ott found a low stool and placed himself uneasily atop it.

Wat merely stood. "No one can hear us in here—I'm quite certain of that," he said. Then he glanced at Ott, as if to acknowledge her secret. Perhaps he wanted Sarra to identify her son, to confirm the rumors, but she would do no such thing. There were important matters at hand, so she ignored his unspoken query.

"You seem like a good man, Wat. We've spoken in passing many times, but never at length. I am going to place a great deal of trust in your hands. I have no choice. I can't run this empire without you."

"You need not worry about my loyalty. I swore an oath to the empire."

"Men swear all sorts of things and most of those pledges are as solid as the air they are carried upon."

"No," Wat corrected her. "I swore my oath to Suten's father. It was a vow I took in blood." He pulled back his sleeve and revealed a scar. "That was the old way, and perhaps it is lost to many, but not me. I bound my promise to my blood. To break it—"

"Is to forfeit your life. I understand. It all sounds very Harkan. They're always drawing blood and making promises. A king once promised me his fidelity, but . . ." She did not elaborate. Sarra wanted to trust Wat, but he *was* a man of Sola. She doubted the truth of what he promised. "Still," she said. "You have the eyes of an honest man."

"And you have nowhere else to go," said Wat with a slight chuckle.

He was right, of course, and she knew it. Sarra flashed him a grin. Perhaps there was more to this old man than she guessed.

"Now let us speak of Harkana," Wat said.

"What of it?"

"We've received a dispatch from Harwen. A new king sits upon the throne and begs for the empire's recognition."

"And?" asked Sarra, her lip curling upward with impatience.

"The boy is a complete mystery. He claims to be your son, and Arko's as well, but the former Ray can hardly confirm the boy's parentage—can you?"

"No," said Sarra. "He's not my son, and this is all news to me. Do not acknowledge the boy, not yet—not until I know the truth of the matter."

"A prudent course of action," Wat said. "Some plan is afoot, but no one knows the truth of it . . . Such are the times."

"In that we are agreed. Is there anything else? Has any other kingdom sprouted an heir?"

"No," Wat said, "Harkana is the only kingdom to be so fortunate."

"That's the end of it?"

"There is the matter of your ascension, my Ray. If that's what I may call you?"

"Call me Sarra—what of it?"

"We must prepare for your journey into the mountain," he said. "The Eye of the Sun is lost, but perhaps the task itself might hold some meaning. It will announce the start of your—"

"No." Sarra was already shaking her head. "I'm not going to wander beneath some damned mountain. There will be no fire upon the hill because there is no jewel to light it. The Eye of the Sun lies beneath the Antechamber. That gem is the last thing I want the people to think about. There'll be no feast and no naming ceremony and the sun shall be the only light upon the mountain. I intend to ignore *all* of the usual formalities. I told Mered as much."

"What do you mean?" asked Wat. He truly did look baffled. "What will you have me do?"

"I want you to draft a declaration. Send out the criers as soon as we've finished our little talk. Damn the traditions, I am the First Ray and when the sun rises tomorrow I will hold my first audience in the Golden Hall."

Wat gave her a pitiful look. "Sarra, you forget yourself. At first bell tomorrow we will be on high holiday. The Opening of the Mundus of Ceres is a two-day event, if I recall. During this feast, as with any other such occasion, it is strictly forbidden for any man or woman to go about their business, to hold an audience or attend one. You know as much." Wat offered Sarra a knowing glance. "You seek to avoid the trap your predecessor stumbled on, but you're already in it."

⇒10⇐

"Harkana has a king," said Merit as she stood on the low hills that encircled the city of Harwen, legs planted on the rocky earth, blue dress blowing in the wind.

"That's generous," said Shenn. "I was going to call him a traitor or perhaps a fraud." He stood uneasily upon the sandy knoll, his leg and chest bandaged, a cane wedged against the palm of his hand. He still carried the wounds he'd taken on the Elden Hunt. Her once-strong husband could barely even stand. She eyed him with pity perhaps, or maybe it was resentment. It was the emperor who married her to a man who chose not to love women. Shenn could not deny his true nature, and she could not blame him for doing it. He was a husband in name only. But he was a friend, the best she had, and perhaps that meant something. He grinned when he caught her eye. "Merit, tell me what sort of man keeps a queen regent waiting?" He pointed to a spot on the wall. "I used to sit at my window and watch the changing of the guard at that very place. I can still see them in my thoughts, coming and going. I know the patterns and I don't see them. These aren't our soldiers."

"Then whose men are they? And how could this happen? We were away for, what . . . three weeks?"

"Perhaps four," said Shenn. "But I hardly think it matters."

"Agreed," said Merit. "None of this could have occurred without a great deal of planning. If these aren't *our* soldiers, they must be mercenaries or they're part of some army we haven't met. They can't be Harkan. This isn't an insurrection—is it?"

"No, this isn't the work of some angry warlord. Harkans don't go stealing thrones in the night. It just isn't done," said Shenn.

"Right. They'd want to cut me down in front of everyone."

"Yes, we're a murderous bunch," said Shenn. "But at least we're honest. We don't steal crowns."

"I'm forced to agree, though I have sent messengers to the warlords, calling them to my camp. Most are engaged in the conflict to the south, but a few stayed behind to protect their lands."

"Will they come to your side?" Shenn asked.

"It's their sworn duty, but these are strange times."

"Barca and his army of traitors," said Shenn. "He's more trouble than we guessed."

"Yes, it's ironic—isn't it? We sent the army south to make certain our kingdom was safe from invasion, and someone took their march as an opportunity to seize the throne."

"Irony's got nothing to do with it. I'm calling it piss-poor luck," said Shenn, grimacing slightly as he pressed his weight against the cane.

"I think not," said Merit, her scowl deepening. "They were aware of my absence as well as the army's, and they knew about this rumored heir to the throne. I'm guessing this new king will claim he is the trueborn son of Arko and Sarra. There are few who can prove him wrong."

"A boy with half a claim to the crown arrived, and with little or no force took the kingdom?" Shenn asked. There was doubt on his face and in his voice.

"Your guess is as good as mine. For all I know he *is* the rightful heir and king, or maybe he's the bastard." Merit ran a hand through her long black hair, her fingers filling up with sand. "We won't know until we walk through those gates."

"And when will that happen?"

"Your guess is as good as mine." She kicked at the sandy earth. "I'm out of patience."

"You are also out of choices. We're not going to breach those walls, not without a ladder or two, and it'll take time to manufacture siege equipment. Our soldiers aren't prepared for this sort of thing. We barely have enough provisions to get us through the night."

"I know as much." Merit settled on a large rock, her eyes fixed once more on Harwen's sunbaked walls, thoughts spiraling toward despair. It was then that she heard the tap of sandals on the hard rock. Sevin had joined them on the hilltop.

"The Ferens are asking to go," he said. "They came to deliver the queen regent, and they did it. There's an uneasy feeling here and the men want to ride out under the cover of night."

"Let them go," said Merit. "This isn't their fight."

"Are you certain?" Sevin asked. "A man can never have too many swords."

"They're not *my* men."

"I'll let them know," said Sevin, but already she could see the Ferens readying their horses for the ride. She knew the men had only enough provisions for the journey there and back, and she had no means to feed them.

"Nearly half my force," she whispered as the Ferens prepared for the ride back to Rifka. And those weren't the only men she'd lost. Three or four had run home to their wives. The sand-dwellers had claimed two, and another dozen had been sent out to man the abandoned outposts. She guessed she had seventy spears at her side, maybe less. They were good men, but it was less than half the force she'd rode out with when she left Rifka, and it made her feel vulnerable. Immediately, she was aware of how tentative her situation had become. She had an escort with limited provisions. They would need additional foodstuffs, and soon. If the new king meant to insult Merit, he'd clearly done so. And if he wanted to humiliate her, she guessed he had done so again, but he had better show his face, or her escort might just vanish.

In the fading light, she looked to Harwen and, unintentionally, caught sight once more of the Battered Wall. It did little to improve her mood. The wall made her think of her father and the times they'd spent beneath it. She expected some pang of grief to strike at her heart, but instead of pain she felt only a sense of hollowness: a space with no feeling—no hurt and no happiness.

She did not even notice when the gates of the city opened.

Riders came forth, two of them, set atop destriers. She had not supped. In fact, she could not even recall when she had last had a chance to eat or change clothes. She wore a decent gown, worthy of a regent but also caked in dust. She brushed at the dirt as the riders approached, trying to look the part of a queen when they arrived, standing erect, chin raised.

Her tent carried the emblem of the king, the silver horns of Harkana emblazoned upon black goatskin. The riders must have caught sight of the crest because they were coming right at her, galloping at a frightful pace. Merit was eager to talk, so she strode toward the approaching soldiers, eyes fierce, teeth bared.

"Out with it," she said. Neither man had spoken his name.

"The king will see you," said the first of the two riders. He was an older man, hair white and a bit short for a Harkan, his skin a little too pale. He didn't look like a deep-desert man. His teeth were too clean, but she followed him, gesturing for Sevin to rouse the men.

"No guards," said the other soldier, a clean-shaven fellow who looked to be no older than a boy, "but you can follow along behind us if you'd like."

Merit clenched her fists. She'd wanted a triumphal return, seventy soldiers at her back, banners raised, but she was once again denied.

"No soldiers, none at all. That's the king's command, not mine," said the older man, voice gruff. "You may enter along with your husband," he added, as if Shenn were some kind of protection.

"I will enter as I left the Hornring," she said.

"And how is that?" asked the older man, the one with the pale skin and white hair.

"As queen regent—it is the law."

"Queen, eh? Well, we don't have one of those, but you can enter all the same. Come," said the rider as he galloped off toward the gates.

The walk from her camp to the Blackwood Bridge was not far, but Shenn's stumbling made for slow going and the journey seemed to last hours when it might have been minutes. They passed over the bridge and beneath the arch. They were home, but nothing felt familiar. The court was empty, a ghost yard where once there had been a thriving castle. Where were the merchants and the soldiers? Where were the proud banners and the lookouts upon the towers? Even the *badgir* seemed to slump, as if the wind itself had abandoned this place. It was late in the day, sunset, but surely that was no excuse. The Harwen she recalled had bustled at every hour of the day.

The corridors of the Hornring were no different from the streets.

The halls were quiet, empty almost—no servants rushing about their business, no soldiers or workmen of any kind. Even the mice seemed to be in hiding.

Everything's wrong, Merit thought, but she went along with it anyway, dread filling that hollow place in her heart as the doors to the throne room opened and she waited to see what was inside.

⇒ 11 ⇐

The lamps went out and Mered's soldiers surrounded the Harkans, taking up positions but not advancing. They held, waiting for the ransoms to surrender themselves to the empire. No one came forward, so Admentus told the ransoms to take the night, *to think things over,* he said with a chuckle. Then the red soldiers encircled the exposed portions of the cistern. They blocked the Harkans from leaving through the open archways, but the backside of the cistern was shot through with pipes and passages. Thus, when Admentus billeted the red army, Ren went looking for a way to escape.

In fact, he'd been at it all night.

"What's this? Tye asked. "The twelfth passage—the thirteenth?" They'd obviously lost track of the number. Not one of the corridors had led to the surface. In truth, they'd each ended in a brick wall or some other obstruction.

"No." Ren picked up the conversation. "I think it's the fourteenth. Remember that narrow one?"

"Ughhh." Tye shook her head. Ren had tried to force his way through the slender passage but had only gotten himself stuck. It had taken the black shields an hour to free him, and time was in short supply. Nevertheless, they'd been through every imaginable sort of passageway. Some were new, others ancient. A few were dug in mud and clay, while most were set with carefully laid stones. Ren had put every last bit of his strength into the search. He wanted to find a way out before the morning came around and the soldiers in red advanced, but that was not his sole motivation. He feared that if he slowed for a moment, that if he gave up the chase, he might have to think about what Admentus said. He'd need to reckon with the truth, if it *was* indeed the truth: Ren was a bastard and not the true heir of Harkana. If that was the case, then he'd suffered in the priory for nothing. He'd claimed a throne that might not even belong to him. Arko made Ren his heir. He'd acknowledged him in front of the guard, but did he know Ren was a bastard?

"It's darker up ahead," Tye said, breaking his chain of thought and drawing his attention back to the task at hand.

"Is that good?" Ren asked.

"Damned if I know." Tye held up the tiny lamp, trying to illuminate the passage, but she was too late and Ren slammed into a wall.

"Definitely not good," said Ren, shaking his head, fingers rubbing at his temples.

Tye held the guttering flame up to the wall, illuminating her face. In spite of all they'd suffered, there was still a glint of hope in her eyes, a bit of red blossoming across her pale cheeks and nose. This was the girl he'd saved from the burning ruins of the priory, the same girl he'd fought Oren Thrako to rescue. He'd once stood beneath the sun for five days, baking like a bit of bread, just to spare her the injury, and he'd do it all again. Ren wondered if she'd noticed all he'd done, if she cared.

"These stones are freshly set." Edric, one of the captains, interrupted Ren's thoughts. "Someone laid them recently. The grout has only just set." He dug at the mortar. It was hard on the surface, but when Edric poked at it with his sword, the top layer chipped off and the cement beneath was damp.

"They're blocking the passages," said Ren.

"Yes, but they're not far ahead of us," said Tye. "If we'd come this way first, perhaps we'd have beaten them to this tunnel, maybe . . ."

"I know," said Ren. "Maybe we wouldn't be in this damned mess. They must've paid off every smuggler in Solus, bribed them to reveal their passages, making certain we'd never find our way out of here."

Edric grunted.

Ren was exhausted, hungry. He hadn't eaten, and the amber he'd swallowed was worse than foul.

"All the fucking corridors are blocked," said Kollen. He came upon them unexpectedly, appearing out of the darkness, beard caked in sweat.

"How many did you find?" asked Ren. *And must you always curse?*

"A measly six."

"We found twice that number," Tye said, a bit proud, but not too haughty. After all, the passages *had* been blocked.

"There could be other paths," Ren ventured.

"And there might be a golden stairway that leads us straight up to To-lemy's fucking brothel, but we're not going to find it," Kollen said.

"Not if we don't try," Ren shot back, his anger making his headache clear.

"All we've done is try," said Kollen. "It must be morning, or it soon will be. They offered us a night and we spent it. The time has come and gone and we've got nothing to show for it. Just a few headaches and some empty bellies. I spoke to your captain, Gneuss. His soldiers crowded into every hole they could find, but they were all blocked. He sent a dozen men to test Mered's line. None of them returned."

"I didn't know that," Ren said.

"Of course not, you've been smacking into walls. I saw the red soldiers slaughter those men," said Kollen. "They cut them up and left them to bleed out. Gneuss had to shoot them full of arrows just to put a stop to their whimpering. Not a pretty end."

"Did you think it would be?" Ren asked.

"No, and I doubt we'll find a better one, not unless we surrender."

Ren shook his head. He knew what Kollen was after, but he didn't want to talk about it. He didn't want to consider their surrender until they'd exhausted every other option. He had escaped death more than once already and walked through a wall of flame. He'd done plenty, and all of it had seemed impossible right up until the moment he accomplished it.

Hence he retraced his steps, hurrying back down the passage toward the great drum of the cistern, where the body of the kingsguard waited. There, they bided their time, some sleeping in shifts, others chewing at the last of their provisions, pissing behind rocks, or tossing their waste into the black stream. There were almost five hundred of them and they filled nearly half the space. He smelled them before he caught sight of the guard and, in the distance, he glimpsed the men in red, aligned in rows, waiting

in the darkness, standing idle like tokens on a game board, ready for someone to set them in motion.

"It must be morning," said Tye. "I wish I'd slept."

"I don't," muttered Ren. He needed to keep the promise he'd made.
Bastard or not, he'd named himself king and told every one of these men
he'd find a way out of the city. He'd made this mess, and he wouldn't rest
until he'd done something to clean it up.

"What's happening?" Ren asked when he caught sight of the captain.

"Happening? We're about to be overrun by four armies, maybe five."
Gneuss grimaced. "The men in red are repositioning their soldiers and
we're up to something similar. Our boys slept in shifts while my captains
worked up a defense. I've got most of the men in place for the counterat-
tack. We're as ready as we'll ever be."

"It's morning—isn't it?" Ren asked.

"I've got no way to know the hour, but the red army started reshuffling
their troops a while back, so I guessed it was time," Gneuss said. There
was something bitter in his voice. Maybe it was anger or just some last
bit of defiance. "Take a look," he said. "Seems they have a present for the
men."

In the distance, soldiers upended great sacks. Rats scurried in every
direction, but Mered's men had already blocked most of the ways. They
used torches to corral the rats, to send them scampering toward the archways of the cistern. The patter of a thousand little feet made tiny echoes
in the dark.

"Back," said Ren, but Gneuss wouldn't budge. He refused to even look
down at the things.

"I've eaten rat for midday meal. If this is the worst they can offer, we
might as well have us a snack." Gneuss stood tall, but when the rats came
he seemed to change his mind. "In rows," he told his soldiers.

The men made a wall with their shields. They tried to hold back the
creatures, but their armor wasn't meant to repel rodents. The rats scurried
over the soldiers, tangling themselves in the men's cloaks, looking for
food or a bit of flesh to snack upon.

"They must have emptied the stores of every haruspex in the city,"
said Gneuss, explaining where all the rats had come from and why they
seemed particularly hungry.

"What is this?" asked Tye, who had clasped a hand to her mouth.

"They want to make certain that your lot surrenders. You didn't come
when they first called, so they're going to soften you up a bit before they

make their second offer," said Gneuss, and again his voice was tinged with bitterness. Gneuss knew what waited for his men, or maybe he'd just guessed at it.

"Why don't they just attack?" Tye asked, hand still clasped to her mouth, eyes filled with disgust.

"It's damned obvious—isn't it?" Gneuss asked. "They've got the numbers, but they want to keep you folk alive. If they sent a thousand swords scurrying into this bowl there'd be no way to know a ransom from a soldier."

"I'm what's keeping you alive?" asked Ren.

"You royal brats are doing a fine job of protecting us. Unfortunately, I don't think it will last. Sooner or later, when they've toyed with us for a bit, they're going to ask for you folk to turn yourselves over."

"That's when we fight," said Ren.

"That is when *my* men fight."

"Your men?" asked Ren. Was he just a bastard? Had he lost his authority? Every bit of him bristled at the suggestion.

Gneuss must have seen the confusion on Ren's face. "These are your men, but we all know that each of you will be a whole lot safer if you hand yourself over to the red army. The kingsguard lives to protect the king, but I'm not sure we can protect anyone down here. Bastard or not, Ren, you should go. This won't end well."

"I'd rather it didn't end at all. I made a promise to get us out of here. I mean to keep it. Gneuss, you must have something to live for. A wife, anything?"

The captain laughed. "No one gives a damn about me. I'm second to Asher Hacal, your father's captain."

"The king?" asked Ren, his interested piqued. He knew so little about his father. The mere mention of him made Ren yearn to know more about the man. "You knew him?"

"I did. We hunted together and killed. I stood with him against the outlanders. I swore an oath to protect your father, but if you ask me, words are just shit. I fought alongside the man and more than once I saw the king take a blow just to protect one of his own."

"You still haven't answered my question."

"You want to know about me? Damn, even your father didn't care where I came from. Mother died giving birth to me. Lost my father when the men from Solus came to take my older brother."

"He was one of the tributes?" Ren asked.

Gneuss grunted. "He died fighting the soldiers. They left my brother, but Erich wasted away a year later. His skin turned black and he vomited till there was nothing left of him. He might have lived if my father let the soldiers take him. They say the servants in Solus eat better than most commoners in Harkana. I was left with no family, so I turned to thieving. I was good at it too. I almost lifted a dagger off the king's belt, but I wasn't *that* good. Your father caught me by the hand and shoved me to the ground, said I'd done a decent job of robbing him, but not a good enough one. He did note that I was fast, faster than most of his men, so he gave me a choice. He could lop off my hand right there and then, in the market, or I could pledge my service to him and join his soldiers." Gneuss held up his hand, indicating that he had chosen the latter.

"You're a one-eyed thief," Ren said.

"And you're a bastard. Aren't we a lovely couple? Look ahead and stop asking your damned questions."

In the darkness beyond, there was movement. A black thing, sheathed in glimmering fur, leapt at the Harkan shields. The creature tore at one soldier's throat, nearly parting the head from the torso, and when a second man stabbed at the thing, it leapt on him and mauled his face, licking up the blood and looking for more.

"What is *that*?" asked Tye.

Ren didn't know what it was, but he worried for Adin. If that thing came upon him, prone and defenseless, he was a dead man. Fearing what might happen next, Ren moved between the creature and his friend, scrambling as he went, trying to find a weapon. "Swords," he said. "Find swords." He set eyes on the red blade he'd stolen in the garden, but Tye screamed before he could snatch it up. Ren spun, thinking she'd been mauled, but Tye had only just caught sight of the beast as it flashed in the torchlight.

"A panther," she said. "Never seen one, but I think—"

"No," said Ren. "It's something else, see those horns?" Like an addax, the creature had a pair of tall and curling horns. Its fur was black, but beneath that pelt there were hints of something shiny and scale-like.

"It's nothing I've ever seen or heard of," said Kollen. "A monster."

"There are no monsters, just men and beasts," said Gneuss. "The darkness plays tricks on your eyes. As long as it bleeds we'll kill it," he said, but his words held little conviction. Worse yet, Ren saw no blood on the thing. The men struck it with sword and ax. One after another they dealt what looked like mortal wounds, but the creature was undeterred, undamaged even, and it was coming toward them.

Four or five men thrust their spears at it. One went clear through the gut, coming out the other side and striking the stones. Two more went elbow-deep into its scaly hide.

"It's done," said Tye, but Kollen was already shaking his head, cursing. The whole thing ought to have been over, but it wasn't. The creature rolled, breaking off the spears that poked from its back before continuing its attack, undaunted, the broken shafts protruding from its black fur as it bounded toward the ransoms.

"It's death itself, Horu in disguise," cried Kollen as the creature leapt at them. It might have struck him, but one of the men managed to knock it aside with his shield.

Gneuss's voice boomed in the chamber, calling the men to his side. The kingsguard surrounded the nameless terror, but the creature flailed about, its tail striking them like a whip made of iron, cutting shields and rending limbs. Once more, it cleared a path to the ransoms. It came charging straight at them and Ren found himself standing face-to-face with the beast. It's slitlike eyes fell on him, but they were not the hungry eyes of a predator. The creature looked him up and down. Then, almost inexplicably, it retreated.

The beast had taken Ren's measure and withdrawn, but for what reason? It had faced the tallest and boldest of the black shields. Why had it paused at the sight of Ren?

"Did you see that?" said Kollen. "The thing looked right at us and turned around."

Indeed, the creature had turned around, and leapt at Gneuss's soldiers. A dozen or more thrust out their spears, but it severed the shafts and tore through their armor. If this continued, the creature would slaughter half their force before they subdued it.

The horn felt suddenly heavy in Ren's pack and that buzzing sound rattled in his ear. Something had stirred within Ren. *I have a weapon,* he thought, *and it is unlike any other.* He lifted the crooked horn. Curling barbs dotted the shaft. It looked like a mud-slathered stick, a twig with too many branches. Ren knew otherwise. The staff was shorn from a god, or something like one.

Horn raised, he went chasing after the nameless creature.

He worried the beast would lash him with its tail, that its claws would sever his hand from his body before he even had a chance to strike with the ivory staff, but the nameless thing refused to assault him. When Ren advanced, the beast withdrew. The pair executed a subtle dance: Ren

following, the creature retreating, slashing at the kingsguard and slaying
them with ease. It was quick to attack, but it would not strike at Ren.
That much was clear. Ren advanced, and when the creature was at last
forced up against a wall, the kingsguard hurled a dozen spears at it while
Ren thrust the horn into its back.

Thinking the task was done, he stumbled backward, but the creature
yet lived. It stood defiantly, thrashing about, but something in that last
blow made its movements slow. It snarled, twisting this way and that,
trying to pull free of the horn, but the bone sword was riddled with barbs
and little bifurcating tusks. It would not loosen.

Froth dribbled from the creature's maw.

The kingsguard retreated and the beast ceased its contortions. Its body
was at last limp, near lifeless, the glimmer fading from its silvery eyes. It
heaved one last breath and Ren caught the creature's eye. Again, the beast
offered him a questioning glance, the eyes of a hound whose master had
betrayed him. It gazed at him with a strange sense of familiarity, just as
the statues in that garden had done. Once more Ren felt that odd buzzing,
that screeching noise that threatened to overwhelm his consciousness. He
felt suddenly dizzy. Something was happening to him. The statues in the
garden, the black creature. They were somehow connected. He guessed
they were pieces in some puzzle, but he hadn't the faintest idea of how to
put them together.

"For a bastard," Kollen interrupted his thoughts, "you're quite handy.
Good to have in a pinch. How'd you manage that?"

Ren shrugged, his head still pounding. He could explain nothing.

It took three of the kingsguard to free the horn from the nameless
creature's back. They returned it to Ren, holding it up with an odd kind
of reverence, as if they were returning a holy relic and not some crooked
horn caked in mud and wet with the fallen creature's blood.

Ren snatched at the horn. He wasn't certain why he was so eager to
have it back. He simply wanted it, as if it were a part of him, something
that he desperately needed to hold.

"That was a feat," Carr said.

"It was more than a feat, it was a king's work," Gneuss said. "The old
blood, that's what that was." The others seemed to agree. Some nodded,
others gathered around Ren.

*Maybe I haven't learned how to lead these men, but at least I've proven I
can fight.* It was a small start, but maybe that was how things worked.
Gneuss had once been a thief, but he'd impressed the king and earned a

position among his honored soldiers. Ren had done something similar and everyone had seen it. He hadn't found a way out of the Hollows but he *had* saved a good number of the kingsguard. The soldiers slapped his back and knocked him jokingly. *They're treating me as their brother.* After all this time, he'd earned a bit of respect from the men. He savored it. Even Kollen had a look of awe on his face, but he quickly wiped it away. Carr did nothing to hide his admiration, and neither did Tye. Gneuss gripped Ren's shoulder manfully and gave it a good squeeze, his eyes on the bloody horn. "You've done well, bastard."

A call rang out from the far side of the chamber. It was Edric, and he was standing at the mouth of the cave. "Find cover," he cried, though, in truth, it was too late for any of them to find shelter. The whistling of a sling followed close on his words. Most such weapons carried bullets made of stone or metal, but these yokes held something a bit less solid. The red soldiers lobbed heaps of entrails at the kingsguard. Coils of rotted viscera splattered on the stones, and the men retched at the sight of it.

"It's your morning meal," cried out of one of the soldiers in red, a tall man with a cleft palate. "You've all done a wonderful job of making it through the night. You've even slain Mered's favorite toy, so we thought we'd send you a little something to eat. We've been nibbling on biscuits and honey, but we guessed your lot would enjoy something a bit meatier," the soldier japed. The men filled their pouches once more and launched heaps of offal into the air. One sling bore the severed head of a Harkan scout. They launched three more before the army parted and the red-robed pair, Admentus and Demenouk, appeared at the far side of the black river. Ren's heart sank at the sight of them. There would be no escape, no smugglers' routes to lead them out of the city.

Admentus and his scribe stopped just short of the black stream, wriggling their noses at the stench and looking eager to be done with this business. The ransoms gathered around Ren. Gneuss stood at their backs, a hand placed again on Ren's shoulder, his touch warm, almost comforting despite the circumstances.

"The guard can take care of itself, so don't go making some sacrifice on our behalf. Someone's got to live through this," Gneuss said, muttering that last part.

"If we leave," Ren said, "they'll storm this place and . . ."

"I know what's coming. This moment's about you folk, so get on with it," Gneuss said, voice cold, emotionless.

"Come now! Time to leave!" Admentus cried. "I don't suppose any of you want to spend another night in the Hollows. From what I've heard it wasn't a pleasant one, though I wouldn't really know. I spent mine in a feathery bed, dreaming sweet dreams, just like you'll be doing tonight. Come, boys." His words echoed with surety. He seemed to think they would accept his offer, so he held out a hand and gestured for them to come forward.

"Give us a moment," Gneuss said.

"A moment. Nothing more." His words were as cold and hard as iron. The time for talk had come and gone.

"Go," said Gneuss, "all of you, just go. What comes next is just a bunch of dying and I'd rather not see children slaughtered."

"No," said Ren. "I stay, but everyone else goes. Adin needs treatment. Down here, in the Hollows, he won't last another night. Take the litter and take yourselves along with it." Ren made certain to look each of the ransoms in the eye.

No one said anything. There was too much pain, too much regret, the moment too charged to permit any of them to speak. Maybe they just wanted this all to be over, so they bent their heads and went about the task. Kollen and Tye lifted Adin's litter and carried him toward the bridge. Adin took hold of Ren's hand as he passed.

"Ren," said Adin, "I . . . I don't want to go, I . . ."

"It's not about wanting," said Ren. "I went all the way to Feren just to save your miserable ass. I won't see it tossed away."

Adin grimaced. He hurt, but Ren could not be certain whether it was the wounds that pained him or his leaving. "I'll come back," said Adin, his voice faint. "I'll march with every fucking soldier in Feren and I'll come back for you. I'm not even a proper ransom. They set me free, remember, so perhaps they'll do it again." Adin spoke the truth, but Ren did not think he would find his freedom, not immediately.

"Goodbye, Adin." Ren said the words he thought he'd never say. "Please, you have my blessing. Share the sun's fate and all that."

Kollen tossed Curst onto the litter, as the soldiers had done once before. Carr went too, and since Ren had not known the boy, he only shrugged as the ransom passed. Tye and Kollen held the litter. A bridge led them over the black river, but they did not cross it. Only Carr made his way to the far side. Kollen and Tye simply laid Adin atop the bridge before coming back to where Ren stood.

Confused, perhaps, Admentus spoke out, "Come now," he said. "The rest of you better gather your things and make your way across the bridge. I won't ask again."

"Go, Tye." Ren blurted out the words. He put his arm around her, stealing one last embrace. "Go on," he commanded. "Spend your days in a cell. But one day they'll set you free and then you can have whatever you desire—a life, and a husband, perhaps." That last bit hurt Ren the most.

He was giving her away.

He would never leave the Hollows, but she could get out. He took her by the shoulders and pointed her toward the bridge.

Tye would not budge. Her eyes were red and glossy and she'd bitten something off her lip. She clearly had something to say, but from the look on her face, she knew it would pain him.

"What is it?"

Tye glanced at the bridge. "I'm not doing it." She paused again, reluctant, but she went on. "I'd rather fight it out down here than go back to those cells. They know about me, Ren. You know that—right? I'm a girl, and they all want to stick their pricks in me." She shouted it out for everyone to hear. "There'll be no safety for me in the priory. No. I don't care about dying in this hole. I'd rather take a sword than suffer a month beneath the sun or half a lifetime in a cage. I'm staying."

He gave her another push.

"No, Ren. I won't."

"Dammit, you have to," he said.

A hand gripped his shoulder. It was Kollen. "I don't think the girl's going." He said it softly, so no one else could hear him.

"Fine," said Ren. "She stays. Your work is done, Kollen. Take your leave. Go and be an asshole somewhere else."

Kollen's hand had not yet left Ren's shoulder. "No. I'm also staying. See, Hark-Wadi, you're a bit of an asshole, too, and as you've often noted, so am I. We're quite alike, the two of us. Stubborn and all that. I'm never going back to one of those stinking cells." To make his decision known, Kollen turned to the red army, dropped his breeches, and aimed a great piss in their direction.

It was answer enough.

Admentus rejoined the ranks of his men, shaking his head a bit as he did it. The soldiers draped the ransoms in heavy woolen blankets and offered them cups of amber and strips of hard meat as they led them away.

Ren thought he spied a bit of fruit, too, a meal like the one he so desperately wanted.

"We're done here," Admentus said, the red army forming ranks in the distance, ready to commence with their attack. "We only wanted the tall Feren, but we'll take the others. We needed him alive and the Harkan dead." His eyes met Ren's. "I suppose we'll have both accomplished in short order."

≕ 12 ≕

A new banner hung in the King's Hall of Harkana. Merit was certain of it, and this was not the only change she noticed. In her father's day, lamplights flickered high in the corners of the room, but that had been the extent of the illumination. As she walked into the chamber, torches blazed from every wall, and two great braziers churned with flame, one on each side of the throne, and the banner had changed. In fact, the changing of the cloth bothered her almost as much as the boy who sat beneath it. The cloth was foreign, much like the king.

Just the sight of him on the throne, pompous and smirking, made Merit want to draw her short sword and cry out to every trueborn Harkan in the room for assistance—assuming there were any. The boy certainly did not belong on the throne, and the men who surrounded him didn't seem to belong here either. Feeling uneasy, she fingered the pommel of her sword, but a guard slipped the blade from her grip before she had a chance to draw it, which was probably best for Merit. Acting rashly seldom led to favorable ends, so she exchanged her anger for calm and addressed the boy politely. "I'm told you are a king?" It was a question. She desired some explanation for how and why this boy had come to sit upon the throne. He gave no answer, so she asked, "Are you the bastard son of Arko, the one that went on that hunt? Did you slay the deer?" She cocked her head as she spoke. Merit already knew the answer. Shenn had met Arko's bastard, so when he saw the boy he gave Merit a subtle shake of the head, letting her know that this was not the boy he'd met on the hunt. She hardly needed the confirmation. Arko's bastard would have already strung her up for treason. But aside from making her wait at the gates, this king had shown no obvious resentment toward Merit or her husband. *So who are you?* she wondered. *And how did you take the throne?*

"Sister," he said. His tone was bright, almost friendly, but it left an ill feeling in her gut. He had no right to address her as such, but he went on speaking. "I am not the man you think."

Well, that was for certain.

"I was born of Sarra Amunet," he said. "I am the true son of Arko and his queen, but I wasn't raised in Harwen. I'm afraid I missed whatever childhood we might have shared. Instead, I was brought up by my mother, in total seclusion, in the city of Desouk."

"And do you have some proof of your parentage? Is my mother here?" Merit would not bend the knee until she was certain of the boy's identity.

"Our mother is in Solus. And your proof," he said, standing, revealing that one of his sleeves was empty except for the shadow of something small within it, the outlines of an odd little arm. "This is your proof," he said. "If Mother had shown me to her king, he'd have thrown me to the jackals. She didn't fancy that, and she didn't want me to be raised in the priory, so she sent the other boy. The bastard son of Arko served in my place, the boy who was born the same week. She sent *him* to the Priory of Tolemy, and our father never knew the difference. Even when he named Ren his heir, he did not know his true identity." The boy forced his lips into a small, slender smile. "All that is in the past though—isn't it? Harkana has its rightful monarch, and we are better off for it. Ransoms make poor kings—do they not?"

"True enough," said Merit. He made a decent case, but she wasn't convinced. *This boy is not Harkan.* He was not her brother, but could she prove it? That was the question. He was already on the throne. *But how did he take it? Did he simply march into the city and sit his ass upon the empty chair?* There were too many questions here and too few answers to make any sense out of them.

"But the horns," she blurted out. "Surely you must undertake the hunt, as my father did and his father before him."

"With this arm? Do you think I'm a fool? I've heard about the hunt and what it entails, the high cliffs and narrow defiles. I could never attempt that, not with this withered little thing for an arm, and I haven't the constitution for a long journey or the murdering of beasts. Why do you think Mother hid me in the first place?" His reply was not entirely unreasonable. She understood the logic, but she did not accept it. To be a king meant something in this land; one did not acquire the Horned Throne easily. She'd kill an eld herself if it would earn her the chair, but the task was already done. The boy in Solus had the horns, or so it was said.

"Traditions are not easily set aside," she reminded the boy who sat on the throne. "To do so might sow unrest among the common folk, and the warlords as well."

"Well, perhaps that is where *you* can assist me, dear sister. You were raised in the Hornring—I think that's what you call it. Surely Merit Hark-Wadi can act as my emissary and explain the uniqueness of my position."

That you are an imposter, she thought, *and an outlandish one at that.* Her mouth moved as if to speak, but she held herself back once more. She maintained her queenly composure. It's what she was good at. In contrast, nothing about the boy suggested the power or presence of a king. He looked like some minor dignitary, or, worse yet, some lowly servant sent to carry out a duty he'd rather not perform. He sat limply in the chair, the great horns making him look small and insignificant.

In the silence that followed, the boy's blank expression resolved into something harsher, the lines of his young face hardening at the eyes. He pursed his lips.

"I've had some time to consider your arrival," he said, and it was indeed true. The boy *had* made her camp outside the city. "I have an idea of sorts. I think it's a rather good one, though I doubt you'll agree with it, not at first. Nevertheless, we Harkans must stand together and we ought to embrace my reign. I've come up with a rather novel way of completing this task. Come forward."

He motioned to Merit, but she did not move. She stood alongside Shenn, wishing he were in better shape, that he were his old self, strong and reassuring, ever deft in combat.

He could offer no help, so all she could do was shrink away as the guards came to fetch her. Two of them held her by the arms and brought her before the king.

"Two things," said the boy. "First, kneel and pledge yourself to me. Do it in front of all who have gathered."

This is wrong, she thought, *and completely without precedent.* She was still queen regent as far as she was concerned, and even if she wasn't, she had no need to swear anything to this child.

"Perhaps we should wait," she protested. "Shouldn't there be a proper coronation?" Surely the boy had not had time to perform one. "We must summon the warlords, the seven. The men must pledge oaths to you. It's our way."

The boy nodded ever so slightly. "All in good time," he said. "For now, it is you I am worried about, Merit, Queen Regent of Harkana and first daughter of Arko. Do you think my absence has kept me from knowing the kingdom's gossip? They say you are king in all but name, that you sat in your father's chair during the Devouring and heard the people's complaints. There cannot be two regents in one kingdom. Thus, it is you that I am concerned with and not the warlords, or the eld horns, or the proper setting of the crown upon my head." He snickered at that last one. He already had a circlet hanging crookedly on his head. It was not the double crown of Harkana, the one she'd taken to Feren and lost in the desert—the boy had found some other one. It was silver and annular, so she guessed it did the job.

What does he want from me?

Did he require a simple act of obeisance or was it something deeper? Must she acknowledge him and at the same time humiliate herself?

The guards forced her to her knees.

Merit kneeled, but she did not allow her composure to falter. She would not struggle or cry out, nor would she beg. This was her home, her seat of power. How it had become such a twisted place in so short a time she did not know, but this was her fault. She'd left the throne and this boy had taken it. Opportunities last no longer than a heartbeat— that's what her father had once said, and it had proven true on more than one occasion.

The false king stood, his ring finger held out before her lips.

Does he want me to put my lips on the damn thing—is that it?

He did not ask her to kiss the hand. Instead, he took *her* hand and held it loosely with his good arm.

"As I've said, I think we need a show of solidarity, proof of your support. If a one-armed man is to rule Harkana, then perhaps his sister, his greatest supporter, ought to have one limb as well—don't you think? A hand will do. This one," he said, and his fingers tightened intolerably around hers, crushing the flesh.

Merit cried out inwardly. *I won't let this boy maim me.* She raised her eyes and it was then that she caught sight of the blade. In his haste, or perhaps his innocence, the boy had left his sword exposed.

Without hesitation, she drew it and pressed the iron to his throat.

Opportunities last no longer than a heartbeat. She knew this, and she also knew what must be done. *Cut him and be done with it.* She had the chance.

One heartbeat. Two.

She called out to the crowd, "If there are any here who are Harkan, come to my side. Join me against this false king." Surely there were a few loyal Harkans left in the Hornring. She hoped they would come to her aid. She could easily slit the boy's throat, but what then? Without the help of others, his soldiers would cut her to bits.

Three heartbeats. Four.

She held the iron to the boy's throat and the coward did nothing to stop her from doing it. He merely shivered, and when she touched the place where his arm was missing, he recoiled as if she'd struck some wound.

Five heartbeats. Six.

She gazed out with fierce eyes, waiting for help, but none arrived.

Her opportunity had expired.

The false king's soldiers advanced and the blade fell from her grip. She'd lost this fight.

I'll win another, she thought, *but not today.*

⇛13⇚

A clarion announced the red army's advance. The groan of a hundred bowstrings followed close behind it. The archers pressed forward, lining up along the black-water stream. Ren searched for Adin, but more bowmen arrived, forming a second line. A third followed close behind, forcing Ren to stand on his toes as he tried to catch sight of his friend. A hand took hold of his shoulder and pulled him backward before he could get a good look at the boy. Someone was hauling him away from the black stream and the archers who straddled its banks, but Ren paid him no heed. He was still trying to get a look at his friend. *Did I make the right decision? And what was that last bit, the words Admentus said before he retreated, something about needing Adin alive and me dead?* Ren wondered what that first part meant as arrows rained down upon the place where he'd stood a moment earlier. *Are they going to march Adin back to Feren and put him on the throne?* That seemed the likely answer. Admentus said he needed an heir, and as far Ren knew Adin was the only heir to the throne of Feren.

"Stay sharp, boy," a voice cried out. It ought to have interrupted Ren's thoughts, but he still wasn't listening. The voice was only a whisper, and a faint one at that. The world felt distant and dreamlike, or maybe he just wanted it to be a dream.

Another volley of arrows clattered against the stones, forcing the Harkans to once more retreat. And when the arrows ceased, the spearmen advanced, the clap of bronze-heeled sandals replacing the thrum of the bows. The men in red marched shoulder to shoulder, heaving deadly spears, staves that were two or three times the height of a man. In the darkness, the red paint of their armor turned to blood, and he realized this was no longer a dream. It might be a nightmare, but even his nightmares had never held anything as terrible as those pikes.

The red army made its slow march toward the kingsguard, and the black shields readied themselves for the fight. Hands clenched spears as lips mouthed silent prayers. Men called out the names of their loved ones or their gods. The worry was palpable, the tension everywhere. The black shields stomped, too fretful to stand idle, packed too tightly to move in any other fashion. The red army continued its slow advance, spears jostling, shields clattering, shouts bounding across the chamber. Even the ground seemed to tremble.

"What's that shaking?" Ren asked.

Tye shuddered, unable to speak.

"They're nearly upon us," said Kollen.

"I can see that," said Ren.

"Can you?" Kollen asked. "If we'd seen how may spears they had or the length of those things, I doubt any of us would have stayed."

"I'm not afraid, not really," said Tye. "There are worse ways to die, slow ways."

"It won't come to that," said Ren. He was looking at both of them and thinking about the promise he'd made. "We'll find a way out."

"Will we?" asked Tye. "Because that's what you promised, Rennon Hark-Wadi." She looked at him, her fist pounding against his chest. "You said you'd get us out of this place, so you'd better do it." Tears welled at the corners of her eyes and she shook uncontrollably. He wanted to take hold of Tye and say that everything would be all right. He went to comfort her, but she slipped from his grasp, deftly moving out of reach. She obviously did not want a shoulder to cry upon; she wanted a way out of this mess, and so did Ren.

A call rang out from the far side of the cistern. The red soldiers were howling some terrible war song, chanting in time. With each grunt they advanced, one foot forward, one thrust of the spear. Stomp. Thrust. Stomp. Thrust. One after another, a grunt, a stab, they were coming, inexorably, or so it seemed.

"Fuck, there're thousands of them," said Kollen.

"Tens of thousands," said Tye. "I've never seen so many spears. It looks like a briar patch."

"And we're stuck in it," said Kollen.

A shout rang through the cistern. It was the first cry of the battle, but others followed close behind it. A shriek. A yelp. The scream of iron as it ground against bronze. The lines shifted forward and back as each side jostled for position.

Ren found the captain.

"They're trying to overrun us," Gneuss said.

Ren saw it. The main thrust of the red army was aimed at the Harkan shields. The kingsguard did their best to hold their position, to dig in and push back, but the enemy were superior in number, fresh-faced and ready for battle. The black shields were haggard, uneasy, uncertain if it were day or night. Their sweaty hands fumbled at their weapons. Gneuss was already shaking his head as he glanced up and down the line.

"The wall's going to break . . . I see it," he said. "We can't hold them back, so listen." Gneuss turned abruptly, grabbing Ren by the tunic and pulling him close. "Here's how it'll go: When our lines break, it'll be every man for himself, or so it will appear, but we've been through this before. The men are grouped in squads. We'll allow the red army to stumble forward when they crash through our lines, and while they're fumbling about we'll re-form our squads into smaller circles. I've done it a dozen times. Stay at my back and remain inside the ring."

It sounded like a good strategy. It would buy them a scrap of time. But what then? What next? Beyond the spearmen there were more sentries, men in a dozen different house colors, all of them with swords and shields and armor. Behind them, past the household armies, in the shadows of a columned hall, more soldiers waited. The yellow cloaks of the city guard stood watch, ready to arm themselves should there be a need. Army stacked upon army waited in the not-so-distant corridors of the Hollows.

"Oh, this is hopeless," said Kollen, his gaze fixed on all those soldiers, voice shaking, sword nearly falling from his grip.

"Hold tight!" cried Gneuss as a solid wall of men slammed into the Harkan line. Shields buckled or were thrown into the air, swords bent, and the kingsguard were either trampled or beaten to the ground, legs bent into odd contortions, bones shattered, men howling in pain. The war cries of the red army continued, unabated, undisturbed by the weeping of the wounded. A second shove sent Ren tumbling, but Kollen caught him and helped him back up to his feet. "Stand or they'll trample you."

"I was trying," said Ren absently, his eyes on the battle, spears thrusting at his face.

"Oh, this is bad," muttered Tye.

"Holy Mithra," said Kollen. "Stay tight."

"Do nothing," cried Gneuss.

Shields locked around Ren and the other ransoms, Gneuss too. Just as he'd said, the Harkans had re-formed their lines. They were safe for now, but that hardly seemed to matter. These lines would soon break, and if they formed new ones those would only break too. Ren saw it. A shield struck his shoulder. They were all jostled, pushed this way and that as the Harkans tried to maintain their new formation.

Meanwhile, the red army drove their spears high and low and in between the Harkan armor. A red stave pierced one soldier just above the ankle, the shaft going clear through it and coming out the other side. Another man took a spear right through his open mouth. Two men fell to the earth and a third joined them, cursing as he bent double, blood pouring from some unseen wound.

"I've never seen so many men, so much red," said Tye. In all likelihood, she was referring to the red armor and not the blood, though Ren guessed it could be either.

"Aye," said Kollen, picking up the conversation, "and so little fucking black."

"There must be thousands in the cistern," said Tye.

"More," said Kollen, "the whole fucking city wants us dead."

The earth rumbled again, just as it had at the start of the battle. Back then, Ren had thought it was Mered's army that made the stones tremble, but the soldiers were no longer marching in time, and their chants had all but ceased.

The rumbling continued.

"Do you hear that?" Ren said.

"What? The Harkans? The ones crying out for the mothers?" Kollen asked.

All around them the injured were indeed whimpering. Dressed in red or black, it didn't matter, a dying man was a dying man, and each of them called for their wives or their daughters or the last good whore they'd bedded. A chorus of grunts and moans replaced the chants of war as the dying heaved their last cries. It was a terrible song, but beneath it Ren heard something else—a sound that was not a part of this battle.

"Listen," he said.

"There's a thousand men screaming and twice that number whimpering—which one should I listen to?" Kollen asked.

"None of them," said Ren. "Just shut up and listen," he said, and for once Kollen did listen, but it was Tye who heard it.

"There's a rumbling. Someone's moving stones," she said.

"Exactly," said Ren, "but where?"

They were all looking around, ignoring the fact that their defenses were about to crumble. In a heartbeat, this second shield wall would collapse and the red soldiers would at once be upon them.

"There!" said Ren. He pointed to one of the cistern's great archways. It was filled in with rock, but heavy wooden posts replaced a missing row of stones at the base of the arch. Someone was removing the wall, but they were doing it from the bottom up.

"What is that?" Tye asked.

"Another trap. Mered's men are clearing the stones and when they've made a wide-enough opening, they'll come at us from behind," said Kollen.

"No," Ren said, "I think someone's trying to open a door, a way out."

"What?" Gneuss came out of nowhere, spinning around, his sword wet with blood, eyes darting. "What door? What sort of silliness is this?" he asked, but the one-eyed man had already caught the ransoms' gaze. He observed the shifting stones with skepticism, with the look of a man who thought he knew a trap when he saw one, a captain who'd lived long enough to know that luck was a thing men seldom encountered on the battlefield.

"Look," said Ren, "they've removed another row." As a matter of fact, a second and a third row of stones had been removed from the bottom of the wall. Wedges and dowels supported the missing blocks, keeping the upper portion of the wall intact.

"It's wide enough," said Tye.

"For you to scuttle beneath?" Ren asked. It was indeed just wide enough for someone as slim as Tye to slip beneath the missing stones.

"The way's open. And I don't see spears, or soldiers either. It's no trap," said Ren. He looked to Gneuss, but a shield slammed into the commander's chest, catching his attention. All around them the men were shifting, the spears pressing deeper into their lines as their shields fell and their defenses thinned.

"We're going to make one last attempt to re-form the lines," said Gneuss. "We'll head for the arches. Then we'll regroup. Maybe we can make a run for it."

"A run for it?" asked Ren. "Just when we've found a way out?" If they rushed the arches, they'd be cut off from this new opening. "See the stones?" Ren said. "They've started at the bottom and they're moving their way up. It's an illogical thing to do. Why not start at the top?" he asked, but he already knew the answer and guessed Gneuss knew it as well.

"Because, if you start at the bottom, you can pull out the posts and collapse the stones behind you," said Gneuss.

"That's our way out," said Ren.

"Or our way *into* a trap," said Kollen. "We all scurry under that wall, then they pull out the posts and trap us. It'll be like walking into our own grave."

"No, someone's given us an exit. Any fool can see it," said Ren.

"Any fool can see that it's a fuckin' tomb," Kollen shot back.

"Oh, shut your mouths," said Tye as she pushed past the boys, slipping between two shields as she left the protection of their ranks. She scurried past the men whose lines had already broken and were fighting sword-to-sword, blades whistling in the dark. She was a slender thing and small. No one paid her any attention and the back half of the cistern was dark, near lightless save for a faint glow emanating from the far side of the gap. In fact, Ren almost lost sight of her as she slid into the narrow opening at the base of the archway.

They waited, wondering if the girl were alive or dead.

The moment stretched.

Perhaps it stretched for too long.

"Time to go," Gneuss said. "We need to re-form ranks, or we'll have too few men to make any sort of wall. I can't wait for that girl."

"I'll wait," Ren said. "Do what you must, but I'm not letting go of Tye."

Ren needed to know what lay beyond the gap. He waited again, but Tye did not appear and the Harkans were readying themselves for that next maneuver, the one that would take them out toward the row of archways and the black river. Gneuss gripped Ren's tunic, but he slipped from the captain's hold. "For Mithra's sake, man, give us a moment."

"Battles are lost and won in moments, and you've lost yours. Soldiers—" he cried, but Gneuss was once more cut short. The shield wall had collapsed. The men ran in a dozen different directions, all except Gneuss. He stood, transfixed, as a spear broke through his chest, entering at the back, blood and sinew splattering in all directions. He fell and Ren caught him as he dropped, the soldiers in black surrounding them.

Ren helped the captain down onto the ground.

Gneuss took hold of Ren's fist. Their eyes met and Ren could see that some notion had formed in the captain's head, some final command. The battle raged, but all eyes were on Gneuss.

"Find my second, Edric, he'll help you," said Gneuss, his words coming in gasps. "Butcher will do the same," he said, nearly out of breath, out of life.

"Help me?"

"Yes, you fool. I'm done. That's plain enough—isn't it? I'll need a replacement and you're the man. It's the only way to secure your position, so don't even try to argue with me. You need the help. Mered named you a bastard. Your crown is in question. If I make you captain, the men'll have to follow you. No questions and no doubts. It's done. You are the leader of the kingsguard of Harkana. You always have been," he said, his voice failing, skin turning pale and white as his body fell still.

Ren removed the spear from his chest. He placed a cloth over the wound. He'd have given the man a moment of silence or a word, but they had no time for either—no time at all.

If he lingered beside the body for a moment longer, there would be no kingsguard left to command. The men had all heard Gneuss's command. Ren was captain, so he wasted no time getting started at his new job. He knew Edric by sight and found him easily.

"We form up at the arch." Ren pointed to the place where Tye had gone. He trusted she was safe, that this was the way out. It was a risk, he knew, but Ren was ready to take it.

He dragged the captain's body. Edric marshaled the guard, ushering them into lines, gathering them up so they could raise shields around their exit.

The distance was short, but they had to fight their way to the arch. Swords clashed and armor crunched, each man grunting and howling. Some cried out their last words while others shouted their victory. Ren could hardly tell the red from the black. The darkness consumed every-thing.

"Put out our lamps," he ordered. "And take theirs too."

The soldiers in red carried lanterns strapped to poles, but the Harkans hacked at them, severing the shafts. One lamp fell, a second shattered; all around them the lights were going out and the already-dark cistern turned a shade darker. *The gloom will be our friend,* thought Ren. In the shadows, no one would be able to tell a red soldier from a black one, and while Mered's men were trying to decide whom to strike the Harkans would make their exit.

It seemed a good enough strategy, but the red soldiers hounded their retreat. Ren held on to Gneuss, dragging him toward the gap. *I won't leave his body.* If the red army recovered it, they'd put the captain's head on a stick for the whole city to witness.

Ren slammed into stone. He assumed he'd reached the wall, so he ducked beneath the stones, pushed between the timbers, and pulled Gne-uss behind him.

Once through, the light made him wince, catching him off guard. He blinked to clear his vision, his eyes adjusting to the lamplight. Around him, priests bearing the simple wrap of the acolyte, a tight roll of cloth cinched against the chest, were busily hauling away stones while others ferried equipment—timbers, dowels, and wedges—to the workers who cleared the stones and erected the supports beneath them. It was an im-pressive operation, well planned and well executed.

"Ren, you made it," said Tye.

"And you're alive!" Ren exhaled. "We've got to get the others." He set down the captain's body and slipped back into the cistern, moving so quickly he stumbled into Edric, the soldier's face revealed by the faint light of the archway.

"There are priests within, safety," said Ren.

"Priests?" asked Edric.

"Yes, do I have to say it twice? Priests. Men without swords, so we might as well join them." Ren was spitting his words out. "What the hell does it matter? It's our way out."

With a nod, Edric vanished. But a moment later, Ren heard his voice, shouting orders in the darkness, directing the Harkans toward that faint light at the base of the archway.

Someone slammed into Ren. He felt whiskers, a beard.

"Kollen?" Ren could not see the face in front of him.

"No, it's Horu come to give you the kiss of death," said Kollen. "What's in there?"

"Safety. Go!"

There was no time for banter. Blades twirled in the darkness and he could not tell if they were black or red, friend or foe.

The Harkan shield men encircled their escape route, protecting the passage. It was the same maneuver they'd used to escape into the Hollows. The black shields hustled through a gap in the line and crawled beneath the stones, some knocking aside the posts that held up the stones, threatening to bring the whole wall down upon them. It was a hasty retreat, and bloody. In the darkness, red soldiers leapt out of nowhere. A blade took one man just as he reached the hole, a second fell just short of it. Something sharp sliced at Ren's shoulder and he spun only to find a man in black staring him in the face. They both held swords to each other's throats, but quickly withdrew them. In the darkness, it was impossible to tell what was going on, but the Harkans were escaping. He knew that much. One after another, four then five at a time, they made their way through the narrow gap while all around them men hollered and blades clashed as the last of the soldiers made their way toward that sliver of light. A crush of soldiers packed the narrow passage, grunting as they dove beneath the stones. Then, abruptly, there was silence.

"We're the last." Edric tapped Ren's shoulder. Butcher had already passed through the gap. In the distance, lanterns swayed atop poles, lighting the way as a fresh line of soldiers appeared, spears leveled, ready for the charge. The army in red had initiated a second advance.

"Time to go," said Ren.

Edric went first through the gap. He pushed aside a timber and Ren kicked at a second as he followed. He left Gneuss's body beneath the stones; it was a good enough burial. The priests did the rest of the work, pulling out the wedges and posts. Stone upon stone tumbled to the earth as a massive pile of rock came crashing down. The rubble piled up so quickly that Ren had to leap backward just to avoid being crushed by it. The dust was impenetrable, but when it cleared, the passage was gone.

In its place, an immovable pile of rock stood between the Harkans and their foes.

⇒ 14 ⇐

The pain woke Merit. An ache in her hip made her squirm uncomfortably on the pallet, and there was something wrong with her right knee. Everything below the joint was numb. She tried to wiggle her toes, but they would not comply. It was as if the lower half of her leg was unaware of the upper. *Am I maimed?* She pondered the matter, but only briefly. Merit had other pains to occupy her attention. A cut on her shoulder stung, and a bruise on her right forearm ached whenever she threatened to move it. Overall, she decided it would be best if she moved as little as possible. In fact, all she dared lift were her eyelids. She blinked them open one by one and surveyed her surroundings, the chamber coming into dim focus. At one end of the room, a window looked out onto the Hornring. A door sat to her right and—

"You're awake." Shenn sat astride her pallet, huddled atop a small stool. "The king's men were not kind to you." He eyed her wounds. "But they were careful . . . in a way."

"Careful?" she shot back. "Tell that to these bruises," she groaned, but, on second thought, perhaps he was right. The men who attacked her carried swords. They could have easily cut her to shreds, or maimed her in some more permanent fashion. She could not wiggle her toes, but at least she had all ten of them. Her attackers had not severed her hand as the king ordered.

"Perhaps you're right then."

"They left your face."

"How lucky. Too bad my good looks are all out of uses." She'd always been better at using her head than she had been at using the curve of her breast, at least when it came to what was important.

"Maybe they should have cut my face. I've always wanted a good scar. They're intimidating," she said, almost absently. She still could not move most of her body. She could not even turn her head. "Where are we?"

"South Tower, high keep."

"We're not in the family's quarter?"

"No, I suppose not. Your new *brother* appears to have taken it."

"He's taken everything, but where did he put it? Where did all the

Harkans go? The kingsguard is in Solus and the army is in the south, but there was a small garrison in the Hornring. Were they slaughtered? Or was there no fight at all? Did this boy ride into Harwen with his head held high and announce himself the king returned? Perhaps the guards escorted him to the throne. Maybe they brushed aside the dust and let him sit upon my father's seat—who knows?"

"Not me, and I've heard no news. The men that come, the ones who bring food and tend to your wounds, are soldiers. None of them are Harkan. These are men from Solus, and most have the air of highborn servants."

"Yes, so he brought his own men, but that hardly answers the question. Where are all the Harkans? Locked away in some cell . . . poisoned . . . murdered?"

She looked out through the window. The Hornring was quiet. A scattering of soldiers walked the walls, but she saw little else. Beyond the rampart, though, there was still the city. They had not emptied Harwen. The people, her people, filled it.

"It's obvious they've accepted this new king, at least temporarily. I'm guessing there's a great confusion in Harwen," said Shenn. "But the boy has the throne and he has swords."

"It won't last," said Merit.

"Really? You don't look as if you're in any condition to lead an uprising. And let me remind you—"

"That I'm his prisoner? Harkana will not stand for it—he can't hold me for long. I'll go to the warlords, I'll—"

The door opened and the boy who called himself king stepped into the room. There were four or five men at his back, all had swords but their weapons were sheathed. *He's overdoing it a bit,* she thought. She was hardly a threat, but perhaps the boy was overcautious now. She noted that he no longer wore a sword at *his* belt. *I guess I won't have a second chance to cut him with his own blade.* Then she had a realization. *The boy is afraid of me— that's why he's come with his guards.* It was, of course, a mistake. If she were the boy, she'd have walked into the chamber with a two-handed sword swinging from *her* belt.

"I see you're doing better, sister," said the false king.

"Sister." Merit repeated the word, but it once more left an ugly taste in her mouth. "Call me Merit, or Queen Regent if you want to get it right."

He smiled oddly, then his lips went flat, as if he were not certain whether she was joking with him. The fellow did not appear to be terribly bright, but he held all the cards, at least for now, so she'd have to be careful with him. Merit had no desire to sit for a second beating.

"Like I said," the king spoke again. "You're looking better, so we're going to have to find something to do with you. I can't have the favorite daughter of Harkana wasting away in a cage, and I doubt anyone would be pleased if I sent you to the gallows." He grinned again, but this one wasn't as odd or as curious. He seemed to actually like the idea of hanging her from the gallows, and that gave Merit a chill.

"No, I'll need to find something new to do with you," he went on. "Clearly, my old plan will not work. I can't imagine you rallying the warlords to any cause but your own. No, you're not much use to me." There was disdain in his words.

Merit shook her head at him, though she did it weakly. "It will never work, this thing you're doing. The empire will not acknowledge your authority. You did not serve in the priory. The penalty for this is death."

She expected anger from the boy or something similar, but he only smiled that terrible little smile—the one that never touched his eyes. "No. I don't think that will matter," he said. "I'll be pardoned for not serving in the priory. All in time. You see, I am part of something that is much bigger than you and your kingdom. There is a great movement in the empire—a changing of power, a shift, I guess you could say. Harkana is part of that shift, as is Feren, and eventually Rachis. It's already started in Solus and Feren. Did you know the king was dead, that Dagrun's people cut him down in his bedchamber? Terrible way to go, bled out on his bride, our sister, Kepi. She is queen and Kitelord, but she won't hold the title, not for long. No woman has ever ruled Feren, and there is no need for her to do it. There is no longer a need for little kingdoms and little wars. We ought to be one empire ruled by our greatest citizens and we will be, soon." He stood at the archway, looking out in the direction of the Battered Wall.

"We'll start rebuilding that wall tomorrow," he said. "We have no need for such monuments. They remind us of old wounds, things best left forgotten."

That last one stung, but not as much as the news that preceded it. Dagrun was dead. If the false king spoke the truth, the man she loved was gone, murdered by his own people. She tried to study his face, to find the lie if it held one, but she did not see it.

"Dagrun?" she asked, unable to stop herself from saying the name. "Dead—are you certain?"

"Quite certain. It's no rumor. He is dead and our dear sister is queen, but you needn't worry yourself about such things. You ought to be a bit more concerned about *your* fate."

"Why? What will you do with me?" she asked bluntly, her voice hard, or as hard as she could make it.

"Before I tell you," the boy said, "I want you to see something. I want you to understand your position."

"My position?" she asked. "I came here with almost a hundred Harkan soldiers. Hold me for another day and my captain will come for me. Sevin will scale these walls and cut down every soldier you've stuffed in the Hornring."

"Will he?" the boy asked. He was being coy, and she didn't like that. This child who called himself king was a terrible fellow and he seemed to rejoice in terrible things. Two of his soldiers took her by the arms and forced her to stand. The pain was intolerable when she stood and worse when she took her first step, but she stifled her cries and left her smile flat, her face impassive as they led her to the window. She heard horses neighing and the ugly sounds of war, the grunts of men fighting, the shrill chorus of iron ringing against armor.

Merit did not like what she heard, and she liked even less what she saw.

In the low hills beyond the Harwen's walls, in the place where she had camped with her men, a great battle had taken shape.

"It's a bit difficult to tell one side from the other, isn't it?" the boy king asked. Both sides wore the black of Harkana, though she guessed only one army belonged to her kingdom.

"That's why we all wear our colors and our crests. It keeps us from killing our brothers, though I guess such things are sometimes inevitable," he said, a hint of glee in his voice. "If you're wondering which men are mine and which are yours, just look at the size of the force. You said you had a hundred? Yes? Well, I think it was less when you started and considerably less now. I'd guess that maybe fifty are standing, and I've got ten times that number. I think that makes the matter clear. Your boy— Sevin, was it? He won't be scaling any walls. In a matter of time, maybe an hour or two if they fight well, he won't be doing much at all except feeding the jackals."

"Bastard." It was all she could say, and she did it quietly. Merit did not want another beating, but part of her needed to be out there on that field. A piece of her would rather be dead than see those men slaughtered. She thought of Sevin and her waiting woman, Samia, Asher too.

"Shenn, look away," she said upon seeing him at the arch, his face fixed in some terrible expression. Shenn hailed from an old Harkan family, and he'd often said he dreamed of leading the people, of doing something of worth for Harkana, something memorable. Trapped in this chamber, all he could do was stand and watch as his countrymen fell, the terrible image of it all no doubt burned into his thoughts.

"Look away if you like," said the king. "But I won't call you regent. It's a title you no longer hold. You are Merit, daughter of the former king, sister of the current. There *is* some worth in that. As I said earlier, a great shift is about to take place in the empire, and we are all part of it. I am, at least, and you'll soon join it."

"What does that mean?" she asked flatly, out of patience. She was done guessing at his words. She simply wanted to know what would happen next.

"I am sending you to Solus," he said. "You, Merit Hark-Wadi, are a ransom."

15

"Where're we going?" Ren asked, still out of breath but moving again, up on his feet. He had dust in his eyes, and his ears still rang with the sound of crashing stones, but the priests urged him forward. The kingsguard were well ahead of him as were the ransoms.

"I can talk and run at the same time," said Ren, "so you might as well tell me where we're headed." He pounded the dust from his tunic and coughed.

"I have orders," said the white-robed acolyte at the tail of the column. He appeared to be the one who'd orchestrated the whole thing.

"Whose orders?" Ren asked as he pried miniature shards of rock from the fabric of his sleeve.

"I can't say," the acolyte replied.

"They told you to keep it a secret?" Ren asked, still somewhat dazed. Maybe he was just shocked to be alive.

"Yes," the acolyte said, his voice firm but respectful, distant, as if his

thoughts were elsewhere. Ren guessed he'd memorized their path and was trying to recall the various turns. They rounded six or eight of them, then passed the intersection where Ren at last caught sight of the Harkans. He almost looked away. There were men with severed limbs and broken ones, too, men whose wounds bled and others who were nearly bled out. More than one man needed to be carried, and half the others had some limp or other impediment. Progress was slow. They stumbled down steps and over bridges. Grunts echoed in the black. Men begged for the procession to halt. Some called for water or a crock of amber. They were fresh from the fight, exhausted, but the priests would not allow them to stop.

Death lay behind them. Ren knew that much; he wanted to put as much distance as was possible between himself and the cistern.

"Any idea where we're headed?" Kollen stood in the corridor, waiting for Ren to catch up to him.

"Don't care," said Ren. "Without these priests, we'd all be worm food."

"Speak for yourself," said Kollen, "I took one in the arm." He held up a torn sleeve. "I suppose I'm alive."

"You are," said Ren, "but we left our brothers behind. You think Adin . . ." He wondered if the boy still lived. He hoped the red army was able to mend his wounds. Ren had once risked his life to save Adin. The boy was family, a true brother, but he was gone, fled with the enemy. It seemed impossible.

"He was wounded," Kollen said. "Can you imagine him running like this? He'd have never—"

"I know. I was the ass who made him go."

"Quit worrying over it," said Kollen. "The priests saved us." He slapped the white-robed acolyte on the shoulder. "You have a name?"

"Nester."

"Ah, Nester," said Ren, "Well, now that we have your name, can you tell us about where we're headed?"

"Away from those bastards," Kollen interrupted. "That much is plain. I want to know who sent you, Nester. Why're you here? And who found these corridors?"

"I don't know," said Nester. "If I'd been taken prisoner—"

"I understand," Ren said. The realization had finally come to him. Someone was playing a dangerous game, rescuing the enemy. Such a man would be careful to conceal his identity, especially if things went awry.

"Can you at least tell us how long this is going to take? I can't keep up this pace forever," said Kollen. "We've got injured men, you know. Just in case you missed all that grunting and crying."

"It's not that far," said Nester.

"Oh, that's useful," said Kollen.

"What's your plan? I see priests running in all directions," said Ren.

"We made preparations."

"To conceal our escape?"

"Yes. Some paths will remain open while others will be collapsed. No one will follow us."

"We're free?" Ren could not help but blurt out the words.

"You might be, eventually," said Nester quietly, with more skepticism than Ren anticipated.

"I'll take eventually. That sounds good to me." It was Tye who spoke. She'd just found them. Like Ren, she was dusted from head to toe, the remnants of the pulverized stone covering her in a veil of shattered rock. She wiped dirt from her mouth. "Eventually is definitely a step up from what we had an hour ago."

"You mean back there when we were *definitely* going to die?" asked Kollen.

"We must hurry," Nester interrupted. "There is work to be done, walls to collapse." Up ahead, Ren saw carefully laid stones balanced atop spindly posts.

"Through here," Nester said. Ren followed, and not long afterward the sound of falling stones rattled the air.

"We're going deeper into the earth," said Tye. "I'd hoped to see the sun."

"As had I," said Ren. "Where are we?" he asked again, looking to Nester, who made no effort to reply.

"There're statues," said Tye. "Bloody strange ones."

Carved-stone figures hedged the corridor, some in granite, others in obsidian.

"This must be a temple," said Ren.

"It was," said Nester, "a temple to Pyras, built six thousand years ago and nearly reduced to dust at the start of the Old Kingdom. This is the Well of Horu. It was once the place where the first children of Mithra-Sol chose to leave this world. When they were done with this life, they stepped from the base of the ramp, the so-called Ledge of Dust, and returned to the home of their maker. The shelf has a twin in the Cloud Garden, the

Ledge of Winds, a place where the Soleri were said to pass into Atum. See the ramp?" In the darkness, he traced the faint outlines of a coil that wrapped about the inner face of the well. "This temple is a kind of helix that grips the walls of the great pit, like a spiral stair that winds around the interior of a tower. The ledge rests at the base of the ramp and the Mundus of Ceres conceals the top of the well."

"And what happens when they open Mundus, the holiday?" asked Ren. He knew the calendar. "Won't they spy us?"

"No, they'll see nothing but black. You are deeper beneath the earth than you guess, and that great dome, that opening at the top of the well, will appear no larger than the tip of your finger."

"Then we're buried, stuffed so deep into the earth that no one can find us," Ren said, quietly, a hint of resignation creeping into his voice. With each move, they went deeper into the Hollows, to a place no one could find but from which none of them could escape, or so he feared.

"This's our destination?" Ren asked. "This is it, the end of our little journey?"

"This is *your* destination." The floor became a ramp and they once more descended. Odd symbols blanketed the walls, a language Ren could neither read nor identify. It was drawn in pictures, so he guessed it was one of the old tongues, from the earliest days of the empire.

Nester put a hand on Ren's chest, arresting his movement. "My master waits for you at the base of the temple. I must tend to other matters," he said.

"He's leaving us," said Kollen.

"Picked up on that one," Ren replied.

Up ahead, there was light, a lantern.

"You've come a long way," said a voice.

The lamp revealed a young man of roughly Ren's age and height. He had short hair and a crutch, a priest's robe. The stranger lifted his lamp. "Welcome," he said. "I was unsure if you'd make it." He was silent for a heartbeat, his eyes moving over the ransoms before at last fixing upon Ren. "I am Ott, your brother, and I've waited a lifetime to meet you."

THE MUNDUS OPENS

16

At dawn, the Kiltet clothed Sarra in the livery of the Ray. It was a pains-taking affair that involved six attendants and a set of specially designed ladders. The robe was dropped down onto her outstretched arms, then lowered over her chest and legs, the golden threads bending and twisting as they conformed to the curves of her body. She supposed the garment wasn't made for a woman. As far as she knew, Arko had never worn it, and Suten was a slender man, as thin as a corpse. It hardly fit, but she had no time to mend her raiment and she would not be seen without it. The robe was the great symbol of her office. If she were forced to sit through Mered's feast, she would at least do it in a vestment that announced her place and position, a vesture that was said to be a hundred years old and made from enough gold to ransom a dozen kings and their lands along with them.

Dressed as such and taking small steps, she emerged from the Shadow Gate, the sun catching the golden threads of her robe, casting innumerable streaks of light in every direction. Per tradition, the Ray had no ceremonial guard. No man dared strike the mouth of the god. That was doctrine, words written in the *Book of the Last Day of the Year*. Times, however, had changed. Sarra knew as much, so she met up with a rather large company of priests, as well as a battalion from the city guard. Caution would be the rule of the day; one could never have too much of it.

Ott was absent. She'd requested his presence, sent a messenger, too, but the boy could not be found. In all likelihood, he was lost in some ancient and dusty archive and would eventually appear. In the meantime, Sarra was not without company. Unexpectedly, Wat arrived with a portion of the city guard and made his way to her side.

"My Ray," he said, bowing unnecessarily, almost sycophantically. "They've begun the opening." He gestured toward the Mundus of Ceres, which even at this distance was tall enough to be seen over the crowds. A shout rang out, and a hundred or so workers breathed a mighty groan. They were no doubt tugging at ropes of some sort, pulling aside the dome. She drew closer to the spectacle, watching as the Mundus slid from its moorings. It was slow work, but Sarra moved slowly, her eyes held high so as to avoid the gaze of the crowd. She wanted to be observed, for the golden robe to shine like the sun itself as she wound her way through the masses. The distance was short, but she took her time, making certain to arrive at just the precise moment, when the dome was finally removed and the great well, a pit as wide around as a stadium, was revealed. She stood at the rim, a shock of gold shimmering against the black expanse of the well.

"It stinks like death," she said.

Wat wrinkled his nose. "They say it stretches down and down, all the way to the underworld, into the afterlife itself."

"I was the Mother. I've read the parchments," she said. "When the great Mundus of Ceres is drawn aside, the Well of Horu is revealed and those who have passed from this life to the next are free to walk among the living," she said in a tone that mocked the street-corner prophets who stood around them, warning that the dead were coming, that the seal was lifted and the spirits of the departed were free to roam the city. "The deceased have returned," she continued, "at least until the damned thing is shut." She glanced at the dome. "After two days, they'll drag it back into place and the dead will once more return to their world, or so the story goes. Those are the words written in the *Book of the Last Day of the Year*. It's a feast for the dead, not us. And, given the last few days, all that's happened, I find it fitting—don't you?" She offered Wat a wry smile, but he gave no reply. He did not know Sarra, not well. She saw caution on his face, calculation.

"We certainly have had our share of misfortunes. Let us hope that such things are at an end," said Wat, after a considerable pause. Then he turned as if something had caught his attention. Nearby, children tossed coins into the well. A great many arced through the air. They fell, but never made a noise. If they struck the bottom, no one heard it.

"Curious," said Wat. "The silence. I suppose I should be used to it, but it unnerves me each year."

"A trick perhaps, maybe the bottom is layered with soft things, calf-skins or straw," Sarra ventured.

"I'm sure," said Wat, his voice carrying a hint of placation. He leaned against the well and gazed into the darkness beyond. Following his cue,

Sarra glanced over the rim and, to her surprise, the pit seemed to glare back at her, catching her off guard, pulling her downward, drawing her into the black nothingness of the well.

A hand gripped her shoulder.

It was Wat. "Are you all right?" he asked. "You stumbled . . ."

"I'm fine. It's just the robe. Heavy as a suit of armor and tight as a tourniquet," Sarra said, trying to recover a bit of dignity, still gazing into the pit. *There's nothing unearthly about it.* Sarra attempted to reassure herself of the simple and harmless nature of the well, but lately she'd been less certain where such things were concerned. She recalled those unnatural statues in the Shambles and that strange fire at the Antechamber.

"The entertainments have begun," Wat said, drawing her attention to the far side of the well. A troupe of robed figures ascended from what at first appeared to be the pit. They came over the edge, rising like the dead and shambling out onto the streets. It was a clever trick, but a second glance revealed a slender platform that girded the rim. Clearly, the performers had climbed some hidden stair and jumped from a trapdoor, but the design of the structure made it seem as if the robed men and women were rising from the abyss.

The mummers made every effort to play their part in the spectacle. They flew from the platform, then pranced and capered, mingling with the revelers and dancing with them too.

"The dead walk among the living," said Wat.

"And they drink their amber too," said Sarra. Indeed, one of the cloaked men had stolen a crock of amber and was gulping it down not more than a dozen paces from where they stood.

"Death takes everyone and everything," Wat muttered. "That's the lesson—isn't it?"

"Something like that, it's what the festival's about, but I doubt *we* need such reminders," she said ruefully, as if the very notion of the feast had pained her. *And where is Mered?* He was the only reason she'd attended.

"There," Wat said, as if reading her thoughts, his voice suddenly cold.

Mered had arrived. He entered the scene on a golden chair, which was borne upon a litter and carried by a dozen strong-backed men. An entourage followed his palanquin. There were fifty or so men in it and each wore a false face made of plaster. These were the death masks of the house of Saad, the cast white semblances of the great generals and Protectors, preserved in plaster and worn to commemorate the passing of the former Protector of the Inner Guard, the nephew, Amen Saad. Mered's wives and what seemed like twenty or thirty children completed the entourage.

"If I didn't know better, I'd say he was making up for some insufficiency. Surely no man has the need for so many wives. Look at the children. I doubt he knows half their names," Sarra said.

"Or even one of them," said Wat, "but that's hardly the point. Mered exhibits abundance in all things. His wives are no exception, and look at the crowds. He feeds them and gives them drink. They've come from every corner of the city. For some, it's the first decent meal they've had in weeks. They'll listen to his speech, and most will remember it."

"No doubt," Sarra murmured. The hazy outlines of Mered's plan had already taken shape in her thoughts. The father of the house of Saad had leveraged a lifetime of influence and a king's ransom in gold to place himself in this honored position. He had usurped the roles of both Protector and Ray, and possibly even emperor. She needed to reclaim what he'd taken, but she had not yet named a new Protector; she had only been Ray for a matter of days. She guessed Mered had planned his rise to power for months, for years possibly. There was no sense in forming a hasty response to what was obviously a well-orchestrated consolidation of power and influence.

Mered's entourage halted directly in front of the place where she stood. He genuflected. He gave Sarra her due, just as she'd expected. But he did not sit afterward. Instead, he turned to the crowds—to the commoners and the wellborn alike—and raised his hands. Lanterns burst to life, bathing his already-crimson robe in an even redder light, deepening the color to a shimmering vermillion. He bent toward the crowd, his movements slow and exaggerated. He thanked them for their attendance. They cheered.

Sarra hoped that would be the end of it. It often was, the patron came for his accolades then went off to some private celebration. The wellborn did not mingle with the rabble. The Opening of the Mundus of Ceres was a two-day affair, so she guessed he had much feasting to attend to and that he ought to be leaving. But he did not sit, nor did his palanquin move from its spot. Instead, he lifted his hands and a second set of lanterns burst to life. These burned cobalt blue, bathing his face in a fearsome light.

Her stomach turned a bit, as it often did when she was anticipating some dreadful thing.

"The men bearing the palanquin," Wat said. "Recognize their livery?"

Sarra blinked, shocked that she had missed this detail. The polemen wore the black wraps of the Horu cult, and their faces were sheathed in muslin. *That's why he wears that mask,* she thought, *he's one of them.* Horu was one of the minor cults, small and unimportant, but it was said to be one of the oldest.

"Why Horu?" said Wat. "Is it a show of independence?"

"No doubt," said Sarra. "He's convinced some minor cult to allow him to stand at their head. It gives him a bit of gravitas and perhaps some leverage, but not much more. He's the Father of Horu and master of its twenty-odd followers." She knew little of the cult because, until now, there had been little reason to know anything about them. You could almost count their members on two hands.

A voice rang out, deep and loud, intruding on her thoughts. "It was the house of Saad that raised the Tower of the Protector," said Mered. "We sponsored the first triumph of Amen Re," he continued, going on about his family's history. *And exaggerating every bit of it,* thought Sarra.

"I hail from a long line of leaders," said Mered. "Raden was my brother, but he passed too soon." Sarra was forced to chuckle at that one. *I suppose Raden's son, Amen, thought it was just the right time, since it was he who did the killing.*

"Raden," Mered continued, "found a worthy successor in his son, Amen. The young bull ruled with dignity and strength." *And he allowed Barca to mutiny without even once challenging the traitor,* thought Sarra. *This whole speech is just one lie after another.* She wondered if he'd ever get to the substance of the thing.

"Amen passed into Mithra's light, but I will continue his tradition of service, albeit in a different fashion. Mithra tires of the old ways, just as all of you tire of them. Think on this: The fire at the Antechamber cannot be extinguished. It burns with His light. The god reveals His displeasure. The old faith is done, as are the ways that accompany it. We must forge a new path, and I am the one who will walk it! With the support of this city's wellborn families, I declare myself the First Among Equals.

"What does that title mean?" he continued. "Who is the First Among Equals? I am the one who will unite our great armies. I took charge of the conflict with the Harkans, driving them out of our city and into the Hollows. The ransoms have been recaptured. And as we speak, the Harkans are being put to the knife."

"I've heard other rumors," said Wat.

"And?" asked Sarra.

"They say only a handful of ransoms were captured, the young and the injured. The rest escaped, and the Harkans went with them. They've buried themselves somewhere deep beneath the city."

"Mered's lying," Sarra said. She was thinking aloud. "He thinks he can put them down quietly while they're lost in the Hollows. He's taking credit for a task he hasn't accomplished."

"It's a risk."

"It's more than a simple risk," said Sarra. "It's a mistake, and a clumsy one too. I know the kingsguard, and each one of them is worth a hundred of the Alehkar. And Mered's men are freebooters, mercenaries. Men who fight only for gold are seldom useful."

"We'll see," said Wat. "Mered is not yet finished." He inclined his head toward the palanquin, where Mered was still addressing the crowd.

"I am the one who brought peace to our city," Mered cried out to the crowds, and the people applauded, but he beat down their cheers with open hands. "That was only a small task. With our people safe, I will secure our food stores. As the amaranth grows scarce, we must turn our eyes elsewhere for sustenance. We must demand that our subjects, the Ferens, give their share and more, enough to feed all of Sola.

"It is no coincidence that I speak at this feast. Our gods, like the dead we honor, live in silence. They speak, but only through the mouth of another. Of late, the gods have shown ill favor upon these proxies. We have only one Ray of their light, and I say that it is not enough. We have a voice, an ear, but no fist. I will be that fist. As the First Among Equals I will do the things our city and our kingdom require. We must not allow Barca to abuse our forbearance. Think on this for a moment. Consider the traitor and his revolt. This is the greatest of insults, is it not? A man who was once a simple captain has captured the Outer Guard and turned our holy army into a band of thugs. How long will we suffer this affront? No longer. That's what I say. We will not abide," he said, and the crowd applauded. "We will drive him into the sea, and his traitors with him." Again the crowd clapped, but this time it was doubly loud. People banged cups. Some took flagons and smashed them against the stones. "This is what the first citizen of Solus will do," he cried out to the crowds, and they returned his shout with a great chorus of cheers.

"But I am not simply your first citizen. I am the patron of the Horu, master of the flamines. Why, you ask? Because Horu feasts upon souls, and I intend to deliver up a great many of them. Shall I send the Harkans to my god?" he asked, and the crowd once more erupted in applause.

"Shall I send Barca and his traitors to the underworld?" They applauded again.

Wat bent his head and whispered, "A man cannot rule Solus without a divine sanction, and I think he's just produced one. We know why he chose the god of death as his master."

Sarra had already guessed at what Wat said, but she nodded, her eyes on Mered. He had not yet finished. It seemed this "first citizen" had one last thing to say. The elderly man stood tall and waited a moment while his servants produced another dozen torches. Their light made Mered's red robes glow like some ruby caught in the setting sun. It was a wonderful display and Sarra supposed the commoners must have found it terribly enchanting, but she couldn't wait for him to finish.

"Do I hear any complaints," Mered asked, finality in his voice, "or does my voice echo with the will of this city?" There was no need to wait for an answer; the applause was immediate and deafening.

The city roared its approval.

Even Sarra clapped a bit, just to be a good sport.

⟫17⟪

Merit Hark-Wadi threw open the shutters of the carriage and thrust her head out of the window. She had at last arrived in Solus. It was her first visit to the city of the gods, so it was no surprise that she came here with suspicion, with a heart full of worry and a head stuffed with questions. She had no idea where she was headed or what would happen when she got there. The false king of Harkana had simply packed her up and sent her off to the capital. He knew she held the favor of the commoners of Harkana. She'd spent a lifetime currying it. He could not place her in some cage. If the people heard of it, they'd rise up against him. She'd been all but king during her father's long absences from the throne. *I was their ruler, and I'll rule them again,* she told herself, if only to settle her nerves.

Merit's eyes slowly adjusted to the light. The world came back into focus and her thoughts did something similar. She was in Solus, and everything was strange. The stones of the city's vast promenade were as foreign as the faces that looked down from every window. The streets stretched to infinity, and every corner was stuffed with statues, each commemorating some forgotten hero or long-ago war. There was too much to take in, too many spectacles. There were pools and fountains, great displays of dancing water, dazzling to the eye and decadent beyond all measure. And each monument was taller than the last one. Everything carried a sense of arrogance. It was a pompous place, no doubt populated by pompous folk.

She disliked it immediately.

Harwen was a humble city. Only a handful of structures stretched above a single story. Here, banners waved from buildings of improbable height. Most were four or five stories tall and at first she guessed that was common, but after seeing a few more blocks, the four- and five-story buildings seemed abruptly unimpressive. There were even taller ones near the city's center. Her bruises ached, but the wonders made Merit forget the pain, at least for the moment. The monuments and temples, the great public structures, quickly outnumbered the homes and other smaller buildings. They'd reached the edge of the city center and had come upon something truly novel: the White-Wall district, or at least that's what she thought she'd found. She'd heard of it, of course. It was the place where the wellborn made their homes, where they quartered their armies and tended their vast gardens. The White-Wall district was, in fact, a city within a city, and each domicile was in itself another city within that one. Each had its calcium-white walls, which were twice, sometimes three times, her height. Only through slots and narrow gates could she catch glimpses of the marvels beyond: gardens lush with exotic flowers, trees pruned in the most absurd fashions. This was a place of splendor, and there was something decidedly *un*-Harkan about it. It was a little too clean for her taste, too perfect for the kind of perfection she preferred.

At the curb, she noticed a block of white marble fit carefully among the other stones. The word "SAAD" was meticulously incised into the stone. She guessed it was the street name. The wall stretched the length of the road and there was only one door in it, so she supposed there was only one house behind the wall and only one family inside it. Merit Hark-Wadi was reasonably certain she'd arrived at the house of Saad. It was grand enough, and old. Above the wall, which was already too tall, she glimpsed the ancient structure. Merit knew it by name and reputation. The Cloud Garden was one of the fabled wonders of the realm, a great house whose origin stretched back to a time before the birth of the empire, to the Amber Age of the Middle Kingdom. The long terraces jutted out in every direction, hanging like leafless branches. And at the top, almost too distant to discern, she saw a line of green dangling from the uppermost level of the structure.

Merit was still glancing out the carriage window when the guard flung open the door.

"Come now," he said. His name was Assen, and he'd accompanied her on the journey from Harwen. He was a Soleri man, hair black and cut short at the neck, clean-shaven too. The trip was only a day's ride, but he'd hardly spoken a word to her as they crossed the Plague Road. She'd asked her share of questions, but the man had kept his lips shut. In fact, up until that moment, he'd done little more than trace the curve of her breast with his eyes, and he'd done that more times than she could count or countenance for that matter.

"Ah, you do speak," she said as she let herself out of the carriage. "I thought only your eyes worked, and even those seemed fixed in only one spot," she said, her supple breasts bunching together as she passed through the narrow carriage door. "Tell me, Assen, what's all that going on in the distance?" Farther off, in the city center, voices rang out, sistrums banged. There was a celebration, or so she gathered.

"It's the Opening of the Mundus, a feast my patron sponsored."

"Your patron?"

"Yes, the house of Saad paid for the thing."

"I see, and which Saad is that? I've heard Amen is unavailable of late, so who is it?" she asked, smirking, angry, but most of all tired and not willing to admit it. She was exhausted in every possible way, her body bruised, her thoughts a jumble. Every bump in the road had elicited some ache or other pain. Every inch of her throbbed from the beating she'd taken, but she put on the best face she could manage, and since it was the only part of her that wasn't bruised she did a fair job of it.

"You'll see whomever you see. From what I've been told, you're noth-ing but a sand-eating ransom, so I doubt you'll find more comfort than a servant," Assen replied. He took her roughly by the arm and led her through the tall bronze gates, past two spearmen, and a row of shields. It was early in the day, but there were signs of revelry in the house. Some sort of feast had transpired the night before and was perhaps still in prog-ress. Men and women, obviously wellborn, lay unconscious in the gardens, their clothes and hair disheveled. Some were braced against trees, and more than one had his or her face in the sand. There were noble women half-stripped and others wearing less.

"I suppose I missed the celebration?" she asked.

"Something like that. Yesterday was just the first of two banquets, part of the opening, but I doubt you'd know about such things."

"Feel free to enlighten me," said Merit. It did not appear as though she'd missed much more than a good party. "Is this the patron's house?"

Assen started to nod, but caught himself midway through the act.

That's interesting. It definitely narrowed the list. There was only a handful men who could afford the extravagance of a citywide festival. She guessed this was Mered or Tarkhen Saad, the remaining brothers of Raden, the old Protector, the man who'd stood against her grandfather. She'd committed all of their names to memory. One had to know their enemies after all.

Assen left her with a clutch of spearmen, disappearing without a word or gesture, leaving her to stand alone among the soldiers.

She did not wait long.

Others took Merit. The men, their robes stitched with gold, were more finely dressed than the carriage driver, and they had manners to suit their attire. She guessed they were her patron's private guard. "I am Abet," said the tallest of the bunch. He had a thin face and an even thinner nose, and his teeth were white, which was rare in Harkana but was perhaps common here. She'd never seen a fighting man who bothered to keep his teeth looking shiny. "Up the steps?" she asked. A broad staircase stood before her.

"To the top," said Abet, pointing and bowing slightly. The man was well spoken, his words carrying the accent of the highborn, or at least the servant of the highborn. Abet wore a woolen mantle, which must have felt miserable beneath the midday sun, but he showed no sign of perspiration. "It's a long walk," he said. "Come." And she did. The steps were, of course, shaded, but not by any fixed structure. Servants held aloft great plumes of what she guessed were ostrich feathers, fanning Merit and the soldiers, waving at her as she made her way up the steps. She scaled a series of stairs, doubling back at each terrace and climbing again, higher and higher, until, at last, she could see above the palace's white wall.

She set eyes upon the great city, and a sense of melancholy came over Merit. Her father had ruled here, and these same people had taken his life, all within the span of a few weeks.

She glared at Solus through a red haze.

As she crested the last tread a man greeted her with a slight bow, then straightened himself to reveal flowing red robes and a face sheathed partially in muslin, his hair concealed by a deep cowl.

"Come, Merit of Harkana, I'm sure you're eager to see my garden. It's the only one of its kind," he said, walking with her, waving away Abet. A wide promenade ringed the uppermost terrace, and she quickly realized it was that line of green she'd spotted from the street. Wreathed in folds of leafy plants, the trellis pulsed with color, every inch of it blossoming with life. Merit was a desert girl. She marveled at the lushness of it, at the bright-green leaves and iridescent flowers. From lemon to ochre, a hundred shades of yellow accompanied a hundred different aromas. It almost made her head spin. This might as well be another world. And perhaps it was—the gardens *were* fashioned by the Soleri, gods who were said to have descended from another realm, not this earth but Atum, the home from before time.

"You've imported the flora?" she asked, the question sounding almost silly. But if he wanted to exhibit his wealth, she might as well let him. Merit knew how to play to a man's vanity. And besides, a little courtesy might earn her a bit of kindness. Her throat was dry, and her eyes too, and there was water everywhere. Carried through miniature canals, it trickled down onto the plants. It fed the golden poppies and vibrant blue lotus, but it cooled the air as well, restoring her dry eyes and sore throat. If only she had a cup, she could reach out and catch those droplets as they dribbled from the plants.

The master of the house caught her eye and motioned to some distant servant.

"In past times, I visited these gardens daily," he said. "But of late, I've had little chance to walk here. I am Mered, but I think you've already guessed at that. This is my home, and it has been my family's home for centuries," he said, walking, urging her to follow, red robe billowing in the morning breeze. "Did you know that each of the terraces was once draped in flowering plants? You thought this one terrace was an extravagance—didn't you?"

"I did," she admitted. Though even that admission was a bit of a lie; she had thought it to be beyond all extravagance. A servant appeared, cup in hand. The amber in it was cool and Merit took it down in one long draft.

Mered waited. He seemed to enjoy watching Merit, as if thirst were something he savored, something precious—like his gardens. "We once maintained a dozen such terraces, but now there is only one. See our poverty? The desert takes everything from us, but the sand and heat are not our only foe, nor is the depletion of the amaranth."

"What else ails you?"

"This city, its leadership."

"Is the Mother Priestess not a skilled mouthpiece? Do you not heed the words of Tolemy? I've heard it said that his every utterance is a poem, that his every command is a holy dictate. Am I wrong?" she asked, looking coy.

Mered almost chuckled. "The Soleri are silent. They made this place. The Cloud Garden is proof of their existence. Our greatest builders are unable to replicate the construction of these balconies. They cannot make stones that jab at the sky, hanging in the air as if nothing supported them. These terraces are a mystery, as are the Soleri. These balconies should, by all rights, collapse. The whole thing ought to topple over, yet it has stood here for millennia, undisturbed by the shaking of the earth, or my weight. This is not the work of men. I believe in our gods. They once walked these streets and built these palaces, but it is their current whereabouts that concern me. They are silent, and have been for too long—don't you think?"

"I don't pretend to understand their reasoning."

"You don't?" he asked. "Are you certain of those words?" His voice carried an edge, a piercing curiosity. "We all know the story of the Soleri and what happened after the War of the Four, how the gods chose to seclude themselves behind the wall. I don't believe it. It may contain a piece of the truth, but not all of it. There is a secret history to this empire, or so I believe. Few know it, but I think you're one of them, Merit Hark-Wadi, daughter of Arko, our most recently deceased Ray. Fathers do tend to share their secrets with their daughters. . . ."

"If only Arko had been such a man," she lied. "But he was a distant father, a king who kept his own counsel. It is a tragedy, but there was no opportunity for me to visit my father while he was Ray, though I do wish that I had seen him in your magnificent city." She was worried now. *He knows something,* she thought, *or he thinks I know something, and of course I do. I know everything about the dead gods, but I'm not going to share it.*

They had completed a full circle of the terrace. Having shown her the gardens in their entirety, Mered brought her out to a small balcony, a kind of perch, designed, she guessed, for looking out over the city and admiring it.

"Yes," he said. "Your father's tenure *was* short, but not uneventful. He was after change, but it wasn't the kind of change the city wanted. I'm giving the people what they desire, but that's a different matter. It's your father that concerns me. He sent a great many messages, most of them to Harkana. Many of those were belayed, but I am certain that at least one message reached its recipient. A man you knew carried it. Asher—is it? Asher Hacal, captain of your father's kingsguard."

"He was my father's man, yes," said Merit. The last time she'd seen Asher, he was quartered with her army outside Harwen. She assumed he died there. "I heard he was with my father," she said. "They say he camped outside the wall, waiting for the sun god to take his king's life."

"Asher did wait at the wall. He made a camp on the Field of Osokohn and our soldiers kept watch over him. When your father was made Ray, the doors were opened and Wat's men ushered him into the city. He served in Arko's guard and eventually as a messenger. See, your father, as Ray, was privy to knowledge of considerable importance. I think he shared that knowledge with you, and I believe Asher was the one who carried it."

"Carried what?"

"A message of some sort. Only you would know its contents."

"Ha! I wish I did. If only he'd reached me. I'm certain it must have been something of great importance. You've made me curious now. What sort of secrets do you think my father was keeping?"

"The sort men die to protect. I think you received that message. See, I've already guessed at a bit of what it said. I know why Arko was desperate to send scrolls. There was a secret he wanted to share with his daughter, the queen regent of his beloved kingdom."

Merit colored her face with impassivity, but Mered's eyes were on her now, probing, searching for some reaction. He'd find none. She'd stood up to Harkan warlords, angry over one dispute or another. Surely, she could face this old man. She smirked at him, at his veil and the way he hid his face.

"See that wall?" Mered pointed toward a towering white edifice.

"The Shroud Wall," she said. "The Empyreal Domain, where the gods live and die."

"Do they?" he asked. "I've sent dozens of men over the rim. None returned, but a few shot messages over the barrier, describing what they saw. There are gardens and small fields. There's enough food to feed the Kiltet, but little more, so what do our gods eat?"

"I'm no philosopher, I don't—"

"Know, yes, you don't know. Perhaps the Soleri do not eat anything at all. No one knows what goes on behind that wall, but everyone guesses at it. I make educated guesses. There is no food for the Soleri, so there are no Soleri. No one knows the truth, but it is interesting to note that my spies never once saw the Soleri leave their palace. Don't you find it odd that the sun god's children choose to live in darkness?"

"I don't care where they choose to live or die. In my dreams, they've all got swords in their bellies and their heads are hung neatly on stakes."

"Lovely. It's a shame I seldom dream. I prefer action to thought. You see, I sent my nephew into the Empyreal Domain. I wanted to see what he would find, but he failed to return. Like my spies, he disappeared. This is no coincidence. There are secrets in the domain, and those who witness them do not return. I believe the Soleri have left their holy realm, that they've gone somewhere else, and in doing so they've placed the empire in the hands of the Ray. It's the only logical explanation for Suten's bumbling and your father's too. See, I suspect these things. I have theories, but you have answers—don't you?" he asked.

Again, he peered at her with those dark eyes, the veil somehow making his gaze all the more intense. Merit was abruptly aware of the precariousness of her position, of the balcony and the edge upon which she stood. A little shove, a misstep, and she would tumble to her death. Mered was an elderly man, but he was tall and seemingly strong and she was still weak from the beating she'd taken.

"Do you know why this particular balcony has no rails, why it is an open platform?"

"I couldn't guess."

"The Soleri called it the Avenue of Parting, the Ledge of Winds. This slender platform was the first leg of a journey that led to eternity. When it was time for one of the Soleri to die, they simply stepped off the balcony and their bodies would turn to stars, erupting in a great conflagration. What do you think would happen if you were to fall from it?"

"I imagine my end would be a bit less dramatic," she said. "But who knows, perhaps we should give it a try. I have little and less to lose these days."

"Perhaps we will. Tell me what that message carried and I'll think of some other fate for you."

"I've said—"

"There's no message. Yes, you lie, but not nearly as well as you think," he said, moving uncomfortably close to Merit, pressing against her, moving her toward the platform's edge.

"It would be a pity if your father's last words were lost. I'd like to know them. Perhaps you can search your memories and find that message for me." He gave her a hard shove, one that might have sent her toppling over the edge, but he caught her with the other hand and walked her back a step.

Her breath caught.

"As you've no doubt seen, there is a great feast in Solus, the Opening of the Mundus. It ends tonight. It is tradition, during such feasts, to make an offering at the conclusion of the festival. I intend to carry out that tradition. In fact, I plan to make a great sacrifice, one more generous than any in recent history."

Merit said nothing.

"Do you know how the flamines of Horu prepare their benefactions? Do you know anything of the cult?"

"I've seen the robes, the veils, the markings on their arms."

"Yes," said Mered. "Those red lines carry a bit of symbolism. They remind us of the constant need for sacrifice, that the god must be fed." He lifted the sleeve of his robe to reveal a series of scars that marred the skin of his arm. "The benefactions are cut from head to toe and bled out. It's a terribly slow way to go, a thousand little cuts etched across your skin. It can take hours to exhaust the blood, maybe longer. I've seen strong men bleed for a day before passing. Think on it, and perhaps you will recall some bit of that message. Give me a reason to keep you in my house, alive and unscathed. A woman of your beauty could marry well in Solus, and there are many suitors in the house of Saad. Think on it. Make yourself useful—*everything* must have a use. Find one, or I'll let the flamines do it for you."

≋18≋

Sarra stood before the white walls of the Cloud Garden.

My daughter is a prisoner in this house. That was one of the many rumors. Some said Merit Hark-Wadi was a hostage. Others suggested she was only a guest, but most held that she was in fact a tribute of some kind.

My daughter is a prisoner in the house of Saad.

Mered had invented a new empire and crowned himself the emperor of it, or something like one. Naming himself the First Among Equals was a bold and unprecedented move, and she'd done little to stop him from claiming the title—not yet. That wasn't her way. Sarra had questions that needed answering. So she'd bided her time, but when rumors of Merit's captivity arrived on the same morning as an invitation from Mered, she was forced to make her way to the great house.

My daughter stands behind this wall.

Hence, she had come alone as Mered requested. Ott stayed safely behind, cloistered away in the Empyreal Domain, or so she guessed. She had not seen her son since the day she met him at the Hall of Ministers. Ott had yet to emerge from the archives of the Soleri, but he'd sent messengers. He had requested more acolytes and more coin, more resources to aid in his research, and she'd given them to him. She was more than pleased to see him tucked away in the domain, safe, and outside the reach of Mered. If only she could say the same for her daughter.

Sarra went alone to the house of Saad. She had come dressed as if she were still the most important person in the empire, as if Sarra and the role she played still mattered in this new world of self-declared rulers and men who made themselves emperors of a sort. She wore the golden robe of the Ray. It shimmered like firelight, but it was as stiff as a board and as heavy as a suit of armor, impossible to move about in. It was no wonder it took four servants to place her in it.

Small worries, thought Sarra as she passed beneath the ornate bronze arch, walked through the columned hall, and entered House Saad. As she made her way through the processional, those who took note of her arrival bowed slightly and exchanged brief, awkward pleasantries. *They honor me,* she thought, *but they are uncertain of how to address me. Who am I, and what's my place in the city hierarchy?* Surely those were the questions on their minds.

Mered had made a great confusion out of the empire. Still, the people paid tribute to Sarra. Women in scarves of shimmering muslin bowed and spread their hands. The wellborn were all masters of obeisance. It was second nature to them. Some bent so quickly they did not even interrupt their conversation. Whether they bowed briefly or lingered in the act, not one of them ignored Sarra. She was, after all, the woman who had survived the riots on the last day of the year, the one who had stood in the presence of Mithra's light and survived. Some called her Sarra Twice Blessed, and she quite liked the name.

A man approached. He wore a robe that was the color of madder, the neckline edged with gold. His demeanor was outwardly calm, but he sweated profusely beneath his robe. She considered putting the man at ease, but that would only lessen the power of her position, so she said nothing while he bowed and greeted her as Ray.

"I am Bicheres," he said when he'd finished his genuflections, "and I will be your abettor for the evening." He bowed once more and indicated a gravel path. She walked ahead of him, the stones grating beneath her sandals as her thoughts lingered on his title, abettor. She hadn't heard the term before, and wasn't certain she liked it.

"This is the house of Saad," said Bicheres, in what was an utterly unnecessary introduction. He led her past a pair of doors and a tall stair, then out through a series of waiting rooms, the sounds of laughter echoing in the distance. In fact, a great many voices reverberated throughout the passage, growing louder and more raucous as they went. Bicheres seemed largely immune to the racket. Calmly, he pointed out the various statues and monuments, describing this god or that emperor, taking his time, walking slowly as he led her into a great rotunda. "This is the Chamber of Dancing Waters," Bicheres said, his voice raised in an obvious attempt to capture her attention, but she hardly needed the prodding.

"So this is the infamous hall." Sarra had heard innumerable stories about the decadence that went on here, about the feasts, and the orgies too. Each was said to be more elaborate than the last.

"May I ask," Bicheres said most respectfully, "if you have seen it before, the renowned garden, the famed rotunda?"

She shook her head. "They say the Soleri built it."

"It's true," he replied, barely able to control his enthusiasm. "This was the greatest house of the Soleri, the home of the gods! See the rotunda?" he asked, raising his chin just a hair, his eyes glancing upward. He wanted to remain respectful of the Ray. She saw it in the nervous twitching of his fingers and in the way he dipped his head whenever he spoke, but it was all for show. The man had the airs of an imperial servant. He might be afraid, perhaps even a bit intimidated by the Ray, but he could not hide his pompous nature, his pride. Clearly, it was bred into the man. He believed his master to be the city's first citizen, the most important man in Solus, and, by extension, the most important man in the empire.

"I see it," she said, glancing at the dome and feigning indifference. And she truly was feigning it. The great rotunda, the largest she had ever seen, was slowly, almost impossibly rotating about its axis. Somehow, in defiance of all logic, that massive dome, as big as the sky itself, was turning in a circle, spinning like some overgrown bowl set on edge and given a good twist. And as it revolved, a babbling sound issued from the dome's many-layered walls.

"See the channels?" Bicheres said, pointing to a particular set of fissures that spiraled down the intricately layered dome.

"They're filled with water," Sarra noted. "That's what drives the thing?"

"Most true!" he boasted. "The ancient builders were clever, more so than our people, surely. Take your time and wander the grounds. There is a place for you here among the Dancing Fountains or the Rockery," Bicheres said, pointing to a circle of stools, then a low sort of throne. "And there, in the Garden of Delights." He gestured toward a warren of muslin-shrouded chambers where shadows painted tantalizing images of men and women moving about in ecstasy.

Abettor, the word came to her again as he gestured to the garden. *You are not simply my guide,* she thought, giving him the once-over, looking him up and down. *Perhaps you are less of a host and more of a distraction.*

"I can take you there if you would like?" he offered, an eyebrow arched in speculation.

"If I would like?" she asked, plainly. "I am the eye of the immortal. Do you think Tolemy wishes to see how the wellborn of Solus fuck? What positions they prefer, and all that?"

"It is my duty . . ." he said, voice faltering as he crossed his hands, wringing them ever so slightly.

Sarra set her jaw. "No doubt, but I have my own set of duties tonight, and all of them require me to be upright and fully clothed."

Though I would not mind shedding this dreadful robe, she thought. *It's no wonder Arko never wore the thing.*

Bicheres regained his composure and said, "I'm here to serve you."

"And I am here to address an urgent matter. Fetch me some wine, something dark and red. Strong, too, if you have it." There were some things she could not indulge in, but a drink was allowed. One or two might be necessary for her to stomach the coming ceremony. A sacrifice would end the night. In the past, it had always been an animal of some sort, but the rumors all said it would be human.

My daughter is a prisoner in this house, and tonight someone will die.

Mered had all but implied the identity of that sacrifice, but he had not come out and said it, not directly. Sarra had nevertheless guessed it was her daughter's head that would be on the chopping block or whatever implement they chose.

Where are you, Merit? She searched the room but saw no one who looked like her daughter. She did spy Mered. He was seated on a low stool, not far from Madu of House Entefe. It appeared as if the two were engaged in conversation, but they weren't speaking. A servant ferried messages between them, whispering in their ears then waiting for a reply.

"There are lip readers in the gatherings of the great houses, in all of Solus, to be honest. My master guards his words," said Bicheres.

"But the veil?" she asked.

"It is a part of his livery, as Father of the Horu cult."

"And it also covers his mouth, so why bother with all the whispering? It seems like a lot of work and no benefit." Sarra guessed this was all just a show, that there were no lip readers. Half the wellborn in Solus could barely read a scroll. Reading lips seemed improbable, almost fantastic.

"Do you suppose I could speak to the man?" she asked. Sarra had come here to confront Mered, but she also needed an excuse to rid herself of this *abettor.* She'd fucked kings; the servant did little to excite the new Ray.

"I can arrange for it, though it may take some time—" He came up short. Then he corrected himself. "I am sorry, surely *you,* our greatest light, will not be made to wait."

He left, and Sarra was glad for it. All around her, men and women sat in many-colored robes, some of them indulging in the sort of activity she had hoped the wellborn would limit to the privacy of the pleasure gardens. It gave her pause, made her think. Beyond these walls, where the amaranth was scarce, there was famine. Barca made havoc in the south, working his way toward Solus, and the Harkans fought for their lives in the Hollows. Yet these people feasted and fucked as if they hadn't a care in the world. Sarra shook her head at it. She wanted no part of this feast or this house, so she ignored her appointed place and instead chose to roam the chamber, circling the place where Mered sat.

Madu departed, and a flamine of the Horu cult replaced him in the seat opposite Mered. *He certainly has insinuated himself into that cult,* she thought. It appeared as if many in his inner circle wore the black wraps. Bicheres approached Mered but was waved away.

At the far side of the hall, a procession had begun.

The sacrifices, thought Sarra.

There were two boys, a girl, and a woman of middle age, all of them stripped naked, bodies slathered in a thick red pigment, and each wore an outlandish crown of some sort. The boys bore a golden disk atop their heads, and the woman wore thorns. When the girl came into view Sarra's heart skipped a beat. She was tall and beautiful—young, but still a woman. She wore a crown of horns, and she was about the right age. Merit. Sarra's stomach churned at the sight of her daughter, at her nakedness and the way her body was crudely smeared in paint.

Is this truly my daughter? She hated herself for not knowing the answer, not completely, for not having seen the girl in a decade. She hated that this sad excuse for a funeral was their reunion.

Sarra tried to catch Merit's eye, but she would not look at Sarra, not directly.

"To Horu," Mered announced, his voice rattling in her ear. "I offer not one but four benefactions. I ask that He might speed our victories. War is at hand. So we spill blood here, as a tribute to Him, so our soldiers need not spill it on the battlefield." He gestured toward the center of the chamber. A man dressed in the habit of a haruspex—oxblood leather, face masked—stood before a great table. Knives of various lengths and configurations covered the blackened surface of the wood.

Sarra edged toward the procession, her eyes on the horns. She no longer dared to look at the girl. As Ray, the mouth of Tolemy, she could show no preference toward the Harkan. It would be blasphemy. Yet she moved closer to Merit, her heart a hammer in her chest, the golden robe crushing her beneath its weight. Merit was older, her breasts fuller, but she hadn't changed, not that much. *Merit.* Sarra recalled every letter she'd sent, every attempt she'd made to reconcile their grievance. She'd done everything short of revealing Ott's secret to try to win back her daughter's affections.

A strangled cry jolted Sarra from her thoughts. Wine dripped from the face of the middle-aged woman, mixing with the smudges of red paint that covered her chest, carving tiny rivulets in the pigment as the alcohol dribbled down her naked body. A man in white muslin raised a second cup. To the appreciative shouts of the crowd, he splashed more wine onto the naked woman. Not to be outdone, a noblewoman spat on a crying boy, which seemed particularly cruel. The wealthy and well-to-do patrons hurled clusters of olive pits or half-chewed dates at the benefactions; others tossed cups of amber. A drop of red graced Sarra's robe, but she did not retreat or recoil in any way. In fact, she moved closer to the circle of would-be sacrifices. Two of them were ransoms. Wat's men in the city guard had told her all about them. The girl was Merit. And the fourth benefaction was a stranger, but Sarra guessed she was wellborn. Mered was up to something terribly dangerous. These so-called benefactions were the sons and daughters of kings and noblemen, and Mered planned to spill their blood. It was a bold stroke. Mered and his faction of wealthy and well-bred patricians had made themselves the rulers of the empire and they were daring any who lived in it to challenge them, Sarra included.

The parade of benefactions continued its slow and desperate circle around the haruspex. No music played. There was no dirge ugly enough to accompany this scene. The only sounds were the laughter and shouts of the crowd. The older woman, the one whom Sarra could not identify, shambled past Sarra, her gray hair stained red with wine, body shaking. One of the boys was Carr Bergen—if Wat's sources were correct—and he came next, face dripping with spittle, hair sodden with perspiration. Sarra looked away in time to catch the start of Mered's speech.

"The son of Arko hides like a coward in the caverns below our holy city. He was invited to the feast, but I fear he got lost on the way to my house." Mered gave a laugh, and the people snickered, the drunkards over-doing it just a bit. "We will sacrifice him in the tunnels." Mered grinned a terrible-looking little grin. "It'll be done in no time at all. That is my promise. Death in the sewers. A fitting end for the bastard." Mered cleared his throat, a look of distaste passing across his face. "As I've said, the Har-kan is absent, but we found a suitable replacement. In fact, we came across four of them, one from each of our lower kingdoms." Mered raised a hand to the benefactions. "I give you the highborn sons and daughters of lower kingdoms: Feren, Rachis, the Wyrre, and Harkana. These offerings are symbols of our new order. As the First Among Equals, I propose an em-pire without kingdoms—an empire of one people, the people of Solus. To this end, we take four lives. Carr Bergen, heir of Rachis; Curst Falkirk, son of House Falkirk of Feren; Aeslin Mor, royal daughter of the Wyrre; and Merit Hark-Wadi, queen regent of Harkana prior to the true king's return."

Sarra's heart froze at the sound of her daughter's name, but the part about the king of the Harkans was a bit of a surprise. He said the true king was in Harkana, which meant that he'd accepted a false king and was perhaps the one who was backing the imposter. He'd already con-ceded that Ren was in the Hollows. The king in Harkana would have had to be Ott, which was of course impossible. *You made a terrible blunder, Mered.* Ott was Sarra's son, and he *was* in Solus. She could easily declare the boy in Harkana to be a farce, a false king with no parentage. Mered must have known this, but he'd acted anyway. His boldness had over-taken his reason. *And I will no doubt benefit from this lapse in judgment.*

She pressed closer to the benefactions. Sarra moved directly into Mer-it's path. This was her blood, her daughter, and she had not seen her in a decade. Their eyes met. Merit set her jaw in a careful line, then her lips parted. It was no grin, but it was something close to one, as close as anyone in such circumstances might dare. Her lips quivered. Then she turned and walked away, continuing the procession.

Merit was gone, but she'd stuffed something into Sarra's hand.

It felt soft, like fabric. Sarra stumbled backward, pretending a bit of drunkenness, drifting into the crowds as she peeled open the cloth. It held a single sentence, and there were only five words in it, but they told Sarra everything she needed to know.

⟫ 19 ⟫

Merit Hark-Wadi was no longer a ransom; she was a benefaction, a sac-rifice to the gods, forced to parade before the wealthy and well-bred of Solus. And just to make the whole thing as absolutely unbearable as was possible, she was stripped naked and painted red. A drop of spittle hung from her right breast, and as if that weren't bad enough the horned crown she wore had cut right through her skin, sending slender lines of red dribbling down her forehead. She suppressed the urge to scream—once, twice—but it kept returning. In fact, it doubled when she caught sight of the many knives that cluttered the haruspex's table. She wondered if she ought to grab one and take her chances with the guards, but she did not reach for the blade. She'd chosen to place her hope in the hands of her mother, Sarra Amunet, the First Ray of the Sun.

More specifically, she'd placed that hope in the slip of linen she'd forced into her mother's hand. If it weren't for that scrap of cloth, she would have in all likelihood collapsed, her mind overcome by the sheer hopelessness of her situation. However, she had passed the note, and Sarra had disappeared into the crowd the moment the cloth touched her hand.

It was the one act of resistance Merit could muster, and it had taken considerable effort to produce it.

An hour earlier, she had been an entirely different person, living and breathing under entirely different circumstances. She wore the gown of a queen regent. A bronze cup filled high with amber rested in her hand. She had her dignity, but more important, she had something Mered believed she was willing to trade: a secret. He still clung to the notion that he could somehow force her to reveal it, so he'd plied her with words, and when that hadn't worked he'd threatened her with his torturer. When she still maintained her silence, he offered Merit the haruspex's knife and told her that every highborn man and woman in the city would sit and sup while she suffered beneath it. That was her fate. Mered was quite clear about it. Divulge what she knew or suffer the knife. Merit had accepted the latter.

Afterward, Mered's servant led her down the shaded steps of the Cloud Garden and walked her to a lightless chamber, where she was left alone and made to wait and wonder if the torturer would return with his knife. He did not. Instead, a servant arrived. He guided Merit up and out of the slender space, escorting her through a series of waiting rooms that led to what she guessed was the central hall of the great house, the servant's hand lifted up toward some enormous contraption. "The rotunda of House Saad is the greatest marvel in Solus," he said. "It is surely more elegant than the Cenotaph, and loftier than the Shroud Wall." The servant's name was Bicheres, and he made little more than small talk as he walked Merit through the great hall. "Note the water engine," he said as he pointed out the channels in the face of the dome. "Even our best builders are unable to discern the inner workings of it."

That's no surprise, thought Merit. Imagination was in short supply in the empire. Men of promise dedicated themselves to politics and the pursuit of coin. The people of Solus had stopped dreaming. *All of us have,* she thought, standing beneath the dome, pondering its motion.

"You are no doubt familiar with our history, the stories incised in the dome," said Bicheres.

"The tale of the Soleri?" she asked. "Heard it a few hundred times." She assumed the comment would silence the man, but he went on as if she had not even spoken, raising his voice as he indicated the various scenes, each illustrated in low relief.

"Some worlds begin with a word, some with an action. In some faiths, the totality of the universe is sung into being. But this land was born in darkness. It was the sole province of the Pyraethi—"

"Yes, until the Soleri stole it," said Merit.

"Well, that's one way to put it," said Bicheres. "They brought light to our world . . ."

"No doubt, and they also murdered every living thing in it. They built their empire atop the ruins of another. The victors get all the monuments, but the losers always seem to get skipped over when it comes time to build the big statues and the great halls. There are no monuments to the atrocities we commit. Funny how that works—isn't it?"

Bicheres said nothing, not immediately. Perhaps he was unused to intellectual debate. "I suppose I should leave such matters to more educated men . . . and women," he said at last, his tone hardening as he spoke, his demeanor shifting from the calm composure of guide to something dark and stern. He straightened his back and cleared a god-awful clump of snot from his throat. He swallowed once and spoke, "I am more concerned with mortal matters." He indicated a small chamber. She hadn't noticed it. It was subterranean; a small set of steps led to a door. The chamber beyond had the look of an oubliette or something like one.

"I was only making small talk," said Bicheres, "passing the time while I walked you to the Chamber of Benefactions. We've arrived, so we can forget about the dome and the effort I wasted on our little talk. Once you step over the threshold and walk down those steps you will cease to be the former queen regent. In fact, you will cease to be anything but a sacrifice, a benefaction. Do you understand? Tonight, in a matter of hours, you will be paraded before the great families of our city, our Ray, and our highborn citizens. Then you will be offered up to our god. Nice and simple. A few dozen cuts of the knife and it's finished, give or take a moment or so of slow and painful bleeding. Mered asked that I offer you one last chance to avoid this fate. If there's something you want to say, I'll take you to him." Bicheres inclined his head ever so slightly toward the steps that led back up to the terraces.

Merit said nothing. She would never say anything to Mered. The house of Saad had murdered her father; Amen Saad had set the fire himself. The patriarch of House Saad had led the Protector's Army against her grandfather in the Children's War. This house had tormented her family for generations and they were still at it. The rumors all said it was Mered who pursued her half-brother, Ren, in the Hollows, and that same man jockeyed for power in Solus with her mother. Merit bit down on her lip and Bicheres huffed.

"I don't know what sort of secret you're keeping, but it's not worth a trip to the haruspex's table." He folded his hands and bent his lips into a terrible grimace. "Think on it. Once you enter this room, you cannot go back. Spill your story. Mered promises you a good life, a wealthy life . . ."

Bicheres awaited her answer. He was patient, but Merit said nothing. She would give him nothing. She'd take the knife if it came to that, and she'd grin while it parted her flesh. Merit had made her decision, so she turned her back on him and made her way down the steps and into the little room that Bicheres indicated. She sat on a slender stool, the room's only furnishing, and her stomach dropped when the door sealed shut and the darkness gathered about her, pushing down on her like some terrible weight. She breathed deeply, but it did little to calm her nerves. She sat alone in the tiny cell, but there were other rooms and she guessed there must be others in the cells. She wondered how each of the prisoners had come to be there.

"Who are all of you?" she called out.

They shuffled about their cells when she spoke; she clearly was not alone. A boy in the next cell over screamed something unintelligible while at the same time an even younger boy, who occupied the cell on her other side, began to cry. She feared she might join him. It was terrible to hear a child sob, but the door banged open and her attention was drawn elsewhere. A pair of servants entered the little cell. One was an elderly woman and she guessed the second was her daughter. They carried a large wooden tub, linen cloths, and an assortment of redware jars.

They stripped Merit from head to toe and washed her until her skin was raw. They painted her with tar and madder, which made the whole bath seem a bit unnecessary, if not illogical. She thought of raising the issue, but the servants had no tongues, so there was hardly any point in arguing with them. Merit stood as they painted her with stripes of red and black. The younger girl departed the chamber but soon returned with a horned crown. She placed it in Merit's hands and indicated, without speaking, that she ought to put it on her head. The horns tore a slip of linen from the girl's dress. Merit placed the strange crown atop her head, but only briefly, just to indicate that she'd understood the girl. The gesture seemed to please the pair because they left Merit with the crown, sealing shut the door again.

They'd made a hasty exit and in the process they'd left their lamp in the corner. The flame still burned. Merit sat upon the lonely stool, snatched the scrap of torn linen, took the crown, dipped one of the barbs in the red pigment, and wrote a simple sentence on the fabric. In his arrogance, Bicheres had let one crucial piece of information slip. He'd said the Ray would be in attendance that night. Her mother would be in this very hall, and Merit guessed she could pass a message to Sarra. She curled the linen into a slender little roll and fit it between her index and middle finger, the cloth disappearing into the tar that covered her hand.

A cup of wine splashed Merit's face and her thoughts came quickly and frightfully back to the present. She glimpsed her mother's golden robe, half-hidden among the crowd.

Sarra had the note.

Merit prayed she'd know how to use it.

⇉20⇇

Mered doesn't know the secret.

Sarra had read the note twice. Afterward, she'd folded the linen into a ball and stuffed it into her robe. The benefactions circled the black table of the haruspex, and the executioner was chanting, something low and in a language she did not understand. It was a primitive, guttural tongue—an inhuman voice for an inhuman act, fitting but nevertheless unnerving. He cried out one last syllable, and the benefactions halted their procession, frightened perhaps, or maybe they had been told to stop at that particular utterance. The boy from Rachis, Carr, stood before the table. The red soldiers took him by the arms and strapped him to the black altar. There was no delay, no ceremony to the thing. The haruspex simply pressed his knife to the skin and made the first cut, the boy whimpering as the blade parted his flesh.

Sarra didn't watch, but she did hear the soft mewling of the benefaction. There was a dripping sound, followed by a second chorus of whimpers. The haruspex had made another cut. A third would follow, and soon he'd be ready for another sacrifice. Time was in short supply, so she gathered her thoughts. Merit's letter said that Mered did not know the secret, and since there was only one secret, Sarra was certain that Mered did not know the Soleri were ashen relics. He had said they were absent from the domain, so she guessed that was the extent of his knowledge. Merit also knew the secret. Arko must have told it to her, which did make some sense. She was queen regent at the time. If he were going to trust the secret with someone, surely it would be his daughter, the regent of the kingdom he loved and cherished.

Three people shared the secret of the Soleri. As far as the rest of the empire was concerned, as far as each and every person in this room knew, the Soleri lived and breathed and wielded the power of gods. Maybe they existed outside of the Empyreal Domain. There were some who doubted the faith, but they did not discount it entirely. The appearance of the Antechamber fire had rekindled the beliefs of many, highborn and low. Even Sarra had come to accept such things, if only grudgingly. The gods might be dead, but somehow, almost impossibly, their power endured and Mered had seen it too.

He was careful to honor Sarra, as if he were hedging his bets, just in case he'd gotten the whole thing wrong. The power he took was not the power of the Ray, and he claimed no blessings from Mithra. He'd arrived with his own cult and his own soldiers, building his own empire right on top of the one Tolemy ruled.

It's time to test that empire, she thought. *We will see if his god of death can match my dead gods.* Were the situation any less grim she might have chuckled as she made her way across the room. Everyone else was having a good time. All around her the people pushed this way and that, trying to get a better look at the altar. The feast had reached a crescendo. Everywhere, there were more servants, carrying more plates piled high with more delights. Gold-rimmed platters overflowed with dates, fresh persimmons, and nut-brown sapodillas. The men drank from gilded drinking horns while the women sipped from ornate bowls of colorful glass. Incense wafted from every table, filling the air with twisted columns of smoke, burning Sarra's eyes, filling her nose with lurid aromas. The air was heavy with laughter, with smoldering ash, and the stink of scented oils. Everything was in abundance; everyone had had their fill, and more. The people feasted while the haruspex did his bloody work. To them, this was all a great spectacle, a kind of entertainment. *Too bad I'm about to ruin it.*

"My master will speak with you." Bicheres came upon her unexpectedly. His chin was raised, voice high. In his estimation, it was a great honor to speak to the father of House Saad. Sarra saw things a bit differ-ently, but she had no time to argue with the man.

"Take me to him," Sarra said as she glanced sidelong at the black altar, trying to catch a glimpse of Merit.

Bicheres offered his arm, but she did not take it. The golden robe would not allow them to lock arms. It was simply too stiff, which was a bit of a relief. She had no interest in touching Mered's servant boy, this abettor or whatever he called himself. And he had no right to touch the mouth of the god. Sarra walked with Bicheres at her back. She made her way slowly, with grace, though time was short.

Mered occupied a high chair and his many wives, the chatelaines of House Saad, sat with their children. There were dozens of them, a whole tribe clustered about one another, enraptured by the show. The young-est of the family could not have been older than four or five. Human sacrifice was hardly a decent night's entertainment for a child, but that notion had apparently not occurred to Mered, or to his wives. They were all grinning. It was as if they were watching a puppeteer's show and not some butcher with a body laid out atop his block.

At least one of them had the sense to look away from the altar. Mered stood when he caught sight of Sarra. He made a small gesture with his hand and the wives corralled their children, moving them out of Sar-ra's path. As she walked, cries echoed in the distance, but she dared not glance at the altar. She heard a whimper and prayed it was not Merit's.

When she reached the father of the great house, he bowed and a hun-dred different beads jingled as studs of carnelian and blue faience knocked against one another. It was an awful racket and a silly display of wealth.

"Stand straight," she said coldly, firmly, "there's much we need to discuss."

"Is there?" he asked, his voice sounding higher than she remembered.

"I thought you'd come here to witness my triumph," he said. "To tell good Tolemy of the wondrous accomplishments I've made, of our great feast or our most unprecedented offering to the gods. Sit. There is nothing else for you to do." His words hardened into what sounded like a command.

Sarra was unmoved. "I think I'll stand, and you should do the same. The kingsguard are free." Wat's spies in the city watch had told her the story. "The Harkans have completely escaped, so you might want to stop promising their demise."

"They cannot hide forever," he said calmly. He was not bothered.

"Really? Seems to me that you've lost them completely. You'll look like a fool when word of this reaches the wellborn. You captured only children and tortured them for sport."

"Do not—"

"What? Threaten you? I don't have time for that. I am Tolemy's ambassador. He sent me to save *you* from all this foolishness."

Mered did not reply.

Silence.

Then he seemed to reconsider his quiet. "I require no such help," he said. "I have a ceremony to observe." He gestured toward the haruspex, and Sarra stole a glance at the altar. Merit stood beside it. Their gaze met and Merit's eyes took hold of Sarra. It was a dreadful embrace, and a plea she could not ignore.

"As I was saying," Mered spoke, breaking Sarra's concentration, returning her attention to the task at hand. "Join me and observe the next offering. I believe it's what you came here to witness—is it not?"

"Is it not?" She mocked his words. "No," said Sarra. "And there's nothing left *to* observe." She drew close to him. "You've made a blunder in the Hollows, and soon everyone will know it. But there is still a way to maintain your dignity, First Among Equals."

"And what way is that?"

Sarra was silent. Up until that very moment, she'd bided her time. She'd refused to move against Mered because she knew too little about his plans, but all that had changed. Sarra had learned what he knew of the Soleri and guessed at his larger aims.

"The way Tolemy demands," she said. "Do you think He is unaware of your plans? You allowed the heir of Feren to live. This was no accident. You will support his claim to the throne. He'll be your second puppet—won't he? The first one sits in Harkana. One by one, you claim the lower kingdoms. My priests say you have a Rachin and a boy from the Wyrre." She made up that last one, but she presumed it was true and he made no effort to correct Sarra.

"The king in Harkana is not my son, and I can declare him a fraud at any time."

"Is this the will of Tolemy—or is it *your* will, Sarra? Whose mouth am I addressing?"

"The one you will obey," she said, but it was not quite the wording she had hoped to use. Time, however, was in short supply. The knife was already at Merit's neck.

"I am a mouthpiece," she said, regaining her composure. "You've guessed that our lord Tolemy lives outside of the Empyreal Domain, and I will not deny it. The domain is empty, but our emperor is close and He cares dearly about His city."

"Does He?" Mered asked, and she knew he spoke with honesty, with genuine curiosity. He *was* desperate to know the empire's secrets.

"Yes, Tolemy speaks to me, *and to you*. I will prove it by showing you His wisdom. Send the queen regent to Barca. She has the support of the Harkan generals. Merit was all but king when she left, and little has changed. As his ally, she will enable Barca to forge a treaty with the Harkan generals. This will end the conflict in the south and bring peace to your new kingdom. The Harkan Army will return to Harwen, and you will order Merit to accompany them. She will support your new king, as will Tolemy. If you leave the Harkan Army in the field, Harwen will remain open for the taking, and the bastard and his kingsguard *will* take it. You've already witnessed their fierceness in battle. Your whole army couldn't contain them—"

There was no more time. The haruspex raised his blade, the knife trembled at Merit's neck.

"Stop this!" she commanded. "Get that crown off her head. Have the girl treated decently and sent on her way," she said, gasping.

Mered showed no fear. No disappointment, nor any thanks. She swore he never blinked, but he did raise a single finger and the haruspex rested his knife.

≩ 21 ≨

"Well?" Merit asked Mered's soldiers as they opened the door to her carriage. "Will Barca chop off my head or offer me a royal welcome?"

The two men shrugged. Her escorts—Tehran and Ori, the soldiers who'd ridden her from the house of Saad to the desert camp of the traitor, Barca—had gone off that morning to make some bargain with the rebel. They went out with a scroll bearing Mered's seal and a large chest, which no doubt contained gold. In her experience, a good amount of coin settled an argument better than any sword or scroll. And the chest was gone when they returned, so she guessed it had done the job.

"Barca, will he see me?" she asked.

"Damned if I know," said Tehran.

Ori explained, "They took the gold and said we could ride you to the camp, but you'll be on your own after that—sound fair?"

"It sounds like my only choice. If you want fair, ride me to the Harkan camp and I'll make certain you are both treated fairly, paid your weight in gold—double if you like."

Ori coughed a bit and rumpled his lip. "There's no use in having gold if you can't spend it. If I don't deliver you to Barca, I'll be short both of these"—he waved his hands in the air—"and maybe a foot."

"Ride me to Barca's camp," she said. "The least you can do is save me the indignity of walking." *And that might be the last indignity I'm saved.*

The horses trotted over the low desert scrublands, ferrying Merit to the entry of Barca's makeshift camp, which consisted of nothing more than a line of shields dug into the sand and the dozen or so fighting men who stood before them. They surrounded Merit's horse and looked her up and down, suspicion in their eyes. They wore the bronze armor of the Protector, but they had slashed the symbols on their chest plates, grinding them smooth at the center and replacing the old mark with a new one, a broken circle. She guessed it was Barca's mark, a rather obvious dig at the golden circle of the Protector.

She stepped down from the horse and announced herself, "I am Merit Hark-Wadi, Queen—"

"There ain't one of us who cares to hear a list of your titles. Walk yourself over here. We've got an especially nice place saved for you," said a bucktoothed soldier with a day's growth on his chin, a man from Solus by the looks of him. A curious bit of chuckling followed his words, which made Merit think that her accommodations would be anything but nice.

A short walk past a dozen or so tents, many of them empty, led to a rather large shelter.

"This is it," said the soldier. "Find a cozy place for yourself inside," he said, a smirk on his face, a bit of hoarse laughter.

"I'm here to meet with your master," said Merit. She did not know what title the rebel had granted himself.

"You're here to rot like the rest of the rabble, so get yourself inside that tent," said the soldier. He drew his blade, but Merit had already backed away. Her bruises still ached from her last encounter with a fighting man.

She lifted the tent flap, and a foul smell came rushing out of it, but she entered anyway. Merit expected to find captured soldiers or servants inside the tent, but to her surprise the men and women who huddled within it wore rich clothes, transparent layers of pleated linen, and the air was heavy with the smell of scented oils, the aroma of fragrant lilies filling up her nose. Unfortunately, there were other odors. The smell of rot was everywhere, and no amount of perfume could hide that stink. It was in the air and in their clothes. It made Merit's eyes sting.

"Who are you?" asked a man who wore a silken robe colored green like malachite and a great scarf that wound about his neck, the muslin so fine she could see straight through it to the many folds of his wrinkled skin. He spoke with the accent of a wellborn man, so she guessed these were the highborn of Sola, taken captive during Barca's conquest in the south. *Hardly the rabble,* she thought.

"I'm no one," said Merit. She saw no need to reveal her identity. She covered her mouth with her sleeve and sat, taking stock of her surroundings as she settled in. A lifeless body lay at the far side of the tent. She tried not to wince when she saw it. The corpse had been tossed atop a heap of filth, laid there as if it were just another bit of refuse. These prisoners were obviously wealthy citizens of Sola, but they'd been brought low, lower than low, degraded in every way.

"You certainly aren't one of us," said the man in the silken robe. He eyed her clothes and her eyes too, which were a shade lighter than their own.

"Be glad you are not from Sola," snarled an elderly woman.

"Why?" asked Merit.

"Because each week he hangs one of us. He does it just to make the boys clap. Another rich man dead. His coin is your coin—something like that. That's what he tells them," said the woman.

"He's made them hungry for gold and loot. He's turned the holy army of the Protector into a band of criminals," said an older man with a white beard, his skin amber and wrinkled with age. "Who are you?" he asked, a bit of disdain in his voice. They knew she was not one of them; she had her mother's pale eyes.

"I'm no one," she said again, quietly. She still saw no point in revealing her identity. Sooner or later, someone would come for her, and she hoped whoever it was would lead her to Barca and not the hangman's noose, but no soldiers arrived. The sun beat down on the tent, but there was no water and no food. When one of the men went to complain, the guards beat him without mercy. He lay in the sand, bleeding, and no one came to his aid. Not one of the men or women in the tent paid him the slightest bit of attention. There was no humanity here, no understanding. There was only fear. She saw it. They feared that if they came to the man's aid they'd be beaten as well, so no one moved.

An hour later the guards tossed the body upon the heap, and the stench doubled.

The stink of the place brought back thoughts of the haruspex. She'd waited for her death, but it had not come. Her mother had saved her; she'd made some deal with Mered. Sarra had staved off the impossible and had done it at the very last moment. Merit had not seen her mother in ten years. She'd barely been able to recall her face and they hadn't had time to talk. There hadn't even been the possibility of a conversation. There was only time to pass the note.

That slip of linen had changed everything. Sarra had obtained Merit's freedom with the help of that message, or so she assumed. It was all guesswork. Sarra and Merit hadn't even spoken, but she had stolen a hundred careful glances, studying her mother as she parlayed for Merit's freedom. Well, perhaps the word "freedom" was a bit of an exaggeration. The stench inside that tent almost made her wish she were dead. It certainly made her eyes burn.

The sting abated when the flap opened and a waft of clean air swept past her nose. A soldier entered. Without ceremony, he took hold of the old man, the one who had spoken to Merit. He grabbed him by the arm and twisted the limb until a loud snap pierced the air.

"No," the man cried out in protest. "Dammit, I could buy you a hundred times over. If it's coin—"

The soldier knocked the elderly man across the jaw, drawing blood, but the prisoner was undeterred. "I'll pay you in land," he said, his voice raspy. "There are treasures a soldier—" A second hit disfigured the elderly man's jaw, knocking it out of place, silencing him. The soldier glanced around, his eyes settling on Merit. "Barca wants to see you. Just let me string this fellow up." He spoke with such nonchalance that even Merit—who had often sent men to their deaths—swallowed uncomfortably when he spoke.

The flap closed and everyone inside waited for what came next.

Somewhere in the distance a crowd cheered, and she guessed the deed was done.

"He'll hang you up next, outlander," said one of highborn.

Ignoring him, Merit stood and wiped her dress clean. It was not the shining gown of a regent, but she made the best of it, shaking the sand from the cloth, pulling back her long hair to hide her dusty locks.

"Ah, the girl wants to look pretty while she swings from the rope," said a highborn woman. She cackled a bit, and some of the others did the same. For her part, Merit cast a dour eye on the woman. She wasn't headed to the hangman's noose. The guard motioned to Merit, and she left the tent with as much haste as she could muster. In the distance, a crowd dispersed, leaving a clear view of the gallows.

"I don't envy your position," she said to the soldier. It seemed a gruesome task, but he eyed her strangely.

"You don't? Mine's a place of honor. These well-to-do bastards deserve the rope, and I'm the one who gives it to them. That's a privilege. I know a dozen good men who'd kill for this job."

"Interesting choice of words," said Merit. "These highborn men and women hail from Solus and so do you. Is there really so much resentment among the common folk?"

"Resentment?" asked the man. "I suppose. You've never lived in the city of the gods—have you?"

Merit simply shook her head.

"Barca gives us a bit of respect, or something like it. Why do you think we're out here in the desert with him?"

"I see," said Merit, catching sight of what she guessed was Barca's tent. It carried the golden crest that belonged to the Protector of the Outer Guard, or the former Protector anyway. Barca had murdered the man.

The tent lay in one direction, the gallows in the other.

"What'll it be?" she asked. "Are we off to the tent, or do you have another rope you'd like to stretch?"

The guard chucked at that. He was already walking Merit toward the golden tent.

"I'm to meet the captain, or is he the *general*?" she asked, still uncertain of Barca's title. "I heard he promoted himself."

"It don't matter," said the soldier. "Barca can call himself emperor. Names mean nothing here. And we don't care for titles either." He eyed her dress, which was stained, but still finer than those of the common folk.

"Barca must be eager to meet you, or so I guess. Usually he makes the prisoners stew in their filth for a few days before he sees them. When he does take their call, he makes 'em beg for their freedom, but all they find is the end of the rope." He shook his hand in the air, imitating the snap of the noose.

"I used to enjoy that sort of humor, but now that I've seen the rope I'm having second thoughts . . ." said Merit. She'd have said something more, but they'd come to the golden tent.

"Go on now," the soldier said. "I'll be waiting out here, just in case he changes his mind and wants me to string you up with the old man. We do two in a day sometimes," he said morbidly.

She slipped through the untethered cloth and entered a surprisingly lavish interior. There were broad trestle tables covered in heaps of scrolls, candles burned down to the base, and great bronze flagons of wine. Mounds of treasure sat in half-ordered heaps. A stack of funereal urns was tossed in alongside a pile of great gilded statues. Here and there, precious vessels dotted the floor. A pair of braziers ornamented by dancing fauns framed a rather kingly chair, but no one sat in it. At the far corner, a man in a simple tunic stood among four or five officers, each of them wearing the ceremonial armor of a captain in the Outer Guard.

Merit knocked into something hard and tinny, making a sound she hoped would announce her presence. The man she guessed was Barca whispered something to the others, and a moment later they dispersed. As they did so, he waited at the broad table, sizing her up, perhaps. He did not speak, not yet. He waited, watching the tent flap fall closed with a whoosh. Then he left her, disappearing momentarily, speaking to the guards outside before returning to Merit.

"I needed to make certain we were alone and that no one would enter my tent," he said. It was an odd sort of introduction. For a marauder—a man who was said to be a thief, a traitor, and a murderer—Haren Barca was surprisingly humble *and* courteous. He looked to be in his fifth decade, hair gray, skin lined with deep folds, scars on his cheeks and brow. It was a soldier's face, his eyes hard, his gaze distant. He took her hand and offered her a deep and sustained bow. It was the sort of genuflection one gave to royalty—the kind one presented to the queen regent, not some prisoner in a dirty robe. He bowed with grace, but without explanation. *What is this?* she wondered. *What's going on here?*

He indicated that she should sit. "Please, I know it's been a long ride, and only Mithra knows what they did to you in Solus. I'm sorry you were put with the other captives, but it needed to be done—for appearance's sake." He poured wine for two and offered her the first cup. She was parched and drank eagerly.

"Is there anything else you need? Immediately, I mean. Are you injured?"

"There are many things I need," said Merit. "But the wine will do, and an explanation of some sort. Why the royal treatment?" she asked, her voice blunt to the point of rudeness.

"Yes," he said, pacing a bit, as if he needed to think, to explain something of complexity. "There's much you don't know. This whole thing, my great plan, has become a bit of a mess. But there is time to set things right. I'll need your help, and you'll give it."

"Will I? Perhaps you've forgotten, but the Harkans have somewhat of a grudge against your folk. I'd rather hang than help a man from Sola."

He nodded his understanding. "Yes, yes, exactly. I couldn't agree with you more." He took a deep breath, let it out. "I am not Haren Barca."

"Then who are you? Some bastard son of Solus? Have you come to reclaim a title or perhaps a seat in one of the great houses?" she asked mockingly.

"Yes and no. I've haven't an ounce of their blood, though I was raised for a time in Solus. I spent my early years in the high desert, in seclusion, mostly. It was the only way I could be raised, in secret, always moving, never existing. You see, there is no Haren Barca. It's just a name I chose when I joined the army of the Protector—when I become one of *them*."

"What are you talking about?" Merit was wild with curiosity.

"I'm Barden Hark-Wadi, the younger brother of Arko."

"The one who died at birth?"

"They buried another boy and sent me into hiding. Koren had already fought a war over Arko. He couldn't save me from the priory with his sword, so he chose a different route, a more tactful one but no less difficult. After I was born—my father, your grandfather—gave me to one of his generals. I spent my first years in Harwen, but I looked too much like my father. To hide my face, they sent me into the high desert. I went with nothing more than a cadre of soldiers and enough gold to trade with the outlanders."

"Alive," she said, still shocked. "Barden is alive?" She could hardly believe the words, though they did make some sense. He was fighting a revolt from within the Protector's apparatus, pitting one portion of the army against the other. It explained the ruthlessness of the hangings, the marauding. This was a man set upon revenge.

Merit had a hundred questions. No, a thousand. Who else was party to this secret? And why had Barca not reached out to her sooner? The queries swirled in her head, multiplying by the minute. She did not even know where to start, but he put a finger to her lips before she could speak. "We must be careful and quiet. These men think I am leading a revolt of the common man, the lowborn versus the high, that I am taking them to Solus so they can pillage and take back what the wealthy stole from them."

"I see, so what is it then?"

"This?" he asked, his grin widening. "This is the war your father dreamed of but never dared, the task your grandfather took up but never finished, the battle our forebears fought two centuries ago, the fight Nirus Wadi won then lost." Barca produced the golden sword of the Protector of the Outer Guard. "We're going to fight it again. This is the next Harkan revolt—our final revolt. This time we will not negotiate, we will not even attempt to occupy Solus. No, we're going to burn it to the ground."

THAT COLOSSAL WRECK, BOUNDLESS AND BARE

22

Kepi had forgotten how much she liked to break things. The youngest daughter of Arko Hark-Wadi enjoyed splitting the wood in two, watching the various shards shatter and bounce when the funereal icon broke beneath her blade. She even liked the way her fingers stung from the force of the hit. The queen of the Ferens savored the shock that ran through her hands, the stinging in her thumbs, and the almost electric stab of pain that shot right up the tendons in her arm. She relished the pain because it made her forget the last few weeks, it blotted out the memories that haunted her every waking moment.

She saw the face of her dead husband, and she hacked at the wood.

The voice of her deceased father rattled in her ear, and she chopped at the icon again.

The face of the lover who'd betrayed Kepi flashed in her thoughts, and she hacked at the wood. The howls of the servants who rose up to claim her king's life came unbidden to her ear, so she chopped at the wood until there was nothing left of it.

She lifted her blade and looked for something else to cut, but her concentration broke when the kite's scream shot through the open archway. She glimpsed the great bird, wheeling through the gray sky, and she recalled the way it had circled the chamber when it first came to her side. In her thoughts, she heard again the song she'd cried, the Dawn Chorus, that wild and wordless tune that marked the start of her rule. She felt again the bite of the talons as the kite settled on her forearm in the Chathair while the whole of the kingdom kneeled at her foot. That was the day they named her Kitelord and queen of the Ferens.

For her part, Kepi hadn't wanted any of it. She'd spent the better part of her life trying to escape her royal obligations. In her mind, this new title was just one more of them, another responsibility she'd rather not endure. Her whole life was an endless parade of duties, and today was no exception.

She glanced out through the open window. Past the little bailey and the city walls, beyond the crofters' homes with their pitched roofs and columns of woodsmoke, a low hill hunched in the distance, and a crowd stretched between here and there.

She looked away.

Caer Rifka was quiet today, quieter than usual, and it had been *awfully* quiet lately.

She spent her days in Dagrun's chamber, and she slumbered in her king's bed, her husband's bed.

No, she told herself. *It's just my bed.* She struck the wood again, though there was hardly anything left of it.

She was the queen of a kingdom she did not want to rule—that she had refused to rule. More than a week had passed since the kite came to Rifka, but Kepi had barely left the chamber. Despite dozens of callers, in refutation of an endless parade of well-intentioned petitioners, she had avoided every inquiry, ceremony, and solicitation—and why shouldn't she? She was Kitelord, ruler supreme, ordained by Llyr. With the kite at her side, no one dared question her authority. Hence, she ignored her petitioners. She preferred the company of cold steel.

She always had.

If only I wanted this throne, she thought. *Merit wanted it—she wanted to rule the Gray Wood. I didn't.* She had no interest in governing a kingdom of slaves. Even the ripe tang of the blackthorn sap left an unpleasant taste in her throat—like spoiled wine.

Kepi found one last scrap of wood, aligned her blade with the direction of the grain, and cleaved it in two. The cut exposed the darker sapwood of the tree. It looked ashen, so she stuck the tip of her blade into the wood and tossed it out through the window.

Kepi didn't want to think about ashes.

She looked out that same window, past the long lines of mourners, to the wooded grove at the hilltop. A bit of smoke gathered there, hanging cloudlike above the blackthorns, or maybe it was just the fog. She never could tell the difference, not here. Everything and everyone was unfamiliar. Kepi was a creature of the desert, born in Harwen where water was scarce, a treasure more precious than any jewel. In Feren, all things were green and even the air was sopped with moisture, the fog gathering each day above the trees, hiding the sky in a perpetual gloom.

She lingered at the window.

It's begun, she thought.

The funeral planning had been under way for days, but she hadn't wanted any part of it. The Feren warlords had come to her—first Ferris, then Deccan—and asked her to join in the planning. She'd refused. These were the men who'd stood with her when the commoners raised arms against Dagrun, but she'd sent them away without much more than a wave of her hand or an absent shake of her head. She wanted nothing to do with her husband's funeral or his kingdom.

She wanted to escape, to leave this place, but that wasn't going to be easy. She was the Kitelord. She was free of the need to marry, free of any obligations save those of the land. That was the tricky part. Feren was a slave kingdom. For every free citizen, there were easily two or three who were slaves. *Not much of a kingdom,* thought Kepi. *More like a prison camp, and a crowded one at that.* In Harkana, there were no slaves. She'd had servants, but they'd been compensated for their labors, given food, a bed, and a bit of coin. Here, the slaves did everything from sweeping the floors to wiping their masters' asses.

Her eyes chanced upon the window, and she caught sight of that tall cloud of smoke, billowing upward from the distant hilltop. Dagrun's funeral had begun. Unable to prevent herself, Kepi went to the window, where she once again caught sight of the great bird. It circled the little bailey. In truth, it had not left her side since the revolt, which was less than fortunate for Kepi. The mere presence of the kite brought back memories of the angry mob, potsherds jabbed in her face.

A feeling of bitterness welled within her heart, threatening to burst. *Where are my leathers?* She needed to hit someone. *There must be some soldier here who'll spar with me.*

She went to the trunk, where she stored the sparring clothes her husband made for her, the ones that were so carefully tailored, so beautifully made, and that fit her so well.

She flung open the trunk, but it was empty. Nothing inside. No leathers—not even the tunic was there.

Kepi's heart skipped a beat and her head swung toward that distant hill.

They couldn't have.

She flung open the door to her chamber and ran out into the hall, the guards calling after her and inquiring about what direction she was headed in and how they might assist their queen.

"Leave me!" she told the soldiers. "Lest you find your head parted from your shoulders."

Kepi found the stables. She took the reins from a soldier who was about to mount what appeared to be a well-rested steed. He was probably late for the funeral and would now be even later. Momentarily, he reached for his sword, but when he saw her face he sheathed it and bowed.

There had been a lot of that lately, bowing, and she ought to have acknowledged him in some way, but she had little interest in such things.

The warhorse thundered through the stable's open doors, beneath the Chime Gate, and out toward the northern fields. She rode past the crofters' homes and the packs of mourners who had come to pay their respects to the dead king. She broke through a stand of tall blackthorns and emerged into a great clearing where the warlords of Feren gathered with their sworn men and loyal soldiers. They encircled a yawning basin. A fire, half-buried in a pit, blazed uncontrollably.

She leapt down from her horse and all eyes swung from the pyre to Feren's new queen.

I want my leathers.

She ran to the very edge of the pit, but came up short. Somewhere between the heat and the smoke and her desire to find those sparring clothes, Kepi realized just what she was looking at. This was the funeral of a Feren king. Apparently, such funerals entailed a great amount of burning, more burning than she imagined possible—at least until that moment. Dagrun's body lay atop a stack of wood and all around that stack were arrayed the items of the king's house: his chairs and tables, his chest, his sword, his shield, his every item—from his comb to the polished bronze he'd gazed into each day. Every item of his existence was carefully arranged in the funereal well. His every possession was there, and so, with horror, she realized that his slaves were chained there as well. They kneeled beside their king, the flames licking at their faces.

No. Kepi choked on the smoke, but it wasn't the flames that made her nearly disgorge the contents of her stomach. *This is sick,* she thought. *How can these people simply watch?*

A hundred souls sat in the fire. *And that's what they are,* she thought. *Souls.* Surely that was all that was left of them.

She spied her leathers. *Let them burn,* thought Kepi. *Let this be the price of my silence.*

She'd left her kingdom in the hands of others, and this cruelty was the result. Though she had taken no oath as queen, and there had been no coronation, no ceremony, they'd bowed at her feet in the Chathair. She guessed that was enough.

Kepi was queen, and it was time she did something about it.

⇥23⇤

Ott braced himself atop what appeared to be a hastily fashioned crutch. He was as dirty as the filthiest among the kingsguard, his body as broken as that of any of the soldiers. *He'll fit in just fine with our lot,* thought Ren. Ott's leg was heavily bandaged, as were the fingers on one hand, and he had a withered arm hidden beneath the sleeve of his white robe. It hung, ghostlike, haunting the fabric it failed to properly occupy.

"I . . . I never thought I'd meet you," said Ott, sweating profusely. "You see, I wasn't looking for you. I was searching for something else. Then I found this temple and it was so ancient that history itself had nearly forgotten its name, and it occurred to me that such a place might have its uses—especially for someone who needed to hide . . . someone like you, Ren."

"Thank you, brother." It was all Ren could think to say. "We were . . . well, you know . . ."

"I understand. You owe me your life." Ott spoke bluntly, almost to the point of awkwardness. "All of you"—he waved his hand at the kingsguard—"owe me your lives, and you may have cost me mine." He chuckled oddly at those last words, out of fear, perhaps, or nervousness. The boy possessed an almost indescribable eccentricity, but he held some strength within him and he had Arko's jawline, his eyes, and his wide forehead.

"You never met him—did you?" Ren asked. "Our father?"

Ott shook his head.

"You have his eyes. You're his son. Maybe more than I am."

"I'll never know."

"No, none of us will," said Ren. "He was . . ." Ren did not know where to start. His one encounter with his father had been so brief, the moment so charged with pain and the urgency of Arko's surrender that Ren found it difficult to recall. "He was a mystery," he said at last, wary of the subject. He knew little and less, and all of it was shot through with pain.

"Isn't everything these days?" said Ott. He leaned heavily on his crutch.

Kollen brushed aside a pair of soldiers, his face speckled with dust. "You're the trueborn son of Arko Hark-Wadi and that bitch Sarra Amunet, Mother Priestess of us all?"

"The Mother Priestess—"

"I know she's no bitch to you," said Kollen, "but—"

"No," Ott interrupted, "I wasn't arguing with you. I was *correcting* you. Mother is the First Ray of the Sun, right hand of Tolemy the Immortal. In public, I am her scribe, Geta."

"First Ray?" Ren asked. "Your mother, *the* Mother, is Ray? That woman despises me. My father bedded some other girl. Apparently, it pisses her off to no end, and the fact that Arko named me the heir of Harkana and not you"—Ren pointed to Ott—"probably just made the woman doubly angry."

"I don't want it," Ott said.

"Want what?" Ren asked.

"Your throne. I don't want Harkana, and even if I did want it there is already a king in Harwen."

"A king?"

"Yes, but a false one, obviously."

"In Harkana, a man sits upon the throne?"

"That's what I said." Ott's words were loud and clear. "The imposter claims to be me—the hidden son of Arko. The boy who never went to the priory. He sits upon the Horned Throne."

"Well, that's news. I suppose we'll have to do something about him— won't we, then?" Ren's gaze went to Edric and the rest of the black shields. Shouts echoed in the darkness. They were with Ren, but nervous too. None of them knew how they'd get out of this place.

Ren caught Ott staring at the eld horn. The tusk was caked in blood and dirt and a hundred other kinds of filth, but it was still the sacred horn—the symbol of the king, of the hunt, and of Ren having completed it.

"We need not argue over succession," said Ott. "A king sits in Harkana. And to make matters worse, your sister was named queen regent. The chair has three contenders. I'd rather not add a fourth."

Being the right-hand man of the Ray of the Sun was, in all likelihood, preferable to being the monarch of a rebel kingdom, or so Ren surmised. Maybe that was Ott's reason for denying his claim to the throne, or perhaps Ott had just decided to let the three of them fight it out before he joined the fray. It wasn't a half-bad strategy. Merit was a formidable foe, and Ren knew little of this false king.

"Walk with me," Ott said, "if the rest of your people don't mind."

"Oh, they don't mind a bit," said Ren. "You can do whatever you please. Isn't that right, Kollen?"

The older boy shrugged. "Have what you wish. I'm going to sit my ass down and pass out," he said. Most of the kingsguard, except perhaps the captains, had done that already. Tye nodded for Ren to go and sat down beside Kollen while Ott led Ren to the base of the spiral. Nearly five hundred men crowded the ramp. But there was a bit of privacy at the bottom, a chance to speak candidly.

"Do you have a plan, some way to get us out of here?" Ren asked.

"A plan?" asked Ott. "I led you out of the cistern. Isn't that enough? You have no idea how much effort it took to find the right passages and where to collapse them, which ones to close and which to leave open, and how to do it all quickly, properly, to design a path that could not be tracked, that would divert your enemy in a thousand different directions. And I did it in a day. I haven't even slept."

"I'm sorry," said Ren. "Go. Sleep. But let me ask you this one thing: Is there a way out of here?"

"I don't know."

"How about food, have you brought us any?"

"I haven't brought you anything—except time. If I'd purchased a hundred barrels of amber, someone might have thought it odd. I can't take that sort of risk. You are the enemy of both the Ray and Mered. There are two forces set against each other in this city, and both of them want you dead. Every man in Solus would be after my head if my part in your escape came to light."

"But your priests? They're loyal?" asked Ren.

"To the end. Each of them hails from Harkana. They are your kinfolk and they know the risks. I'm taking one right now, disappearing like this—I have duties, and my absence will be noted."

"Then leave."

"I will, but I wanted to speak to you. I'll be plain, because I don't want you to have any illusions and time is short. You are trapped. Mered's army patrols the Hollows and there are men at every gate."

"But the smugglers' routes—"

"Are all sealed, and even if you found a fresh one, the Protector's Army guards the Plague Road. There are what, four, five hundred of you? Five thousand men patrol the desert path and it's the only one that leads to Harkana."

Ren had once walked that road; he knew it.

"Trapped then," said Ren. "And we're almost out of provisions. In truth, we are out. There's barely anything left. Still, you did well, my friend. We're alive."

"I did do a fair job of rescuing you—didn't I?"

"Brilliant's the word."

"Then give me time."

"We don't have it."

"You also don't have a choice," said Ott. "Wait here and I'll find food. For now I must leave."

"Leave?" asked Ren. "There's a way out of this place?"

"There is one, but you cannot follow it. I am the servant of the Ray, and you're the most wanted man in Solus. I passed a hundred sentries before I disappeared and you'd have to pass all of them to follow my route. By decree of Tolemy I am working to unearth the history of the cults of Re and Pyras. I can go wherever I please, but there's nowhere you can go. At least, not with your head attached to your shoulders. I'll find food."

"Good, but don't wait. Throw it over the lip of the well if you must," said Ren, glancing at the orange dot above them. "I'm a good catch."

"If only," said Ott. He motioned to leave, but Ren barred his path.

"Take me with you," he said. "Tell them I am your scribe and let me help you find another way out of this place. I made promises—"

"There is no way out." Ott raised his voice, which seemed uncharacteristic for the boy, though Ren had only just met him. "I'm sorry, I did not mean to. . . ."

"It's all right, but I can't just sit here and wait for you to help us. We'll starve."

"You cannot follow me. We've been over this, Ren. There are too many sentries, too many eyes watching the Hollows."

"You're the son of the First Ray, aren't you? Well, let me tell you something. When you betrayed Sarra, you made your choice. So why wait? Join us. Those aren't *your* people—we are. You're Harkan. I see it in your eyes."

Ott did not respond. His face held no emotion, no regret, no remorse. Blank.

"I'll return," said Ott. He made his way up the spiral, past Kollen and Tye, past the soldiers resting on the stones.

Ren followed Ott. "When will you return?"

"As soon as possible."

"That's not much of an answer."

Kollen followed. "Where's he going?"

"He's leaving."

"Then let's follow him."

Ott was already halfway up the ramp, but Ren chased him to the top. "You and I," said Ren. "We need time—to talk."

"I know," said Ott as he left the temple. "But I can't stay. My absence will be noted." He made his way down a narrow corridor. Ren followed briefly, unable to stop himself. Ott begged him to quit. Then he disappeared down the long and dimly lit passage. Ren stood there, alone, his lamp raised. In the half-light, he caught sight of a black stain on the cobblestones, and when he took a step forward, he took notice of a second, then a third. A whole trail of them was laid out before him. Ott had marked the path that led out of the temple.

24

The cat's ear blossomed to life, its frail petals unfolding like a pair of open hands. Sarra was curious. "Which hour does this one indicate?"

"The third," said the man who tended the garden. "Cat's ear opens at the third bell each morning . . . well, almost. The low sun wreaks havoc on the little things, but they work well enough at this time of year." His knees were half-sunk in the dirt, hands tearing at the roots of some weed that had snuck its way into the otherwise pristine garden.

"Have you seen the clock?" the gardener asked.

"Oh, many times, but it seldom ceases to amaze me," Sarra said. She caught sight of the flowers planted alongside the cat's ear, the sandspurry and crystallinum. Both seemed eager to blossom.

"You know, it was never really the clock that interested me." Kihl Chefren stepped from the shadows of a palm grove.

"Really?" asked Sarra, her voice filling up with mock interest. "I thought this was the pride of House Chefren, the only flower clock in the empire."

"True, but it's the symbolism that interests me," said Kihl, voice dripping with pride. "I built it to show the city just how far my little empire extended, how I could import anything from *anywhere*. Roselettes culled from the hills north of Zagre, from the highest peaks of Rachis. Clianthus, picked at the furthest tip of the Wyrre."

"You told me that story the last time I visited," said Sarra. She really didn't have time to talk about flowers.

"Then perhaps I should invent a new one for your next visit."

"You might want to do that. Everyone knows the Rachin Hills are impassable, but I suppose that is the point of the story."

Kihl allowed a slender smile to cross his face.

"Picking flowers is hardly impressive," said Sarra. "But carting the amaranth? That was an achievement."

"And we did it for countless generations."

"Until . . ." said Sarra, her voice turning sober.

"Yes, until . . ." Kihl furrowed his brow. They both knew what the word meant. The last time Sarra visited the garden she'd seen a hundred carts of amaranth pass the clock before the cat's ear blossomed. Today, the stables were empty.

"Walk with me," said Sarra bluntly, gesturing for Kihl to follow as she traveled the sandy path that circled the clock. Nearby, his palace sat hard upon a plinth of marble. White walls enclosed the estate, blocking out everything but the sky.

"Have you come bearing amaranth?" he asked.

"If only," said Sarra. She made a morbid sort of laugh. "I am no longer the Mother Priestess, and your days of carting the grain are over."

"Are they?"

"Yes, the empire is changing. We're all changing roles—at least, those of us who wish to stay in power."

"Ah, you refer to our first citizen, Mered Saad? The word 'dictator' has been used."

"Not by me," said Sarra.

"No. Never, but the whispers are all around us, Sarra Twice Blessed. Isn't that what they call you?"

"It's whispered—like everything else," said Sarra. She allowed just the faintest shadow of a grin to cross her lips.

"Your priests always were good at murmuring stories in the ears of the people. 'Least you haven't lost your touch. There are plenty of whispers in Solus. Some say the Soleri no longer live within the Empyreal Domain, that the man who worships Horu could not stand and declare himself first citizen while the gods lived within our great city."

"Lies. Well, mostly," said Sarra.

"And which part is true?"

"The part you don't know. Isn't that always how it works?" Sarra grimaced just slightly. Kihl was silent, so Sarra picked up the conversation. "You know, someone once said to me that the gods hide their secrets in the open, so perhaps I should follow their lead. In truth, the Soleri are gone, fled from the domain. Mered knows this and he whispers it in every ear he can find, but it's not much of a revelation."

"Really? It seems like one to me, but I'm not sure what it means. Tell me, Mouth of Tolemy, what's this all about?"

"Nothing."

"And why is that?"

"Because the Soleri live, and they have not forgotten their people. This is what Mered does not know. He feels their absence, but is ignorant of their impending return." Sarra made up that last part. Kihl had looked so disheartened she felt obliged to give him a bit of good news. Any return would, inevitably, be delayed. They walked past the still-closed blossoms of the evening primrose.

"We must, of course, prepare the empire for that return. Our Protectors have done little to *protect* it."

"You're talking about Barca?"

"Yes, that and more," she said, bending to sniff the sweet flowers, wondering what exactly had become of her daughter when Mered sent her off to Barca. She'd sent men to spy on the rebel's camp. Merit had gone into it, but that was all Sarra knew.

"Then you speak of Suten Anu?" Kihl asked, catching her attention. "Surely Suten was mad. How else can we explain the Harkan Ray? Tolemy would never order such a thing. Did you know they're calling this the Year of Three Rays?"

"Hadn't heard that one," said Sarra. She had, of course, coined the term, and her priests had spread it around Solus, but Sarra was still thinking about her daughter. "Suten ignored our gods and was justly punished, as was his Ray. Arko is gone and Tolemy, our emperor, has chosen me to set things right. In fact, he's tasked me with a great many deeds. One of which stands before me."

"We at last come to the point of this conversation," said Kihl. "Tell me what you've come to offer."

"Protector of the Inner Guard. The post sits open, and I know of no one better suited to fill it. You know every inch of this empire, and your house guard is as sturdy as Mered's or nearly so. You have soldiers at your side and commanders who can ably advise you."

"Saad lasted a month, maybe less. Why would I take up that mantle?"

"Riches. Plunder."

"How so?"

"Barca, of course. Your first task will be to put down the rebel, and it's well known that he's spent the past month raiding the southern half of Sola, plundering the deep desert houses, murdering our kingdom's noble citizens and taking their riches." She circled the flower clock, coming upon the late-blooming flora, the moonflower and five-pointed whitestar.

"The amaranth fields lie fallow," she continued. "There is no grain to cart. Those fortunes are at an end. I offer new ones. The man who conquers Barca takes his plunder. You know that, as does Mered. The loot he carries should more than compensate for your losses in the amaranth trade."

Kihl rubbed his jaw and made it look as though he were pondering her offer, but she doubted he'd given it a second's thought. He only wanted to avoid looking eager.

"It's blood money," he said, "stolen from our own people."

"Gold is gold," said Sarra. "And a handful of stolen gold weighs no less than a hard-earned one." She approached the top of the clock, where the smoke grass wavered in the breeze, its blossoms tightly shut in the bright morning light.

"You always were a bitch," Kihl said.

"And you always did what you were told because you knew it was good for you. The priesthood made you wealthy when they chose your house to cart the amaranth. Let the Ray make you wealthy twice over."

"You're not really asking, are you?"

"I never ask."

"Then I suppose you don't need an answer."

"In that you are wrong. Accept my offer. There's work to be done."

"What work? Mered claims the task."

"He cannot defeat Barca. He plays at politics, but war is another matter. Only the Inner Guard has the might to oppose Barca. Everyone knows this. Take up the Protector's mantle, make your commanders into your generals, and take control of the Guard. Five thousand soldiers are billeted outside of this city. With Tolemy's divine authority you command these men."

"Then it's done." They'd reached the place where they started, where the cat's ear blossomed. "I'll miss the garden." Kihl raised his chin, his eyes set on the black tower of the Protector.

"That's your tower. Summon me when you've taken it and are ready to march on Barca," Sarra said, and she was already motioning to take her leave, wishing him the sun's fate as she went to the gate where her priests waited, four dozen in all. They clustered around her as she passed the iron bars.

In the distance, hiding in the shadows of a portico, soldiers in red observed her exit. They were Mered's men, but there was hardly any need for them to spy on Sarra. She'd named a new Protector of the Inner Guard, and by midday she'd have the news posted on every street corner in Solus.

⇒ 25 ⇐

"You'll forgive me if I have questions—won't you?" Merit asked the man who claimed to be Barden Hark-Wadi. She'd already encountered one purported relative. Another stood before her, so she looked at him with doubt, studying him with every bit of suspicion she could muster. He offered her an alliance that was difficult to refuse, but she needed to know more about the man. This whole empire was filled up with imposters, and she worried she'd found yet another.

"If you are Barden," she asked, "why didn't you contact your brother when he was Ray?"

"I tried. If you recall, Arko's tenure was brief, and I spent most of it in the Wyrre. When my soldiers reached the mainland, we sent messengers to Solus, but Amen Saad's men held the roads. My letters never reached your father."

"Still, he named me queen regent. I own that title, so why didn't you send messengers to me?" asked Merit, though she already knew the answer.

"I did, but you weren't in Harwen. At first, I was told you were lost on the desert road. Then it turned out you were a prisoner of the sand-dwellers. When you were released, you headed straight to Rifka, and afterward you rode back to Harwen. You never stood in one place long enough for a man to find you."

"I'm forced to admit that I have been somewhat difficult to locate." All of it was true. She'd spent the past few weeks traveling back and forth across the empire. "You were unable to contact the family," she said, her voice tainted by mild irritation.

"I sent letters to Sarra."

"My mother—why would you do that?"

"She was queen once, and she raised you. I said nothing of my true identity, but I urged her to send an emissary. It's an unusual request, but I am reasonably certain it led to your arrival at this tent. I told her enough to make her curious, to compel our Ray to send someone out to my camp, just to see what I was up to."

"Is that what led me here—some letter?" Merit had puzzled over the matter ever since she was stuffed into that carriage and ridden to Barden's camp.

"Your guess is as good as mine. She must have known I'd find a use for you even if she didn't know my true name or purpose. As you know, I've been trapped up against the Harkan lines for weeks. It was never my intent to fight them. When I seized the Outer Guard at the Gate of Coronel, I wanted to head straight north to Solus. Raden had just died and his son was still stumbling about as he tried to gain control of his father's generals. It was the right time to strike at the city, but the men had other ideas."

"The men? Are you not their general?"

"There are no generals in this company. This isn't an army, not any-more. It is a body of men drawn together by a promise. I told them we'd loot the south, that we'd plunder every house from Scargill to Solus. That pact bound them to my service."

"Apparently, you made good on your promise. There's hardly a coin left in the south—complete and utter conquest."

"I'd hardly call it conquest." Barca glanced at the tent floor, as if he were stricken by some uncomfortable memory. "It was more of a massacre, but it did the job. We took more loot than we could carry before we marched on Solus."

"Never made it, did you?"

"The Harkans blocked our approach. Fools thought we were trooping toward Harwen. I tried to negotiate with your men, but they have no leader."

"No leader?"

"Seems there's a bit of confusion in Harwen. There's a king, but the army won't follow him. There's an heir, but he's stuck in Solus. And the queen regent . . . well, she's nowhere to be found." He cocked an eyebrow. "Heard she was in Feren." Barden tossed down the golden sword, and it made an awful din as it struck the pile.

"Feren . . . what a waste of time," said Merit. It was her turn to glance sideways and try to forget the past. "Tell me what happened. No leader, no negotiations, straight to the sword?"

"The Harkans struck without warning. I think they were trying to discourage an eastward march and using the point of a spear to do it."

Merit furrowed her brow. "That's one way to get things done. Did you attempt to tell them the truth?"

"The truth?" Barca asked. "Who would I tell it *to*? The king in Harwen? Even the army won't follow that fool."

"So?" Merit asked.

"I retreated. I did not want to spill Harkan blood, not if I could help it."

"And you've been stuck here since?"

Barden didn't bother to answer her question. His soldiers' tents might be golden, but the men were covered in dust and sand, and all of them had the look of hunger about them. They had their plunder. They'd grown rich in the south, but a few weeks in the desert had obviously left his army short on supplies, low on morale too. *A good time to begin our negotiation,* thought Merit, but Barden caught her off guard with his next remark.

"Let me take you to see my men," he said.

"Your men?" asked Merit, confused, but only briefly.

"Can you ride?" he asked.

"Better than most."

"Show me."

A soldier in bronze mail brought horses. The mounts were lightly weighted, so she guessed it would be a short ride. The man tried to help Merit up onto the saddle, but she swatted him away with a wave of her hand. She was mounted before Barca had a chance to put his foot in the stirrup. "Where are we off to?" she asked.

"To see my armies," he said, his voice low, as if he were concealing what he said from the soldier.

"I thought . . ." she said, but Merit caught herself. He was holding something back, that much was clear.

A short ride led to a narrow defile. It was late in the day and the slender walls of the gorge blocked the sun's last rays. There were no lamps here, so she was forced to slow her horse's pace, but the fissure soon opened, revealing what she guessed was a great caldera. Soldier upon soldier packed the crater. Campfires lit the sky and the air was punctuated by laughter and the occasional hoot of some drunkard. *Well-fed, drunken men,* thought Merit. *What is this?*

"Ride with me a bit further," Barden said, leading her up to a slender promontory, where he leapt from his horse and offered her his hand. She took it this time, clearly impressed.

"You've hidden your army," said Merit. "All those sicklings, the piles of butchered bones, that stench—"

"It's a deception, a ruse. We have men and provisions, though I dare not speak of them. I sleep with the dying while my army feasts on what we plundered from the wealthy of Sola. You have no idea what riches the wellborn hide within the great houses."

"But," she asked, "who were those men, back in the camp?"

"Conscripts, mostly from the Wyrre, men who joined our raiding parties or were press-ganged into service. Think of them as camp followers. They seldom leave that ring of shields, and there are other fissures in this crater. My men never pass through that camp. Every day the Harkans send scouts, but all they see are the dying, the severed limbs, and troughs overflowing with waste. We've kept our numbers hidden from the Protector as well as the soldiers in red."

"Mered."

"Yes, Mered. His scouts are everywhere."

"You've concealed your numbers."

"I gave it my best try. This is not simply the remnants of the Outer Guard, though they do form a small piece of my force. We drew volunteers in the Wyrre. Most were sell swords or freebooters, but we also took on fighting men from the royal houses we conquered. We offered them all the same bargain: Join us and you'll be wealthy. We aim to loot Solus, to sack the city of the gods. There'll be plunder aplenty. The Grim Companions are here. You've no doubt heard tales about them. Freebooters, eight hundred in all, and they are not the only company to hear my call. The Blue Spears have come and so have the Storm Men. There are the outlander clans. I spent half my life living among them. They know and respect me. I've built alliances. The Hykso camp with my army, each one as fierce as any soldier in the Alehkar. These are hungry men. I've promised them much and I intend to deliver more, but their patience is at an end—I'm out of time. We need to march, but I'd rather not fight a war with Harkana." Barca drew his blade. "Can you end my standoff with the Harkan Army? Are you with me?" he asked.

"I am. I can name every commander in Harkana and their wives too. I know how many striplings stumble about their homes. I can hand you a Harkan peace treaty," she boasted, "but there may be a catch."

"What?"

"We don't know if that traitor in Harwen has made changes to the army, murdered generals and the like. I can only command the army of my father. If it's intact, I'll have this skirmish sewn up in short order."

"You will. If the boy king controlled that army, he'd have them in Harwen."

"Good, then the task will be simple. I will ally your army with Harkana's and we'll march with you to Solus. I'll be there when the Shroud Wall falls, but there is something that must be done first."

"What business trumps this one?"

"Harwen. We take back what is ours."

"Harwen? You waste time. Solus is the prize."

"I'm not negotiating."

"If I march on your city, I'll reveal my numbers."

"Then I'll ride with the Harkan Army," said Merit. "There is only a garrison in the city. They won't have a chance against the full force of our legions."

"Then go, make our treaty. Take your army and your kingdom," said Barca, an ill look passing across his face. "Do what you must, but know this: I've made a pact with these men." He hardened his jaw. "I offered them plunder. I promised it to the sell swords and the outlanders too. These are pacts drawn in blood, and they'll end in it too if I'm not cautious. If we don't march on Solus, then we'll need to go somewhere else. Understand me?" Barden shot her a furious glare. "Harwen is the last city I wish to raid, but it's close and there's wealth in it. Listen closely." He swallowed twice before finishing. "I cannot control these men, not fully. They're held together by the desire to plunder without recourse. I've offered them Sola and you've committed to that course. If you're unable to make a pact with your generals, my army will put the Harkans to the sword and we'll lose half our men doing it. The mercenaries will find better work, the outlanders will flee, and we won't have enough men to challenge Sola, but we'll still have enough swords to best our black-leathered brethren. When that happens, there will be no soldiers left to protect your precious home—our home."

Barden steepled his fingers and met her gaze.

"This army will sack Harwen, and there'll be nothing either of us can do to stop it," he said, his fingers unwinding, one hand gesturing toward the flap. "Go, and don't even think about failing."

⇒ 26 ⇐

A red torch arced through the purple sky, glowing faintly as it plummeted through the mist. It struck the long and spindly bridge with an almost silent thud, a second torch following close behind it, then a third. The flames shot out across the trestles, enveloping the ancient wood.

"That's the last one," said Kepi. "We've burned every bridge, north to south, up and down the rift. We're cut off from the empire."

"It was Dagrun's last wish," said Deccan Falkirk. He'd ridden with her to the rift. Ferris Mawr was there as well. They were warlords of Feren, and they had both stood with Kepi in the Chathair. Deccan was older than Ferris by several decades. He was a sheepish man despite his height, and she could not help but notice that he was constantly fiddling with his beard and mustache, trimming and grooming the thing. She found him vain, but loyal. He'd stood in the ring when the commoners turned against Dagrun, and he had the scars to show for it. Ferris had more than his share of blemishes, but he was by far the youngest of the warlords. If she had to guess at his age, she would venture to say that he was not a year older than ten and seven, but he bore the scars of a man of twice his age and the maturity of a boy who was half it. The young warlord had a striking face, blue eyes, perpetually unkempt red hair, and a chin that always seemed to have a day's worth of scruff poking from it.

"It's done," said Kepi. "The bridges are burned. It *was* Dagrun's last command. It was almost the last thing he said to me, so I made it my first task as queen." She kicked at the ashes left by the torch. "These flames are the start of a new Feren."

"Or the end of it," said Ferris.

"How's that?"

"Well, I don't argue with the act," said Ferris, "but I am compelled by my great and virtuous sense of honesty"—he offered Kepi a wry grin— "to point out the consequences of your actions. You've cut off all trade with the empire, and put a stop to the tributes. These things are owed to Tolemy. This's a provocation, my lovely queen." Ferris grinned again and flashed his blue eyes, but she wasn't certain if he was flirting with her or testing her nerve. She found it impossible to gauge the man.

"Tolemy will not allow Feren to leave the empire—especially when we're the ones feeding half of Solus," said Deccan. He spoke in a high voice, acting as if he were somehow correcting Ferris.

"I know as much," said Kepi, a bit taken aback. She wasn't certain if it was appropriate for these men to address her in such a casual manner, to second-guess her decisions, or to tell her how to manage the kingdom. She'd seen her father strike a Harkan warlord for speaking as such, and he'd used the sharp edge of a sword to do it.

"Feren needs its crops," said Kepi. "I have plans. I won't say them, not yet. I've got more than one provocation in mind, so if you don't like this one you might as well put down your sword and let some other man pick it up." The funeral made Kepi wary of the Ferens and their customs. She intended to put an end to more than one tradition, but she knew enough about the politics of kingdom to keep her plans to herself.

Still, Deccan wrinkled his nose. He was careful where Ferris was headstrong, wary where his counterpart was brash. "I am loath to admit it, but this bridge burning *is* an act of war. When his grain does not arrive in Solus, Tolemy will send soldiers to retrieve it."

"And I'll be the one to fight 'em," said Ferris. "My men hold the rift," he said, plainly. It was no boast.

"You just happen to have the southernmost caer," said Deccan.

"And you happen to live in the north, in the tranquility of the forest, with nothing but the mountain lords at your back. We all know those poets and scholars are never going to pull their quills out of their asses and come marching down those hills."

Deccan flashed a grimace. "We do our part. While you quarrel with the locals, we raise the crops that feed your men—forget about that?"

"Never. Every time I bite into a week-old turnip I think of Deccan."

"Enough," said Kepi. This was her decision, her command. And these men could fret over it on their own time. She turned and showed them her back, ending the conversation. She'd wanted to see the flames gutter out, but the last of the fires had vanished. Darkness followed, but it was not complete. Faint lights appeared in the forest.

Ferris gave a whistle and several of his men jumped to their feet; more approached from the north.

"What's that?" Kepi asked, eyes suddenly wide.

"Torches," said Ferris. "Looks like someone's come to watch the bonfire, or maybe they've been watching all along—eh?"

"Perhaps," said Deccan, "but who are they? Harkans? I think not."

A man in dark desert robes broke through the tree line. He wore no armor, and he held only a scroll.

"I could take him down with an arrow," whispered Ferris.

"And what would be the point in that?" Kepi asked. "He's a messenger."

"We've burned the bridges," said Ferris. "So why wait around to hear what this man has to say? We're already at war."

"Point taken," said Kepi, yet she *was* curious. Who had come to the rift, and why had he appeared at this very moment—when the queen herself was here and had burned the last of the bridges?

A faint crack rippled through the air as the man broke the wax and carefully unrolled the scroll. A second figure appeared at the back of the first, a torch held high above both of their heads. The firelight revealed the color of their robes, which was pale red—something like madder or the red clay of the Feren earth. Kepi eyed the parchment. *Perhaps I ought to be the one to read it first.* The thought had barely entered her head when she saw the kite circle then dive. Its movements were as quick as her thoughts. Even as the notion formed in her head, the great bird stole away the parchment. The man in red had no opportunity to move or react in any way. The parchment was simply gone from his hand, leaving his fingers held aloft, a look of bewilderment on his face.

The scroll fell into Kepi's hand. Ferris chuckled a bit, impressed, perhaps, or maybe he just enjoyed the look of agitation on the other man's face. The manners of the red-robed man betrayed him as a servant of Solus: pompous, arrogant, annoyed at having the parchment ripped from his fingers.

Kepi made short work of the message, reading it quickly, then tossing it to the earth.

"Well?" asked Ferris. "Is it a love letter from Tolemy? If not, you might as well share it."

"The scroll was inked by Mered Saad, a man who calls himself the First Among Equals. He's concerned about the food shortages in Solus. Says we ought to triple our annual tributes. He wants food and tribute, everything an empire needs to function, and he wants Feren to provide it."

"Somehow, I doubt you'll comply," said Ferris. "Shall I go ahead and put an arrow through the messenger's head? Maybe his friend can drag him back to Solus. That plump body ought to feed a dozen pigs."

"Can you quiet yourself—for just a moment?" asked Deccan, his voice raised. "I know this man, Mered, and he maintains a great army." Deccan lifted the parchment and read it. "He asks Feren to increase the already-agreed-upon tributes threefold."

"By what authority?" asked Kepi.

"None but his own and his army's," said Deccan. "Though this scroll does bear the signature of three others, heads of great families. He is not alone in his endeavor, and each of these families maintains an army. Together they could muster a sizeable force."

"Let them try to cross the rift," said Ferris.

"I fear they will," Deccan replied, "but not yet. They've given us time to ready the first shipment. It says here that Mered intends to ratify this new agreement in person. He asks the queen to meet him at the rift. Three days' time."

How does he even know I am queen? She'd held the crown for barely a week, and the ride from Rifka to Solus was almost that long. Had news of Dagrun's death traveled that quickly? She'd heard of Mered; she knew his surname well enough. Raden Saad was the man her grandfather fought, the old Protector, and his son was the Protector after him. Kepi had hoped to leave the empire behind, to avoid the wars that were brewing in the south, to keep the forest's riches here, at home, but that hope seemed foolish now.

She looked out across the rift, but the two men were already gone. They must have seen her read the scroll and known their work was done.

They had not come to talk. This was no negotiation.

If they did not give Mered what he asked, he'd take it.

≋ 27 ≋

In the lamp's flickering light, they traced the marks left by Ott's crutch. It was not an altogether difficult task, but Ren had already lost the trail twice, the marks having grown lighter as Ott made his journey out and away from the black, soot-stained ramps of the temple.

"There's another one," said Kollen. He was rubbing his eyes and squinting at the thing, trying to discern if it was a smudge or just one more bit of dirt in an already dirty place.

"You've got better eyes than me," said Ren. They'd gone a good distance, but each corridor looked like the last one, and none of them led to the surface.

"No," said Kollen. "My eyes aren't any better. I just don't have my nose stuck to the earth. Stand up, man. This'll go quicker. And another thing, this trail, it seems rather easy to follow—don't you think?" Kollen arched an eyebrow. "Are we certain this isn't some sort of ploy, a trap of some kind? Can we trust your brother? I mean, how do we know he's the genuine article? He could be anyone. Might be Mithra's mad child, or Mered's for that matter. And even if he is Arko's son, he's also the Ray's son. Ever think about that? Maybe he saved us from Mered so he could hand us over to his loving mother. Perhaps we're some sort of gift."

"No," said Ren flatly. He projected certainty when in truth he *had* considered the possibility. It was all he'd thought about. Ren had no way to confirm whether Ott was indeed his brother. He had only a feeling, a hunch. Something deep within him told Ren that Ott shared his blood. He had the eyes of Arko, but that might just be wishful thinking on Ren's part. He hoped he wasn't letting his emotions overpower his reason.

"I don't know," Ren admitted. "I've a hunch, nothing more."

"Oh, and those hunches of yours . . . they've worked out so splendidly in the past."

"They kept us alive," Ren said. "I reckon that's more than you've done. I'm trying to find a way out of this place. You seem bent on nothing more than annoying me."

The sound of boot steps thudded in the corridor. Ren reached for his blade, but Kollen placed a cautioning hand on Ren's shoulder. Edric appeared with a dozen black shields at his back, filling up the narrow stone space. None wore armor, but they carried swords hidden beneath linen robes.

"I don't recall inviting you," said Ren, his eyes meeting Edric's. "These passages are watched by the city guard, and at some point we're going to run into them. We might pass for beggars, but your lot is another story."

"I asked the boys in black to chase after us," said Kollen. "Figured we might need a little help. You know, if things go astray. I've said what I think of Ott. For all I know, this trail leads straight to the Hall of Ministers, or maybe we'll come upon the Ray's privy."

"You've made your opinions abundantly clear, and I've tried to make it equally obvious that I don't care what you think, so—"

"Sorry," Edric interjected. "If we end up butting heads with the city guard, you'll be happy we joined you. Trust me. You spot someone you don't like and we'll knock them over the head—deal?"

"No deal. Just keep quiet and follow along," said Ren. He didn't feel the need to make any kind of agreement. He was in charge. Gneuss had said it and Edric heard the command. Ren turned without saying another word, and the captain did not challenge him. He served under Ren's command; Kollen was another story. The boy served only his ego. Undeterred, he continued his rebuke of Ott. "I don't think there's a single soldier in this passage. We haven't seen one. That brother of yours was just trying to scare us. That's what I think. Maybe he doesn't want us following him around, catching him while he nibbles away at cheese while we bite at our fingernails for nourishment."

"Now you're just imagining things."

"No, I'm not. He said there were soldiers, that if we followed him we'd be discovered. But we haven't found a single one. *He's a liar.* Plain and simple."

"Maybe they're just up ahead," said Ren, the irritation mounting in his voice. "Or they've spied us and run off to grab the rest of their men."

"And maybe they're just in your fucking imagination." Kollen stepped ahead of the others, moving into the larger chamber that was just up ahead of them.

"Quiet," Edric ordered in the stentorian tones the captain so ably pronounced. Ren took note. He'd need to learn how to bark an order if he wanted to command these men or to silence Kollen.

They'd lost Ott's trail, but they'd found something else. Up ahead there were oil lamps, and they illuminated a dark space. It was large but cluttered with pillars. The place was of indeterminate size. He saw no bounds, no limits, no walls. There was nothing but oil lamps, hung here and there from the columns, their pale lights drifting off toward infinity. They followed the lamps, moving through the darkness, a distant light appearing on the horizon. Somewhere far off, he glimpsed a dozen or so shelters, glowing faintly in the black. As he moved closer to them, he saw there was in fact a great number of structures, all of them stacked into some kind of pyramid. It reached upward until it was truncated abruptly by the ceiling of the chamber.

"Are those tents?" Kollen asked. "Are the fools waiting for it to rain?"

"No. It's a market," said Ren. "Those are stalls, not tents. Weeks ago, when I first entered the underground, we passed through a similar place. The priors called it the Night Market; this must be part of it."

Edric pushed ahead of Ren. "Well, looks like we've found a way to fill our stomachs. Only problem is this: we've got no coin." He gripped the hilt of his sword. "Things could get messy if they've got guards." The captain looked to Ren. "You might want to wait this one out."

Ren cast a doubtful look on Edric. "You said something about staying quiet and knocking heads when I asked?" said Ren, cocking his head and waiting to be acknowledged.

"I'll do as you wish. I only thought it should be said," Edric grumbled, his fingers drumming on the pommel of the sword he kept beneath his robe.

Eyes wary, they moved slowly, cautiously. Their stomachs grumbled and they were sleep-deprived and thirsty, too, but Ren dared not hurry. He did not want to draw attention to their little group, so he forced himself to walk at a measured pace, taking in the scene. Everything was bathed in the oily residue of the lamps. It covered their sandals, making their toes black. It even gave the stalls a waxen sheen. This market was old—ancient, possibly. The flames must have burned for centuries to accumulate such a large quantity of residue.

"If you'll allow me to offer a bit of advice," said Edric. "I think we ought to circle the market. Let's see what's for sale and who has all the swords. It might be best to target a few of the less well-defended tents."

"I wasn't going to charge the man with the ax," said Ren. "I think we've all got the same plan in our heads."

Ren had passed through the market once before, but he had no memory of the pyramid. He guessed the underground bazaar was vast and he had not glimpsed this portion of it. The place he recalled was packed with stalls and poorly lit. Now there was light and a bit of space, and instead of running from his foes he was leading a band of soldiers. Ren decided it was a small but decided improvement in his status.

Old jars and broken ladles rattled as he pushed his way through the warren of dimly lit tents. Stalls of frayed linen flanked him on all sides, the dirt-faced hawkers crying out their sundry wares. One sold rusty knives; a second offered nothing but entrails. Not far from where they stood, a moldering pig's head sat atop a barrel, and heaps of intestines oozed from an oilskin sack. The earth was wet with bile. There were plenty of stalls, but all of them were selling entrails, discards from the city butchers or the knacker's yard. It seemed as though there was nothing but offal in these tents, but when they climbed to a higher level, up above the ground, along the spiraling path that wound about the pyramid, they found stalls hung with exotic herbs, blue lotus, and red poppies. In hopes of finding even better wares, they climbed higher, up the winding path, past the hawkers selling everyday goods: homespun fabrics and siltware of every sort. Nothing they needed, so they went a bit farther, moving this way and that, scurrying between the stalls as they scaled the ramp. Higher up, near the top of the spiraling path, the smell of salt saturated the air and Ren at last laid eyes on what he sought. Well-preserved hocks of ham hung from iron hooks, and salted racks of lamb dangled in nets.

Ren retreated, nearly colliding with Edric, who was standing in a space concealed by a pair of oddly juxtaposed stalls, conferring with his men. "I think we've found our spot," said Ren, but Edric shook his head. "If we start the fight here, we'll have to battle our way down the whole damn pyramid."

"Got that," said Ren. "Wasn't planning on a fight. There're too many swords in this market."

"Well?" asked Edric. "You have some suggestion?"

After a brief pause, Ren spied an unattended torch. It had nearly guttered out, but the coals were still hot. Perhaps the owner had forgotten about it. Ren slipped the shaft from its mooring and carefully laid it alongside the threadbare linen of an adjacent stall. The cloth burst into flame. The kingsguard retreated from sight, but Kollen found a lamp and flung it down onto the next lower level of the pyramid. It struck a small black tent, bounced, then hit a large stall with a roof sewn from a patchwork oil-stained silk. Both took to flame.

"Time to knock some heads," said Ren. Indeed, the services of the kingsguard were at last required. Several armed men had spied what Ren and Kollen were doing. They drew blades, but they were few in number, and there were twelve men from the kingsguard. A couple of bloody swings left the sentries prone and unable to fight, most likely dead. Ren didn't know. The kingsguard had already set about plundering the little stall, taking everything they could hold before the flames snatched it away from them.

"I found another torch," said Kollen. He appeared out of nowhere and nearly collided with Ren. He carried an oil lamp in his other hand.

"I suppose that's for me," said Ren. He took the lamp and lobbed it down onto an even lower level, where it struck a tent, bounced twice just like the last one, then landed atop a large stall, which immediately burst into flame. They tossed one torch after another and before long they didn't need to light the fires. The flames had taken on a life of their own, jumping from tent to tent.

"Take this." Edric tossed Ren what appeared to be the butchered hind leg of a wild boar. It had a briny odor that made his eyes water. Most of the kingsguard had sheathed their swords and taken hold of whatever they could lay their hands on. Of the dozen soldiers, only two kept their blades in hand. The others carried great jars, wooden kegs, or sacks of wheat. Some held casks of lamp oil or barrels of amber, all of them stumbling as they made their way down the path. Around them, a general panic had ensued. Everyone was trying to protect their tent or their sundry wares, pulling at the already-burning fabric of their stall or dousing the fires with whatever liquid they had at hand. Ren had never seen a man try to soak a fire with an urn full of blood, and he guessed he'd never see it again.

"Thief!" a hawker cried. "Bandit!" howled another and another, but they weren't looking at the kingsguard. When the fires struck, more than one man had joined in the turmoil, stealing from this tent or that one.

"I'll be damned," said Kollen. "I do believe this is actually working. We might just get out of here alive."

"Alive," said Edric. "Yes, we beat back the guards, but we might just be roasted by that fire if we don't hurry." Momentarily, a tendril of flame wound its way across the trail and the black shields ground their sandals against the stones. Armed men leapt onto the path. They'd come from behind a burning tent, jumping from what seemed like nowhere and slaying one of the kingsguard, a man who carried a great barrel and had sheathed his sword. Defenseless, he fell to the cobblestones, the barrel tumbling from his hands and rolling downhill.

"What in Horu," cried Kollen, who stood next to the fallen man. He must have feared he was next because he nearly stumbled, but the kingsguard dispatched these new attackers with precision, coming at their flanks, cutting down both with a pair of stabs and a thrust to the gut. In a heartbeat and a half, two men fell to the cobblestones and Edric was already leaping over their bodies.

The flames parted and they made their way down the ramp and into the fleeing crowd, trying to look as though they were a part of it, which did not take much effort. Almost everyone had something in their hands. Those who didn't were ripping open tents or overturning pots and taking what they could carry while the vendors did their best to beat back the flames or the thieves, whichever they could manage. The path was choked with men wrangling over stolen goods, with hawkers struggling to put out the flames or to take hold of their wares and run before the fires overwhelmed their stalls. Half the sentries had stowed their swords and were carrying pots. Greed overtook the rest. One seller stole from the next, and by the time Ren and the others reached the base of the spiral, no one could tell a thief from a hawker. No one cared.

"Through the columns," said Ren. "Back the way we came."

They did their best to look as if they were not hurrying too much or trying to hide where they were going. When they reached the place where they first spied the pyramid, they stopped to watch the flames, acting as if they might be hawkers lamenting their lost inventory or thieves who were just glad to be free of the flames. They retreated into the narrow passage that led back to the temple, the path between the walls. Ren let the others pass him.

"What're you waiting for, Hark-Wadi?" Kollen asked.

"Just an idea," said Ren. "We've done well. Why not leave our mark on this thing?"

"Don't," said Kollen. "No, don't be a fool, Ren!" he cried out feebly, but Ren was already running and he could scarcely hear what Kollen said. He went a good distance away from the passage, out into the open, where he stood among the people who were fleeing the market. He did not want to reveal their escape route, but he did have something he needed to share. He'd been simmering with resentment ever since he escaped the priory. This city, its soldiers, and its highborn men had caused him to endure more suffering than an average man accumulated in a lifetime, and there seemed to be no end to it. Mered hounded his every move, as did the city guard. Thus, it was only natural for Ren to feel some small stab of joy when he at last struck a blow against his foes. He decided to tell the people of Solus who had done this work. "I am Rennon Hark-Wadi and—"

Kollen slapped a hand over Ren's mouth, and before he could say another word the older boy was dragging Ren back toward the hidden passage.

⇥ 28 ⇤

The kite wheeled through the mist, soaring at an elevation that might have escaped a less keen pair of eyes, but Kepi saw it, darting through the clouds. She felt the wind flutter across its wings. For days the kite had circled, sketching arcs and ovals in the clouds while below it the queen of the Ferens made camp at the Rift valley.

"Three days, that's how long I've stood here." Kepi plunged the tip of her sword into a blackthorn stump. "Does the man think I will simply wait for him?"

Ferris Mawr cleared his throat. "That question seems to have answered itself." As a matter of fact, they had waited three days.

"Are you trying to insult me?" She enjoyed his honesty. In fact, she found it refreshing, but everyone had their limits.

"Just stating the obvious," said Ferris. "Mered's put us in a bit of fix. It's five days' ride to Rifka, five days back—you know as much. Our reinforcements are seven days out. If he's got an army in those woods, we can't fight it, not if he's brought the Protector's soldiers."

"What do your scouts say?"

Ferris dipped his head. "Apologies, my queen, dead men offer scant details. I've lost seven scouts in the last three days. I haven't a clue what's out there."

"We don't even know if Mered is here. Might be an emissary, could be the army," said Kepi, her voice filling up with frustration, hands hot, sweat beading on her forehead. She pulled the sword from the blackthorn stump. "We should retreat. It's the sensible option. We join your soldiers with the men from Caer Rifka. Then we talk."

"Sounds reasonable," said Ferris. "I wanted to regroup with the army as soon as I saw that messenger. You were the one who wanted to wait it out."

"Well, I've done that," said Kepi. "We sent Deccan to Rifka, and I think it's time we join him." The older man had gone north to rally the army at Caer Rifka and march them south to the rift. Mawr, whose keep lay less than a day's ride from their camp, had stayed with Kepi, preferring to remain at his queen's side while his sworn men had ridden with haste to marshal his soldiers. The main body of his army gathered in the wooded hills just north of the rift while small bands of soldiers huddled among the tall stones that lined the rocky edge of the valley.

Kepi sheathed her blade and was about to turn north and join Ferris when she caught sight of some small bit of movement. "Hold," she called out. "Someone's come." Kepi drew her blade and raised it, indicating a patch of trees at the far side of the rift.

"Can't see a thing," said Ferris.

"Wait."

A man in red leather broke through the tree line, emerging from the shadows, his armor seeming to turn from deep crimson to a lighter shade of red as the sun fell upon it. He did not speak, and neither did he gesture to them.

"Did they send us a mute?" asked Ferris, a smile creeping over his face.

The man in red walked to the edge of the rift, turned, then strode off without even looking at them.

"Imperial folk," Ferris said, and spat. "That bastard's toying with us." Ferris stumbled over the rocky terrain as he made his way to the jagged edge of the escarpment. "You there!" he cried. "Got something to declare? Speak."

The man said nothing.

"Do we play their game?" Ferris asked, his big blue eyes bearing down on the queen. It felt strange to have a man of such obvious experience and strength, however young, look to her for instruction, but she *was* the queen. She ought to get used to that.

"We waited for three days, so we might as well see who's come to meet us," said Kepi. She'd taken a bit of time to answer, which made her once more feel somewhat self-conscious, but he only grinned.

"Oh, I figured you'd say that," said Ferris. "But people in charge like to feel important, so sometimes you just have to ask them to state the obvious so they can feel like they're in command."

"Well, you can skip that business with me," said Kepi, annoyance in her voice. "We haven't had time to set Dagrun's crown on my head. I'm new to all this, but I'm not a fool. Don't treat me like one. Walk." She indicated the trail that ran along the north side of the rift. The man in red followed the southern rim and was a good ten or twelve paces ahead of them.

Ferris whistled, and a pair of soldiers came running out of the forest. He whispered some order and they took off at a sprint, vanishing into the deep shade of the blackthorns.

"Scouts?" she asked.

Ferris winked, a gesture she thought to be almost as annoying as his last comment. "I don't like surprises," he said, "or secrets. And men who don't speak tend to have both. We'll find out what's up ahead."

"Perhaps we should start by asking the man's name," said Kepi. The cloaked man intrigued the queen, and they'd nearly caught up to him.

Ferris called out to the man. "You there! Have a name?"

"I am Quintus, servant of Mered."

"Oh, wonderful, Quintus, glad you're speaking. Care to tell us your purpose?"

Quintus gave no reply. He simply went back to walking, and they were once more forced to follow him.

Kepi looked to Ferris. "What do you suppose this is all about?" They'd left behind her camp, but Ferris's soldiers were still with them, their numbers concealed by the forest.

"Oh, I don't know," said Ferris. "Maybe they guessed I have a whole army stashed away in these trees, so perhaps they are looking for another place to talk. Somewhere a bit safer for their folk?"

"You can hardly blame them. There are more swords than trees in that forest."

"And there is a bridge across the rift," said Ferris.

Kepi's head spun around.

It was true. In the distance, a slender bridge straddled the gap. It was an odd sort of contraption. It looked like a hundred trestle tables, one set beside the next. At one end, a great counterweight hung from a network of cogs and winches, and the whole apparatus sat upon wheels.

Ferris's scouts came rushing up to them. One of them, a young Feren, unarmored, hair long and hanging over his eyes, spoke. "I swear, I walked this patch of dirt just an hour ago, and none of this was here." A tent sat beside the bridge.

"I believe you," said Ferris. "Now, make yourself scarce. We needn't reveal ourselves, not yet." Ferris was looking at the wheels on the bridge, at the freshly trampled grass. He scratched at his scruffy chin. "It's old," he said, eyes on the bridge. "The way the wood is weathered and white. Blackthorn turns pale with age. The oldest is stark white, and that wood is paler than an old pile of bones."

"Some toy of the Soleri, something left over from the birth of the New Kingdom?"

"No doubt," said Ferris. He was looking at the complexity of the tres-tlework, and the machinery connected to it. "Looks like it can extend and withdraw. And the length of the thing, its thinness . . ."

"I know. It's as slender as a needle," said Kepi.

"And as deadly. With this device, they can cross the rift at any point, and we burned our bridges. What a bunch of—"

"Fools," said Kepi. It was true enough.

"Too late for regrets. Where do you suppose they found that thing?"

"Mered is quite wealthy and influential—an old family, right? Who knows what machines of war he's unearthed, or what tools the Protectors of old squirreled away within their vaults."

"Well, hopefully they stashed only one of those things."

"With my luck," said Kepi, "they've got a hundred of them, each one wider and longer than the last. They're probably swarming the rift—"

Ferris raised a cautioning hand.

A man emerged from the tent, a sentry of some sort.

"Looks like someone's ready to meet the queen," said Ferris.

"Not quite," said Kepi. "I still haven't seen the man himself, Mered. We've met only soldiers and servants. I'm tired of waiting." She set out at a brisk pace, hurrying right up to the lip of the bridge, Ferris following, eight of his sworn men hurrying to his side, more soldiers coming out of the trees, shadowing their queen.

From the far side of the rift, the sentry approached. She recognized him; it was the man who'd delivered the parchment three days prior. "Only the queen may pass," he said. "We guarantee her safety under the empire's conventions. She meets on neutral ground and treats with a sovereign of equal standing. No soldiers need be present."

"Don't," Ferris whispered, but she pretended as if she didn't hear him. Kepi was not alone. The kite circled, far above and out of sight.

"I have all the help I need," said Kepi. She raised a finger to the sky, and Ferris grinned.

The bridge was sturdier than she guessed. It did not flex, nor did it sway as she crossed it.

At the far side, the sentry led her toward the red tent. The man, Quintus, stood at the flap. She tried not to appear wary or nervous, to be calm, but her eyes went this way and that, expecting betrayal at every step.

The tent flap flew open. A boy emerged, limping slightly, his arm in a sling.

Kepi quickly retreated. "This is treachery," she said. Mered was an elderly man, not some skinny child with an awkward walk.

"Who are you?" she asked, still withdrawing, nearly at the bridge. If Mered had not come, there was no sense in any of this. She intended to leave, and to do it now. Kepi was nearly halfway across the bridge when the boy spoke.

"I'm Adin Fahran, son of Barrin, and rightful ruler of the Gray Wood." He was dressed in the gray woolens of Feren royalty, though she did not know where he'd gotten them.

"Are you the heir of Feren?" she asked. There was skepticism in her voice, maybe even a bit of mockery. For all she knew he was a stable boy dressed up in the king's raiment. Aside from his attire, he didn't look like the sort of man who could command a kingdom or earn the respect of the kite. He had a sickly appearance, and the gaunt eyes and yellowy-white skin of a malnourished child. "Is that your true name?" she asked. "Adin Fahran? Perhaps you weren't told, but my late husband deposed your father. Dagrun ended his line, and no one in Feren gave a care. The former king of the Ferens, your father, was not exactly the toast of the Feren court. Even his own men turned on him when Dagrun took the crown, and the people were glad to see it done." *Until recently,* thought Kepi. Dagrun's reign hadn't lasted very long. Still, he'd deposed the previous king and the empire recognized Dagrun's rule. It was obviously news to the boy. His face paled, turning almost as white as the bridge she stood upon.

Perhaps he is the heir, thought Kepi, *fresh out of the priory. He certainly looks troubled.*

Adin walked to the edge of the bridge, and he and Kepi stood facing each other, one at either end. "I'm sorry," he said. "I don't know you, but I've heard what happened at Caer Rifka. The whole empire knows about the people's revolt. Seems your husband wasn't any more popular than my father. Both are dead, and patrimony *is* the rule of Feren. I'm the only living son of either man. This *is not* treachery. You meet with one of equal standing. I come to you as heir, but I'll be king soon enough."

"The kite chooses the king," said Kepi. "It's our custom. And the kite has settled the matter, so put off your claims and limp back to your master in Solus. Tell him that Feren needs no king—it has a Kitelord."

"I'll find my kite," said Adin.

Kepi shook her head. "There is only one kite."

"Then I challenge you," he said, "to a contest of arms. Here and now, I question the legitimacy of your rule. Llyr will settle this issue, and the kite will come to the victor," he said. Kepi gave no response, so he spoke again, sweetening the deal. "If you are victorious, I will leave the forest and put off my claims, and if you decline I will take my throne by force."

Kepi bristled at the insult and the brashness of the one who'd given it. She was already queen. She hardly needed to prove herself.

Ferris was yelling something. She heard his disembodied voice, but she could not quite make out the words. She was instead studying the boy, his thinness and the way he limped. It wouldn't be much of a contest.

"*You* want a fight?" she asked. Kepi took a step forward, advancing on the would-be king.

She was nearly at the center of the bridge when Ferris cried out in what must have been an even louder voice, because this time she heard it clearly. "Get your queenly ass back to our side of the rift. If this fool wants a fight, I'll give him one," said Ferris, and even as he spoke his soldiers booed at the sight of Barrin's son. The old king truly was unpopular.

Kepi ignored Ferris, but she did enjoy the ruckus his soldiers made, the jeering and hissing. Some soldier tossed a stone at Adin, and it nearly struck him on the head. He winced, withdrawing slightly as he bit down hard on his lip, clearly unnerved. The boy must have come here expecting the queen and her men to cower at the might of Mered's army, but he'd found only mockery.

"I accept your offer to duel," said Kepi, advancing, crossing to the far side of the bridge, stepping off, and following Adin as he retreated toward his tent. She was already pondering the contest and how she ought to engage the boy when a group of red soldiers drew heavy iron blades and advanced upon her position. Adin quickly retreated, hiding behind Quintus and the soldiers.

"What's this?" she asked, but Kepi knew the answer. This *was* treachery, plain and simple. As if to illustrate the point, the boy stumbled over his own feet, let loose a terrible cry, and fell flat on his ass. Adin Fahran was in no condition to fight; he could hardly even walk.

Behind Kepi, wheels roared to life. She turned in time to see the bridge raise itself from the ground and retract, moving swiftly back to the Feren side of the rift. One of Ferris's men leapt at the thing, trying to grab at the trestles. He caught the last plank, but only one hand gripped the wood. His fingers parted and he plummeted into the rift, disappearing from sight as the device completed its machinations, withdrawing completely, the gears still whizzing as they spun to a halt.

"Trapped," she muttered as she whirled around, looking for Adin. If she could capture the boy, he might serve as a hostage, but soldiers stood between Kepi and the fallen heir of Feren. In fact, there were more of them coming out of the forest, men in red-painted mail. Hundreds appeared, maybe more. They came from every direction, or so it seemed.

"I'm sorry," said Adin. She could not see his face. She saw only a line of shields, but he sounded honest enough. "It was the only way," he went on, "the quickest way to end all this . . . You see, I don't want to go to war with my own people. I *am* the heir and I survived the priory. I only came to take what is mine. Mered gave me that opportunity. If you surrender, I'll set you free. You can even go back to Harwen, unharmed. Just go," said Adin. There was honesty in his voice, but his actions told a different story.

"I don't treat with liars," said Kepi. "And screw patrimony. Forget your claim to the throne. I am Kitelord and I rule Feren. Crawl back to Solus, boy. My men laugh at you, they howl at your lies," she said, and indeed the Ferens *were* howling at the boy, at his deception, at his fearfulness. They'd seen him fall.

Ferris's archers lined up alongside the rift, bows drawn, fingers trembling with anticipation. He called to Kepi, something about ducking, she thought. Perhaps the red soldiers were in range of his arrows, but Kepi did not think she would need his help.

She gave Adin a sad little smile, a look of pity really. Then she took one step backward, then another and another until she'd reached the rift's edge.

"What are you doing?" Adin asked. He was still sitting in the dirt, but a pair of soldiers helped him up to his feet. "Surrender," he said, mustering as much dignity as any man could summon after falling flat on his ass in front of a crowd. "You're surrounded," he continued, acting as if he were in charge. "There's no sense in fighting . . . or in anything else." His eyes darted toward the rift.

"I know," said Kepi quietly, curtly. She edged closer to the valley's edge, sending grains of sand skittering over the brink.

"What's this?" the boy asked again, still confused. Maybe he *had* hoped she would surrender.

"You want the Feren throne?" Kepi asked.

Adin said nothing.

"Fair enough," she replied. "Let me offer you an illustration. Watch how the Kitelord of Feren rules. Follow me if you can," she said before leaping blindly into the rift.

⇥29⇤

The Harkan kingsguard feasted on suckling pig and gulped amber from the keg, gorging themselves on the spoils of the Night Market. They'd been at it all night. Ren had joined them, but only briefly. He'd taken a slap or two on the back, but he could not bear the men's praise. It felt hollow. They were trapped so deep beneath the earth he feared they'd never find a way out. Frustrated, lost, and unsettled, he slipped from the crowd. Ren was filled up with every sort of anxiety, uncertain of where they'd find their next meal or if this one would be their last. Out of sheer desperation, he set about looking for other ways to exit the temple, pacing the ramps, exploring Ott's passage. He found little more than a drainpipe. It was made from red clay and too small for any soldier to pass through, but Ren guessed he might fit within the slender tube. He crouched low and peered at the darkness within, observing the way the pipe curled upward, following the contour of the well.

"It might lead to the surface. I think it's a drain of some sort," said Ren.

"A drain?" asked Kollen. He'd followed Ren up and down the ramp, gulping amber as he went. "What use are those? It hasn't rained in decades." He took a long draft.

"It did once, and this place is old," said Ren.

"That wasn't my point. What if it's a sewer? I'd hate to be caught—"

"As would I," said Ren, "but we need a way out of here."

"Don't you mean *another* way out of here?" Kollen tossed his empty cup to the floor of the ramp. "We *had* a perfectly fine one until you shouted your name to the whole damned city. Mered's men are no doubt tearing through the ashes, trying to find where you went."

"They won't find us," Ren said.

"They will."

"Well, that's why I'm trying to find us a second way out, another exit." Ren thrust his head into the pipe. "I'm climbing, so you might as well join me."

"Me?" Kollen asked, suddenly trying to look busy, his head swinging back and forth as if he were searching for some other task that might occupy his time.

"Yes, you," said Ren.

"I'll come. I'm smaller than you bastards," Tye said. She must have come to see what the boys were doing. "I'll go first," she said, and with characteristic charm she stuck out her tongue and dove into the pipe. "It's not so bad." Her words echoed faintly from the shaft.

"You first," said Kollen, his gaze falling with disdain on Ren. "It's your dumb idea."

It was his idea, so Ren followed Tye into the tube. It was relatively smooth inside and sloped upward at a fairly steep angle, but it was narrow enough that he could wedge his legs against the curving walls and use them for leverage as he climbed.

It wasn't long before the two boys caught up to Tye.

"I wish I'd stayed to eat a bit more," she said.

"You?" asked Ren, "you swallowed half a ham. It's a wonder the soldiers had anything to chew on."

"Funny, I think I saw you do the same, though neither of us ate more than him," she said, nodding at Kollen.

"What, me? Fuck, I was the one who grabbed the leg. Why shouldn't I be the one to eat it? Don't go lecturing me. We left enough for those lazy bastards. We were the ones who risked our asses, so why shouldn't we be the ones to reap the reward?"

"Not the charitable type are you, Kollen?" Ren asked, a faint smile crossing his dirt-stained lips.

"Charity's for fools."

Ren only nodded. He'd made a habit of ignoring most of what the older boy said. He went back to climbing, but when he went a little farther and his hand hit the pipe, it came up black. From somewhere behind him, Kollen cursed.

"It *is* a damned sewer pipe. I told you we'd be ankles deep in shit before this ended," Kollen whimpered. There was anger in his voice, but it was also tinged with resignation. He'd known what he was getting into. For his part, Ren still wasn't listening to Kollen; he'd already guessed at the tube's purpose and was now studying its shape, peering through the occasional crack in the clay. "We're circling the well, that's why the passage is always curling."

"The Well of Horu—isn't this thing at the center of the city, the site of some festival?" asked Kollen. "Don't you think there'll be soldiers up there? Ready to lop off our heads as they poke from the drain? Maybe we'll find your brother with a dozen sentries?"

"Still going on about that?" asked Ren. He saw no need to defend Ott. He saved their lives and that ought to have been the end of it. Unfortunately, everyone else seemed to think Ott was a spy or some scout for the First Ray.

"He's had plenty of time to betray us," said Ren. "If the yellow cloaks were going to storm the temple, they'd have done it. And if you doubt me, go ahead and stick *your* head out when we reach the top. You'll be the first to know if the guards are waiting for us."

"Splendid. The heir of Harkana has once more found his sense of humor. Too bad you're laughing at our deaths. I'm serious about this one."

"Oh, we are too," said Tye. "We'll make certain your body is sent home to Rachis."

Kollen didn't laugh, but Ren did. Covered in a dust made of something that had likely come out the backside of a horse, he did his best to chuckle at the boy's fear, and just to spite the two of them, Kollen did take the lead, passing Ren and Tye, climbing higher up the pipe. Still, there was no end in sight and they began to tire.

"Feels like we've been at this for hours, two or three," said Tye.

"Maybe longer," Ren complained, "but I think we're close." The inevitable light at the end of the tunnel had at last shone itself in the form of dim stripes, glowing faintly on the side of the pipe. There was a grille somewhere up above them and the distant sounds of the city followed: vendors crying out their lots, beggars thumping their cups, someone singing for a crescent, a soldier shouting at some cutpurse.

Kollen halted, his upturned finger indicating the grille. He raised the metal up and set it quietly aside. It took two hands to lift the thing and both trembled as he clutched the grate, but he managed to move it aside without making the slightest noise. He only grunted when the task was done. He thrust his head from the hole and Ren was glad to see it return fully intact.

"It's nearly dark outside," said Kollen.

"What do we do?" asked Tye.

"We wait," said Ren.

"Until it's dark," Kollen agreed. It was the sensible thing to do, so they retreated from the opening and fed upon what food they had left in their pockets. In the meantime, night descended upon the city, the darkness drawn like a veil across the streets.

They waited while the last of the soothsayers cried out their prophesies and the fortune-tellers made one last bid for a patron. The buskers ceased their songs and the sellers of trinkets packed up their wares. The three ransoms listened until the plaza was at last quiet and the darkness had safely enveloped their narrow exit, then they gathered their things and made their way back to the opening.

"Let's go have a look around," Ren said as he put his hands on the grate.

Kollen grinned, but Tye bit her lip, clearly nervous despite her earlier show of enthusiasm.

"What's the matter?" asked Kollen. "Lost your nerve?"

In fact, it did look as though she had lost it. Tye sat there, wedged in the tunnel, feet and hands pressed to the pipe so she wouldn't tumble backward down the passage.

Meanwhile, Ren and Kollen lifted themselves through the narrow opening.

"For once, being half-starved has come in handy," said Kollen. "I don't think we'd have fit through that pipe otherwise. You coming?" He was looking at Tye. "Or shall I toss the grille back into place?"

"Oh hell," Tye said as she lifted herself from the pipe. "With my luck, someone'll decide to have themselves a good piss in this hole if I wait here for the two of you."

"Good, I was about to have one myself, so you might want to get out of there," said Kollen. Ren, in a decidedly kinder gesture, offered Tye a hand. A moment later the trio stood upon the streets of Solus, but they were still hidden from view. A kind of platform surrounded the well. From beneath it, Ren saw a great dome resting crooked on its tracks. It appeared to have fallen off the rails. He guessed they wouldn't be closing the Mundus anytime soon, which was good for all of them. If the great dome *were* set in place, it might cover the pipe. *We truly are the dead,* thought Ren. *When they close this thing, we'll be trapped.*

Through the planks, Ren glimpsed a white wall. There was a fire in the distance, an orange light flickering amid a great heap of broken stone. "C'mon, Tye, Kollen," said Ren. "Let's have a look around. There're people out there. I see beggars. I'm certain we can blend in with the rest of them." Ren slipped out from behind the platform, crouching and trying to look sickly. It took little effort.

He glanced back at the dome. He guessed it would not be difficult to find the Mundus. It was the tallest thing in sight. In all likelihood, they'd be able to see it from almost anywhere they went. As they wandered through the evening crowds, they saw it from every corner, and they also spied the provisions they so desperately needed. Unfortunately, the ransoms had no swords.

"I don't think we'll be swiping anything from these people," said Ren. Men with axes or clubs stood at every stall, and the red soldiers were out in great numbers, patrolling the streets. *Probably looking for me,* thought Ren.

"There," Kollen said, pointing to a white edifice. Even in the half-light it glistened ever so slightly, and it bore a pair of doors carved from pale-white marble.

"The temple?" asked Tye.

"Exactly," said Kollen. "Plenty of food, offerings to the gods, that sort of stuff, and priests don't carry weapons—right?"

"They don't," said Ren. "That's what they taught us anyway. I've never actually set foot in a temple, but there's something oddly familiar about this one, those stepped walls."

"Sort of looks like the temple in the Night Market, the one we roasted," said Kollen.

It does, thought Ren. *In fact, it looks like the missing top of that pyramid, the part that that went straight through the roof.*

The outer doors of the temple stood open, so they passed through the pylon and into the columned hall, moving slowly, carefully, picking their way through the inner chambers, moving onward toward the sanctuary, pretending they were beggars or pilgrims come to kneel before the statues. At the golden doors, Ren entered with Kollen, Tye following reluctantly behind them.

Inside, Ren at once shielded his eyes. Every surface was polished to a mirror sheen and the light was near blinding. It was dark outside, but it felt like high noon in the temple.

"What is this?" asked Ren.

"Maybe that fire we set has made its way to the surface," said Kollen.

"No, look there, you idiots," said Tye, a hint of smugness in her tone. She pointed to a dozen braziers, each one tall and wide and brimming with flame.

"Forget the flames," said Kollen, "look here!" He pointed to a plinth where twelve golden statues sat upon a stand of marble and beneath them ripe pomegranates, rich brown dates, and olives lay in great heaps. They were wilted from the day's heat, but still good, still edible.

At the sight of all that rich fruit, Tye lost her fear, and perhaps her dignity too. She dashed forward, feet shuffling on the polished stones, eager to pick at the gods' offering. Kollen went after her, making his way to the great marble plinth, where he stuffed olives into his mouth with one hand while the other shoved clumps of nut-brown dates into his pockets.

In spite of his hunger, Ren walked in the opposite direction. Something had caught his attention. A low chant echoed off the marble walls of the temple. He went looking for the source and found a portion of the temple that was recessed into the floor. He glimpsed white-robed priests.

"Not going to eat?" Kollen asked, his voice sounding distant. Ren glanced back at the boy in time to see him stuff handfuls of plums and other fruits into the sleeves of his robe, which he used as a kind of sack. *Inventive,* thought Ren. *The threat of starvation does do wonders for the mind.*

"Just a moment," Ren replied softly, not wanting to be heard by the priests. He edged closer to the center of the temple, coming up behind one of the great braziers as he stole a glimpse of what lay on the temple floor. In the sacred heart of the temple, there was a great stele. The carved relief was as tall as a desert palm and the scene was familiar. It depicted Re, first of the Soleri, as he descended from Atum, the home before time.

Beneath the stele, the priests were engaged in some sort of ceremony. A man chanted in a low voice, singing in a language Ren could not understand, while the rest of his companions kneeled. The chant ceased and one group of priests stood while the other did not. Those who chose not to stand remained completely immobile. They did not move the slightest bit as the ceremony resumed and the singer took up the song. Once more, Ren was struck by the strangeness of the tune. The rhythm was out of kilter and there was no harmony to the thing. It was pure dissonance— like the humming he'd heard since he struck that statue. *What is this place?* he wondered. *And why is that chant so odd and yet so familiar?* He guessed this ceremony had something to do with those statues in the garden and his strange vision. He wanted to know more. In fact, he wanted to march right down there and ask those priests just what the hell they were doing, but he guessed they'd simply turn him over to the yellow cloaks, so he hunched behind a brazier and watched.

Below, on the sanctuary floor, a young priest drew forth a staff and held it aloft. It was gnarled in places and it glimmered oddly.

It can't be, Ren thought, but he knew what he saw. The staff was an eld horn. Perhaps it was an old king's sword, stolen from the Harkan Repository. There were dozens of them, some in Desouk, too, he knew. These were the swords of dead kings left for future generations to admire. But what was it doing here? And what in Mithra's name were they trying to accomplish with it?

The priest held up the eld horn, dangling it over the twelve who kneeled. He said some words then bent his gaze upon those below. It seemed as if he were expecting them to react, but they did not. The moment stretched. The staff wavered in the young priest's grasp. He appeared to be waiting for some moment of importance, but it seemed to not materialize. And after a while, the young man lowered the eld horn.

"Ren!" Kollen shouted, his voice shattering the still air. "They've found us!"

A man with an unkempt beard and a lazy eye bounded toward them with a wooden mace, swinging it this way and that while a second man, a tall fellow with a missing tooth, held something similar, a barbed club of some kind. Kollen held a great stack of persimmons and was carrying heaps of fruit within the tied-off sleeves of his robe. Tye balanced a mound of fresh pomegranates against her chest and, like Kollen, she'd stuffed her sleeves full of fruit. Neither could fight, and they certainly could not run, not in that condition. Unburdened, Ren dashed toward the exit, throwing out his hand to catch the door, a soft whine buzzing in his ear, the moan of an ancient hinge rotating about the pin. He reached the handle, but he was too late. The gap had shut. His hand slapped against the closed door, and the terrible sound of a bolt sliding home rang throughout the temple.

≋ 30 ≋

The Harkan scouts descended upon Merit and her guards. The men were as swift as thieves. One had already nocked an arrow, and the second held a spear to her chest.

"You might want to point that in a different direction." Merit took the offending spear by its point and pushed it calmly to the side. "It would be a tragedy if one of you were to slay his own queen," she said, speaking in her most regal voice, the one that was as unrelenting as their charge, as hard and steely as their blades.

"Queen? No one knows where the queen regent went and you"—the spearman eyed her bruised skin—"you look like a dog who's been set upon by his own pack. Like—"

"Enough," said Merit. "I'm aware of my god-awful appearance, but it does not diminish the truth of my position. I am the queen regent, and your generals, Tomen and Enger, will know my face. I know theirs and the names of their wives."

"Names can be learned. They're not secrets." The bowman looked her up and down. He was young, his hair long and wild, skin as yet unblemished by war.

"And neither is my reputation. I'm not known as the forgiving type. If my words prove true, your crudeness might cost you the hand you've got wrapped so tightly around your bow. Lower your weapons and ride us to your camp. I'm in no shape to fight and the camp's location is no secret. Surely the Harkan Army isn't afraid of an unarmed woman and a pair of soldiers."

"No one said anything about fear," said the spearman, "but you might be spies. We'll ride you through the gates and maybe, if you're lucky and one of our great generals has the time, he'll take a peek at you from inside his tent. If he knows you and what you say is true, then all is well. Elsewise, we'll ride you around back and let the men use you for sword practice. Sorry, my lady, but with all those bruises, I do not think you're fit to be a camp follower. There are all sorts of tastes and desires that a soldier might develop, but—"

"Deal accepted," Merit said. She chose not to comment on the latter part of the man's offer. Maybe she feared it was true, or maybe she was just too used to her good looks and the way they made men bow to her desires. Maybe it hurt too much to have that taken from her, for a time at least. She ignored the slight and they rode to the gates of the encampment, where the captain of the watch, a young soldier she did not recognize, greeted Merit and her entourage.

"Leave your men with your horses," said the captain.

"No," Merit replied, "I'll take my men, they are unarmed and hardly a threat to the army."

The captain uttered a low sigh, which she assumed to be some sort of grudging acceptance of her terms. He nodded to the spearman, issuing orders for him to guide Merit to the general's tent.

"You must be new," she told her escort as he led them through the camp.

"Why's that?"

"Because you don't know me. I've made a habit of knowing not just my generals but their men as well."

"Well, you've guessed that bit right; they've been recruiting up and down the countryside, parting men from their wives and their goats—just to bolster this army. I was a free man two weeks ago, a sword for hire."

"You have no idea how much that explains," said Merit. "I think I'll spare your head after all. You've never set foot in Harwen or seen the first family?"

"Not once."

"Then shut up and show me Tomen's tent," she said. There was no point in wasting her breath on this man. He was just some free rider. She knew the general's tent better than him, so she cast her eyes over the camp, looking this way and that. "That one, there, take me to it," she said, and a trace of fear flashed across the spearman's face. It was obvious she'd spoken the truth. He bowed his head and quietly led her to the general. As they went, she pointed out three or four other tents and named each of the captains that slept within them just to make clear her knowledge of the army.

"Tomen, I hope you're not banging some whore," Merit cried out when they reached the general's tent. "Your queen regent has arrived." She used her loudest voice, startling the spearman.

A moment passed before the flap parted. "If this is some jape I'll have the head—" He caught sight of Merit, and his expression changed from outright anger to one of surprise, and perhaps even pity.

Gods, thought Merit, *I must look like death itself.*

Tomen welcomed her inside.

"My guards as well," she said, and Tomen allowed it.

"Where have you been?" the general asked, almost without hesitation. He'd always been an abrupt man and it was good to see that he had lost none of his vigor.

"I've been everywhere," she muttered. "Where would you like me to start? At the Battered Wall?"

"That's when I last saw you."

"Yes, I seem to remember leaving the kingdom in *your* hands."

Tomen wriggled his nose at that.

Merit squared her shoulders and swallowed.

There was a matter they needed to address, and Tomen's response would mean everything to her cause. She needed to know if he had accepted the false king, but she stumbled over her words.

"What is it? What do you mean to ask?" said Tomen.

"The king in Harkana."

"That imposter?"

"Thank the gods," said Merit. "How did you come to know the truth?"

"The truth? It was plain as day. I've sent emissaries to the court. He's a fraud, a mummer, and a cheap one at that."

"That's why the army is camped in the desert?"

Tomen let forth a great sigh. "We're stuck between two foes, Barca on one side and the false king on the other. There's nowhere for us to go, nothing for us to do but wait until the heir returns from Solus."

"That boy died in the Hollows or is as good as dead," said Merit. "And even if he did return, he's a bastard."

"My king named him heir—"

"He's lost beneath the city, but I am here and I was named queen regent in my father's stead, a title that still holds. Ren has not returned, and you've already spoken your thoughts on the false king, which leaves only one person to lead the people." Merit grinned slightly.

"I don't contest it," said Tomen, ever loyal.

"You'll follow me?"

The general cocked his head, his mouth fixed in a snarl. "Follow you where? There *is* nowhere to go, not with Barca on our heels. If I ride to Harwen I'll leave my back exposed."

"That won't be a problem." The voice came from behind Merit. One of her soldiers threw off his hood, revealing the face of the rebel and one-time captain of the Outer Guard.

"Barca?" Tomen's sword was in his hand before the word left his mouth. The general was well past his sixth decade, but he moved with the speed of a man half his age, bending his knees, sword outstretched, ready for the kill. His men were no less impressive. Three held blades to her guard and the others had already surrounded the man they thought to be Barca.

"There's no need to draw blood," said the man Tomen thought was Haren Barca. "Clear the tent, Tomen. Just the three of us."

"I'd sooner—" Tomen started, but Merit shot him a glance that told him to comply, that he was safe or safe enough. He raised a hand and the men lowered their blades. Merit ushered them out of the tent.

When they were alone, the swords went back into their scabbards and Tomen took a step back, taking a long sip of amber and savoring every drop. "It's been a while since I've drawn a blade at such close quarters. I was looking forward to using it."

"No doubt," said Barden. "But you would have made a grave mistake. I am here as a friend—no, a countryman, a brother, if you will. My name is Barden Hark-Wadi."

Tomen shot Merit a sideward glance, but she nodded. The empire was filled with bastards and false kings, but she'd accepted this man's story. She hoped Tomen would do the same.

"Barden?" Tomen asked. He was tugging at his beard, looking the man up and down. "You're the dead boy, the one we buried?"

"They buried the stillborn son of the butcher, or so I was told. I lived in Harwen for a time, with Taren. Did you know him? He was one of my father's trusted men."

"I knew him well enough, but he never spoke of you. He left for the high desert—"

"He took *me* to the high desert." Barden told the rest of his story, from his time in the high plains to his rise through the army of the Protector. Tomen took it all in, nodding, still suspicious.

"Truly, I've got no way to know if you're Arko's brother, but I can see a bit of him in your face, and maybe that's enough." Tomen was shaking his head. Merit guessed he shared her skepticism, her doubts.

"I know about your soldiers, the ones in the caldera, not the starve-lings you've been parading around for the past few weeks," Tomen said.

"You found my true army?" asked Barden.

"Your secret's safe with us. I camped out in that crater when I was ten and eight. There's a cave that leads up to the rim. Your scouts missed it, but we've been running ours up and down it for the past week."

"Unfortunate," said Barden. "I went to great lengths to conceal my numbers."

"And what are those numbers?" Tomen asked. "I've made guesses, but you might as well show your hand."

"Six thousand outlanders. A thousand freebooters, maybe more. Five hundred of my own men. Double that number in conscripts."

"It's not enough," said Tomen. "Those conscripts won't be worth much if they're forced to stand against imperial men, and the outlanders are as likely to fight as they are to flee. Same goes for the freebooters. You don't have the numbers."

"I will if you join me," said Barden. "My army cares only for Solus. We never meant to cross swords with your men. My goal is to sack and burn the city of the gods. The promise of plunder is the only thing that keeps these men together. Greed. Avarice. Call it what you will. It is the force that drives this army. I've lived in Sola, and the wealth there is beyond imagining. Statues of silver grace forgotten corners, and every temple is piled high with rich offerings. While the empire starves, they toss away their meals half-eaten. I've offered the fortunes of Solus to these men. It's a hard deal, I know, but it's the one I made—the only one that could forge an army large enough for the task. We'll plunder the city, then burn what cannot be carted away. Join me and you buy your freedom from the empire. There is a civil war afoot. A man who calls himself the First Among Equals threatens to take the empire as his own. He wields power in the city of the Soleri, yet the old gods are silent. Some say they've fled, that they care not for their city. The rise of Mered Saad is proof enough for me. Solus is ripe for the taking. Your queen joined me, so will you lend me your hand?"

Tomen didn't say yes. He just stood there as if he were contemplating the weight of the thing, picturing every battle, every maneuver it would take to reach Solus, to prepare his army, to provision his men and protect those who would supply his soldiers.

Tomen caught Merit's eye, "Is this your will?"

"It is," said Merit.

"Then I need not speak on the matter. I'm just a general. I do as I'm told," said Tomen.

"Well," said Barden, "I believe your queen has some unattended business she wishes to discuss."

"What business is that?" Tomen asked, a hint of exasperation creeping into his voice.

"My throne and that sniveling brat who sits on it," said Merit.

Tomen grinned just a bit.

"I don't believe I've ever seen a smile on your face," said Merit.

"No, you haven't, and I doubt you'll see it again. The whole thing shouldn't be much trouble. We've been scouting the Hornring for weeks. He's poorly defended. We saw only a single regiment. Mered thinks Harkana has accepted his puppet."

"How do you know this is Mered's doing?" she asked.

"We've intercepted messengers, tracked a few of them."

"You were always my father's best."

"Still am."

"We'll see," said Barden. "Can you take the city by yourself, as you've said? I prefer not to reveal my numbers, not until the march on Solus."

"I can," said Tomen. "Mered's army is split between Solus and Feren, or so my scouts report. He thinks our armies are in a stalemate, so he's left the Hornring relatively undefended. We've got more than enough men to take the city."

"Good, then go," said Barden. "And I'll return to my camp. Send messengers when you've taken the Hornring."

Tomen bid him farewell, nodding his goodbye.

Barden left, drawing down his cowl and rejoining his soldier, the tent flap closing behind him with an almost silent whoosh.

Tomen was quiet.

"What is it?" Merit asked.

"That man, there's something about him, a coldness."

"I know, I've seen it. They sent that boy into the desert and told him to avenge his family. As we rode, he went on about his first years, how the outlanders singled him out, how they hunted him as if he were a jackal, and mocked him for his dusky skin, told him he was cursed. They tortured the boy, but no hunter ever caught him and no blade cut him deeply enough to deter his rise to power. The outlanders follow him as if he were their king, and these traitors do the same. He's made an army out of men who are bent on conquest, angry, and out for revenge, for looting and for pillaging."

"Aye."

"I cannot agree with his methods, but I do share his sentiment," said Merit. "Look at what Tolemy did to me. My father is dead; my sister and I do not speak. I've been beaten and tortured, stripped bare and offered to their god. I saw my mother for the first time in a decade, and it was only days ago. We've suffered much and more, but when Mother sent me to Barden and I discovered his true name it made me think there might be some hope for the family, the possibility of some sort of reconciliation."

"I'm not much for hope."

"I know. It's a fool's hope. Like Barden, we're all ruined folk."

Tomen gritted his teeth, his leathery skin folding back at the lips. "Sometimes, in the taking, the revenge is worse than the crime that spurred it."

"Yes, but only Mithra knows the future. He's been silent of late, so while the gods sleep let's take back our kingdom."

"It won't be easy. I wasn't entirely honest with Barden."

"What?"

"He commands an army of cutthroats and outlanders. I won't let them march on our kingdom, so I told Barden we could take the city with ease, that the false king has only a small garrison."

"He doesn't?"

"No. Mered is no fool. When he sent you to Barca, he dispatched a large force to Harwen. He's anticipated this move, but his armies are still split. On that one account, I told the truth. Most of his men are in the north, in Feren, and there are still a great number in Solus. We outnumber the traitor's men, but they hold the Hornring and its walls are tall. I spent a lifetime standing atop them. I ought to know. We'll march on the kingdom, but don't count on taking it."

⋛ 31 ⋚

"When he hit me with the club, I think a dozen pomegranates exploded," said Kollen. "The stuff was everywhere: red in our hair, red in our faces. By the time the priest wiped the juice from his eyes, I'd knocked him on the jaw and nipped his club. After that it took just a few knocks here and there and those priests went running."

"The way he tells it, it was Kollen that did all the fighting. Seems I saw Ren take a swing or two with that club," said Tye.

"Yes, well, that was after Kollen dropped it." Ren laughed. "He left out that part of the story."

"Quite conveniently," said Tye.

"It slipped from my fingers," Kollen explained, holding up his hands, which, even after the climb, were stained red and slick with juice.

Ren, Tye, and Kollen were back on the ramp, in the strange temple that wound about the well, explaining to the black shields what they'd done. Edric was there, nodding, holding back a chuckle as he looked them up and down. Their robes were smeared with lamp oil, caked in dung, and slathered with red. All in all it was a humorous, if not disgusting, sight.

"We took what we could carry," said Tye. "Ren got the door open and we flew."

"Did you?" Edric asked. "The three of you, out on the streets, hands filled up with dates, and no one took notice?"

"We hid it in our robes," said Tye dismissively. "It was dark outside."

"The captain of the guard went out ranging, and returned with food for the men," Ren said. Indeed, a sizeable pile of fruit stood in front of them. "Also, I found a second way out of the Hollows."

Edric eyed the tube with suspicion.

"Don't worry," said Ren. "The end of that pipe is concealed by some platform. No one saw us come or go. No one even goes near the thing. Perhaps they think the dead are still rising out of it."

"Oh, the dead are rising," said Kollen, "and they're hungry too." He drew forth something ripe and brown and tossed it to Edric. "Eat, fool, and stop asking questions. Last I checked, Ren was in charge." Kollen inclined his head toward Ren, who had already turned his attention elsewhere.

"Sorry, Kollen, I'm not much for restating the obvious," said Ren. "I rule the black shields. Anyone who disagrees is free to leave our company. I've got other things on my mind."

"Such as?" Kollen asked.

"That temple. They were up to something, some ritual, but it seemed to fail. It was a curious thing," said Ren. "I'd like to go back there, but I fear they'll double their guard after this incident."

"I'm sure there are other temples we can loot," said Edric. "I'll see if any of the men can fit through that pipe. If I can find enough soldiers to field a squad, we can mount more serious raids and perhaps gather more than just a pile of dates."

"Do it," said Kollen. "If we can't leave Solus, we can at least survive here."

"No," Ren said. "That's not enough. I saw palaces and temples. They weren't far from the Mundus. With soldiers at my side, we could raid them by night. Surely there is food there, but there is also an opportunity."

"For what, Hark-Wadi? Are you going to yell out your name again?" Kollen asked.

"Something like that. Let's show Mered we aren't afraid. If we can't leave Solus, we might as well make a bit of noise."

"I'd relish the chance to wreak a bit of havoc," said Kollen.

Edric was quiet for a moment, his dark face looking reddish in the lamplight. "I think we'd all like a bit of that," he said. "I'll talk to the men and find volunteers. The task will not be difficult." He scooped up a ripe date. "Almost forgot to tell you, *Captain*. You have a visitor. Top of the spiral."

"Ott?" Ren asked.

Edric grunted, his eyes lifted toward the apex of the ramp, a place cloaked in darkness.

Ren scaled the spiral.

Already out of breath, the walk made him doubly tired, and when he reached the top he could barely speak.

"You're in worse shape than I am," said Ott.

Ren was still licking the pomegranate juice from his lips. "It tastes sweet."

"No doubt. I see you found another way out of here," said Ott. His voice betrayed a hint of knowing.

"You meant to leave those marks, the black stains on the rock, didn't you? It might have been easier if you'd just led me to the Night Market."

"Doubtful. I've spent a lifetime distrusting others, questioning their intentions, their intelligence. If you couldn't follow a trail as obvious as the one I left . . . well, then you didn't deserve to find it."

"You're not a terribly pleasant fellow, are you?"

"I wouldn't know," Ott stuttered. "I had a pair of friends once, but the old Protector took their lives, if you must know. Since then I haven't talked to a lot of people . . . or trusted them. This is all new to me. It is . . . a challenge."

"Family isn't worth much, not unless you want it to be. You saved us. I trust you, but I don't expect you to return that favor—not yet. Besides, we're doing well. We even found a nice little temple full of pomegranates."

"Yes, the old temple of Re. Curious story. Apparently, some gutter rats ran off with the god's offering. Word travels quickly in Solus. Three little mice crept into the temple and sped away before anyone could catch them. By the look of it you were one of them?"

Ren's pomegranate-stained grin answered the question.

"Tell me what you saw in the temple," Ott said. "Mother tasked me with a bit of scholarly work, scroll-studying, and some of it involves the old temples."

"Yes, well, I didn't see many scrolls. None at all really." Ren described the curious ritual.

"That sounds right," said Ott. "It matches Noll's story."

"Noll? Who's that?"

"Noll is the priest you saw in the temple, the one with the eld-horn staff. Noll!" Ott cried out, and a figure in shabby white robes emerged from the darkness. It was the same priest Ren saw in the temple, the one with the horn.

"That was awfully quick," said Ren. "How in Mithra's name did you find Ott, let alone this place? I just got out of the tube."

"I knew exactly how to find Ott. There is a door that connects the temple of Re to the Empyreal Domain. They told me where to find it."

"They?"

"The twelve. They sent me to find you," said Noll.

"What do you mean by that? Someone else's after me? Well, I've got quite a list of enemies, so I don't suppose one more will do me any harm."

"They're not your foes. In truth, they're your kin," said Noll.

"Kin? I'm not terribly fond of family. Who are you talking about?" Ren asked, and at that very moment he felt that curious buzzing at the back of his head, that noise he kept hearing since he bumped into those statues in the garden.

"The twelve. You know what I speak of," said Noll.

"No, I don't," Ren lied. He knew this had something to do with the statues that moved. He looked to Ott. "Who is this fellow anyway?"

"He's an old associate. I murdered him with poison, handed him the cup myself. That was a long time ago, so to speak. Back then I believed in death. In the past few hours, since he found me in the domain, I've come to believe in other things."

"Sounds like you've got a lot to explain," said Ren. "What was that ceremony and why were you holding the eld horn? Who were the twelve who kneeled? Why were they frozen like that? It seemed unnatural."

"They are statues . . . of a sort."

"Of a sort?"

"Yes," said Noll. "You encountered twelve others in the garden. They are stone and yet they are not stone."

The buzzing at the back of Ren's head doubled, and he felt as though his head was about to burst at the temples. Still, he tried to gather his focus. "If they are not stone, what *are* they made of?" Ren asked.

"Stars, if you believe it. Each weighs less than a feather, less than a quantum of light."

"The Soleri?" asked Ren. The buzzing was still there, but it felt more distant. "I thought they wore golden masks and all that. You're telling me *those* things were the twelve?"

"They are what remains of the line of Den, or so I thought. That was their resurrection ceremony—or at least an attempt at one. I said the words and raised the staff, but nothing happened. Well, almost nothing. When I failed to revive the twelve, the priests became angry."

"Yes, we know all about their clubs," said Ren. "Not a terribly pleasant bunch."

"Agreed," said Noll. "When the ceremony proved . . . unsuccessful, the priests claimed I'd somehow misled them, that the failure was my fault alone. The twelve knew otherwise. They told me how to find you. You see, I did not locate those statues by accident. They called to me. Ever since I was a child, I've heard voices. I can read the language of the gods, words that no other living person understands. I recorded each of their symbols. I made it appear as if I'd discovered the words through some scholarly research. In truth, I was born with that knowledge, born with a calling. Someday I would meet the twelve. I knew that. They beckoned to me, so I traveled to Desouk. I led Ott and Sarra to the last resting place of the gods. It was my work, my charge, to find the twelve and revive them. I failed, but the gods said there were others who could complete the task. I was not the only child of Mithra they called to Solus."

The buzzing in the back of Ren's head redoubled, but he fought it back so he could speak. "You're talking about me? Well, sorry to ruin your little fantasy, but I was the one who decided to come back to this miserable city. Also, I guess I missed that part about the Soleri being dead or statues or whatever. I thought they were lounging behind that wall of theirs, sipping wine and singing songs. This's news to me."

"Is it?" Noll asked. "Tell me if my words do not ring true." His eyes bored into Ren's. There did seem to be some truth in what he said. Ren was forced to consider the twelve he'd seen in the garden. He recalled the old story, the one about the children of Mithra-Sol. There were two families of twelve, the Soleri and the Pyraethi, and there were two sets of statues.

Ren gazed into the endless gloom of the well, and in it he saw again the statues that walked and heard the voices of the twelve echo in his thoughts.

"You feel them, don't you?" Noll asked.

"The statues?" Ren shook his head in disbelief.

Noll nodded silently, knowingly. "Trust me, friend, I know your thoughts. Some things are not easily accepted. In fact, sometimes the most frightful truths are the ones we won't dare admit to ourselves."

⇒ 32 ⇐

Merit crumpled the parchment and threw it across her general's tent. It landed at the foot of the false king's messenger. "Go," she said, "and strip off those leathers before you depart. You're no Harkan."

"But my lady . . ." The messenger balked at her command, but when Tomen's men brandished their swords he quickly undressed, leaving him clad in little more than a loincloth.

"Away with you," said Merit, who had turned her attention from the messenger back to the parchment she'd crumpled. "I suppose I should have expected this from the pretender. He held on to Shenn, and some part of me knew he'd take his head if we marched on the city."

Tomen laid a comforting hand on Merit's shoulder. "Threats are easy to make. Shenn's a royal hostage if there ever was one. It would be foolish to lop off his head at the first sign of an attack. A smart man would hold on to such a prisoner."

Merit kicked at the parchment. "That's the problem, there's nothing smart about this boy. He hasn't an ounce of sense in that tiny head of his, so yes, he might do exactly as he claims."

"Then we march," said Enger Adad, the commander of the Outer Guard, her father's second general. He was younger than Tomen, less experienced, but well suited to his job. The Outer Guard often skirmished with the outlanders. It took a young man with a quick mind and an even quicker hand to keep the sand-dwellers at bay, and Enger had accomplished that task more than once.

"I agree," said Tomen. "There's no sense in trying to guess at what the boy will do."

"I know as much," said Merit. "I can't allow the life of one man to stand in our way." Shenn was the last bit of family she had left. Her brother was a foe, her sister was estranged, her father was dead, and Sarra was simply a mystery. "I don't think I can bear to see his head on a spike."

"We'll send an advance party, a dozen good men. They can infiltrate the Hornring, steal cloaks, and weapons too. They'll do their best to find your husband, but there are no guarantees in such things," said Tomen.

"Do it. Send them and don't bother reminding me about guarantees. I'm well accustomed to disappointment. It's all I have of late. Also, how did the boy come to know of our advance? The false king must have a spy, or he's spying on us from afar. How else would he know about our impending march?"

"I'll send out more scouts and we'll tighten the perimeter, but that's all I can do. We've doubled our numbers in the past few weeks. I've press-ganged every farmer and fishwife into my service. One of them could easily have been Mered's man. It's the risk you take when these things are done."

"I know and I understand our need for numbers," Merit replied, "but your eagerness has cost us the element of surprise."

"Would you like me to undo the past?" asked Tomen. "What's done is done." His words held no remorse. The discussion was ended. They would march, and her husband's life would hang in the balance. *Shenn.* She had not even had a chance to say her farewell, not a real one at least. It had been foolish to think she would see him again, Merit realized. He *was* a prisoner after all, the captive of a king she was hell-bent on deposing. *I'm sorry, Shenn. I failed you, but I won't fail Harkana.*

"We march on Harwen and we do it now," said Merit. "They know our intentions, so there's no use in giving them time to prepare or to call for men. If we leave camp within the hour, we can arrive at sunrise."

"Now?" asked Tomen, his eyes suddenly wide.

"Yesterday would have been preferable."

"Such things take time I—" The general caught himself. "I'll do what I can. Make it two and we'll march." He bent his head toward the table as if lost briefly in thought, then he raised it and motioned to his men.

"Enger," Merit addressed the general, "will you have one of your men find me a suitable mount, one that is well fed and lightly barded? I'm guessing we'll need to ride hard to reach the city before dawn."

"It'll be a race, but I'll find you the right horse," he said, and he left the tent.

She followed behind him, waiting nervously, roaming the camp while the army assembled for the march. It was all done in haste, with men running this way and that, tying on armor or gathering up their pack, loading into some carriage, or fitting their horse with the proper tack, but Tomen accomplished the task in the time he claimed. The cavalry rode at the head of the company while the infantrymen were packed into horse-drawn carriages. This was a sprint, nothing less. If the boy king had any sense, he would have first sent his messenger to Solus. Once Mered had delivered a suitably large number of soldiers to fortify the Hornring, it would be safe for him to order his message to be sent to Merit. It's what any sensible leader would do, but she didn't know if the boy had any sense. He certainly hadn't shown much in her company. Hence, her thoughts were clouded by uncertainty and her mood turned dark when the hills outside Harwen came into view.

"We'll need to slow our advance," said Tomen. "The lowlands are fraught with dangers: narrow valleys, caves, slender ridgelines. The best course is to move slowly and scout out each advance."

Merit knew the landscape and she knew the risks it carried. "I'd rather we marched right up to the gates, but I'll take your counsel," she said, though she soon regretted her words. Their approach was slow and full of starts and stops, hiding in valleys and riding roughshod over ridges. Tomen was a cautious man and the hills held dangers as well as opportunities. He was mindful of both. At every crest, he sent out watchers. Each basin might hold a battalion of red soldiers, or, if empty, a place for the Harkans to shelter while they contemplated their next move.

"I think your knowledge of the terrain is working against us," said Merit. "You know too much."

Tomen shook his head. "In the dark, they could be on top of us in a heartbeat, flooding out of this fissure or that valley. Better to be watchful," he said, and the man *was* watchful. They waited silently, huddling behind the crest of a sandy hill, for another round of scouts to return, then dismounted and bent low to avoid being seen. There was no high ground in the vicinity so there was no one place where a man could scout out the whole field, Tomen had explained, so they simply had to do it piecemeal, one hill at a time.

The pace of it wreaked havoc on Merit's nerves.

At each ridge, they knelt and waited for the scouts. If the way ahead was clear, they would traverse the hill and send out another round of watchers. It went on like that for what felt like hours, hill after hill, shuffling over ridges and slipping into crevices, always observant of an enemy that had as of yet remained unseen. It wasn't until they crested a particularly tall and rocky hill that Merit finally set eyes upon their target. The jagged outlines of the *badgir*—those spiky wind scoops that poked above Harwen's walls—loomed on the distant horizon.

"We're home," she whispered. Yet this was *not* her home. A false king held the throne, and who knew what damage he'd done to the kingdom. Had he plundered Harkana's coffers or sold off the family's riches to pay Mered's soldiers? Any number of foul things might have been done in her absence. What had become of the castle attendants and the waiting women Merit left behind? Had they found their deaths or just a cell beneath the Hornring? Were they bedded each night by Mered's soldiers or sold off to traders? She'd have her answers soon enough, but Merit wasn't certain she wanted them.

"Where's that last scout?" she asked Tomen.

"No one knows, which means he's dead or lost. I tend to assume the former," Tomen replied.

"Are we discovered?"

"Possibly."

"So much for surprise."

"We never had much of that," Tomen reminded her. "But we still have time to retreat."

Merit gazed out over the ridge, toward the *badgir.* She watched the wind scoops, but they weren't swaying from side to side. They moved up and down. "Those aren't *badgir,*" she said, taking Tomen and pointing at the horizon where the first purple rays of the sun were breaking across the desert, painting bruised shadows on the gray sand. "Those are men. There's an army assembled before Harwen."

33

Ren said nothing. He simply listened while Noll shared his story. Ott had long ago left their company, claiming he had agreed to meet with the Ray at some important house and could not fail to attend the engagement.

"It makes some sense," said Ren when Noll had at last completed his story. "But I don't accept all of it. How many generations did you say?"

"Nine," said Noll. "Nine generations have passed since Aryn Hark-Wadi's wife, Koriana Hark-Wadi, lay with the last emperor of the Soleri, Sekhem Den. As I said, Aryn was a proud man. He wasn't willing to admit that his wife carried the child of another man, so he raised the boy as his own. These were different times. The Harkans were proud men."

"Oh, don't lecture me about the Harkans. Little has changed."

"Well, then you understand, don't you? He raised the boy as a Hark-Wadi, and you are his direct descendant. Your blood and the blood of your siblings is the only living relic of the line of Den."

The buzzing had returned, but this time it wasn't at the back of his head, it was everywhere, threatening to overwhelm his thoughts.

"Are you . . . feeling all right?" asked Noll.

"I'm fine. I'm very excited about all of this. Great news. I'm sure it'll be a big help down here." Ren stopped to take a deep breath. He was babbling and needed to get a hold of himself. "Tell me how this happened. Was it common practice? Did the Soleri simply rape whomever they wanted?"

"No, I don't think it was common practice. In fact, I believe it was forbidden. The family interbred. There were always twelve: a husband, a wife, and ten children. Five boys and five girls. The children were married to one another to keep the bloodline pure, but it's hard to deny your urges when you are all but a god."

"They cheated? That's what you're saying. They broke their own rules."

"Something like that. It was common practice for the Soleri to murder their bastard sons and daughters, but a beautiful face can sway even a god. Perhaps Sekhem could not bear to murder the son of a woman as lovely as Koriana."

"And you've got the same story. They took some Wyrren servant and kept it a secret."

"Yes, but that was four hundred years ago, give or take a decade. The blood in my veins has only a fraction of the strength in yours. I can hear the voices of the twelve, but that is apparently the extent of my gift."

"And you think I can succeed where you failed?"

"There is hope."

"Hope?" asked Ren. "None of this makes any sense. Why didn't they come straight to me?"

"Perhaps they did or they will. The Soleri do not see or experience time in the same manner as us. I cannot pretend to understand their minds. You spoke to the statues in the Garden of Den. That is proof enough that you share a connection with the children of Mithra. And you said you saw them, the living gods, looking straight at you—right?"

"Well, I'd just had my head smashed against a block of granite, so I'm guessing that's what caused my divine vision. It's been giving me a headache ever since."

"I disagree. When I touched the statues, I heard the living Soleri."

"Yes, but I think we've got a bit of a problem. There's one set of statues in the garden and another in the temple. There can't be two sets of Soleri—am I wrong? There are only twelve."

"Yes, twelve Soleri. I found twelve statues in the Shambles and I carted them to Solus. There were others in that chamber, and I saw the place where they stood."

"Others?"

"The other twelve, the ones who pursued the Soleri, their adversary."

"And . . . who are they?"

"It's not difficult to figure that one out. Two sets of twelve. Two children of Mithra, two divine families. Pyras, eldest son of Mithra and first of the Pyraethi, founded the first empire; and Re, second son of Mithra and first of the Soleri, founded the second empire on the back of his brother's."

"So the gods fought each other . . . or something like that. Two hundred years ago, during the great war, when the Harkans took Solus and the Soleri fled their domain, their old foes went looking for them?"

"True enough," said Noll. "As far as I know, Ined Anu, the first Ray, found both sets of statues, but he took only one to Solus. He placed them in that garden; it's recorded in the city's history. He named it the Statuary Garden of Den, so he must have believed they were the Soleri. And for some perverse reason, he placed them in public view. For two centuries, the secret of our dead gods has stood in plain sight."

"How did he know which set of twelve to take?" Ren asked.

"I've wondered about that same thing. He must have believed they were the Soleri, but the statues I found made the same claim."

"One of them is lying?"

"So it seems," said Noll.

"I'll be damned," said Ren. "We've got two sets of dead gods in this city and we can't tell them apart. As far as I know, the Soleri were a bunch of murderous bastards. I can't imagine their foes are any better."

"They are both your kin," said Noll.

"Yes, got that, but what exactly can they do for *me*?" asked Ren.

"Help you," said Noll.

"You mean to say that the gods themselves, the ones who made this empire and enslaved my people, are going to help me? Why in Mithra's name would they do that?"

"Curious phrase. *Mithra's name.* You are one of His children. Like me, you hold some piece of His light. Why do you think your father's grave still burns? What made the fire that cannot be extinguished? Why does the Mundus refuse to close? You, your father, and your return to the city of light has caused a great change. You have strength in your blood. Suten Anu felt it. It's why he brought your father to Solus. The eld saw that strength in you. That's why it gave you a piece of its horn. That beast you killed in the cistern, the arrarax, is a creation of the gods, and only they can strike it down."

"Wait a moment, how did you—" Ren stopped. How did he know about the cistern? And the Harkan hunt was supposed to involve the killing of the eld, not the cutting of its horn.

"How did you know the secret of the Harkan hunt?" asked Ren.

"We've been over all this," said Noll. "When I touched the statues, I gleaned more knowledge than my brain could hold, things that have already happened, things that have yet to come. I'm still remembering it all, trying to piece together the puzzle—if there is one. They kept certain things from me, or so I suspect."

"Like which set of statues is really Den and which is some ancient breed bent on killing the other? If you ask me, we ought to set them both free and let them work it out."

"That may be their goal," said Noll. "They want to find their freedom. Two hundred years ago, the children of Mithra-Sol fought a great battle. It was supposed to have been the last battle in a fight that stretches back to the beginning of time. I traced the lines of that conflict with Ott. We saw chambers reduced to ash. We unearthed the remnants of a war that raged between the gods."

"And that's where it ended . . . in some secret palace in the Shambles?" Ren asked.

"Yes, as far as I know, the twelve Pyraethi, the descendants of Pyras, gave the last of their strength to defeat the Soleri. The Pyraethi became something like stone, as did the Soleri. Two sets of gods, diminished, nearly lifeless, dead but not yet dead."

"They fucked up their own revenge, and now they've both come back. All twenty-four of these gods are in this city and they think I'm the guy who's going to help them—me? The dead boy who can't get himself out of Solus."

"This *is* your way out of Solus—don't you see it? You'll never make it out on your own. Go to them and they will tell you what to do."

"Go to them?" Ren asked. "I'd rather be skewered at the end of Mered's spear than bring those bastards back into this world."

"You may not have a choice," said Noll.

"What's that supposed to mean?"

"When I touched the face of Den, he showed me the fate of Solus. He called it a 'Devouring.' It's happened before. Three thousand years ago, the Soleri conquered and destroyed the empire of the Pyraethi, and these are the ruins of that empire's capital"—Noll waved his hand at the Hollows, the temple—"the last remains of the empire of the Pyraethi, destroyed in the First Devouring and built upon by the Soleri."

"The Soleri literally built one empire on top of the other one?" said Ren. "That's what all this is down here—these old temples and worn-down walls?"

"Yes, one city built on another. There is a cycle, as with all things."

"A cycle? Like the seasons? The hot and cool? And we are about to witness the end of one? Is that what this is all about? Tell me, what's coming?"

"The Last Devouring, if you can believe it," said Noll. "In their minds, it has already happened. Each brother had his time upon this Earth."

"Oh, how sad for them," said Ren. "Let me tell you this: Not one of us will shed a tear when those bastards cut and run."

"I hope that's the case," said Noll, his hand trembling slightly. "I hope we're all around to witness it."

"Oh, don't go all sad and gloomy on me. You said those statues were my way out of this city," said Ren.

"They are," said Noll. "Unfortunately, their return to this world will not be peaceful. I cannot claim to know what is to come, not fully. I've seen only glimpses. Nevertheless, if you see enough of the past, the future comes into focus. I saw three thousand years of history flash before my eyes. In a lifetime I could not tell you the things they packed into my head. It's given me a bit of perspective. I can say with some certainty that before this is over, before you leave this world, those statues will walk."

⇉34⇇

"A smart man would place his army behind the ramparts and let us crash upon them," said Merit as she stood on the ridge, gazing out at the spears that protected Harwen's mud-brick fortifications.

"They know we can breach those walls," said Tomen. "We laid the bricks and we cut the tunnels that run beneath them. That's why they put their army *in front* of the walls. They fear we'll slip beneath them and come 'round behind their lines."

"That *was* the plan."

"Yes, and without it we should retreat," said Tomen, who was furiously stroking his beard, looking up and down the enemy lines, trying in all likelihood to gauge the size of the false king's army.

"No." Merit was firm. "Again, you're too cautious. The longer we wait, the better fortified our enemy will become. Give him a week and he'll have Mered's whole army at our back. Our siege will turn to a rout and that'll be the end of us. We'll be begging Barden for aid, and I'm not certain that's something my pride can stomach."

"I'd rather beg," said Tomen, "than kneel to the traitor."

"We're in agreement, but let's hope it won't come to that. Do we have options? What about the southern flank?"

"We tested that route, and no scouts returned. If we go that way, we'll be heading into unknown territory," said Tomen.

"I'd rather head toward the unknown than ride toward an impenetrable wall of spears. Ride south," said Merit.

The army did as the queen regent commanded, but they immediately found resistance, soldiers tucked away in the belly of a sand dune.

It was a small enough group, a half battalion. "We ought to just dispose of them," said Tomen. The old general led the charge, but the younger soldiers hurried past him. The first clash of swords rang out over the sandy dunes. A brief scuffle ensued, but the fight was over before it began, the false king's soldiers retreating without hesitation.

"Pursue them," Merit cried, and the Harkans followed them over the crest of a hill and into a wider valley, not far from the city. Harwen's walls were within sight. Merit saw the real *badgir*, swaying gently, the first light of day kissing their sharpened tips.

Tomen followed her order, but as he rode past the crest of the hill worry colored his face.

"What is it? What's getting you?" Merit asked.

"This valley. Half the walls are too steep to climb. And the way those men retreated, it was almost as if they had given up without a fight." He swallowed bitterly as he surveyed the landscape. "Back!" he called, but it was already too late. A volley of arrows arrested their charge. Archers appeared at the ridgeline, three rows, arrows nocked for a second volley.

"The damn thing was a ruse, and we fell for it," Tomen muttered.

Tall ridges blocked their path on the one side and archers covered the other. They could only retreat, which was the intended effect. "Move," Tomen cried, but his captains were already ushering the men backward, over the hilltop and out of the archers' range. Harkan after Harkan fell as the arrows claimed their retreating targets.

Merit and her generals rode beneath a wall of shields, the constant patter of arrows drumming in her ear. One bolt pierced the shield above her head, splinters shooting this way and that. She pinched her eyes shut.

Humiliated, their force rode farther south, but when they caught sight of more soldiers, Tomen called a halt to their ride. "They've obviously blocked the southern approach."

Retreat again seemed the best option. Merit saw it on Tomen's lips, but she ushered it away with an angry glare; she'd have no talk of running. No, they needed to press onward. "We retreat a bit then go around that valley. If they can hide in the hills, we can do the same," she said.

Tomen relayed the orders. His captains were tired, grim-faced, but not yet finished. Where once they had eagerly accepted her commands, Merit saw reluctance. They questioned the quality of her decisions, but she would not let their lack of faith deter her from this path. "Tell them to hurry it up," she spoke out over Tomen. "And wipe those bloody scowls off their faces." She stepped out ahead of her generals and spoke to the men. "You're Harkan, and this is your land. Be glad to give your lives for it!"

Hearts heavy and bodies wrecked with exhaustion, they went back the way they had come, over the hills, sending scouts and waiting for their return, repeating the old patterns. They had long ago lost any chance of surprise. The cloak of night had vanished; the desert was pink with the day's first light. Tomen stood upright on his horse, his chest moving in and out in slow, controlled motions. She envied his calm. Her brow was damp with sweat and her leathers were wet through with perspiration. But the old man just stood there, eyes distant, watching, listening to the desert. Perhaps he heard things she could not, maybe he felt the shuffling of distant sandals. For all she knew he was dreaming about fucking his wife.

Merit was too anxious to stand in one place, so she climbed to the crest of a nearby dune, hoping to once more catch sight of Harwen. She shuffled up the gray and sandy slope, her leather armor feeling heavy on her shoulders. Tomen had asked Merit to stay below the ridgeline, but she stood boldly atop it, eyes trained on the horizon.

Without a moment's pause, she called for the men. "We march toward Harwen. No more scouts, no more hiding. We ride straight to the Black-wood Bridge." Merit did not ask; she commanded.

The sun had risen, illuminating the city.

Smoke rose in great columns from the Hornring. Men hurried back and forth upon the towers, and the army that had once stood before the walls had now dispersed. The city was in open revolt. There could be no other explanation. Hearing of their queen's return, the people must have turned against the false king. The army that had once stood at Harwen's gate had gone off to fight the insurrection. The bridge was lowered and the way was open.

⇒ 35 ⇐

Sarra stood before the doors of House Chefren.

Her new Protector had done well. He'd elevated the leaders of his guard to roles in the army of the Protector, but he'd left many of the mid-level commanders, the holdouts from House Saad, in place. He'd struck a balance between the old and the new and had thus stepped into a position of power without rumpling too many feathers. He'd remade the hierarchy of the Protector's Inner Guard without causing much trouble or resentment among the commanders or the soldiers who served them. She envied his savvy and looked forward to working with the man. It was good to have friends, especially talented ones like Kihl Chefren.

Sarra had allies within the imperial cults. The high priests of Bes and Sen were loyal, but the amaranth trade had made a different sort of ally in the house of Chefren, the kind that grew wealthy and prosperous. Kihl was chief among those men, but the trade had allowed her to forge bonds with at least half a dozen other houses in the White-Wall district. With Kihl in place, it was time to call upon those other houses. There were appointments to be made, positions that could make a man wealthy, or wealthier, if he knew how to use the influence that came with the post. When Arko Hark-Wadi was named Ray, many of the great houses had declined their family titles, leaving the posts open or unattended. Mered Saad had refused to continue his work as the Overseer of the House of Crescents. She needed to appoint a new master of coin, and there were dozens of other posts that needed filling.

Mered was first citizen. He'd won a victory of sorts. He'd carved out a new position in the empire, and half the city stood at his back. But half was still only half. He'd given himself a title, but Sarra was the master of a hundred different titles. For two centuries, the Rays had ruled Solus. Their reign could not be unmade in a single day. Already, Mered's hold on the city faltered. The bastard king, Ren, had dealt the first blow. Mered had all but declared him dead, but the boy lived. He'd set fire to the Night Market, turning a centuries-old structure to ash in a matter of minutes. He'd raided the house of Re, desecrating one of the city's oldest temples. The gods themselves were offended; that was the talk of the city.

Rumors abounded. There was news of a run on the granary, and someone had looted the armory. It seemed the Harkans were everywhere, but
no one could find them.

She tapped on the bronze knocker that hung from the door of House
Chefren.

No one answered.

Sarra tapped again. At her last visit, a guard had stood at this door.
Odd, she thought.

Ott approached, escorted by a cadre of priests. He was late. In fact, he
had been late the last time she saw him. He was always hurrying about
and covered in dust—completely occupied by his studies. It was as if he'd
fallen into some abyss and she had to drag him out each time she wished
to speak to him.

His guards carried weapons, clubs studded in bronze. Priests were forbidden to bear such implements.

"You've hired mercenaries and put them in the white?" she asked.

"One night in Mered's dungeon was enough for me," said Ott. "I won't
chance a second."

It was blasphemy. Only an ordained priest of the Mithra cult was permitted to wear the white, but Sarra had committed her own share of
sacrilege. She could hardly begrudge Ott for doing the same.

"I'll ignore this," she said, appraising him. Each time she saw Ott, he
was a new man. His hair was longer and he stood a bit taller despite the
crutch. Sarra pressed her back to the wall. "Apparently, the guards are on
break."

"Odd," he mused.

"That's what I thought." Sarra looked again at the door. "You've been
acting a bit odd yourself, always missing. What are you up to? What discovery has captivated your attention?"

Ott swallowed bitterly. "Academic matters. The history of the gods.
The Soleri and the Pyraethi."

"Yes, what about them? What have you learned about those statues?"

"Nothing. Nothing yet, but I'm close . . ."

"To what?"

Ott stumbled over his next syllable. He went quiet and she saw a drop
of perspiration on his brow. He was lying. She was almost certain of it.
The boy was terrible at such things. He was honest to the bone and could
hardly suppress his nature.

But why is he deceiving me? In recent days, she had assigned several priests to a covert task. She'd asked them to follow Ott through the Hollows, but they were not yet certain what he was doing down there. Time would provide an answer.

Sarra tapped on the door again. This time she hit the bronze a bit harder, trying to make a sound loud enough to bring the guard. It made a brassy thump and the door gave way, squealing faintly on its hinges as it swung open.

"Gods, what's going on here?" she said, stepping past the door and into the garden. Ott followed, his guards quickly encircling the two of them. "Call the yellow cloaks," said Sarra. The city guard waited just outside the white walls of House Chefren. She preferred to approach the house alone, to show that the Ray needed no protection. But when real danger was present, she walked with sharpened iron at her side.

A gray-cloaked man dashed through the garden, trampling what she guessed was the midday portion of the flower clock. He carried a great urn of some sort, gilded in electrum and sparkling in the morning light.

"Thieves?" she asked. "What's happening here?"

"We should go," said Ott. "Leave now, there's something amiss."

"No, not yet. These are our allies. Where are their guards?"

Sarra hurried down the garden path, past the great flower clock, which had been trampled more than once, perhaps even on purpose. All those delicate flowers, drawn from the farthest reaches of the empire, had been uprooted or mashed. The whole thing had been desecrated, the clock, the garden. The doors of the great house stood open, revealing a pair of bodies.

"Kihl's house guard," said Sarra.

"And they both died fighting," said Ott. "Look at the cuts. There was a battle here," Ott said, leaning hard on his crutch. "Why haven't we left?"

"Because we have guards. Perhaps we can be of assistance." Her alliance was too important to allow harm to come to this man. *Where are you, my friend?*

The house was built around a lavish pool with fountains that sprinkled water into the air, only now there were three dead men floating in the water and the pipes were clogged with viscera. Overturned jars sat atop smashed urns. Heaps of ivory lay in piles. Shards of glass dotted the marble floor. There was no sign of Kihl or his personal guard, so they went deeper, around the pool, following the faint sounds of what she guessed was a battle.

They passed the shrine, smelled the sweet scent of this morning's offering, laid out fresh beneath the statue of some ancestor. The idol was knocked aside, but the offering was still in place, the smoke of the incense winding upward from a censer. There were lavish halls with lotus-topped columns, and stele depicting the great flower clock. It was a place of beauty, but it echoed with the sounds of distant battle, the cries of men, the clash of bronze and iron, wood and leather. Guards littered the floors; waiting women lay with their throats slashed. Dancers, scribes, and cupbearers all lay dead before them.

They scurried through the menagerie, where baboons sat limply against the bars of their cage, where an ostrich roamed freely, wandering, lost and looking for something to do with itself. They chased the roar of the battle, Ott growing more nervous, his men gripping their clubs. Beyond the pool, in the wide hall of House Chefren, a great conflict raged between men in kohl-stained robes and the guards of the house. Her allies were easily outnumbered, perhaps three to one. The house guard fell quickly, one after another, the thieves drawing ever closer to Kihl.

Are these the Harkans? she wondered. *Had they turned to raiding the houses of the wealthy?* It was possible. It was said they wore gray, oil-stained robes and disguised themselves as beggars. These men certainly fit that description, and they fought with the fierceness of soldiers. Beggars and thieves hardly had the skills to cut down the personal guard of one of the great houses. Kihl employed the best.

He stood with his house guard, but they were few in number, and there were at least sixty or seventy attackers. The assassins moved with astounding speed, cutting down the guards and quickly dispensing the last of his men.

Kihl Chefren stood alone.

For a span, the room was quiet.

Sarra caught his eye.

I've brought this man his death, she thought.

A sword rippled through the air, catching a bit of red as it crossed Kihl's neck.

Before the father of house Chefren hit the stones, the assassins were fleeing, rushing this way and that. They paid Sarra no attention.

She went to Kihl and lifted his head, but his eyes were turning gray, the skin growing cold to her touch. His chest did not move. He was dead. Everyone here was dead. She saw his wife, dead. His children, dead. All of his servants were dead, everything smashed. Potsherds littered the ornate tiled floor, an ostrich feather drifted through the air.

"The Harkans, of all the houses, why pick this one?" she asked.

"This wasn't the Harkans," said Ott. "Their intent was to murder Kihl. You saw it yourself. When the man fell, they fled. This was an assassination. The Harkans steal food; they don't murder innocents."

"What do you know of the Harkans and this Bane of Solus?" she asked, suspicious. In recent days, the boy had earned a reputation for looting and burning. The common folk had given him a title, calling him the bane of their city and assigning him an almost supernatural ability to slip in and out of the great houses and temples.

"Ren is . . ." Ott stuttered.

"What? Your brother? You think because you share a dead father that you have some kinship with that boy? The Harkans destroyed my best chance at restoring order to this city."

"This was not the work of the Harkans."

"You may or may not be right. Those men could easily be Mered's soldiers disguised as the black shields, or they might be the genuine article. The truth is irrelevant. That is what you fail to grasp. The kingsguard have made Solus into a lawless city. Mered knows this and takes advantage of it in more ways than one. Whether or not he committed the crime, Ren is the cause of our troubles!"

At her fury, Ott shrank, his hand shaking.

You lied to me, she thought, *and it has something to do with the Harkans.* He'd defended them far too quickly. *What are you up to, my son?* He'd always been loyal, but the boy had grown into a man. He had his own ideas, his own thoughts and agendas. As a slender plume of smoke rose from House Chefren, Sarra wondered if those goals aligned with her own.

≋36≋

Ren leapt from the pipe, bounded onto his feet, and dropped a pair of urns on the stone floor of the temple. One shattered, sending golden crescents tumbling in every direction. After his conversation with Noll, he'd needed to clear his head, and a night raid had seemed like a good way to do it. He'd welcomed the priest into their ranks and then he'd gone off with his friends, roaming the streets of Solus and looking for trouble. He'd found his way into a white-walled palace and pilfered a bit of food, some coin.

"Bane of Solus." Edric repeated the name the people of Solus had given to Ren. "While you've been out looting, we did some real work."

"What's more real than gold?" asked Tye. She held two urns full of crescents, which she set down on the floor, coins clinking as the clay thumped against the stones.

"Yes," said Kollen, picking up the conversation. "What *is* better than a heap of crescents? I've never owned a single one and now I've got thousands. You do realize we can buy things with these little pieces of gold, don't you?" Kollen had no jar, but he held a sword. He'd been their guard as they looted the house.

"Well," said Edric, "we plundered the cellars of some wealthy bastard, snuck behind his white walls and took every bit of grain in the house, took their bread too, but I don't think they'll mind. I'm sure they'll have more by tomorrow."

"More for us to take?" said Ren.

"Something like that. We ran afoul of some guards, but we managed to slip out without much trouble."

"How much trouble did you run into? We're only in it for the grain. We're not killers," said Ren.

Edric shook off the remark. "You've said as much, and we did as you asked," he said as he picked up a gold crescent and held it to the lamplight, his face a wide grin. He walked off with the crescent, returning to the company of the kingsguard.

Ren studied Edric as he stood among the men, slapping one soldier on the back, uttering some joke Ren could not hear, laughter echoing in the chamber.

Are you lying to me, Edric?

Ren could not be certain. He could not follow every raid, so he had to trust the men would obey him, that they weren't out there murdering the house guards. Such folk were often pressed into service. They hardly deserved the point of a sword shoved in their face.

"Why so glum?" Kollen knocked him on the chest. "We did well. We're doing splendidly and your brother's going to find a way out of this place for us. Stop your worrying. You think too much."

"That's what Tye always says."

"It's true enough." Kollen knocked him again, harder this time. "I mean it, man. Thinking's a symptom of laziness. Sit around too long and you'll fill your head with all sorts of dreadful thoughts. I try not to think at all."

"That much is plain."

"I'm talking about you, Ren. When I see a boy staring at the wall I assume he's deaf or dumb." Kollen tried to slug him a third time, but Ren caught the blow midstrike.

"You know, I always hated you," Ren said. "I mean it. In the priory, more than once, I nearly cut you open with my shank, and now you're my friend. What sense does that make?"

"Well, if it's any consolation, I was a complete ass. I arrived at the priory when I was twelve, not three. I was heir to the throne, a fucking prince of Rachis. I was a freeman, so don't blame me for not savoring my time in captivity. If pain makes the man, it made me into a terrible one. You, on the other hand, that pain never seemed to bother you. You were always defiant. Annoying, but defiant. I envied that—ya little bastard. Thought you were a fool, a total fucking fool, but I envied you."

"How touching," said Ren. "Did you come here to confess your deepest emotions?

"No, didn't plan on saying any of that. In fact, do me a favor and forget every word of it. The darkness does strange things to a person's mind. I came to you with an entirely different purpose. I want to know a bit more about this fellow Noll, the priest that arrived with your brother. He speaks to no one, eats little, and spends his days meditating like he's off in some other world. Edric wants to lop off his head—thinks he's a spy. I'm inclined to agree. You're the only one who's spoken to him, so what did he have to say for himself?"

Ren heaved a mighty breath, uncertain of where to start. In truth, he wanted to confide in someone, to tell them everything Noll shared. Unfortunately, Kollen didn't seem like the sort of fellow you told such things. Still, it was a burden and Ren had enough of those. His head was still buzzing, driving him mad, and he needed the distraction so he told Kollen what Noll said.

The older boy was oddly quiet as Ren spoke, and he said nothing when he finished. He just sat there in silence, the well looking dark and empty, that dot of sunlight hovering somewhere in the distance. The chamber was cold and Ren felt a shiver; he had only his threadbare tunic for warmth.

"Say something," said Ren. "I've just shared with you the whole history of the empire. That ought to elicit some response, don't you think?"

"Well, it's obviously horseshit. The whole point of the twelve was the interbreeding, five boys and five girls. That was the way of it. The blood stayed pure. Now you're telling me some other story. You claim the blood is in all sorts of folk, everywhere. There are bastards in every kingdom. Two of them in this chamber! Horu's eight hells, Ren, how does someone hide such things?"

"How can an empire exist for centuries without an emperor?"

"Well, you've got a point there," said Kollen. "Hell, maybe *I've* got a bit of that blood. My old man is the king. Wonder why Noll hasn't come knocking on my door."

"It's been a while since the mountain lords left their homes. You might want to venture down from the clouds if you want to mingle with the rest of us," said Ren.

"Why?" asked Kollen. "The moment I get out of this lightless well, I'm heading north and never looking back."

"I don't blame you."

"Wasn't expecting blame from you. I simply want out. You were practically a newborn when you showed up at the priory—am I wrong? As I've said, I was ten and two when I arrived. I can still picture Zagre, the palace at Musket, the onyx columns and gilded fretwork. There are eight frozen waterfalls that surrounded the courtly palace, and each is as tall as this temple. I want to see them again."

"You will," said Ren. "I'll make certain of it." He'd gotten into the habit of making promises he wasn't certain he could keep, so he saw no point in stopping. He'd dug himself into more holes than he could count. He figured he'd find a way out or he'd be buried. Either was just as likely to come to pass, or maybe that buzzing in the back of his head would simply drive him mad and that would be the end of it.

Ren drew one of the gold coins from the pile. This one was a perfect circle and it held the face of the Sekhem Den at its center. Ren hadn't seen the emperor's likeness among the living statues. For that brief moment when they'd come alive in the garden, he'd witnessed their true faces, but he had not glimpsed Den's. There was only one grown man among the twelve, and it wasn't the one on this coin. This was a revelation of sorts. It meant that the statues in the garden were the Pyraethi, and the figures he'd seen in the temple were the Soleri. It was a guess, of course, but he trusted it. There were two families of warring gods in the city. Once, they'd fought each other to a standstill. And for two hundred years after that, the gods lay frozen and inert, dreaming in some strange sleep while they waited for their return. That wait was at an end. He sensed it. The sons of Pyras had tried to put an end to this empire, and he guessed it was time for them to finish the task.

⇒ 37 ⇐

Ott was absent from the barrel-vaulted chamber at the heart of the Hall of Ministers. It was late in the day, but Sarra had somehow expected to find him at one of the tables, toiling away amid a stack of scrolls. He was always working, or so he claimed. She tapped impatiently on one of the desks. A weary-eyed minister lifted his gaze from a cracked roll of parchment.

"Have you seen Geta, the priest with the crutch? Curious fellow, bandaged hand, always working?"

The man tipped his stylus toward the ceiling and cocked an eyebrow, indicating the upper chambers. The rooms at the topmost level of the hall were once reserved for the emperors and their audiences. They were lavish in detail, grand in scale. Sarra kept an office in one.

She found her way up a broad stair, passed a waiting room, and another one after that. The walls of these slender chambers were each adorned in a different stone, agate in the first, sardonyx in the second. Both were similar stones, translucent in nature, shining, and lined with a thousand undulating stripes of white and brown, or sometimes black with a hint of blue and red. The beauty of the place made the guard at the carved wooden door seem out of place. She was unaccustomed to the presence of sentries within the House of Ministers. The yellow cloaks stood outside. They guarded the doors, but the men were not permitted to venture inside. The scrolls and tablets compiled by the ministers were often of a sensitive nature, so access was strictly regulated. Apparently, someone had made an exception.

"Ott posted you at this door?" she asked.

The man grunted, which was, perhaps, the extent of his language skills. He was dressed in the white linen of a priest, but he was no holy man. She knew that much from his appearance. His muscled physique belonged to the streets, as did the odor of his body.

"You may want to wash a bit more regularly if you're going to impersonate a priest," she said. "We do it on first and seventh bell and we make sure the same is done with our linens. Wet them and soak them in natron if you want them to look right. Ask a washerman about it, or better yet, hire one. I assume you are well paid?" She flashed some semblance of a grin, enough to make the man nod. "Now move," she said. "I have business with your master."

The man hesitated. He'd clearly been instructed to turn back any that might approach the chamber.

"Have you ever heard of a vessel?" she asked.

"Like . . . a pot . . . or something?" He did his best to reply.

"Yes, like that. It is something that contains something else. I am a vessel of Mithra-Sol. As the right hand of Tolemy, I hold a piece of His light. When you bar my path, you are barring a vessel of Mithra-Sol. Not a smart thing to do, is it? Should some of his light spill from that vessel—are you following me—I would not expect you to survive."

"I . . . understand Your Rayship, if that be the right title. I was only . . . followin' orders and I didn't recognize you . . . at first. You'll forgive me . . ."

"I might, if you get out of the way," she said, flashing a small grin once more.

At that he did move, though just a bit, as if he could not allow himself to do more.

Sarra slipped past the man.

Inside, scribes sat at trestle tables, translating old tablets or deciphering scrolls. A map occupied the south wall. It was stretched on a wooden frame and it appeared to contain a chart of Solus, complete in every detail, but difficult to follow. The parchment was impossibly thin, and there was another sheet behind it. A map beneath the map, and this one she did not recognize. The shapes of the second conformed roughly to the ones of the first, but in places they diverged or there were only columns indicated where a structure stood in full on the upper map. There were great streams, buildings, too, and places marked with characters drawn in kohl. She recognized the symbols, which belonged to the gods' forgotten tongue. Ott held Noll's translation of the script, but Sarra had requested a copy, which she studied from time to time.

Above what she guessed was the temple of Re, she saw the familiar character that indicated the House of Stones and Stars. In another place, one she guessed was the Mundus of Ceres, a black mark stood in bold relief against the map. The mark meant "king." *The king in black,* thought Sarra. She cocked an eyebrow when she saw it.

"I see you've found my maps. Impressive, aren't they?" The voice belonged to Ott. He stood a few paces from the entrance, balancing on his crutch, a drop of sweat on his brow. She guessed he'd just completed a long walk. The hem of his robe was black with soot, his sandals brown with mud, toes stained. It had been a very long walk indeed, and she guessed it had been through the Hollows.

"Yes," she said, answering his question, "they're quite impressive, though I'm not certain they have anything to do with the task I assigned to you. I asked you to learn more about Noll and that chamber in the Shambles, about the children of Mithra-Sol, the descendants of Re and Pyras."

"I've done that," said Ott.

"Really? It looks like a map of the sewers. That's what this is, isn't it? A drawing of the Hollows. I've never truly seen one. Some must exist, but I doubt one of this detail has ever been attempted. It's like mapping an ant hive. There's no logic to the thing."

Sarra again took note of Ott's dirty sandals, the map, and the many scribes. She had allowed him to work unsupervised, and this was the result. Fifty or more men toiled in the chamber, and there were another seventy or so who were, in all likelihood, digging tunnels. She wondered how much coin he'd wasted on this folly.

"Get your scribes out of here, and I don't want them listening at the door," she said, then changed her mind and decided to do it herself. She was Ray; she might as well exert her will. "All of you. Out of here. Now," she said in loud but carefully enunciated words, ones she needed not repeat. The last man out sealed the door.

Ott stuttered, trying to form words, but nothing of substance came to his lips.

"Are you going to admit the truth, or must I say it for you?" Sarra asked. She waited, but Ott gave no reply. *He is going to make me say it.*

"I've had you followed, through the Hollows, and these passages you've excavated."

She tore off the upper layer of the drawing, revealing the map of the underground.

"House of the king, isn't that what this symbol indicates?" She pointed to the black mark. "A bit presumptuous—isn't it? He's a bastard. *You're* the heir. The bastard boy calls himself king, and I suppose this sewer is his castle, his attendants a bunch of dead men. Still, it is good to confirm the location of his hideout. He is, after all, the boy who cannot be found, this Bane of Solus—isn't that what they call him? He's confounded Mered, desecrated temples, looted markets. I might have allowed this to go on for a bit longer had he not murdered my only ally. What do you say to that? This work of yours almost wrecked me. You are assisting Rennon Hark-Wadi, the bastard of Harkana? Say it."

"I . . ." Ott stammered, which was answer enough for Sarra. She had given Ott coin and the freedom to do with it as he pleased, and he had betrayed her cause. "Ren didn't murder Kihl," said Ott. "You were there . . . you saw it. The men were a poor imitation of the kingsguard. They weren't even Harkans."

"You miss the point. You gave shelter to our foe." She indicated the temple, the black mark. "I wouldn't be surprised if one of them popped through that door right now and lopped off one of our heads. That's their game, but they aren't going to win it. Their end is a foregone conclusion. You saved them from Mered, but not from me. There's no way out of Solus. The passages are sealed; the army sits in waiting. We may not have a Protector, but we *have* an army. There are thousands upon thousands of soldiers quartered outside the city and only a handful of Harkans within it. You're torturing them. Is that not apparent? Let them die a quick death. It's the only real favor you can offer the black shields."

"I . . . can't. I'm sorry. I can't . . . do that," said Ott. Droplets of sweat blossomed on his forehead and pooled at his eyes, making them red. "You're right, they should've died in that cistern . . . but I stopped it. I saved Ren. He *is* safe."

"If only that were the truth," she said plainly, knowingly. This next part would be particularly difficult for her son.

"What do you mean?" Ott asked, his voice quickening, the stuttering gone. "What're you going to do?"

"Going to do?" asked Sarra. "I'm not going to *do* anything. I've already done it. I had you followed. This map simply confirms what my priests told me this morning. The Harkans hide in the Well of Horu. Their location is revealed. Don't you see what this means for us? We'll be the ones who dispatched the *Bane of Solus*. Not Mered. It's a chance for us to show power and influence. We'll take the boy, then we'll end Barca's revolt. My men say your sister, Merit, has joined with the rebel, strength-ening his cause and making his force too large for Mered's house army to dispatch. Only the well-trained soldiers of the Protector are fit for such a conflict. I'll find a new man to command them and we'll stamp out the revolt. Even if we fail at the task, it'll hardly matter. I alone have the power to bargain with Merit; she's my daughter and I recently saved her from a rather unpleasant encounter with the haruspex. She owes me. I will find my victory, and I will have you to thank for it."

"I . . . you can't do this. Ren'll think I betrayed him, that I led the city guard—"

"To him? Didn't you? The Harkans were always careful and quick. They left no trails, but you are an entirely different story. A lone boy hobbling with a crutch in the darkness. Did you not think you would be noticed? That white robe glowing in the black? Don't worry," she said, "Ren was always a dead man. Dead since the day he came to Solus. Dead as that body beneath the still-smoldering Antechamber."

Ott wrinkled his lip, making her guess that last line may have been in poor taste, and perhaps it was. He tugged at the door with his good hand while still balancing on his crutch. The door creaked open.

"What're you doing?" she asked.

"Isn't it obvious? I'm sending a man to warn Ren."

"You don't grasp the situation. It's too late to warn him. I've already sent the city guard to the temple. They're on their way. I would not have come here unless the task was done. I'm no fool."

"Is that what you think *I* am? Some fool, some pet you've kept clos-eted for all these years?"

"You're my son."

Ott gripped the door, swinging it wide with unexpected force. The crutch twisted beneath him and it slipped, sending Ott tumbling to his knees, where he knelt, chest heaving. He drew in a great snot-filled gasp and looked up at her, eyes watering. "He's my brother, my . . . my friend—I think. I had a pair of friends once, from Rachis. The only others I've known are the beggars I feed in the plaza."

You have me, Sarra wanted to say, but she held her tongue. She knew the hurt she'd caused.

"I'm sorry," she said quietly, almost reverently, as if she were already speaking of the dead. "There was no other way."

Ott fumbled for his crutch. Taking hold of it, he righted himself once more and headed out the door.

"You're not going after him, are you? The task is done," she said.

"I don't care."

"It'll be a terrible mess down there," she said. "You shouldn't go, not alone. Mistakes are easily made in battles. You don't want to find yourself on the wrong side of the line."

"Don't you understand?" Ott leveled his gaze at Sarra. "I've already crossed it."

⪥ 38 ⪤

The Blackwood Bridge groaned beneath the weight of twenty or thirty destriers, the mighty timbers flexing as the great warhorses thundered their way across. Merit rode with the forward guard. They made their way through the open gates of the city, past war-riddled streets and rows of dead soldiers. They found little resistance in the outer districts. Her cavalrymen cut down a dozen soldiers, maybe less. The people of Harwen had fought the real battle—that much was plain. Their bodies littered every street and alley; the dead clogged the very roads they trod upon. The people of Harwen had waged what looked like a quick but bloody fight, clearing the path for Merit to ride unmolested through the inner city, all the way up to the gates of the Hornring itself.

"Shields," cried Merit as they entered the tunnel that would carry them past the fortifications, but the men had already raised them up above their heads. The vault was littered with murder holes, but no arrows flew from the slender openings. Unchallenged, they rode out of the long passageway and into the Hornring, Harwen's keep, a look of naked triumph on their faces. They'd met almost no opposition and now, as they rode into the great courtyard, they saw the reason for it. When they came upon the field of battle, Merit traded her joy for something altogether different. Dread perhaps, horror in all likelihood.

Body lay upon body, thousands of them resting where they'd fallen. Everywhere she looked there were commoners with common weapons, men who'd fought with hooks and hoes, shovels and potsherds. They'd brawled with the red army and triumphed, but they'd done it through sheer numbers. There was no military genius here, no cunning. The entire city had risen up and it looked, for a moment, as if the whole of the city had fallen upon some sword or spear. Merit had never seen such carnage. It was total. The bodies lay in heaps so dense they eclipsed the cobblestones. Tomen slipped from his horse and kneeled, bowing his head while his captain coughed up the contents of his last meal.

Merit searched for Shenn. She looked for a head upon a spike or some similar vulgarity, but she saw none. There was, however, movement among the bodies. A man stood, hand pressed to his bloody chest. He could not speak. He simply pointed toward the King's Hall, waving them onward. Merit would have followed his direction, but there was no way to ride through the courtyard without treading upon the dead.

"Come," said Tomen. "We'll go on foot from here."

Merit slipped from her horse and drew her blade.

"Are you certain you want to march with us?" Tomen asked. "There may well be soldiers left alive, men who guard the false king. This is the end for them, and desperate men are known for desperate measures. There's no telling what'll happen in the throne room."

"I know as much," said Merit, "but I need to be there. I have to be the one who holds the sword to his chest, and there is still the matter of my husband. We haven't seen him or his head. Perhaps he lives, maybe your men . . ."

Tomen grunted bitterly, "Shenn's the least of my worries. Harkana has an abundance of kings. If you lose your head . . ."

"I know the risks, so make certain I'm safe, Tomen. Now, march!"

With that, the Harkans did march, making their way into the Hornring's inner chambers, picking through the bodies, trying not to step on the dead. Up ahead, sounds echoed in a nearby chamber, men cried out, and wood broke upon iron. The fight was nearly upon them, and Merit was close to the head of the charge. She peered over shoulders and shields, glimpsing the damage as they swept from corridor to corridor, stepping over more bodies, more dead and wounded. The Hornring was utterly upended. Every chair and table lay broken or shattered. There were more bodies than any man could count, all of them bearing improvised weapons, shards of glass made into daggers or the legs of chairs turned to spears in the haste of battle. In places, the people of Harwen had barricaded themselves behind stacks of tables. None of it saved them from Mered's spears. As Merit and her army played games in the desert, a terrible battle had raged across the Hornring. The blood was still fresh, still warm. Among the dead, there were those who clung to life, jerking about and crying, missing limbs bleeding out upon the stones. She wanted to go to them, to order her men to tend to their wounds, but the march could not be stopped. Dozens of soldiers charged ahead of her and hundreds shoved at her from behind. None would halt. All of them drove forward, toward the entrance to the King's Hall, a pair of doors, wide open, a yawning mouth at the corridor's end.

Merit leapt across the threshold; men dashed past her on all sides. In her father's hall, the false king stood upon the throne. Men with tall shields encircled the platform, while archers and spearmen stood upon the dais. A hundred or so commoners gathered around the false king's men, throwing themselves haplessly at the soldiers, dueling with stolen weapons, hurling rocks or shattered urns.

"To the side," Merit cried.

At the sound of her voice, the commoners turned and caught sight of their regent, joy breaking across each face. The queen had returned, as had the army. The fighting men of Harkana drove forward, but the commoners would not stand aside. Stewards and scullions fought beside well-trained soldiers. Waiting women and weavers stood among captains and infantry. The strong men of the Harkan Army charged the false king's soldiers while the carters and cooks nipped at their heels.

The Harkans trampled the shield wall. It shattered in a single stroke, and the men who held it were crushed by boots, cut with swords, their shields cloven, limbs shattered. The Harkans cut through the archers and spearmen, eliminating what remained of the false king's army.

"Stop!" cried Merit. "Tomen, order them to stop!"

Her general echoed her command, and his soldiers lowered their arms.

All eyes went to the queen regent.

Merit made her way carefully now, lifting her bloodstained dress as she climbed over the fallen, as she tromped past broken spears and cracked shields. Swords slathered in viscera poked from still-moving corpses. The soon-to-be dead pawed at her ankles. Some cried out in agony, others made only some gurgling sound as their lungs filled up with blood.

The false king stood upon his dais.

"Tell your men to lower their shields. You've five, and we've five thousand. The fight is done," said Merit.

The false king's men turned to their master, who himself seemed to look around for some answer or exit.

"Lower your shields," she said with patience, with the confidence of a victor, her voice eliciting a quiet calm to contrast the frantic demeanor of the boy. "Drop them or I'll take them myself," said Merit, who was within striking distance of the king. Tomen eyed her nervously. His men swarmed at her heels, but she pushed them back.

The king made a sad little gesture with his good hand. "Drop your arms," he told his men. "Let them fall. There's no use in any of this."

"Indeed," said Merit.

The king's men parted for the queen regent, and she passed through their lines while behind her Tomen's men sent his soldiers stumbling to their knees with a swift kick here or a punch there. They were not gentle.

Only the false king stood, alone upon the Horned Throne, the great horns of Ulfer curled up behind the boy, that shiny black banner still hanging from the wall.

Merit joined him upon the dais, much as she had a few weeks prior. Again, she held a sword in her hand. He, too, was armed, a blade at his side, but he dared not unsheathe it. A dozen Harkans stood within striking distance, swords raised, the men trembling with eagerness, their blades wetted with blood.

"You're too late," said the false king. She did not even know his name.

"Late?" she asked. Then it came to Merit. *His threat, the letter,* she thought. *He's slain Shenn.* In the heat of the moment, in the glorious charge, she'd almost forgotten about her husband. *Almost.*

"Yes, late. Too late to save your man. Terrible, isn't it? While you dallied in the hills, the commoners fought the real fight."

"Quiet yourself, imp, and show me my husband."

At that, the false king complied. Shenn was there, among the rebels, his body piled upon a dozen others, caked in blood, spear wounds in his chest and leg, his right arm mangled beyond recognition.

She ran to him and knelt. His blood, still warm, wetted the fabric of her dress.

She stroked his black hair and the blood-soaked strands made knots around her fingers. The eyes were open and she searched for life within them. They still glittered, teasing her, making her think he was somehow alive, but it was only a trick of the light. The breath had long since faded from his chest. Her hand touched his heart. It did not beat. He was warm, but growing cold. She slid his eyelids shut and laid him gently, reverently, upon the floor.

His blood, still pouring from his body, limned the corpse in red.

Her stomach churned and she nearly disgorged its contents upon the floor. Her skin went cold and sweaty and her heart beat with such thunderous strength that her ears rang. A shock ran through Merit, her breath coming in gasps. Her eyes stung. She did not care who witnessed her grief. For once, she allowed herself a moment of uninhibited sorrow.

Then she turned to the false king, the nameless boy, the one who dared call himself brother. She stood, but she did not advance on him. A voice had caught her attention.

"It was Shenn who led us." A woman stepped forward and Merit knew her face.

"Akti—isn't that your name?" Merit asked. "What did you say?"

"Your Grace, I was just saying that it was your husband, Shenn, who led us. One of the helpers at the prison cells was Harkan, you see, and Shenn convinced him to set us free. The king had us locked in the cells beneath the Hornring"—she pointed to the boy who stood upon the throne—"he chained us like dogs, but Shenn led us out of there. He told us to go to the gates, to open the Blackwood Bridge and clear the wall walk. He did all that, my lady, called every man and woman in the city, and they all came running. They knew his face; they knew what had to be done. Shenn was at the head of it all. He led us here, all the way to our king's throne room, and we almost took that bastard's head." Again she pointed at the false king, her finger trembling with anger, tears running down her cheeks. There was blood on her dress and cuts on her arms, a bruise turning the left half of her face purple.

Shenn led the revolt, thought Merit. *This was all his doing.*

It was a bold act, a heroic undertaking for a man who had seldom been heroic in life.

He'd done the hard work and taken the hardest of hits.

He'd given his life for the kingdom, she supposed, and for her—so she could have her throne. They'd never been lovers, but perhaps there were other kinds of love, and maybe that was what they shared.

"That's how it went?" Merit asked the nameless boy, the one who claimed to be her brother. "You marched into Harwen, proclaiming yourself the son of Sarra, the heir that was rumored to have been born in Harwen but raised in Desouk. The true son of my mother and father?"

"Something like that." He stood alone upon the throne. "Does it matter?"

No, thought Merit.

She went to him, her heart overflowing with rage. She ripped the finely woven robes from his chest, revealing the place where his arm was sawn off and sewn shut to make him look as if he were Ott.

"It must have hurt terribly when they cut it off," said Merit, her eyes lingering on the stump.

"It did," he said, twitching uncomfortably, "but Mered promised me a kingdom, and even if Harkana is nothing but an awful patch of dirt, I thought it might be worth a lost limb." His eyes flashed with anger. "It's a notion I've since dispelled."

"Enough," said Merit.

She was already wiping his blood from her sword when the boy collapsed, his neck striking the throne, red spraying on the chair and the shiny banner her soldiers tore from the wall.

The Horned Throne was empty.

She did not loiter.

Caked in the blood of her husband, Merit took the throne. This was her moment of triumph but her face was blank, expressionless, drained of all hate, love too, and hope.

THE LONE AND LEVEL SANDS

≋ 39 ≋

Ren gripped the familiar grille at the top of the pipe that wound itself around the Well of Horu. It dangled a hair's width above its seat, but he did not move it to the side as he often did. Something made him pause. He had decided to go out ranging with Tye and Kollen. They'd made it all the way to the top of the pipe, but some change in the plaza above made him reconsider his plans. The platform appeared to be missing and the streets above were silent. Where was the chatter? The cries of the hawkers, or the buskers crooning for one last crescent before the day's end?

"Did they all go on holiday?" Tye put her head next to Ren's, trying to catch a glimpse of the streets.

"Most definitely," said Kollen. "I think they've gone and left the city for us to plunder."

"No doubt." Ren set the grille aside and stole a glance at the street.

"Well?" Kollen asked.

"Empty. Not a soul. No soldiers, no one, and it might as well be midday up there. They've hung lamps from every ledge and door." He set the grille back into place.

"It had to happen sooner or later," said Tye.

In truth, Ren had hoped for a little more time.

"They must have guessed at our location," said Kollen. "The temples and houses we visited are close to the Mundus."

"Yes, they've guessed at the general area, but they don't know *exactly* where we are," said Tye, hopeful.

Ren shared none of her enthusiasm. "I have a terrible feeling. We should go."

Sandals tapped on the stones above, the ring of bronze heels beating on the ground.

"Soldiers," Tye whispered.

Ren held his breath. Kollen was already backing down the pipe, Tye hot on his heels.

"They could be coming for us in the Hollows and above," said Ren.

"Or this might just be caution," said Tye. "Perhaps the whole city's locked down, a curfew or something like that, an attempt to stop us from prowling in the night. The temple might be safe."

"Or there might be a thousand red soldiers storming it as we speak," said Kollen.

"Listen," said Ren, "none of us know what's happening."

"Which means we ought to get our asses moving," said Kollen, and that was the last thing any of them said.

Kollen led, followed by Ren, then Tye, all of them shimmying their way down the long and winding passage. It was slow going and every creak, every sound, made them stop and listen. Was that a soldier? Had they just heard the distant clamor of battle? They listened, eager to learn what waited for them in the temple. Silently, one in front of the other, feet forward, sliding on their asses, they went, the air filled with dust.

"This is killing me," said Tye, "not knowing what's down there."

"How far have we gone?" asked Kollen. "I forgot to keep track of the turns." The tunnel wound around the shaft eighty times. They'd counted it once, but never again.

"Don't know," said Ren. "Maybe halfway."

"Should we call out? Maybe they'll hear us and send up a man with some news," said Tye.

"Or perhaps Mered will send up the whole fucking army," Kollen ventured.

Ren agreed. "We ought to stay quiet until we know what's down there."

Uncertain and afraid, they descended the tube.

Kollen said nothing—not a word or a jape. The boy was deep in thought, or trapped in some web of fear.

As they neared the base of the pipe, a notion occurred to Ren. "Tye, maybe you should stay a good way behind us. Me first, then Kollen. Just in case."

"In case of what?" Tye asked. "In case our asses are in danger? I don't need savin'. I've wanted to sink a blade into one of those bastards for days. If this is the end, I want to be the first out."

"First to get a sword in your belly; good luck with that," Ren muttered. He'd gone all the way back to the Priory of Tolemy to save Tye, and nearly lost his life along the way. He still cared. He still saw that bright-eyed girl he'd met in the priory, the one who grew her hair long to hide her girlish face and strapped cloth to her chest to maintain a boyish appearance. Even among the kingsguard, he still reached for his blade whenever some soldier looked at her for too long or lingered in her presence. They all knew she was a girl, the only girl in the company of five hundred men, but Ren had made it abundantly clear to the captains that any man who came near Tye would find a sword in his back. He was still protecting her, just as he'd done in the priory, just as he'd always do. It didn't matter if she cared for him or knew what pains he took to make certain she was safe.

A rattle echoed in the tunnel, an odd sound. Ren looked for Tye and spied her just up ahead.

"What was that?" she asked.

"Who knows," said Kollen. "There're more rats than rocks down here. It's hard to know what you're stepping on."

"Quiet." Tye pushed past Kollen, moving to the head of their group, just as she'd promised. "There's something going on down there."

"If it's a battle, it'll be over by the time we reach it," said Ren.

"Yes, and there'll be a hundred men in red waiting for us," said Kollen.

"They don't know we're in the shaft," said Ren.

"Good," said Tye. "Let's go. Out the top and away from whatever's down there."

"I thought you were up for a fight? Change your mind at the smell of blood?" Kollen asked. "Those empty streets are more dangerous than some rattle in the tube. I say we have a peek at what's down there before we make any decisions. Weren't there a few openings near the base of the shaft, places for all this muck to overflow?"

"I wouldn't know," said Tye. "I'm not an expert on shit."

"I agree with Kollen," Ren said. "We need to know what's down there."

Tye did not argue the point further. They did their best to ease their way down the remainder of the shaft, but every moment was torture. A crash made them stop.

"That wasn't a rat," said Kollen.

"I know," said Ren, his words hushed, resigned. The sounds of battle grew louder. The rattle turned to banging, the squeaks to shouts.

"Let's run, up the shaft," said Tye. There was fear in her voice, trembling in every word. "What's the point in going any further? We all know what's down there."

"I need to see it," Ren protested, "and we're here anyway."

A dim glow emanated from the bottom of the tube. Shouts penetrated the opening, a choir of battle cries rising about them. Then it was all muffled and the light was gone. A rustling sound echoed in the tube. Someone was climbing, coming at them fast.

Ren gripped his dagger.

There was no light, nothing. There was only the sound, and even it had stopped.

"I've been waiting for you." Edric's voice. Ren recognized it, though he could not see the young captain's face.

"The city guard came out of nowhere. They knew where we were hiding. Someone betrayed our location, or they finally just followed one of our squads. We don't know how they found us, but we were ready for their attack. We blocked the top of the spiral. They could only come at us one or two at time. We're holding them back, but it won't last," said Edric. He placed a bit of parchment in Ren's hand, pulled out a tinderbox, and lit a rushlight. "Read this. It's from your brother. It arrived just prior to the first soldier."

"How was it delivered?"

"Attached to a rock and dropped over the edge of the Mundus," said Edric. "It nearly killed one of our men." Ren took the scroll but noticed the wax was already broken.

"You read it?" Ren asked.

"I had no choice—I needed to know what it said."

Ren glanced at the writing. Ott had sent Ren a warning, saying the city guard had discovered their location. It laid out rough directions for a retreat. Ott claimed to have found a second place where the black shields could shelter.

"Do you know this tower?" Edric asked.

"No, we'll just have to follow the map, and that won't be easy—especially with the yellow cloaks on our heels. It'll be a miracle if we find this place."

"Well, this is the city of miracles . . . perhaps you'll find one. We need you alive, Ren. Lead the men, and I'll stay here and try to hold back the—"

A great explosion interrupted Edric. They eased down the shaft a bit, to a place where there was an opening in the pipe that allowed them a view of the temple. The yellow cloaks had used some sort of ram to demolish a portion of the wall. At the temple's midpoint, they had opened a second avenue of attack. A shout rang out as chunks of stone went flying in every direction. Men in yellow cloaks threw down their ram. They tossed earthen jars into the air. The clay shattered against the stones, exploding in red and yellow flames. It lit the black temple, allowing the city guard to take stock of their foe.

"Arrest that charge," said Ren as he hurried down the last few turns of the pipe and leapt out onto the ramp. "Clear a path and I'll lead the men out of here."

Edric didn't bother to answer; he was already shouting orders.

The yellow cloaks were everywhere, hopping over walls, leaping down onto the lower levels of the ramp, and striking at the Harkans from every direction. There was no charge to arrest, just a seemingly endless parade of soldiers. And Ren did not see Tye or Kollen. Soldiers hurried in every direction, some trying to hold back the city guard, others looking to Ren for direction. He turned and ran straight into Tye.

"Where's Kollen?" Ren asked.

"Don't know. Thought he was with you."

"Gone," said Ren, who was already running, shouting for the men to follow him. Ott's directions called for the black shields to exit through the top of the spiral. Having read the letter, he guessed Edric had cleared the way.

"Go," he said to Tye. "Through the passage. Start running and I'll catch up. Lead the others." Ren was not ready to leave, not without Kollen. He searched the sloping ramp, glancing up and down it, but the temple was a mess of men and armor, swords clashing, torches hurtling through the air.

The city guard had the numbers, but the temple was essentially one giant ramp, so the guard could not gather in one place or form a sizeable group. This made it easy for the Harkans, who were superior at combat, to break through the slender lines of the city guard. Ren guessed that a good number of his men would make it to the top of the ramp.

"Kollen!" Ren cried out, but there was no reply. He doubted anyone had even heard him. The clash of steel was near deafening and the hard, smooth walls of the temple made every sound reverberate a dozen times over. Ren pushed his way through the fleeing Harkans, down the ramp to Edric. He grasped the captain by the shoulder. "Have you seen Kollen?"

"The Rachin? That ass?"

"The only one."

"Thought he was with you."

"He was," said Ren, a lump forming in his throat. Kollen was gone and Ren held the directions required for their escape.

Edric eyed the parchment.

"You need to go," he said. "Our men are fleeing, and if you're not at the head of the column they won't know which way to go."

Ren turned to leave him, but just then a dozen yellow cloaks came hurrying down the ramp, swords drawn.

"You should have gone when you had the chance," said Edric, his words tinged with regret. He thrust a blade into Ren's fist.

A moment later the yellow cloaks were on top of them.

≈40≈

Kepi sat with her back propped up against the stony wall of her chamber in Caerwynt. She stared out at the forest beyond, the rift carving a narrow wedge in the distance. Eyes fixed on the great valley, she massaged the aching muscles in her shoulder, kneading the place where the kite's talons had caught and held her arms.

"Fool," said Ferris as he threw open the door. He had ridden ahead to prepare the fortress and had only now come to visit Kepi. "Queen and Kitelord, ruler of the Gray Wood and all that, but a bloody fool. How did you know the bird would catch you?"

Kepi's fingers fell away from her shoulder. "I asked it. The kite circled. I saw it approaching, navigating the narrow rift, preparing to take hold of me."

"You whisper to some damned bird?"

"To the forest god," said Kepi. "If you believe in such things," she said, almost silently, before she went back to massaging her shoulder.

"Well, I'm glad the two of you had a chance to talk before you took that leap. I was a bit concerned when you stepped off the cliff's edge. Most folk do not recover from that sort of trick. I was quite angry over the whole thing, and I may have killed one or two of Mered's men. Well, all of them, actually, or at least the ones who didn't run." Ferris took a long draft of amber. "The boys in red retreated, but I doubt they went past the tree line. They are readying themselves for war."

Kepi shrugged. The world felt distant, almost unreal. The thrill of flying held her in its clutches. Her heart thrummed, and she did not care about petty politicians. She had flown through the air.

Ferris must have seen the way she ignored him, how she shrugged at his concerns.

"Well, I suppose you're quite pleased with yourself. That *was* impressive. The boys are calling you *the queen who flies*. That was no small feat. I thought we'd lost you, all the way up until the moment when you flew out of the haze and landed at my foot."

"Well, from my point of view, you were at my foot. I am queen."

"No doubt."

She ached all over, but it had all been worth it, in her estimation. She had found an unexpected pleasure not simply in the act of leaping blindly from the cliff and plummeting through the air, but in the coming of the kite as well, in the way it dove to meet her command, soaring to her aid and rescuing her from the fall. She'd discovered something in that moment, a thing she'd suspected since that first night in Cragwood but had not been sure of until the moment the creature latched onto her shoulders. The kite was not simply some protector; it was a part of her, an appendage she hadn't known she possessed. They shared the same blood, or something similar.

"And as I recall," said Kepi, "you were the only one laughing when I appeared. The rest of your lot had faces as white as ghosts."

"They thought you were dead."

"And you thought the whole thing was funny?"

Ferris shrugged and took another drink. "Few things frighten me. Pain makes the man."

"That's the priors' mantra, isn't it? It's what they said in the old priory house, the one that burned on the day my father died."

"I drank for two days straight when that hole in the earth crumbled and fell," said Ferris, his smile abruptly turning flat. He placed his empty cup on a table.

"I didn't know you were a ransom."

"Ransom," he muttered. "I haven't heard that name in years." He tried to look as if the word hadn't bothered him, but the man's whole demeanor had changed. He was abruptly sullen, resentful even. "It was a short stay. We can thank the spindly little bones of the fennec for my early release. Seems my father ate one every night—had a whole herd of them, but they got the better of him. He choked on a leg."

"I was wondering why someone of your . . . age, ruled Caerwynt. The other warlords are—"

"Older? That they are," said Ferris. "I'm the exception."

"Not unlike this new *king* of Feren," said Kepi.

"Mered's little boy?"

"He looked to be about your age," Kepi said. She raised an eyebrow.

"Maybe, but the boy is a weakling, a coward, and an injured one at that. You heard the way our men jeered, how they hooted and hollered as the *heir* limped away into the forest. He's already proven himself a liar, and he'll find no family in Feren. Dagrun was not a forgiving man. The line of Barrin is utterly gone, wiped out at Catal."

Kepi found it odd to hear Dagrun's name mentioned so casually, as if Ferris knew him. Maybe he did. She'd barely had the chance.

"Well, whatever that boy had hoped to achieve, it's failed," said Kepi, her face impassive, her thoughts still clinging to Dagrun.

"Has it?" Ferris asked. "This was just some opening ploy. They thought they could take the kingdom without the effort of a full-scale war. Mered has an army in Harwen and another in Solus. He's stretched thin. That's why he wanted you dead. He's scared of fighting an all-out war in Feren while he's occupied in the south."

"They set a trap?"

"And it failed, but don't get cocky," said Ferris. "Mered's armies are split, but they *are* large. I don't think he'll shy away from a fight, and if he can bring the Protector's Army to his side, we won't stand a chance."

"I know as much, but I must confess something. Ferris, I itch for a fight. Solus took my father. They burned him like livestock and threw a feast on the next day, something about the dead, some holiday. It's a sick place, Solus. Feren will never again send their children to that city."

"Then it's war. Fortunately, we have a queen who flies." Ferris tapped her on the back, careful to avoid the place where the kite had gripped her shoulder. "I think Tolemy himself might have moved his bowels if he saw you rise from the mist. There's been a shortage of miracles in this world." He patted her again, but the second touch was not as hard as the first. That one possessed all the roughness of a soldier's clap on the back, while the second felt more personal—a little too soft, by her estimation. Kepi shied from his touch. She'd had enough romance for one lifetime. *I have two dead husbands,* she lamented. She'd watched one choke and die and her onetime lover had murdered the other in cold blood before her eyes. Seth. Things had moved so quickly, she'd hardly had time to consider her first love. *Where are you? Locked away with all the other traitors?* She didn't even know what had become of him. He'd simply been hauled off with the rest of the mob, probably lost in some cell. She'd only had time to bury her husband and carry out his final wish. Then this war had started, and she'd forgotten all about Rifka, Seth, and the life she'd once led in Harwen. There was an army on the far side of the rift and a boy who claimed her throne, enough problems to occupy any mind.

She slapped Ferris on the jaw, but only lightly. "Do not touch your queen," she said.

The young warlord reeled, pretending as if she'd knocked him over, long hair flailing, feet stumbling. The man was incorrigible. "Hit me again if it makes you feel good," he said. "Pain makes the man. It made me."

"I'll take your word for it. We have a war to fight—or had you forgotten about that?"

"No, but I can think of two things at once. Three on a good day. Right now, I'm wondering what other tricks you can perform with that bird, trying to figure out how to get more scouts across the rift, calculating how long it will take Deccan to return, and wondering in general if I've got enough men to hold off Mered. What's on your mind?"

"You're bragging," said Kepi.

"And you underestimate me because I'm young. I doubt you're any older than I am."

"You'll never know," said Kepi. "Focus on the war. You are a warlord—isn't that what they call you? So fight the war."

"Well, I'm not the one who can lead the warlords into battle—that's the king's task, or in this case the queen's. You've got my loyalty and Deccan's too. We were there when the people revolted. We saw the kite settle on your arm. You don't have to convince us that you're Kitelord, but Feren has twelve warlords."

"They were at my wedding."

"And they rambled on with their bloody speeches. Personally, I had my eyes on the new queen. It seems her dress was a tad low in the front, if my memory serves me well."

"Are you looking to be knocked on the jaw again? I am your queen."

"And I have more soldiers than you—at least until the rest of the army arrives. Feren is a kingdom of warlords. You have the allegiance of two, but you're going to have to convince the others to fight at your side if you want to take on Mered's army. It's time for you to speak to them."

"What do you mean?"

"Deccan summoned the lords. Only Caer Rifka and Caerwynt have standing armies, but the others can still muster a great number of men. They spend the wet season farming, and the dry in military training. They'll throw down their plows if their lords command them to do it. You need to convince their masters to stand at your side."

"Convince? Isn't the kite enough?"

"It might be, but there's more to Feren than some oversized bird. Come," he said. "There's something I need to show you. The sun is nearly set and I want to catch the light."

He offered her his hand, but Kepi kindly refused. She was injured. Her shoulders ached, but she could stand without the help of any man. She rose uneasily from her seat, realizing belatedly that she had erred. No one cared if she could stand with an aching back. She was a queen. They cared if she could lead, if she could command men. Ferris had offered his hand as a sign of supplication, but she'd blindly turned him away. Kepi grumbled inwardly. She had the kite, but what skills did she possess as a ruler? A little politeness might have helped. She ought to have allowed him to help her rise in a queenly fashion, but it was too late for that.

A frown crossed the warlord's otherwise unflinching grin.

I'll make it up to him, Kepi thought. She needed friends. She'd lost Dagrun and Seth too. Kepi was alone. She wanted a companion but was uncertain of how to approach Ferris. *Where do I look for friends when everyone I know is my subject?*

Like Caer Rifka, Caerwynt held a small forest at the center of the stronghold. Ferris led her out into the yard and up a winding stair that followed the trunk of a great blackthorn, up and up and up until they pierced the canopy. There, above the treetops, she was in another realm. The blackthorn canopy was so dense, so thick with leaves and branches, that it formed a kind of ground, an earth made of leaves covered in centuries of dust and dirt. Grass grew upon this second earth, this ground above the ground. Misty air settled atop it, and stray trunks poked from the canopy. The wood was carved in strange patterns, depictions of a many-limbed creature, something like the squid that Wyrren fishermen pulled from the Cressel.

Ferris waited for her at the top of the stair, leaning against one of the totems.

"What's that you're propped up against?" she asked.

"Llyr."

"The forest god?"

"Yes, these statues are old. The oldest in the kingdom."

"They're strange."

"Are they? A tree has no face, only a trunk and branches, roots too. Like the trees, Llyr is nothing but limbs, hundreds of them."

"It's frightening."

"Aren't all gods frightening? Llyr's a forest god, some say. Others call her mud god, *kitemathair* to some, *kitefaethir* to others. After the first Feren kings abandoned Catal, they came here and made their home at Caer-wynt before moving onward to the high city. This is our second oldest fortress, but this temple is the first of its kind."

"I didn't know that."

"That's why I brought you here. Do you see the kite?"

She hadn't, so she shook her head.

"The kite was not always a part of our religion, and not *every* king has ruled with one at his side. Your former husband was our most recent example."

"Why are you telling me this?" she asked, unnerved by the mention of Dagrun. "The people revolted because no Kitelord stood upon the throne."

"They did, and many believe that a man cannot rule Feren without the kite, but others do not. Some don't think the kite is even a creature of Feren," he said.

"Is this really about the kite, or is it about Adin Fahran?" she said.

"He has a legitimate claim to the throne."

"No, he doesn't, and we don't even know if he is the *true* son of Barrin. Does anyone in Feren know his face?"

"I do."

"What?"

"I served in the priory—or had you forgotten? I was taken at eleven and set free at fourteen. I knew Adin Fahran. He was your brother's friend. I thought you ought to know that."

"My brother, Ren? The bastard?" News had come to them as they rode toward the rift. A great confusion surrounded the Horned Throne. No one knew who was king and who was not, and now someone had come to Feren, sowing more dissent. "This is Mered's work," she said. "He was the one who supplied Adin with the soldiers. They say Mered is the one who chases Ren through the Hollows. This is all one scheme. This title he's taken, the First Among Equals—he's the father of all these false rulers."

"I doubt he'll strike at the Wyrre," said Ferris. "They say Barca left only bones and rock, but the rest is true enough. This may be some ploy by the man in Solus, but that's not the issue. If the boy has a claim to the throne, he is free to chase it."

"As long as he lives."

"Yes, well, it is difficult to pursue one's claim when you no longer draw breath."

"I could have ended him."

"You should have. It would have made your life a lot simpler."

"You spent three years in the priory—as his subject?"

"I'm no—"

"But you thought you might one day be his subject?"

"There was the possibility."

Kepi sighed at that. She'd thought she might find a friend in Ferris, or maybe a confidant, but he made her doubt his intentions. He supported or at least acknowledged Adin's claim.

She sighed a bit and he took notice.

"You are the queen of the Ferens, Kitelord, through and through. Have no fear and don't doubt my loyalty. I'm simply telling you what you need to hear. When the warlords arrive, you'll have to convince them to follow you into war. You've persuaded me and every other man that stood with you at Caer Rifka. It's a good enough start, but that's all it is. You have my word and Deccan's, but you'll need ten others if you want to take on the empire. And there's another issue . . ."

"What?"

"You know what I speak of . . ."

"Oh, no—not that."

"We cannot ignore the obvious. These other men are a bunch of bloody pigs and not one of them has ever bowed to a woman."

"Things change."

"Have no doubt. I bent the knee, as did Deccan and Gallach before I took his head."

"For better or for worse, the moment is burned into my skull," she said, her words sounding harsher than she'd intended. There was too much mention of Dagrun and the revolt. She wanted to put all of that behind her, but the whole thing stuck to her like a shadow in the bright sun.

"You need the twelve, it's a tradition. The warlords must vote for the kingdom to go to war. If Dagrun were here, he'd have bribed them all—if it's any consolation."

"It isn't, and stop mentioning the man. I lack the coin, and I have no notion where he kept it." She groaned a bit, her thoughts lingering once more on the uprising in Rifka. The beauty of this heavenly place, of the setting sun, was lost on Kepi. Her thoughts turned dark as she imagined the kite tearing out each of the warlords' throats. Perhaps by the third they would all follow her—too bad that was a poor way to rule a kingdom.

The day's last light limned the treetops with streaks of purple and red. Past the tree line, horses and carriages moved in great numbers, their dark silhouettes appearing no larger than dust on the horizon.

"It's Mered," she said, gesturing to the south, past the rift. "His army approaches, and I must beg Feren's to fight it."

⋛41⋚

Under the cover of darkness, Barden rode into the city of Harwen. He came alone, posing as a messenger, his soldiers waiting in the hills beyond. He brought his horse to a halt as he entered the Hornring and left his mount with a boy while a Harkan soldier led Barden to the Hornring's inner court, where the bodies of the dead were laid out in rows. Thousands lay lifeless upon the stones, the corpses gutted, washed, and stuffed with natron. Soon they would be smothered in salt and left to sit for forty days. It's what a proper interment demanded, and when it was done and the corpses were oiled and wrapped, the bodies would be removed. Harkans remembered their dead. Merit's father taught her that lesson the first time they stood before the Battered Wall, when he told her how the fortification was left unrepaired after the first revolt so each generation could witness the harm the empire had inflicted upon their kingdom.

She wanted Barden to set eyes upon the dead, to witness this new but temporary memorial. He was her father's brother, but he was not raised in Harwen. She was not certain he knew their ways, not truly. He acted Harkan, but it seemed more like a performance and less like a part of the man. Merit had been six when her father took her to the wall and told her about the men who died there, how their ancestor had torn out his own stomach after he'd been forced to eat the still-burning coals of the charred fortification. Barden might be twice her age, but a man was never too old to learn.

He did not even bother to glance at the bodies. If he was stirred in any way by the dead, he did not show it. He moved at a measured pace, his gray desert robes fluttering about in the evening breeze. All day the storm had blown across the city. Of late, even the desert was restless. It seethed with bitter winds, blowing sand into the air, into Merit's eyes. She found it beneath her fingernails, and in the hinges of doors that would not quite shut. The desert heaved a great breath, the sky darkening to a muddy shade of gray.

Barden climbed the steps and for a moment Merit swore she was looking at her father. The people of Solus wished one another the sun's fate. They said each man would rise again, and now it seemed that her father *had* risen, if only in a way. Here he was, returned, and ready for the reckoning her true father had wanted but not achieved.

"Leave us," Barden told her man, though she did not think it was his place to do so.

"We left a thousand bodies at the Coronel. That's how this whole thing started," said Barden. "I'm no stranger to the dead, and I know how you took the city. My scouts observed your advance. The battle was hard-won, but it *is* done. You have your kingdom. You are the ruler of Harkana. There's still an heir or two who might challenge your seat, but I doubt Mered will trouble you."

"I hardly need the reminder, but I do think you ought to show these people a bit of respect. My husband's body rests on that field. Did your spies tell you that?"

"No," said Barden. "But there'll be more bodies if we go forward— more dead Harkans to bury. Surely you know this? We'll mourn when the battle's done. By my estimation, it's only just begun. I came here to collect on a promise, to see this battle started, not to mourn the one you finished. Tell me, Merit Hark-Wadi, queen of the Harkans, will you do as you promised?"

Merit offered her uncle a withering look. "After all this?" She motioned to the bodies. "You think I'll quit? You doubt my intent?"

"Doubt is a habit I learned in Solus. They trust few, and in the high desert we trust no one. I'm not from Harkana, but my heart is here, somehow. I've spent my whole life dreaming of this place and its freedom."

"I know as much," said Merit. "It's why I brought you to the wall, so you could see the city."

"And its dead." He exhaled his words, at last expressing what sounded like grief. "There's news from Solus," Barden said. "The boy, Ren."

"Lost in the Hollows, dead possibly, or so I heard."

"Ren is very much alive. They say he escaped Mered and the city guard. Neither was able to arrest him. He moves about the city with impunity, striking the rich and the holy, stealing whatever food he needs, taking gold from the wealthy, and laughing all along. They call him the Bane of Solus. The boy has wrought mayhem upon the people who trapped him. He knows he has no way out of the city. He's trapped there, but he fights. He has hope, and the boy has shown remarkable bravery. They say he can enter any house, that he could steal the pillow from beneath Mered's head, or dine with the emperor, and no one would know how the task was done. Rumors abound. Some are no doubt half-truths or outright lies, but not all of it can be false. The boy lives."

"The bastard," she corrected him.

"The bastard king," said Barden. "They say my brother named him heir in front of the kingsguard."

"He is a bastard," said Merit. "And Arko had no idea who this boy was when he named him heir. My father was ill informed. Ren is the son of a servant. We're not going to discuss it, not if you want me to march on Solus."

"I wish the topic was more easily abandoned."

"What are you talking about?"

"You won't like what I'm about to say."

"Then don't say it. Have some discretion."

"I can't. Ren is our best chance at making a quick entry into the city. He has five hundred men. It's a small number when compared to the might of the Protector's Army, or even Mered's, but it *is* a sizeable force, and the soldiers of the kingsguard are already inside the city walls."

"What are you getting at?"

"I need to get a message to Ren. They say that someone in the Hall of Ministers assists the boy. As a newly crowned monarch you are expected to visit Solus. All kings and queens have done it. You'll go to ask for the emperor's blessing, but you will in fact seek out Ren. Make contact and convince the boy to join our cause. His army is large enough to secure at least one of the city gates. If his force could seize the east one, the Rising Gate, for half a day or even less, we could storm the city. We could take

Solus in a single stroke. Without him, we'll be forced to lay siege to the capital. It will take time and a considerable amount of patience to breach the city walls. There will be risks. If the siege is long, if it takes months or even years to break the fortifications, my army may grow restless and they will turn their eyes toward less hardened targets. If we strike swiftly and decisively, we'll have an army that dwarfs all others and an open door to march it through."

"I grasp your tactic." Her voice was shrill, harsh, just as she'd intended. "It's a good enough plan, but I'd rather you left me out of it. I'm not on good terms with the boy. If I go to him, he might just have my head and add it to his collection of trophies. Perhaps we should send a simple messenger."

"A courier will not suffice. Ren will be undertaking sizeable risk, and I don't think he'll do it unless we offer him something of equal value."

"My life?" asked Merit.

"Your words, not mine, but you're not too far off the mark. When you go to Ren, you'll be forced to join his men. You will tie your fate to his. Such an act will prove our sincerity. He will know that I am marching on Solus, that I will storm the open gate and take the city. In return he will at last have his freedom. He wants a way out of that city, and we can offer it to him. On scrolls, I have detailed these plans. You must find the boy and convince him to follow these instructions. Go to Solus and he *will* agree to our plan. He's trapped. A dead man if there ever was one. If he joins us and we take the city, he goes free. The past is the past, Merit. Forget what you've done. The boy has too much life in him to squabble with you. Ren wants to fight. He will not refuse you. I'm certain of it."

"Certain? I'm not. Nothing is ever certain. This plan of yours is as risky as the assault on Harwen. I'll be putting my life on the line, but what will you be gambling—nothing? It's what you hazarded when I marched on this city."

"I intend to risk everything when we move on Solus," he said. "Believe me, if I had another plan I'd follow it.

"The Protector's men have already cleared the countryside and evacuated the villages near Solus. When my army came up against the Harkans, I lost any chance I had at catching the Inner Guard by surprise. Weeks have passed, and despite the absence of a new Protector, the guard is well prepared for our assault. A desert siege is not an easy thing, and with those villages gone, with even the cactus shorn to the ground, it will be an impossible task. I believe we must act while Ren lives and the Ray of the Sun squabbles with Mered Saad. A civil war is afoot. The time is right. We must—"

"Strike," said Merit, her voice quiet. She understood it all and agreed with most of it. She needed no convincing of Barden's logic. It was sound enough. The choice was made, but she dreaded it nonetheless.

⇒42⇐

A bell chimed in the distance, but Sarra paid it no heed. The marshal of the city guard—a man named Stiris, tall and gaunt, face littered with bruises—stood before her, his cloak stained black. A day had passed since the yellow cloaks went chasing after the kingsguard. It ought to have been a rout, but something had gone awry. "My men're still down there," Stiris said, his voice brimming with distaste. "It's not finished—it won't be done for some time, actually."

"It *is* over," said Sarra. "The bastard king, this Bane of Solus, escaped. You're no better than Mered. He allowed Ren to elude capture, and you gave him that same opportunity. Is he so slippery that no one can catch him? He's just a boy, some runt from the priory."

Stiris swallowed deeply, unpleasantly. He appeared to be wondering the same thing as Sarra because he simply shook his head, spat, and held up a pair of open hands. "It's not over, but there is a chance you are correct and the boy has escaped." He swallowed once more, deeply. There was blood on his hands, and dirt as well. He picked at it as he spoke. "The Hollows are the real enemy. We have your maps, but they aren't complete. And to make matters worse, someone carved new corridors, dozens of them. It's a mess down there, and each of those Harkans fights like five of the Alehkar."

"Spare me the details. Just tell me when you've put an end to that boy."

In the distance the bell chimed again, though faintly. Sarra stood behind doors of ironwood. No common chime could pierce that wood. Someone wanted to be heard.

"You took prisoners?" she asked.

"A dozen or so," said Stiris. "Wat told us to bring them here."

"Where?"

"In the gallery."

"I'll find them," said Sarra. "You have work to do. Do it." She brushed past the marshal. The door opened and she once more heard a bell chime, a little louder this time. It was a distinct sound, a note she'd heard often. This particular chime was used to summon the Ray of the Sun from the Empyreal Domain. It was the only way Wat could communicate with her when she was on the other side of the wall. But she wasn't in the domain, and Wat ought to know that.

She led the marshal into the corridor, sending him down the stairs as she climbed up them, making her way into the gallery. The long corridor-like space was lit by an open-air clerestory, which admitted not simply light but the cries of the people as well, the ones who gathered at the Antechamber. The crowds had grown despite her best efforts to dismiss them. She'd placed a curfew over the city. She'd hoped it would keep the Harkans off the streets and the petitioners inside their homes, but it had failed on at least one count. The city guard refused to arrest the mob; it was too large and too unruly. The crowds huddled about the great, golden conflagration, their numbers growing by the day.

There were hundreds of them. Some came to pray, or to beg for the Soleri to show their faces. Some arrived in the morning and left at sundown. Others camped at the wall, spending their days and nights in protest, waiting for their silent gods to appear. Worse yet, there were some who had dedicated themselves more wholly to this cause. They followed an ancient tradition, one known as the stylite. The men sat atop tall and spindly columns, eating little or nothing at all, starving themselves as they petitioned the dead gods for help. They called them pillar dwellers, but they looked like fools to Sarra, men who were looking for a little attention from the crowds and not the gods they claimed to worship. Sarra doubted any of them would stay the course. A true stylite, so dedicated, would remain atop his column until he died or his prayers were answered, whichever came first. In this case, the outcome would no doubt be the former. Dead gods do not talk—at least, not yet.

The bell chimed again, louder now, sounding through the open windows.

Inside the gallery, Wat sat idly atop a small stool. His head jerked upright as she entered. He stood uneasily and bowed as deeply as his aging back would allow. "These are the prisoners the city guard captured in the

Hollows. They are here for your review," Wat said, his voice gruff from age or exhaustion, perhaps both. The last few weeks had in all likelihood carried more events than the last decade of his life. "Also, I located one of the men that worked in Tolemy's house, a prior. I think he might prove useful."

"A prior?" she asked.

"You'll see," said Wat, a slight chuckle in his voice.

"Go on. Show me what you've found and stop your man from ringing the bell. Was it really necessary for you to strike the thing? I wasn't in the domain."

"And I didn't ring the Chime of the Ray. In fact, it was stolen last night."

"Stolen? So who's ringing it?"

"Your guess is as good as mine," said the old man with a shake of his head. "Should I send someone to have a look?"

"No," said Sarra. "Show me the prisoners."

In the long gallery, the city guard had assembled the captured men. They stood, hands bound behind their backs, feet shackled. They wore soot-stained rags, but most carried armor beneath their tunics. The men of the kingsguard were giants, each one standing a head above even the tallest of the city guard, but one had no armor. He had the look of a beggar or a sickling of some sort, his beard ragged, face slathered in something black.

"Who's he?" she asked the commander, a man named Padiset, she thought, the marshal's second overseer. She looked to him for an answer, but someone else spoke in his place.

"That one is mine," said a man Sarra did not recognize. "Kollen Pisk of Rachis. A ransom."

"A ransom?" Sarra asked. "How do you know this?"

"As Wat said, I was a servant in the priory. My name is Nevan, if you need know it."

Sarra crossed the long room to the place where the ransoms stood. "There were three of you," she said. "That's what my emissaries tell me: three in the temple of Pyras, three stealing from the houses of the wealthy. Where are the other two? Where is Ren and the girl?"

Kollen did not speak, so Sarra turned back to the prior. "This ransom, Kollen," she asked, "did he have any friends in the priory? Was he close to the Harkan?"

"This one?" The prior lifted a finger to indicate Kollen. "If memory serves me, he was not particularly fond of the Hark-Wadi boy; he has-sled him to no end. I'm a bit surprised the two stuck together. I'd have thought one would have strangled the other by now."

"Things change," said Sarra. "War can easily make friends out of enemies."

She addressed the ransom. "The house of Pisk must be quite small. You've been loose in the Hollows for some time but they've sent no soldiers to save you, nor have I seen a petition from the mountain lords asking for your release. Seems as if no one cares about you."

"That don't bother me a bit, Your Rayship," said the ransom. "My father's probably taking bets on how long I'll last. He was always a bit of a bastard. I never expected help—never wanted it. We had plenty of fun before these pricks ruined it for us, but that's all right. I see only a dozen or so prisoners here, so I reckon there are still hundreds left in the Hollows. I bet they're out there right now, raiding one of your palaces. Did you know the kingsguard are starting to get fat? Too much plunder, I suppose."

Sarra was unimpressed by the boy's crudeness. "It's only a matter of time," she said. "It's easy to grow fat when you're stuck in a cage. Get-ting out is the hard part, and I don't think they'll manage that one." She looked to Wat. "Show me someone else."

Wat led Sarra to a boy who appeared only slightly older than the first, but this one wore armor and his breath was calm, a sharp contrast to the ransom's frantic demeanor. "He's one of the commanders," said Wat. "We heard the Harkans talking. His name's Edric. He's not their leader, but I gather he's a man of some importance."

"Good," said Sarra. "A ransom and a captain. Send out criers. These men—the kingsguard and the boy from the priory—will stand and face Horu's trial. They'll suffer until the Harkan kingsguard and their bastard king surrender themselves. Do it now, and make certain the prisoners are well guarded. If the Harkans come for them, I want to be prepared."

"Aye, Your Rayship. I'll put every man I've got available on it. We'll stand them in the plaza that faces the statuary garden. We won't fail you."

"Good. The Harkans have had too much luck and too little loss. Let's put an end to that, shall we?"

Padiset gave a nod, turned, and addressed his men, ushering the pris-oners out of the gallery. Sarra watched. She knew full well that it was not good luck but was instead the aid of her son that allowed the Harkans to twice escape capture. However, the kingsguard had lost their guardian.

She'd taken Ott's maps, sent his scribes to prison, and sealed his chamber. She'd put an end to his endeavor. Unfortunately, Ott was missing. He could not have reached the Harkans before they fled the underground temple, but perhaps he knew the location of their new hiding place and had joined them.

The thought made her stomach coil into a tightly cinched knot.

She'd given up much and more for that boy. She'd left behind two daughters and a kingdom, but he'd betrayed her at the first possible opportunity. And he'd left her for Arko's bastard. The whole thing made her sick.

The door creaked open. "Who is it?" she barked, but it was only another of Wat's pages. She could not tell one from the other. They all wore the same golden robes, and each boy had the same bowl of black hair tossed over his forehead. He offered her a scroll and took his leave when she granted it, wishing her the sun's fate as the door closed.

Sarra cracked the wax, straightened out the parchment, and looked it up and down. It was a message from her daughter, Merit, the apparent queen of the Harkans. Sarra's hunch had paid off. She'd known there was something to this traitor, Barca, some secret he wished to reveal. He must have somehow come to an understanding with Merit that allowed her to retake the kingdom. She offered no details except to say that the people of Harkana had risen up against the false king in Harwen, taken his head, and dispensed with his guard. Mered was finished in Harwen, which was a great relief for Sarra. *A victory,* she thought. Her daughter occupied the Horned Throne and she sought the empire's recognition. It was good news all around. Merit offered her loyalty to Tolemy and his Ray, not Mered. As was the custom, the Ray anointed each new king—or queen, in this case—as they came to power in the empire. Dagrun had traveled to Solus, and Dolen, king of the Rachins, had also.

Sarra called for the boy and asked if he had parchment and ink, and when he produced some she drafted a hastily composed letter, inviting her daughter to meet with her in the House of Ministers. She sealed it when the boy brought wax.

The bell chimed again.

Only this time she knew it was not Wat who struck it. Hence, she went looking for the bell, chasing up and down the long corridors of the House of Ministers. It was nowhere to be found, so she went to one of the balconies that looked out onto the city.

Mered Saad stood before the House of Ministers, dressed in bronze, a cord grasped between two gauntleted fingers, the bell hanging from it, red cape draped from his shoulders. It was not the suit of armor that Amen Saad, his nephew, had worn. That one lay rotting in the Empyreal Domain. This armor was newly fashioned but made in the style of the Protector's livery. Sarra knew immediately what was afoot.

Mered gave the bell one last strike when he caught sight of Sarra.

He wore the helmet of the Protector, but he had not removed his veil. Behind him, in jumbled lines, the generals and captains of the Protector's Army stood before the mighty ranks of the Alehkar. There were thousands of them, more men than the streets could fit. The soldiers were forced to peek around corners, and there were others in the distance, crouched on curving paths, all of them come to show their allegiance to the new Protector. Her man, Kihl, had owned these soldiers, but they'd found a new lord, a richer one, she guessed. Mered must have spent half his fortune to gain the allegiance of this many men in this short a time.

"Hail, First Ray of the Sun, Wife of Mithra-Sol," said Mered. "Hail and witness your new Father. I, Mered, in this time of crisis, as first citizen, First Among Equals, claim the name of Father Protector, a title the great families of Solus have humbly bestowed upon me. These men stand at my back, eager to put the empire in order, to silence the rebel and the boy who runs amok in the Hollows."

He went on, but Sarra had heard enough—seen enough too.

He'd ruled the day; there was no sense in denying it.

Mered had won yet another skirmish. She knew as much. Sarra was well accustomed to failure and smart enough to know that the victor in this war had yet to be decided.

⇒43⇐

Merit Hark-Wadi arrived at the tall and formidable gates of Solus with considerable pomp. Her war carriage was appropriately adorned for a person of her standing. Hewn from graythorn, stained black, and edged with silver, it caught the eye of all who passed it. She was the queen of the Harkans and her authority was without question, or it soon would be when the empire acknowledged her position. That was the pretense, anyway, so she made certain to look the part. The army of Harkana rode at her back. Five thousand horse-mounted soldiers gathered at the city gates. She looked more like a general riding at the head of an invader's army than a woman who had come to pledge her loyalty to the empire, but she supposed that couldn't be helped. She was there under false pretense, after all. She needed no Ray to bless her reign. She had earned her throne. The whole of Harwen had earned it, but she guessed Sarra, and perhaps Mered, would believe that she wanted the empire's approval, that she was afraid of the young upstart, Ren. It was a logical assumption, or so she hoped.

A soldier bearing the bronze armor of the Alehkar rode out atop a rather pompous-looking steed. The horse was barded in gold and bronze, and an ostrich feather dangled from the creature's headpiece. The man dismounted and raised his hands to show that he bore no weapons. He had only a scroll and his marvelous armor, emblazoned with a thousand different prayers. A Harkan soldier took the parchment and rode it to Merit.

The letter was brief. The Ray of the Sun had granted Merit access and audience and assured her safety. The Alehkar would escort Merit to their meeting place in the Hall of Ministers. The Harkans, her army and their swords, must remain outside the city gates. There was nothing further in the message, which was fine with Merit. She had exactly what she wanted.

≩44≩

Sarra walked with a cadre of loyal city guardsmen. Even in the House of Ministers she no longer moved without sentries. For all she knew, Mered's men were storming the hall at that very moment. Every sound, every creak in every door startled her. Nothing and no one could be trusted. Mered had taken the army. It was only a matter of time before he found a way to take her office. Sarra needed allies, and Merit had just arrived. She'd come with an army and Sarra needed one of those. Hence, she went to the place where she'd arranged to meet her daughter, but the room was empty.

"Wondering where you'll find the queen?" The voice came from be-hind Sarra.

"No, not really, Mered. I assume you've waylaid Merit?"

"Something like that," said Mered, who had only just entered the chamber. "You're surprisingly quick-witted for someone who is so ter-ribly slow in all other regards. You admitted the queen of the Harkans to our city and watched her arrive at the House of Ministers, but you did not make certain she reached *this* chamber, the one you requested. She went to mine, and she's there right now. See, you haven't enough men, not enough loyal ones. I have the yellow cloaks at my back and the Protector's seat. I own the armies of the great houses. I've given out titles. Inni will be the overseer of the House of Crescents, and when these conflicts are settled, my son, Evin, will be Father Protector. I've assigned nomarchs and called the viziers to a congress."

"I see you've thought of everything."

"Indeed, I've even thought of a place for you. Though I do not serve Mithra and my body does not belong to his cult, I honor his traditions, his mouth. I'm offering you a new title, just as I've done for the rest of Solus. You will be Tolemy's emissary to the First Among Equals. What do you think? A bit long? We could just shorten it to messenger."

Sarra forced her lips into a hard line. *He means to put a leash on me, to tie me with a rope woven from meaningless titles.*

"I think Ray is a fine title, but I can always add another. Titles have a way of accumulating in number, but not meaning. Go ahead. Add two more, call me messenger or call me scribe. It changes nothing."

"In that regard, you are wrong. We need a messenger. A *real* messenger. The people demand the presence of the Soleri. Bring forth the gods, or I will find someone else to do it. You *are* a courier, so take this message to Tolemy and his folk: The people will not tolerate the silence of their gods. They cry out and you ignore them. They gather at the burnt ru-ins and your god does nothing to address their needs. They say the fire burns with the light of Mithra-Sol. That is why the pilgrims cling to it. The city cries for its gods." He brushed his hands together as if he were washing himself clean of the matter. "We will not speak again. You have your task." There was finality in his words. He'd have her life if she did not comply, if Sarra did not produce the impossible.

The ruse was at its end.

The Soleri had been silent for too long; too much had happened. Too much faith was lost. With Barca and his hordes approaching the city, with famine in the air, with the drought and the sandstorms, with the threat of war all around them, the people demanded their gods.

This was no time for illusions or blind faith. It was a rough time, a time of testing, when all things would be questioned and those found false would be put to the sword. Sarra saw this, saw herself standing atop the greatest lie in the history of histories.

Mered motioned to go, his red robes fluttering about him, delicate bells dangling from his sleeves. He was leaving. She guessed she would never see him again, so she did the one thing she had wanted to do since meeting the veiled man. She took hold of Mered's robe and swung him around. She flung back his cowl and tore free his veil.

"Let me at least know the man who will bring me my death," she said, but Sarra did not *see* a man.

The eyes were still kohl-black, but they'd lost all their masculinity. Freed from the disguise, a woman stood before Sarra.

"You are dead anyway. You might as well know my secret," said Mered. "It's not much of one; most of my loyal household knows it."

"But why?" asked Sarra.

"Why?" the woman who called herself Mered asked. "Why? Because Raden Saad, Protector of the Empire, would not admit to siring a girl, not as his firstborn. He could only give life to men, to soldiers. His seed carried the blood of a hundred generations of warriors. It bred only hounds, so when his firstborn turned out to be a bitch you can imagine his indignation, his disbelief. He named me a boy and I was one thereafter. The deed was done. I have no memory of ever being a woman. My father thought he could bend the world to his will, and in some ways he did. He made me into what I am and I have accomplished more than he ever dreamed possible."

"But your wives, your children?"

"Bastards, and the women, my wives? I let my generals fuck them for sport. I have no need for such things."

"Apparently," Sarra muttered. As the young queen of the Harkans, Sarra once had those needs. She had wanted a family, but those desires had led only to pain, to hurt and more hurt. She envied Mered's indifference. Sarra had no such luxury. A part of her still yearned to see her daughter, and the rest of her thoughts lingered on Ott. Her son had vanished and she no longer had the city guard at her beck and call; she had only her priests to hunt him down.

The woman in red retreated.

Their congress was at an end. She slipped the veil once more across her mouth and nose. She wrapped her hair back into a red turban. A cord drew down her cowl and she became Mered Saad, the First Among Equals, the Father Protector who was not even a man.

⇒45⇐

"This is the place," said the man who led Merit through the Hall of Ministers.

"The place for what?" she asked.

"Waiting."

I've done enough of that, thought Merit, but she kept her mouth shut. The stern look on the soldier's face told her that complaints would get her nowhere. He departed, leaving her alone in an antechamber. It had two doors. She'd entered through one. She knew where it led, but the other was closed. *Should I open it?* She could knock or give the ring a tug, but the soldier had told her to wait. For once, she chose to heed the words of an underling. She settled herself on the golden bench, and the door at the far side of the chamber—that second door, the one she had almost knocked on—opened, but just a bit. Red flashed in the narrow gap between the door and its jamb.

Mered.

Merit went cold and the bench felt hard against her back, the chamber too small, too much gold in too little a space. A hundred different thoughts flooded her mind. Had she been led astray? Merit stood, seated herself again, then eyed that sliver of light, wondering if someone had wanted her to know what lay beyond or if the door's opening had simply been an accident. Perhaps a small draft had caused it to pivot just slightly on its hinges.

She wondered if her dispatch had even reached the First Ray or if it was waylaid by one of Mered's soldiers. Worse yet, had the Ray of the Sun received the message and handed it over to Mered? That last one seemed improbable. On the last day of the feast, Sarra had saved her from the haruspex. Why would she turn on her now?

A slight creak issued from somewhere in the room. A portion of the golden paneling spun, revealing a concealed doorway. In the gap, a boy appeared wearing a simple red robe, holding a cup in his hand. She had seen such robes in the house of Saad, so she guessed he was one of Mered's servants.

"I have no need for drink." Merit looked away. She did not want anything offered by the house of Saad. There were no guest rights in Soleri culture.

"My queen," the boy spoke, his voice loud, which she thought rude. "Turn around and look me in the eye."

"In Solus, are all servants as rude as you?" she asked.

"I wouldn't know," said the boy quietly, a soft stutter in his words.

"Well?" she asked. "Apologize or leave. I hardly have time for you." Indeed, her attention was fixed on that chamber.

The boy gave no reply, which made her at last turn and face him. *Have you no manners?* she thought to ask, but Merit came up short. He had a false arm. She could see it now—a sleeve stuffed full of feathers and straw, a gloved hand that did not move. *Could it be?*

"You're him?" she whispered.

"And you are in danger." Ott returned her quiet reply with an even quieter one. "This is Mered's doing. He'll meet with you, but he won't place a crown on your head. Enter that room and you'll never leave it."

"My brother, Ott," she said, almost involuntarily. He had her father's nose and eyes, but there was a bit of Sarra in the outlines of his cheek and brow. His hair was lighter, not dark like hers, but pale like his Wyrren mother.

"Quit gaping," he whispered.

"What now?" Merit asked.

"You have only one option. Mered is Father Protector. He owns the army and the city guard and he's imprisoned the Ray of the Sun, or so it's said. No one really knows what's happening in Solus, but I do know that you will not find the First Ray of the Sun on the far side of that door. You were led to a chamber of Mered's choosing, and I followed you by another route."

"Is there a way out of here? That door? Does it lead somewhere safe?" She indicated the narrow panel through which he had entered.

"Perhaps, but we must go," said Ott. "In a moment, those doors will open."

He retreated a bit. He was trying to keep his back straight, but he was clearly in pain and limping slightly with one leg. He was leaving, and she needed to decide whether she was going to follow him.

Merit's gaze swung toward the door at the far side of the chamber. Flickers of red appeared in the gap. Mered had declared himself First Among Equals and Father Protector. He was making a play for power, dueling with the Ray, and Merit was somewhere in the middle of that conflict. It was possible that Mered, in his desire to enlarge his reign, would acknowledge her power and send her back to Harkana. After all, she had presented herself as an ally of the empire. She had come to feign loyalty to the Ray. She could just as easily feign loyalty to Mered.

"Perhaps I *should* go through that door. What if they name me queen?" she asked, whispering still and feeling foolish. Ott was leaving.

"Decide," he murmured, and somehow she knew it was the last thing he'd say. He was hell bent on departing before those doors opened and the men inside had a chance to steal a look at him.

Her gut told her to go, to leave, to flee from Mered, but a part of her wanted to enter that room. It was the part of Merit that had ordered the lavish carriage. She wanted her power to be acknowledged by the empire, by everyone—Mered too. She wanted him to name her queen, but he'd never do it.

"Ott," she asked, "do you know why I'm here?"

"You're here to see my brother, the bastard," said Ott as he disappeared down the lightless corridor.

The boy *was* clever.

The great doors at the far side of the chamber at last opened. Merit heard them grinding on their hinges, but she never saw what was inside. She had already shut the hidden panel and was hurrying after Ott.

≋46≋

"This is the tower," said Ren. Though, in truth, he only guessed it was the one indicated on Ott's map. It might just have been the threshold to yet another corridor, a temple, or a stair that led to nowhere. He'd encountered an endless parade of dead-end passageways and circular paths. He'd escaped the yellow cloaks, but it had not been an easy task, and not all of them had made it out of the Well of Horu. Edric had fought his way to the top of the ramp, and he'd held the passage while the kingsguard fled. He was the last to leave and the first to go running off in an alto-gether different direction, leading the yellow cloaks astray.

Ren and Tye and most of the others had escaped the city guard, but there were casualties. Noll was lost, Edric too, and Kollen was missing. Ren hadn't seen his friend since they left the pipe. Maybe he'd gone back into the tube and made it to the surface, or perhaps he'd found the sharp end of a sword.

Ren shook his tired head as he stumbled into a tall space, and Tye was close behind him. He guessed that it was in fact the tower Ott described. Slotted windows covered one wall and a large ironwood door with three drawbars stood at the far side of the chamber. He half expected to find Ott, but his brother was absent, replaced by an older man—a Harkan, perhaps. He had the burnt skin of the desert folk, the deep wrinkles. He'd spent a lifetime beneath the sun, and much of it must have been in battle. His hands bore a web of disfigurements, deep cuts that welled up into bulging scars.

"I'm Asher Hacal," he said. "And thank you for bringing my soldiers to me."

"Your soldiers? Asher?" asked Ren, Tye at his side, voice weary from the long dash through the Hollows. Exhaustion hindered his thinking, but he knew that name—Gneuss had mentioned it. Asher was the true captain of the kingsguard.

"How?" croaked Ren, his throat dry.

"We have spies," Asher said.

"We?" Tye asked.

"Harkana. The army has emissaries inside the city. We walk among our foes just as they no doubt circle the Horning. I escaped the false king in Harkana. My man in the city found your brother. We traded messages. Ott produced a map and I followed it here. Didn't expect to see the kingsguard come chasing up the stairs. And you, you're the boy my king named heir."

"My father's gone." Ren was still exhausted from the fight, barely able to form words.

"I know as much," said Asher, "but it changes little. In fact, your father's death is the reason I came back here, to retrieve the kingsguard and lead you home."

"Fair enough," said Ren, still out of breath. "I don't suppose you have a plan to get us out of here. That would be awfully useful right about now."

Asher shook his head. "One man can easily enter the city. I killed a soldier at the Dromus and stole his armor, but it won't work in the reverse, not with a whole army. Who commands the black shields?"

"I do," said Ren. He ran a hand through his sodden hair. "Gneuss named me captain . . . when he passed." Ren winced ever so slightly. "Edric's gone as well."

"I suppose it was to be expected." Asher's face paled, but only slightly, his mouth drooping at the corners. "How many others?"

"We don't count," said Ren. His words sounded more ominous than he'd intended.

"If Gneuss made you captain, the order stands."

"Good enough. Any idea where we are?" Ren asked. There were slotlike windows in the tower walls, so he pressed his face to one, wanting to get a sense of where they stood. Ren caught sight of the Shroud Wall and the flames at its base. He'd hoped they were closer to the outer walls of the city, but they were still trapped in the Waset.

"That's the Antechamber, if I'm not mistaken," said Asher. "I lived in one of its lower chambers while I served your father."

"The flames still burn," said Ren.

"That's the rumor, but this's the first I've seen of it," said Asher. He, too, was looking at the crowds that gathered around the distant blaze. There were men atop poles, people in tents, and others who were simply pacing, arms raised to the sky. There was unrest in the city. Ren didn't know whether he was the cause of it. He hoped he'd had some small effect on these people, that he'd been some minor nuisance to his captors.

"We're deep in the Waset, which means we're a long way from the city gates," said Asher.

"We always have been," said Ren. "We've been stuck here in the center, at the Mundus and the Night Market. We've never even come close to finding a way out of the city."

A voice boomed in the distance. Outside, a cloaked man walked the broad avenue, crying out the day's news in a strong, steady baritone. The words were loud, but largely unintelligible. Ren and the others had to wait until the man came a bit closer to hear what he said.

"The Harkans and their captain, Edric, and Kollen Pisk, heir of Rachis," the crier's voice rang out, "have been set about in the Plaza of Miracles, beside the Statuary Garden of Den, where, in accordance with the *Book of the Last Day of the Year*, they shall stand and bear Horu's trial, as all who insult Mithra-Sol must do . . ." He went on, repeating the news with some slight variation, adding detail as needed, but Ren didn't need to hear the rest of it. They had Kollen and Edric too.

Tye listened, her head hung low in frustration. Ren was quiet too.

"It's a ruse," said Asher. "They've given us the place and dared us to go to it."

Outside, a second crier followed the first, this one with an even lower voice, a booming bass. One after another, he named the captured soldiers.

"They're taunting us," said Tye.

"Yes," said Ren, "but they can't find us. That's why there're wandering around, calling out to the heavens like a bunch of fools and hollering about Horu's trial, whatever that means."

"I wouldn't know," said Asher.

"I don't either," said Tye. "I missed that lesson, but it's named for their god of death—"

"I know," Ren snapped. He hadn't meant to cut her short, but they all knew the gods' names. There was no sense in guessing how such a trial would end.

"We need to do something," said Ren.

"No, we don't," said Asher. "It's a ploy. Our men will be heavily guarded—don't you see that?"

"I do," Ren shot back. *But I can't accept it.* He needed to go there, to the plaza of wonders, or whatever it was called. He could not sit and do nothing while his friend suffered. *And the statues,* he thought. *I can't escape them, either,* or so it seemed.

Ren was still lost in thought when Asher and Tye gathered at another of the narrow windows. Something or someone had caught their attention.

"It's Ott," said Tye. "He's headed for the door."

Asher shook his head. "If we open it, we'll reveal our location. It's midday and we're in the heart of Solus. No one bothers with this tower because they believe it to be some sanctuary of the gods; that's what Ott's messenger told me. But if we open the door . . ."

"I know," said Ren. "It's a risk, but I'm captain and it's my decision. Ott helped you, he helped all of us. The least we can do is return the favor."

Outside, the plaza was busy. After the criers moved on, the people had gone back to their business. The temple singer resumed her song, continuing whatever vigil her god demanded, and the beggars started up with a chorus of banging pots and clanking wooden cups.

"Remove the bars," Ren commanded, but the men hesitated, so Ren drew his blade. Ott was alone and possibly in distress. Ren would brook no dissent.

It took a dozen men to lift the first bar from its sleeve.

As the soldiers worked, Ott circled, shaking visibly. Things must have gone sour for the boy. He was limping badly, hair soaked in sweat, robe caked in dirt and wet with perspiration.

"Hurry," said Ren.

"We are hurrying. Would you care to lend a hand?" Asher asked, a hint of sarcasm in his voice. Taking him at his word, Ren threw down his sword, put two hands on the bar, and helped lift it. The weight of the thing *was* immense. It hit the ground with a thud that made the stones tremble beneath his feet.

"Open it," said Ren. "Slowly, quietly, and just a crack."

They tugged at the door. Ren poked his head into the widening crack, but found himself thrown back by Ott, who fell tumbling onto Ren as he lost his crutch. The two of them landed awkwardly on the floor.

Ott spoke without hesitation, "Close the goddamn door before they find us!"

Ren helped Ott to his feet and handed him his crutch.

"Ott, tell us what happened. How did they find us in the temple and why are you here?"

Ott told him everything, what Sarra did, how her priests followed him to the temple, how she'd found his maps. "I was a fool," he admitted. "However, I've learned my lesson. I chose an indirect route, one that follows the newer passages, the ones that aren't on the map. I was careful."

The men went to fit the drawbars back into place, but Ott raised a cautioning hand. "Stop, or at least wait until you've heard me out. Your sister is here."

"Which one?"

"The one you don't want to meet."

"Merit?" Ren asked.

"Queen of the Harkans."

"Is that what she calls herself? Seems like everyone's giving themselves titles these days," said Ren. "Mered is first citizen. Your mother is the Ray of the Sun . . ."

"And what about you, Ren?" asked Tye. "First Asshole?"

"Fine by me, King of the Harkans does sound a bit pompous."

Ott shook his head at both of them. "It hardly matters what title our sister carries. She is here and in peril. Mered sent Merit to Barca. She was a gift, a bargaining chip to secure his puppet king in Harkana, but she made Barca an ally and took back the Horned Throne—an act you might appreciate as a fellow Harkan."

"I would, had she not put her ass upon it," said Ren.

"That battle is over, yet a second looms. The rebel's army rides toward Solus, but Merit and the Harkans struck out ahead of Barca and his army. She journeyed to the city of the gods as each of the kings or queens of the lower kingdoms have done, so that Tolemy might recognize her authority."

"I don't recall Arko making that ride," said Asher.

"That is beside the point," said Ott. "Merit is here under false pretense. She is here to see you, Ren, but our first citizen struck before she could make contact. I intervened."

"Why?" asked Ren. "Why's my sister in Solus?"

"Can't you guess?" asked Ott.

"Well," Ren replied. "I suppose it would be helpful to have a friendly army in the city you are about to invade."

"No doubt," muttered Ott.

"She's close by?" Ren asked.

"Yes," said Ott. "She's with Kara, my scribe. If you will allow it, Merit will come to this tower. She knows the location and waits nearby."

"Allow it?" asked Ren. Could he truly allow the woman who had thrice tried to end his life, who had sent her own husband to put a dagger in his back, to come and treat with him?

"Yes," said Ott. "Will you allow it? I've guessed at her sins, that she's kept you away from Harkana by force of arms when necessary."

"Force of arms?" asked Ren. "That's one way to put it. You have no idea what that bitch did."

"I have a rather large imagination," said Ott, "and a mother who has more spies than friends. We know most of it, but only you can tell the full story."

"When there's time," said Ren. "For now, Kollen needs me. My sister can wait."

"No, she can't," said Ott, his voice filling up with irritation. "Barca rides toward Solus. The pace of this thing is set, and there is no time to stall. Make your decision."

47

The door opened and Merit stumbled into an empty chamber. She'd expected some welcome or other greeting, but the room was empty. Men *had* occupied it. Their sandal prints littered the floor, and someone *had* opened the door. She'd seen it pivot ever so slightly as she ran toward it, but they were gone. She was alone and forced to wonder just what she was doing. Would Ren lop off her head or greet her as a sister? The former seemed the most likely, but Ott claimed he could convince Ren to speak with her in a civil manner. Merit had simply nodded. She had little choice in the matter. She was alone in the city of her enemy, and Ott was her only ally. She hoped to find a second one in this tower.

Looking around, she noticed the chamber was round, with a stair at one end and slotted windows at the other. There were two doors: one large and one small. She'd entered through the big one, but now it was the smaller door that opened. A boy appeared, a servant, judging by his clothes and the way he kept his eyes downcast. He bore a silver cup brimming with red wine. She took it and watched as the boy sealed the larger door, silencing the distant cries of the city guard. She was surprised by his strength and the ease with which he closed the thing. The door groaned louder than a house full of whores, but the boy pressed it shut, leaving just the two of them in the chamber.

"Where is your master?" she asked. "The boy, Ren, the bastard of Harkana?"

"My master?" the boy asked, still not raising his eyes. He'd been a servant for years, she presumed, or perhaps he knew she was a queen and was just giving Merit her due.

"Look me in the eye when you speak, there's no need for pretense. I came to see the boy, Ren. Is he here or are there a hundred of Mered's soldiers behind that door? Tell me who sent you." She was out of patience, done with waiting.

"Ren's here, mistress, if that's what you'd like me to call you."

"Queen will do. You are Harkan, aren't you? Maybe some servant gone over to the rebel's side—is that it, boy? Were you one of the tributes sent to Sola to serve some foreign master?"

"Something like that," he said.

"I thought as much; you have the look of a Harkan, but not the demeanor. It's barbaric, this practice of sending our children to Solus. It's something I intend to end, and promptly. Now, tell me when I'll see your master."

"Soon enough."

"That's hardly an answer. Where is he? Out raiding, pillaging, like in the stories we've heard?"

"I can't say," said the boy.

Merit quickly remembered that she was not among allies. Even though this boy was by all rights her subject, he had sworn his allegiance to the bastard. It was a muddy situation at best. The kingsguard of Harkana served Ren, but he was not the king.

"Do you remember Harkana much?" she asked, making conversation, hoping this servant was simple enough that she could pry some information from him while they waited.

"No, not much at all. I was there once, but I don't remember it, not a single memory."

"Not one," Merit echoed. "Perhaps it's better that way, when they take them young. You can't steal away something you don't have. If you never had much of a childhood in Harwen, or wherever they took you from, then there is nothing for you to miss, no memory of your mother to cry over."

"If you say so."

"It's only a guess," Merit admitted. "I lost my brother, my mother too. I had a father, but—" She caught herself. Merit was feeling vulnerable. Perhaps too much so. Her pains were none of his business. She was the one trying to wring secrets from him and not the other way around.

"Tell me, what happened? How did you join the bastard's little rebellion, and how many others of you are there? Has he raided every house in Solus? Built himself a little army of dissidents?"

"An army—of servants?" the boy asked. He was clever, this one. He'd not only ignored her question, but he'd returned her inquiry in his own, questioning the very logic of how she questioned him.

"Yes, how many of you are there?"

"Not many, none like me, really," he said. "You haven't had your wine. I swear it's good. The best in Solus. We haven't much in the way of food. A good cup of wine's a royal treat."

"I'm not thirsty." She lifted the cup, but did not drink from it. Then she returned it to the boy, who frowned as he placed it on the stones. When he bent, his tunic lifted to reveal studded leather and the hilt of a blade.

Servants bore no weapons, but she guessed he had given up that life. He was a rebel, but the blade made her wonder about him. Merit had made a life out of distrusting others, and she wasn't about to change her nature. She stepped slowly away from the servant, circling the conical chamber, making it seem as if she were studying the place, which was quite grand and no doubt belonged to the structures of the Middle Kingdom.

"Is he coming soon, this master of yours? I haven't a place to sit and it's been a long day. Also, is Ott here? We met only briefly, but I'd like to see him again."

Merit wondered what lay beyond the little door. The Harkans had to be back there somewhere. She was half tempted to rush past the boy, but he was armed and she was not. *Best not to tempt fate,* she thought.

"He'll arrive," said the boy. He must have seen the worry on her face. "When he's ready, I suppose."

"The bastard wants me to wait? I might as well. I've waited in every chamber from Harwen to the Hall of Ministers and none of it has come to anything. Are you sure your master's here?"

"Oh, most definitely."

"Well, that's good news. You didn't by chance serve in the house of Saad, did you?" she asked the boy.

"No, nothing like that," he said. There was contempt in his voice, bold un-servantlike contempt. He was a soldier, she guessed, or maybe just her assassin. Merit turned to defend herself with the only thing she had, the only weapon she had ever wielded: words.

"I don't know what the bastard told you about me. Perhaps he said I've named myself queen without having the right to do so, that I rule with neither the sanction of Tolemy nor the eld."

"He's said nothing, but those *are* the rumors."

"Well, they are both true, so let me tell you this, boy. I fought for my kingdom, our kingdom—if you think yourself Harkan. I've dealt a blow to the man in red. I've done more to fight him than your master and his meager raids. I took back our kingdom and now I've come to take Mered's—to return the favor, I suppose. Don't you think that's a worthy cause? That maybe I ought not to be left waiting? Perhaps you should go find your master and tell him to hurry his ass over here, because, like it or not, I am queen and I command the army of Harkana. He is a boy without a throne or a kingdom. He has nothing but his guard, but they'll all be dead soon enough. He'll be dead. Barca races toward Harwen. Time is short. If the boy wants to help our cause he'll need to show his face."

"And what cause is that?" he asked, but before he'd finished his sentence he drew his dagger and pressed the tip to her chin. She yelped, shocked not just by the blade but the realization that accompanied it.

"You're him!" Merit exclaimed. "The bastard of Harkana."

⇥48⇤

Ren fought the urge to use the knife.

No, he thought, reversing what had only been blind impulse.

He loosened his grip on the blade, but the desire to wield it resurfaced just as quickly as it had vanished. A life for a life. That was what the people of Solus said. His sister had thrice tried to kill him. He ought to at least return the favor this once. It was only fair. The knife had already pricked her pretty skin, and with just a bit more force it would break through that perfect surface. He found his grip and his knuckles went white. Merit trembled, her body quivering against his own. She twisted, attempting to free herself, but his hold did not waver. Ren had thought he'd enjoy the ruse, that it would give him some time to take stock of the sister he had never met, whom he had never even seen before she stumbled into the tower. But the whole thing had done little more than frustrate him. His anger had bubbled over and, unexpectedly, he'd found his dagger pressed to her throat. In truth, he didn't even know if he *could* take revenge on Merit. He certainly hadn't intended to do it. He'd set Shenn free and bound the man's wounds after he tried to take Ren's life. He had returned Shenn's violence with kindness, so he held back whatever urge drove him to dig that blade into Merit's skin. He'd run through fire and killed the black beast of the Soleri. He'd been told he had the blood of some otherworldly being in his veins. The queen regent didn't frighten him.

He sheathed his blade and set her free.

"Hell of a way to meet," he said, "but you earned it, didn't you?" Ren asked, half grinning, fingers sore. He hadn't realized how much pressure he'd put upon the grip of that dagger—not until his fingers came loose from the thing. Every bit of pain she'd inflicted on him had poured itself into that hand. He swore he could have driven the blade clean through her skull. Even if it wasn't his way, she'd pushed him to the edge, nearly forcing him to become something he was not: a creature like her.

The queen did not answer his question. Perhaps she was waiting to see what he would do next.

"The knife could not be helped," he said. It wasn't an apology, just a statement of fact.

"I know," she replied, her voice quiet, accepting. She would not shy away from what she'd done. Ren saw that.

"Still unrepentant?"

"In a way, yes, and in another, no," Merit said. "As regent, I did what was best for the kingdom. They were not proud deeds, but I thought them necessary. I feel no emotion toward my actions—nor should you."

"We do as we must," said Ren.

"Exactly."

"Well, screw that. If I had done *what must be done* I'd have cut you down for treason, for plotting to kill the heir of your own kingdom, for fratricide, and for pissing me off without end. I know what *your kind* does and does not do, and I want none of it! I do what I think is *right*. Have anything to say to that?"

"I have terms," Merit said, and afterward she was silent, undisturbed. She acted as if her case were immune to his own and perhaps, in her estimation, it was.

Ren resisted the urge to unsheathe his blade.

I have terms. The words echoed in his thoughts. She wanted to treat with him, to begin whatever negotiation she'd planned. Ott had already explained her intentions; Ren knew her offer. He hardly needed to hear it, and he wouldn't—not until she'd addressed *his* concerns. By hearing her terms, he would acknowledge that she was a regent, or something like one, that she held power in Harkana. *That she is my equal.* He wanted none of that. In truth, he wanted to throw her back into the street.

There was no family here, no reunion, no love. His only family was Tye and Kollen, Ott. They were loyal.

"Terms," he said the word with as much scorn as he could muster. "Not even a moment to speak, to embrace, to welcome the half-brother who was stolen from your home? I don't recall your face, but you were ten and six when they took me. You must have known mine. Are you not happy to see it? Did you not want to hold the boy that was once your little brother?" Ren asked, angry now, irritated that she had not even bothered to acknowledge him.

"The blade," she said, calmly indicating the dagger. "It may have prevented me from embracing you." Her voice was quiet, impassive.

"True enough, but would you have acted differently if I hadn't drawn it?" He unsheathed his father's dagger, toying with it. Ren answered her cool countenance with naked aggression. He saw no need to veil his emotions. Briefly he wondered if he should have used the knife.

Too late for regrets.

"We cannot second guess the past," said Merit. "When you returned to Harwen, I did want to see you, and I told Father as much. I said he'd robbed the family of our reunion when he sent you away on the hunt without even setting foot in the Hornring. I wanted to meet you, but in a way I was glad I did not. Call me a coward, but I thought it better that I did not see your face."

"No doubt," said Ren.

Merit shook the dirt from her robe. He supposed she was trying to improve her appearance, and she almost pulled it off, but the filth of her garb undid whatever queenly aspirations she held.

"I *was* ten and six when you left. I said goodbye to my three-year-old brother. Do you think that was easy?" She drew closer than he preferred. "It's been a long time. In my thoughts, I see you as a child, stumbling in the dirt and plowing into urns. There is nothing afterward. No one visits the priory. It's forbidden—at least for the family. Whatever happened to you in Solus is a mystery. A stolen life. Your whole identity was taken from you, but not by my hand. Blame the men who took you from your home, the ones I've come to overthrow. Join me."

"I—" Ren broke off. He heard nothing but honesty in her words, but he hesitated. He was no fool. She'd once sought to claim his life, and now she had the audacity to argue that they were allies. He resisted the urge to speak. He kicked the little door, and a dozen or so men from the kingsguard shuffled out. Asher was there, and he embraced Merit as he said he would, confirming that she was indeed the first daughter of Arko and not some imposter sent by Mered. Ott came, too, and greeted Merit.

Eyeing the crowd, Ren made his decision. He would not bargain with his sister, not one-on-one. He would allow her to talk. He'd let his companions hear her case.

"You are here to speak, Merit of Harkana. Get on with it," said Ren.

He withdrew into the ranks of the kingsguard. He stood among his men, beside Ott, next to Tye.

"I make no argument," said Merit. "I offer only facts. Haren Barca is not the man you think. I share a secret with you and trust that it will not leave this chamber. He is not from Sola. He is Barden Hark-Wadi, brother of Arko, nurtured in the High Desert and in Solus. He was raised in hiding, where he spent his life preparing to strike at the people who forced him into exile. He is our kin and is in need of our help. As we speak, he rides toward Solus with his rebels, with a horde of outlanders, with freed servants, and with sell swords. Barden travels with the storms, coming with the dust and sand to meet up with the Harkan Army. He force-marches his men through secret passages beneath the Dromus. He will reach the city by daybreak. This is a fact. Barden will strike at Solus while it is weakly defended. Mered's eye is on Feren. The empire must eat, so he's sent half his men to the north. His army is stretched thin. Barden knows this and plans to take advantage of this weakness. Within a day, he will besiege Solus. When he does that, he will trap you within the city. You have only one option. One way out. Join us. Use your men and take hold of the Rising Gate. Capture the pylons and the winch room. Secure them so Barden can ride unmolested into the city. I have drawings and instructions. The scrolls explain how the structures are accessed and how they can be breached." Merit produced the parchments she'd carried from Harwen. "With this advantage, Barden will take the city. He will strike swiftly and put an end to the empire." She turned in a circle, looking at all of them. Many she knew well, Ren saw it in their eyes and in the way they nodded as she spoke. "The Rising Gate is the doorway to your freedom." Merit raised her voice. There was power in her words, strength that came from constant exercise, from a lifetime of ruling. Ren had none of that, no practice and no polish. His elocution could be outmatched by a goatherd. *I'm no politician*, he thought. Hence, he gave no rebuttal.

Ren needed a way out of Solus, and she offered one.

⋛49⋚

"What did the great warlords of Feren think of their new queen?" Kepi asked, her voice betraying a mix of mockery and annoyance. She stood outside the makeshift council chamber at Caerwynt, leaning against a narrow stone parapet that overlooked the rift. She'd spent the better part of that morning making her case to the warlords of Feren, explaining her intentions for the coming war. She described the army that stood on the far side of the valley and the need to confront rather than placate Mered.

"They were all very thrilled to see the kite," said Ferris. "Only one of the twelve is old enough to recall Barrin's kite, and he was just a boy at the time. No one doubts that you are the Kitelord."

"But?" Kepi saw reluctance in his eye. There was something Ferris did not want to say. "Was the kite not enough, were my words unconvincing? Mered's army masses at our border, and he's already shown he has the means to cross the rift. What further motivation do they require?"

"A man."

"You joke."

"If only. The laws of patrimony determine who is and is not heir to the kingdom. The laws say that Adin is heir."

"That makes no sense. They bowed to Dagrun. He had no kite, nor did he have any of that royal blood they've put so much value upon."

"Dagrun's reign was unique and it didn't—"

"We both know how it ended. Honestly, though, let that boy try to earn the kite's loyalty."

"You might wish you hadn't said that."

"Are they seriously going to escort this tool of the empire to the stone forest so he can prove his worth?"

"Some think that is the best of course of action. Let the kite choose the king. It is our way."

"It *is* your way, and the matter's settled. There is only one kite; the choice is made. If that boy sets foot on Feren soil, I'll have the kite tear him limb from limb. That ought to quiet the lords."

Ferris laughed. "Between my garrison and yours we don't need their men, but we do need their coin and their provisions. If the battle is protracted, if we are besieged or if we take the fight to Solus, we'll need these lords to provide a proper supply train. Soldiers do not win wars, not by themselves. We need resources."

"I know as much, so cut to it. How many voted in my favor?"

"You had my vote."

"Only you?"

"Old Arni raised a hand, which was good."

"Why?"

"He's wealthy."

"What about Deccan? He was in the Chathair. He doubts me?"

"No, he voted in your favor."

"Anyone else?"

Ferris shook his head.

"Three of the twelve voted in my favor and the rest want to give Barrin's son a go at it?"

"That is the consensus. Those men were not in the Chathair, except Deccan. They didn't fight at your side or see the arrival of the kite. I did. You have every soldier in the Feren Army at your back; many of them were there as well. It's not a weak position."

"Nor is it a strong war footing."

"No. In fact, I half suspect they are using this heir as an excuse to avoid fulfilling their oaths. They'd rather keep their men at home, farming their fields and making crops. They're a bunch of cowards. The bastards want us to do the fighting and they don't want to pay a single crescent for it."

"This is Mered's doing," she said. "He's bribed them, hasn't he? This man from Solus has found a way to divide us. He's driving us apart before the conflict even begins." Kepi drew her blade and looked around for something to slash.

Ferris smirked. "You're going to have to learn to fight with words as well as iron. Mered knows that you are young and inexperienced. He is no doubt aware of the uniqueness of your position. You are the first woman to be chosen as Kitelord, but that's not the only issue."

"Enlighten me."

"Our army, Feren's army, it's not . . . how do I say this . . . ?"

"Up to the task?"

"Dagrun spent a considerable amount of coin to enlarge the standing army at Caer Rifka, but it's not an imperial force."

"We're not fighting the empire, not yet."

"I know, but there are rumors from Solus. Word has reached my ear that Mered has declared himself Father Protector. We could have bested his house army, but if he sends the army of the Protector north . . . well."

"I understand," said Kepi.

"We cannot fight the empire and Mered knows it, but our news from the south is not entirely bad. Barca is on the march. My men say he is a day's ride from Solus, maybe less. If he attacks the city, he may draw off Mered's armies, but they *will* return. The issue will not go away."

"What do we do?"

"The warlords believe we should comply with the imperial demands, that a little suffering at the dinner table is preferable to spilling blood on the battlefield."

"These men call themselves warlords?"

"Goatherds and lumbermen would be more suitable titles," said Ferris.

Kepi leaned against the parapet, craning her neck to get a look at the rift and what lay beyond it. A distant rustle caught her ear. "Who is aware of this little conference of ours?"

"Just the warlords. No one knows about the meeting. It was kept secret, the scrolls sealed. We are at war and we hardly want our foe to know that we are all gathered in one place."

"Yes, a good strategy, were we not betrayed."

"What do you mean—" Ferris drew his blade as he caught sight of the approaching soldiers. "The red army gathers on our doorstep," he muttered. "How convenient."

"No," said Kepi. "It's worse. Look there!" She pointed to a legion of bronze-armored soldiers who had assembled on the far side of the rift. "That's the army of the Protector, isn't it? Only they wear the bronze."

"I see it, and they've brought more than just bridges. Look there." Ferris indicated a distant stand of trees and beyond that a line of catapults, followed by what seemed like endless rows of armored chariots. "Those are the old machines of war, the ones the Soleri built to conquer the lower kingdoms. I've never seen anything like them . . ." Ferris came up short, out of breath or perhaps out of words.

Kepi stood beside him. "This is impossible . . . we need time. We're not ready, we're not even united . . . not yet."

"What do you mean?" asked Ferris.

"Well, if this attack isn't reason enough for the warlords to gather at my back, I'll give them another. They want me to prove myself, don't they? They wish to give the boy a shot at my throne? Well, then I suppose I'll have to comply. We need to stall for time, and this ought to buy us at least another day. Adin offered me a duel once. I think it's time to hold the heir of Feren to his promise."

⇒50⇐

The sky was still dark, the air quiet, when the kingsguard of Harkana threw open the tower door and marched into the empty streets of Solus. The alleys and avenues were dimly lit, the air filled with sand. The black shields moved three abreast, sandals tapping on the cobblestones. They traversed a narrow street, trampling a city guardsman, a beggar, and who knows what else.

Ren led, Asher pressed to his shoulder, Tye following beside them. Ott was there, too, strapped to Butcher's back, carried like a child and protesting as if he might actually be one. Ren had seen the humiliation on his brother's face as they fastened him to the larger man, but it could not be helped. Ott could not march alongside the Harkans. He could barely walk, but he refused to be left behind, and he had given them reason enough to carry him with them. Ott knew the roads and was perhaps the only one in their company who could lead them to the Rising Gate. The rest of them—Ren, the kingsguard—were strangers in the city of the gods. Even with a map, they might quickly find themselves lost or confused.

Merit remained in the tower, alone save for a single guard. Ren said he'd send soldiers to fetch her when the battle was over, but she'd waved away his offer. *Barden will come for me. Have no worry,* she said. So he let her go without even saying farewell or attempting some form of embrace. He had wanted a reconciliation of some kind, but she remained distant. She was a monarch, a woman whose every act spoke of calculation, not emotion. *She's afraid,* he thought, *scared to let down her guard.* She'd spent her whole life at court. He knew that, and he understood that he could not match her poise or the tone of voice she used to capture the ear of every servant and soldier. Ren guessed that was why she never let her queenly demeanor slip. She was too afraid to lose whatever respect she held with the men. *Too afraid to be my sister.*

He was motherless, and he'd lost his father the day they met. He'd finally met one of his sisters, but she hadn't acted like one. She was a queen who'd come to negotiate with a reluctant ally. Nothing more.

The whole thing stunk.

Hence, Ren turned his attention to Barden's plans, to the streets, to Tye, and to making certain she never left his sight. Even in the dark, he watched the girl. He observed the fearless determination in her eye, and the way her fingers wrapped the pommel of her sword. The weapon was meant for a man twice her size, and the scabbard dragged on the cobbles. She'd strapped on a bit of leather armor. Along with the sword, it must have weighed as much as Tye, but she marched alongside the rest of the guard. She was one of them, and she wanted this victory as much as any man. He followed her until she caught his eye and slapped him once on the cheek. "Get your head together, Ren. Focus on the streets or you'll end up tripping over them."

She was right, of course. There was work to be done. Their task was to find a postern marked with a black cross. Inside, a man loyal to Barden would grant them access to the pylons that flanked the Rising Gate, as well as the winch room. From what Ren could gather, the walls of Solus were vast in size, complex in scope, ancient, and well fortified. Three bulwarks protected the city: a low scarp wall, followed by the city's first great rampart, a mud-brick construction erected during the Old Kingdom, then a second one built of stone during the New Kingdom, when the emperors' relentless provocations brought about the need for better defenses. All this stood in Barden's path, but he did not intend to breach these walls. Barden wanted to ride his army right through them. The Rising Gate was in truth not a gate but a long tunnel that ran from the scarp wall all the way past the third and final fortification.

Barden wants us to hold that passage for him, Ren thought. It was no small favor.

"This," said Asher as he knocked against Ren, "is either the start of your reign or the end of it—your last march or your first."

"Fuck's sake, man. You have a penchant for drama," said Ren.

"And you're leading the kingsguard against an empire. There's a reason why no army has breached these walls in two centuries."

"Damn the reasons. No army's been trapped in here either."

"Quiet," said Ott. "The sun'll be up soon."

"Can we find the gates before the first light?" Ren asked, hopeful, but

Ott only shook his head. None of them knew how long it would take to reach the gate or what trouble they might find on their way.

They rounded a corner and Ren glimpsed a distant shimmer, a bit of light hidden behind a cluster of temples. It was nothing more than sand glowing yellow in the predawn sky, but he knew what lay below it. Even at this distance he felt the presence of the twelve. And again, he heard that buzzing at the back of his head. It was louder this time, and it almost resolved into something he could understand. He wished Noll were at his side to explain the noise in his head, but he was gone. Ren guessed he'd slipped out in the confusion, that he had come to deliver his message and then gone off to do whatever bidding his gods demanded, leaving Ren with more questions than answers. He recalled the ceremony in the temple of Re and the way Noll had held up the eld horn. The kings of Harkana carved the antler into a sword, a weapon, but he guessed it wasn't meant for fighting. In all likelihood, it wasn't anything more than a ceremonial sword. Its true purpose had been forgotten or concealed. After witnessing that ceremony, Ren guessed it was a wand of some kind, the holy standard of an ancient ruler, or just some half-forgotten tool of the Soleri. He'd seen Noll lift up the horn as if it were some great and twisted staff, as if he were some shaman poised in the middle of his conjuring—and maybe that wasn't too far from the truth. Ren knew what Noll had tried to invoke.

As he glanced once more in the direction of the garden, he felt something stir within him. He'd sensed it when he took the eld horn and when he'd slain the black beast. He felt it in that strange buzzing in the back of his thoughts, and he focused on it briefly—

Tye stumbled into Ren, breaking his concentration. "You're shuddering," said Tye. "You closed your eyes and were speaking some language I couldn't understand. Get it together, man."

Ren massaged his temples. He'd almost forgotten Tye was moving alongside him. He'd forgotten the march, their mission, and Asher as well. The former captain of the kingsguard was looking at Ren and shaking his head. "This is no time to lose your nerve," he said.

Ren nearly growled. "I'm not losing my damned nerve. There are things you don't know. Things none of you—"

"It's all right, Ren," said Tye, her voice sounding warmer than usual. "It doesn't matter what's in that head of yours. Just keep your eyes on the street. We're nearly at the pylons and daybreak is upon us."

It was true. The golden rays of the sun shot like spears through the dusty air, catching every mote of sand, making them shimmer and dance in the day's first light.

Asher coughed, covered his mouth, and barked at Ott, "How far?"

"We're close, so shut your mouth. I need to focus," said Ott, stuttering, coughing up a bit of sand as he studied the map. He pointed to a narrow street that veered to the right, and the army hurried in that direction. Sand whipped at their faces and the soldiers jostled one another from every side. A high and tinny note pierced the early morning air, a horn calling out from some distant tower.

"What's that?" Ren asked.

"A call to arms," said Ott.

"Then it's too late," said Asher, "we've been discovered."

"No, that sound has nothing to do with us," said Ott. "The alarm belongs to the Protector, and his men are *outside* the city walls." Ott was quiet for a moment, pensive. "It can only mean one thing: Barden has reached the gates. The battle is under way."

As they came upon the Rising Gate, the Protector's Army swarmed the wall walk while rows of archers gathered at the pylons, readying themselves for the first volley. Men ran in every direction, but they were all focused on the desert beyond, not on the city at their backs.

"Barden's distracted them," said Ren. "They're protecting themselves from the wrong attack."

"He must have ridden through the night," said Asher, "or he used the storm as cover."

"Or both," said Ren.

"He's taken them by surprise," said Tye.

"Perhaps," said Asher, "but it'll do him little good. We're late."

"Maybe he was early," said Ren. The soldiers on the wall walk did appear to be unprepared, as if Barden's army had materialized out of the sand itself and surprised them. Some were still gathering their armor, tying leather straps, fitting bronze plates to their bodies, or tossing arrows into a quiver. No one looked at the black shields as they crept up to the pylon. The door with the black cross marked on it stood before them, and the postern was indeed open. They never saw the man who turned the lock and pulled back the drawbar.

Ren darted toward the door, but Asher caught his sleeve, making him wait while a foot soldier entered. Ren shook himself free and was second to enter, Asher at his heels.

Darkness enveloped them.

"We go our separate ways," said Asher, "just as we discussed."

"I'll see you when it's done," said Ren. The Harkans needed to secure the two pylons and the winch room above the passage, so they split into smaller groups. The men went this way and that, stumbling through the dark passages inside the walls. Ren agreed to secure the winch room. If Barden could be trusted, it was the least-fortified position. The main body of the Protector's guard occupied the pylons. The heaviest fighting would be there, so Asher claimed that task.

Tye held up a lamp she took from the wall, giving them a little light as they made their way up the stone-carved steps, across a narrow traverse, and over to the winch-room door. Ren drew his sword, Tye still holding the light, Butcher carrying Ott, the boy giving directions, though no one was listening to him.

"Quiet," said Ren.

A door banded in iron and cut from blackthorn barred their path. He pressed his ear to the wood and listened, but no sound penetrated the stout timbers. He raised three fingers. The fight was nearly upon them and he felt it, in his veins and in his muscles. Ren's hunger was gone, his fear too. He lowered his fingers, one at a time.

Three. Two. One.

He hit the door, which gave way easily. It wasn't locked. Clearly the men hadn't expected an attack from within. Ren and the others stumbled upon twenty or thirty archers, bowstrings taut, arrows trained on murder holes in the floor. Past the bows, men poked staves through narrow grooves in the floor, driving them down on the invaders. Others manned trapdoors, heating oil, and tar, the smoke filling up the room.

An enormous scuffle had broken out in the tunnel below them, and it occupied all of the workers' attention. Barden's army must have made it past the first gate, but Ren guessed they were caught, blocked by a second barrier. The bowmen let loose a volley and the passage echoed with a dozen different cries. The defenders nocked arrows and readied themselves for a second volley.

Ren didn't hesitate. The Harkans crowded into the long and narrow winch room, ready for a fight, set to meet whatever resistance was in store for them, but they saw only blank stares and looks of complete astonishment. The workers were completely unprepared for a fight. The archers had no swords, and their bows were hardly useful in such close quarters. The men with staves could not remove them from the slots, and the pots of oil were bolted and hinged. They could only rotate them this way and that, between the fire and the trapdoor. The archers had some skill, but the rest were technicians of a sort, men who were practiced in the use of all the various contraptions.

"They're defenseless," said Ren. A swift knock across the jaw from one of the bowmen corrected his arrogance. He tumbled backward into Butcher, who had just laid down Ott. The stout Harkan caught Ren with one arm and used his massive hammer to smash the bowman across the chest while all around him the Harkans filled the winch room, surrounding their foes and quickly overwhelming them. Ren recovered his wits and raised his sword. He was ready for the fight, but there was none to be had.

Without any sort of discussion, the defending bowmen simply dropped their weapons. The others abandoned their staves or left their pots to simmer. These were not soldiers. They were outnumbered and unprepared. The workers scurried to the far side of the chamber, fearful perhaps that the Harkans would slaughter them.

"You're him?" asked one of the workers.

"The Bane of Solus, the one who's been sticking it to Mered?" said another, a hint of admiration in his voice.

"You're the Harkan bastard," said a third.

"I am," said Ren, not with pride or any another other emotion. He no longer cared whether he was a bastard. "I'm the king of the Harkans."

"We know as much," said one man, face stained with oil, tunic burned at the cuff.

"Go then," said Ren. "There's no need for bloodshed. Leave this place."

These were clearly the words the men had wanted to hear. As quickly as he spoke them, the workers cleared the corridor, throwing off their tools and hurrying out the door.

"We've done it," said Tye.

"We've done nothing," said Ren. "Listen."

Indeed, the fight was not yet over. Through high windows and half-open doors, the sounds of battle rattled the air. The kingsguard had not yet taken the flanking pylons. Only the winch room was clear. Sounds of hammering and scraping rang through the murder holes. Barden's men were trying to cut through some barrier, but Ren doubted they'd have any luck.

"There must be a gate or some other contraption that's blocking Barden's army. Find it," he ordered. But when he looked up Tye was already taking hold of a great wheel, pulling at one of the spokes and glaring at Ren with annoyance.

"A little help," she said. "This damn thing was made for a dozen men to turn."

Ren went to the wheel, as did the others. Twenty or so hands made the first turn. The floor rattled and the soldiers below let loose a great cry of joy. A few more turns and the path would likely be clear.

With a cry, they pulled at the great wheel—one turn, then another. In a moment, the task would be complete, but when Ren put his hand to the next spoke he found himself fumbling for his sword instead of the wheel.

The red army had entered through the door at the far side of the chamber, blades glistening in the firelight.

⇒ 51 ⇐

A barren stretch of earth served as the dueling ground between the queen of the Ferens and the would-be king. Both sides had agreed on the place. It was neutral ground, or the closest thing they could find to it. Hence, when the sun rose above the horizon, both sides rode out from their camps and met at the rift's edge. It was an ugly place, but perhaps that was appropriate. This was a duel to the death. Blood would be spilled. For her part, Kepi quite liked the spot. The sand and rocks reminded the young queen of her desert homeland. She dropped from her saddle and handed off the reins to one of her soldiers. Ferris rode out with his sworn men. If the duel turned ugly, if it went from a civil contest to a brawl, he was ready for a fight.

On the far side of the clearing, a red soldier held Adin by the waist as the boy slid awkwardly from his mount. She looked for the limp he'd shown at the rift. *Is it there?* she wondered. The boy walked with confidence, but his pose was awkward, his movements slow. He was thin, and tall. His arms were awkwardly long, his body malnourished. She pitied him. Kepi yearned for an honest fight, but she wasn't certain she'd find one.

Ferris had volunteered to be her substitute, so he stood at her side. Kepi leaned in close and whispered, "When you speak with Mered's man, ask him to call it off."

Ferris shot her a questioning glance.

"Look at the boy—he's all skin and bones," she said. "We're here to stall for time. Killing him will be like swatting a fly. I can't do it."

"You may not have a choice," said Ferris. "Don't forget. You asked for this duel."

"I know. I thought he was injured. He looks more like a sickling, and a weak one at that. They must have pulled him right out of the depths of the priory."

"No," said Ferris. "Tolemy set him free after the emperor recognized Dagrun's rule. I heard the boy was taken by traders, who sold him to one of my fellow warlords. He was sent to Rifka as a wedding gift, but the boy escaped."

"He was at my wedding? He's the servant who escaped?"

"Yes, so I suppose he's seen your tits just like the rest of us."

She knocked him not unkindly on the jaw.

"It must have been terribly cold that day."

She hit him again.

"I am bloody serious and that boy *was* at your wedding, and if he hadn't run he would have been one of *your* servants. Come to think of it, if Dagrun hadn't taken the throne in the first place, Adin would have one day been king. Strange to ponder the paths fate offers us, isn't it?"

"No," said Kepi. "Not at all. I make my own fate, but I can't stand an unfair fight."

"We don't pick our enemies," said Ferris.

"And I don't want to fight—not after seeing him again."

"I'll do what I can."

He shuffled off, exhibiting his usual swagger, hand on the pommel of his blade, whistling a bit, as if he were off to hear a busker sing and not standing between two great armies, negotiating a fight that would cost one opponent their life.

What a complete ass, thought Kepi. *If I had the stomach to love another, I might be interested.*

A red-robed man spoke for Adin. He called himself Admentus and he wore another of those madder-colored mantles, this one jeweled with lapis and sparkling in the first rays of the sun. A deep cowl hid his face, but he threw it back when Ferris approached. She watched the young warlord talk, his fingers resting on his blade, daring the man in red to give him a reason to draw it.

Then Ferris turned, spinning on his heel at what appeared to be the end of their discussion. As he walked back to the place where she stood, he rolled his eyes, which was his way of saying that the fight was still on, or so she guessed.

She waited while he walked the last of the ten paces, returning to where she stood.

"So?"

"The terms remain intact," he said, his tone mocking. She guessed he had just repeated the last words spoken by the man in red. Ferris leaned in close and spoke. "I did what I could, but he wanted none of it."

"It'll be blood for blood," she said. "We fight until one of us is dead." Kepi eyed the sandy earth.

"Are you still trying to figure a way out of this?" Ferris asked. "I'll kill the runt if you like."

"And break the terms? No. I set this thing in motion. It's my duty."

She drew her sword and gave it a spin. It was a newer blade, forged in Feren and perhaps a bit heavy for her taste, but it was the right length. She measured it against her hip bone, and the balance felt good in her hand. She'd chosen an angular blade with a pointed tip, one that could be used for piercing armor at the joints. She'd hadn't bothered to don the queen's raiment. It might have made a good show, but she'd come here to fight, so she wore leathers. It was light armor, but speed had always been her advantage so she didn't think it an error to wear such slender protection. *Make it swift,* she thought, *get it done and end this war.*

Chalk formed the circle in which they would fight.

She kicked at the powder, stirring a pale cloud at her feet.

At the far side of the ring, the boy removed his mantle while Mered's soldiers fit the last bits of armor to his hands and neck. They placed a helm atop his head and secured it with a strap. He wore the gray mail that was common among Feren soldiers.

Kepi tried to meet Adin's gaze, but he looked away, choosing instead to study his feet. Maybe he was too fearful or too nervous to meet her eyes, or perhaps he was afraid he would betray whatever deception he planned.

"Blades," called a voice.

"Ready?" asked Ferris.

"Do I have a choice?" said Kepi. She called out to the other side. "Stop fussing with the boy's armor and let's get this over with."

The Ferens gave a hoot. A few clapped, but the rest came up short. It was hard to find humor in such a moment. Everyone was tense, even

Mered's men scanned the horizon, seeking some betrayal. *It's always the dishonest types who expect treachery*, she thought as they fiddled with the buckles on Adin's armor.

Kepi planned no deceptions. She sought only to buy time, not to kill a boy, though she guessed she'd have little choice in the matter.

Her foot crossed the white ring, initiating the fight. She raised her blade, but Adin was still fussing with his mail. Seeing that she had engaged him, he threw off his attendants and stepped across the line. He advanced a step or two before he realized that he had no sword.

Kepi whistled when she saw the empty scabbard.

The Ferens all whooped again, louder this time.

She cocked her head and pointed with her blade. At the far side of the ring, a boy ran out with her opponent's weapon. She could already see it was the wrong type of sword. They'd chosen one that matched Kepi's, but he needed a longer blade to suit his height and reach. It ought to have been the flat kind of sword that was commonly used for slashing at leathers. The red army was as inept as it was bold, apparently.

Adin stuck out his hand and the blade fell crooked into his grip.

One hit, she reminded herself. *I am queen. All I have to do is kill this hapless boy and my throne will be uncontested.* She advanced, careful to stay outside of Adin's reach.

"What did Mered offer you?" she asked plainly, openly.

"My throne," he said, his words sounding as honest as her own. "What is rightfully mine."

"The kite begs to differ." She raised her eyes toward the sky. The great bird circled, its shadow darting across the field.

"Perhaps it came to see my victory, to land at *my* side," said Adin.

"It came because I called it," she said, and the kite flew low and settled upon her shoulder.

"It's our duel," said Adin quickly, fearfully. "One-on-one." The great bird was no doubt intimidating. She told it to fly, but it did not go far and its great wings cast whirling shadows across the field, reminding all of its presence.

"You'll never be anything more than a rich man's puppet," she said, advancing a bit, blade held level.

"I'll have a throne," said Adin, who mimicked her stance.

"Yes, you'll warm it while Mered is out wielding the power that should be yours, Adin. He'll own you." Kepi took one careful step forward followed by another.

"No one will own me. He's just—" Adin's feet froze in place, stuck like his tongue.

"A means to an end? He'll be the end of Feren. The kingdom will be a warren where servants grow crops for the empire." Kepi took another step forward.

Adin shook his head, angry, maybe even a bit confused. Perhaps the boy had not fully thought through what he'd done. Regret colored his face bright red. He took two long strides and thrust out his blade, but she had already moved out of the way before he finished adjusting his feet. She tapped his sword, teasing him.

In anger, Adin struck again while the two stood close together, but she knocked his blade aside. The edge of his sword grazed her armor, but it did not pierce the boiled-leather hide.

"A first hit for the Feren heir," said a voice in the distance, someone in Adin's camp.

Ferris howled, then he must have uttered some joke because the Ferens all laughed. Adin's strike was more of a miss and she guessed he'd said something to that effect.

She breathed deeply and circled her opponent, feet shuffling in the sand. *One hit. One hit and it'll be over.*

"Why don't you go?" she asked. "Strike out north, beyond the Gray Wood. Find your own place, in the Northwoods or beyond. There are great, uncharted territories you might occupy. Leave this kingdom, Adin. Don't give up your life for some bloody tract of land."

"It's my land. I survived the priory, and I went back and saved every ransom from it. We are owed these kingdoms. I can't give that up. Your brother shares my sentiment. He's my friend—did you know that?" he asked, still recovering his strength, chest heaving, blade not quite level.

"I heard you betrayed him, left him in Solus." She was guessing, mostly, but she must have struck a chord because his face darkened. He struck again. This time in great anger, and again clumsily. He raised his sword above his head before he brought it down. It was a silly and somewhat theatrical move, and it gave her more than enough time to prepare her riposte.

When his blade missed the mark, she caught it with the tip of her sword and used all that unexpended energy to send the sword spinning out of Adin's grasp. It was a dueler's trick, not the sort of stunt you pull on the battlefield, but it worked wonderfully in the ring. The Ferens cheered when his blade struck the dirt, a cloud of dust briefly concealing the sword.

Kepi might have killed him then, when he showed her his back, but there was something too easy about it. She allowed him to retrieve his blade.

She retreated. One step. Two.

She felt suddenly cruel. She was toying with the boy. *Time to end this,* she thought.

One hit and it'll be done.

Strike.

This time her words were transformed into action. She leapt with such speed and agility that the boy did not even perceive the attack. To his eyes, she guessed she had simply appeared out of nowhere with the blade driving downward at him. It was a killing blow, a strike at the top of the spine. It would have been a perfect kill, a quick and painless death, executed in half a heartbeat's span, but the boy jerked desperately to one side and the blow went wide of its intended point of entry. The iron went deep but struck only muscle, driving into the flesh, delving so deeply that she could not pull the blade out. Kepi stumbled backward.

"It's finished—he's finished," she said, and he truly was finished. The boy could not move, let alone fight, not until the blade was pulled from his back, but Adin could not reach the hilt and the rules of the game forbade anyone else from entering the ring. Adin knelt, writhing in pain, trying in vain to snatch at the blade.

"End this!" she cried. "End the contest or I'll pull the blade myself."

"It ends when one of you dies. Kill him," said Mered's man, his face blank, voice cold.

"No," she said. "The matter is settled." She backed away from Adin. He needed a physician. If the blade were carefully removed, he might live, but she doubted he'd fight again, certainly not today. He would struggle against death from this moment onward.

Kepi took a slow step backward, crossing the line of white chalk. "It's ended."

"No," Admentus said, voice as cold as iron. "You violated the rules of the contest. If you'd killed him you would have been the victor, but in failing to do so you have forfeited our agreement." The man in red drew up his cowl and retreated. Soldiers clustered around him and she realized he must be their commander, the one they'd been fighting against all along. He looked at her with a scowl, with disdain.

"We are finished here," he said. "Tomorrow, we take Feren by force."

≋52≋

The red army advanced on the black shields, making their way across the winch room, spears wet with blood. Perhaps they'd slaughtered their own workers as they fled the chamber. That would explain the blood, or maybe the red army had met up with an unlucky group of Harkans. Ren didn't know, and it hardly mattered. The men were coming for him, slowly navigating the long and narrow corridor, two abreast, spears bobbing as the soldiers dodged pots of bubbling oil and long wooden staves. Beneath them, Barden's army howled in frustration.

"It's not too late to fall back," said Butcher. "There's no shame in it. You're the king's son and we're just a bunch of killers. Let us do what we're good at."

Ren might have taken him up on the offer, but the soldiers in red were already upon them. Butcher crushed a spear midshaft, shattering a stave that might have split Ren in two.

"There's only room for one of us, so stand aside," Butcher said. He swung again, this time taking down a pair of spearmen, crushing their staves in a single blow. Another Harkan, a man named Arix, shouldered past Ren, throwing himself over the fallen spearmen, squeezing into the ranks of Mered's men, where he drew a pair of daggers and cut all who stood within his reach.

"I can't tell if I've wetted my steel or if the damn thing is just covered in red paint," Butcher cried. He was nearly out of earshot. The Harkans rushed past Ren, and Mered's soldiers advanced. Soon, they were all pressed so tightly together they could hardly move. Ren was shoved backward and he clambered into one of the trapdoors, nearly falling through the open hatch as the ancient wood broke loose from its hinges and fell to the tunnel below. He found himself gazing down into the passageway. A dozen soldiers stared up at Ren, eager to join the battle. Ren cast about for a ladder or something like one. Chains operated the pots of oil. The one nearest him had already been emptied, so he yanked at the bronze links until they came loose from the pulley. He cast the chain through the open hatch, where a soldier caught hold of the end of it.

A moment later, he came climbing up it, another man following close on his heels. Ren stumbled back as Barden's men made their way into the winch room. The soldiers flipped open another set of trapdoors and cast down the chains, bringing more men into the fight. Quick to respond, Mered's soldiers hurled themselves through the doors. They struck at the climbers and hacked at the chains. Mered's soldiers found the still-burning vats of oil and tipped them onto Barden's soldiers. One man howled in pain, but that was the end of it. The invaders were too quick for the red army.

Barden's men came one after the other, rising up into the already-crowded chamber and generally making a mess of things. The fight was short but chaotic, and more than one man struck his brother as each side struggled for control of the room. Ren found himself pushed hard against the wall, Harkans on both sides of him. The number of men had just doubled, and with every passing heartbeat a dozen more men squeezed into the thick of it. The melee was so close, so intense, that half the soldiers were forced to abandon their swords in favor of their fists; they were the only weapons a man could wield in such tight quarters. Several of the kingsguard broke the heads from their spears, forging makeshift daggers. It was a close fight, a dirty fight, and the black shields appeared to savor every moment of it. They fought with elbows and fists, with anything that could be used as a weapon. They beat back their foes in a bare-knuckled brawl that left the once-crowded chamber blanketed in red. Bruised and disfigured bodies littered every inch of it. Cloven heads and cloven shields lay mangled and mixed together.

"It's done," Ren said, the words coming out in great gasps.

Ren eyed the wheel. He was the first to reach it, but Tye was not far behind him.

"Where were you?" he asked.

"Hiding," she said. "I know when to stay out of the way."

"Good enough," said Ren. He gripped one of the large spokes and gave it a turn. More hands clasped the wheel. One rotation, then another, and soon a cry of joy rang out from the tunnel below them. The passage was clear.

≋53≋

The cloth caught the wind, billowing into a bold and black flag, fluttering from the window of the tower where Merit waited for Barden's arrival. This slip of cloth was her signal, the one that would tell her uncle or
her generals where to find her. With the flag raised, all she could do was
wait and watch for their armies to approach. If Ren had done his task, the
way was clear and the sack of Solus had begun.

All her hopes rested on that boy. She prayed she could trust him. Ren
had looked younger than she imagined, but it had been difficult to see
his true face through the ash that smeared his brow. He had the look of
a soldier who'd just come from the fight, or was still in the midst of one.
It was a hungry look, desperate too. He wanted more than anything to
get out of this city. She saw that. The boy brimmed with determination.
It overwhelmed his every aspect. He'd give his life to get those men
out of Solus, and the kingsguard would do the same just to keep the
bastard alive. They truly were a desperate bunch, caught in desperate
circumstances. She doubted the soldiers at the gate would have half a
chance against the Harkans. She wished her people well, and Ren too.
Merit still recalled that little boy, the young heir to the kingdom, tearing
through the Horning, knocking over urns—just as she'd said. He'd been
her brother once. She'd sworn never to regret what she'd done to him,
how she'd tried to keep him out of Harwen. Again, she told herself that
she had acted in the interests of the kingdom, but she knew it was a lie.
She'd sought to preserve her power by suppressing Ren's. She'd believed
her lie all the way up until the moment she met the boy. Ren had spared
her life. He'd shown mercy on her and agreed to Barden's plan.

An alarm rang in the distance, a bell of some kind. A moment later, the
first of her uncle's soldiers rode into view. Their charge was unexpectedly
swift. With only the city guard to stifle his push, Barden's soldiers rode,
almost without resistance, through the streets.

Merit's heart warmed. In war, as in life, few things went as planned.
Nevertheless, this one time all things were in place. Barden and his
armies went their separate ways, the free companies going in one direc-

tion, the outlanders in another. Both set about plundering the city, and Barden joined in the mayhem. His soldiers threw torches on every hut, hovel, and house they passed. The people of Solus packed their roofs with firewood and foodstuffs, lamp oil too. The blaze spread quickly. The palm-leaf-shaded markets took to flame just as easily as the linen-draped alleyways. A red haze followed Barden's charge, glowing more brightly as he approached. Soon he would reach her tower, and she'd join him. She'd lead the charge, and their army would meet with Harkana's at the Shroud Wall. That had been the plan, at least.

As Barden's riders came upon the Waset, he passed the great Circus of Re, where the crowds still cheered at some unseen spectacle, unaware of the terror that swept through their city. Apparently, no one knew what transpired in the streets outside the ring, so the applause continued and the invaders rode past, skipping the circus altogether, leaving it for the outlanders perhaps.

Barden rode at a frightening pace. He must have decided that shock was the best mode of attack, that if he rode all the way to the Shroud Wall the fight would be done before it was started, their foes demoralized and confused.

He only slowed at the steps of the Waset. At a trot, he moved down the wide stair, down into the heart of the old city, to the place where Merit waited atop the tower, black banner calling to him in the breeze. Once more she felt a surge of pride at seeing what her uncle had done, what she had in fact done. They'd dealt the blow her father had only dreamed of. The Harkans had once more taken Solus, but this time they weren't going to occupy the city.

When Barden ran out of torches, his men shot flaming arrows. They hurled burning tar from slings, setting fires wherever they went. If the dust and sand could have been lit aflame, he'd have put them to the torch as well.

Barden passed a garden of what appeared to be golden statues, then a great and towering arch of white marble. He rode to the mighty Shroud Wall, then turned and galloped straight at Merit's tower. The sun had risen, but it was only a faint glow on the eastern horizon, a smoldering ember in an already-ashen sky. The windows were too narrow for her to poke her head out, but the cloth waved and she guessed he'd spotted it. He rode so close to her tower that she could almost see the color of his eyes, and her flag caught the wind once more as if to assert itself, but

Barden simply shrugged and rode on, disappearing behind a high wall
and a long line of riders. He was gone, and Merit had no idea if he had
seen the banner or not, but the man *had* disappeared.

She waited, hoping he would circle around or send back soldiers to
fetch her. She allowed him a bit of time, in case he was engaged in some
unexpected conflict. She strained to get a look at him, moving from
window to window. She saw house soldiers of every color, and the yellow cloaks were out and about, trying to hold back the flames, probably
wondering what was the greater threat to the city: the fire or the man
who lit it. Everywhere, the city buzzed with activity, but she'd lost sight
of her uncle.

The realization came slowly to her, but it struck her nonetheless:
Barden would not come to her aid. His plans had changed, or he'd never
revealed their true nature. Whatever the case, he'd seen her banner and
ignored it. For some reason, he'd chosen to leave her in the tower. Perhaps
he thought it safe. She could not guess at his intentions, nor were they her
concern. She worried for herself and no one else. Merit needed an armed
escort. If Barden refused or was unable to supply one, the Harkan Army
would have to suffice. They knew the signal and were instructed to search
for it. The army in black had besieged the north gate, but she didn't know
if they'd entered it. Perhaps something had gone awry. Maybe that was
why Barden had ridden off. It was possible that he had gone off to help
the Harkans, just as Ren and the kingsguard had assisted Barden. *Is that
why he left me? Perhaps he'll come back*, she thought, but only briefly. Merit
knew false hope when she heard it.

In the wake of Barden's charge, the outlanders followed. They came
wearing rags or furs or nothing at all, their skin caked in woad or ash.
Some looked as if they had emerged from the sand itself, the desert come
back to reclaim the land it once owned. With clubs and axes, they tore
statues from plinths and pried golden urns from temples.

The mercenary armies rode behind the outlanders. They marched an
ever-increasing crowd of men and women in front of them. These must
be the wealthy of Solus. Perhaps they were prisoners, or maybe the free
companies planned to use the wellborn as a kind of shield, to deter an
attack from the city guard or the house armies of the wealthy. Barden's
initial charge had ended; the city was on fire. The army of the Protector
stood outside the walls of Solus and the various house armies were all
chasing after Barden's legions or trying to defend their palaces.

Only the Harkans were absent. She looked out to the many ramparts and pylons that composed the city walls, but the sand rose higher, obscuring her view of the city.

Who will come for me?

Wars were a messy affair, and she knew well that the Harkans might not reach her position, not for some time at least.

Something struck the tower wall. *Someone's at the door,* thought Merit.

A second hit, this one loud enough to shake the stones, smacked the tower's base. She pressed her head to one of the slots. The outlanders had taken a great beam, the kingpost from some half-destroyed roof, and were using it as a battering ram to strike the narrow stones that stood between the slotted windows at the tower's lowest level. If they dislodged one of the columns, they could clear a space just wide enough for a man to slip inside.

The outlanders were coming.

She scrambled down the steps, calling out to her guard as she went. "Pull back the drawbar! Pull it back!" Once the outlanders entered the tower, she'd be trapped, and Merit knew exactly how that would end.

Her guard, a man named Garen, balked, so she slapped him on the cheek. "I am queen. Pull back that bar and thrust open the door. We're going out into the streets. We'll find some other place to shelter, perhaps the Temple of Mithra. This place is done."

Garen hesitated once more, but she glared at him, so he went to work. Head shaking, he drew forth the heavy wooden plank, the wood screaming as it left the bracket. The door opened with equal resistance, turning slowly, by painful degrees, the man grunting as he went about his work. When the crack was wide enough, she slipped through the door's opening and bade him follow. He made for the gap, but something held him back. Pale, dirt-encrusted hands pawed at his armor. Fingers wrapped his arms and chest, clawing at his face. The outlanders had entered. Garen stood his ground, blocking the door, pushing it closed as he pressed his back against it. A terrible scream echoed through the wood.

Merit did not dally.

She ran blindly through alleys and streets, not knowing where to go, or even where she was. Among the free companies and outlander clans, few knew her face. They might not recognize her as an ally. She had already once been a prisoner of the sand-dwellers. After that ordeal, she vowed never to let them take her again. Hence, she hurled herself through the crowded streets, stumbling this way and that, but the invaders were everywhere. One by one, they pulled women and children from their homes, looking them up and down. Some were killed right there on the spot, while the richest, the most well-attired, were tied in packs, kept for ransom. Any house servant with a strong back was tied hand and foot, knotted into a gang, to be sold as slaves.

Up close, the outlanders were far fouler than she recalled; they did not even walk like common men. Bow-legged from having spent a lifetime atop a horse, they moved in odd, staggered motions, like some devilish race not meant to tread upon this earth. In the city of light, where every statue was gold and every house was plastered in white, these men wore rags sewn from the skin of rats, their bony limbs looking more skeletal than human. Even their horses were gaunt and malnourished. She'd seen her stable master put down steeds that were healthier than the outlanders' best mount.

Yet these same men raided the houses and temples of Solus. They took whatever held worth and cast everything else aside. The outlanders pried gems from obelisks and scraped gold from pillars. They wrested pearls from the eyes of great statues and scraped electrum from urns. When the obelisks were small enough and carved from precious stone, they too were carried away, loaded on carts, tossed one on top of the other. The great stone monuments, the ones that were too big to be lifted or carted, were stripped in whatever way was possible. A gilded mask was pried from a funerary placard and the gold was chipped from the stele that ran along the base of some temple. There were great heaps of looted treasure, precious vessels of every sort, wine cups and wine jugs, vessels for mixing or storage. Golden statues lay in great heaps, sacred images of the gods tossed to the stones. In the dust and haze, Merit could not even ascertain which god these men had offended. *By the end of the day they'll have offended all of them a hundred times over,* she thought, but these men gave no care. They had their own gods.

The invaders stripped the city bare. Where they could not easily find riches, they took men and women and dragged them from their homes, demanding to know where their gold could be located, insisting that each man produce his every possession for them to paw through and plunder. Men were forced to produce keys and open the sepulchral chambers of their ancestors. The bodies were ripped from their resting places, the desiccated remains torn apart to free a golden bangle or an electrum-studded collar. Each body was given a second death by accident, their souls lost for a bit of metal or a few old gems.

Resistance came seldom, but when it did, the results were disastrous.

Merit saw a man flayed before his wife's eyes. She ran from the sight of it, but she could hardly escape the depredations of the invading army. Bodies littered the streets. Great rolls of fur and fine muslin lay in haphazard stacks. Men tied hand and foot sat alongside sundry casks of oil, wine, and amber. And the parchments that had once filled a hundred repositories lay stripped of the gold rings that bound them, the scrolls tossed to the fire, the gold thrown in sacks. In fact, anything that was not precious was given to the blaze. And after each house was cleared, it, too, was set aflame. Such were the ways of the outlanders. She knew this, had seen it during the wars with the pale-skinned warriors of the west, but was nonetheless shocked by the scale of their plundering and the foulness with which it was executed. Had even Barden anticipated such bedlam, such vulgarity? Perhaps. He was reared among these people.

It took three thousand years to build this city and a day to sack and burn it, she mused. Seeking to avoid the outlanders, she found herself swept up into a crowd of people who were moving away from them. All of Solus had joined her in the streets. Barden's attack had come so swiftly that no one had had a chance to flee the city in advance of his assault. The gates were barred in the east by Barden's soldiers and she assumed they were blocked in the north by the Harkans. Only the southern gate was likely open. There were a thousand different posterns and smugglers' routes that one might use to exit the city, but she knew the location of no such places. In fact, no one in her proximity seemed to know how to get out of the city. The only solution was to run. From the lowest beggars to the highest of the highborn, everyone abandoned their homes or hovels, fleeing the outlanders, trying to find shelter or to hide.

A rooftop overflowing with people collapsed inward, drawing its inhabitants down upon whatever lay below, which happened to be a chamber that was itself overflowing with people. Bodies crashed upon bodies, bloody limbs mingling with broken beams and cracked tiles. No one paused. No one even gave the devastation a moment's notice or stopped to aid those who had fallen. The crowd surged forward, prodded, perhaps by the destruction, by the desire of each and every citizen to escape whatever death they'd just witnessed. Merit saw the panic in their eyes, the fear mingled with resolve. Half of them already knew the truth: they would die, they'd be burned or bludgeoned. The other half was just too panicked to put it all together, but the realization would come to them soon enough. It came to Merit. She needed to get out of these streets. She had to find Barden or her generals, but she saw little of either. Even the mercenary armies stayed clear of the outlanders. Perhaps they, too, were frightened of the sand-dwellers and had taken their wares and moved on to safer territory. She did her best to push through the crowds, but her progress was slow and Merit was still uncertain of where to go.

Barden could be anywhere. The Harkans were in the north, but who knew how long it would take them to reach this part of the city. They were set to face the Protector's Army, and that battle might last a day or a month. No one knew or could predict how such a thing might play out.

I can't count on the Harkan Army to find me, and I can't rely on Barden either. He rode past my tower. She would have to save herself, and quickly.

A notion formed in her mind. To others, this might have been an obvious idea, but it had taken some time for it to come to the queen of the Harkans. There *was* one place she could go for protection. The Shroud Wall was tall and impenetrable, and her mother stood behind it, so she made her way toward the white edifice. She might have reached it, but something arrested her flight. A rope fell over her head and tightened around her neck. Her hands were bound with sinew. She was thrown bodily to the ground, tossed in a pile like the rest of the loot. Merit kneeled and out of desperation she lifted her eyes to the Shroud Wall.

Behind a veiled window, someone moved.

⋛54⋚

Sarra looked out at the city through one of the bronze screens that dotted the Shroud Wall. She saw little. The storms had transformed the sky into a swirling haze of dust and debris, so she climbed to the top of the wall, exposing herself to the winds and achieving almost nothing for her effort. She looked down at the Shadow Gate, at the ceremonial entrance of the Empyreal Domain, to see if the way was clear, but it was blocked. A barricade made of wood and stone choked the passage, and Mered's soldiers crowded about it.

They've sealed me in, thought Sarra. *Trapped me in the domain.*

She was alone, cut off from the city and the people, severed from everything but the wail of the crowds, the winds, and the crackle of a hundred fires. Solus burned, but there was little or nothing she could do about it. She was trapped like some animal in a menagerie, pent up in a cage, even though it was a lavish one. The gardens of the Empyreal Domain might be a glorious place to spend a sunny afternoon, but the sun was gone and it had taken the sky with it, leaving behind nothing but smoke and sand. The air was as lethal to the nose as it was to the skin. Every gust of wind sent sand hurtling toward her, and it stung like an insect's bite. Still, she stood amid the gale, waiting for the winds to subside. When they did, and the sand settled briefly to the earth, a hazy panorama of red and orange flashed before her eyes. More fire than she imagined possible. From the outermost districts to the great temples of the faith, the inferno raged. It was in the streets, the markets, and the barracks. It had even touched the Golden Hall, and to her surprise, the White-Wall district bristled with flame. In fact, it burned brighter than anything in sight. The glistening walls reflected and multiplied the fire-light. It was a wonder to behold, the houses of her foes slowly reduced to ash. However, one conflagration caught and held her eye. It burned among the clouds. *It can't be,* she thought, but there was no mistaking it. No other structure held such lofty terraces. The house of Saad had fallen, taken by the outlanders, Barca, or some nameless company of freebooters. For all she knew, the people themselves had flung torches upon the Cloud Garden of the house of Saad, their anger spilling over into violence. The storied house of the gods burned like the rest of the city, the fires leaping from terrace to terrace, climbing ever higher, making it seem as if the heavens themselves were aflame.

And why not? The rest of Solus was on fire. Why should the wellborn and wealthy be spared? Everywhere she looked, the people were forced out into the wide plazas and broad ceremonial ways. Shouts reverberated from every alley and plaza. There was war in the city and unrest. So where was Mered? Where was the army?

The answer came in the form of a low rumble. Beneath the cries of the people, somewhere amid the crackle of all that flame, she heard the well-choreographed march of the Protector's Army. Drums banged and a clarion pierced the air. The army of the Protector had arrived, and she guessed Mered was with them. They'd formed a long procession, oc-cupying the full width of the Rellian Way, but when they entered the Plaza of Miracles the men split off into groups, each going in a different direction, creating some new formation, laid out in great squares at the base of the wall.

When the last man fell into place, the soldiers lifted their chins in a pompous gesture that only the army of the Protector could muster. It was an impressive show of force. Unfortunately, no one watched it, and almost immediately after the men had all found their spots, a good number of them were forced to put down their spears and join the city guard. They lifted buckets of water or bags of sand, fighting fires instead of men. However, the remainder of the army stood at attention, shields raised and spears leveled. *Mered wants a fight, but there isn't going to be one, not with Barca's forces.* The rebel had already ridden through the Waset, and she doubted he'd return.

Still, Mered looked this way and that, observing the city from his ornate perch. He was seated on a golden chair that was itself carried atop an elaborately adorned palanquin. It would have made an impressive sight, but a thick layer of ash had already covered the thing. The city burned, but Mered was still searching the ancient streets, as if anticipating some attack. There was defiance written all over him, but there was no one to defy. Seated atop his perch, the First Among Equals appeared utterly irrelevant. He had ruled Solus for a day before the city was put to the torch. *He's the Emperor of Ashes,* Sarra thought.

Mered sat up from his chair and his soldiers tightened their ranks. A mob approached, but they were not the invaders. The people of Solus had come to the Waset, seeking shelter or a bit of aid. They were trying to escape the outlanders, but there was nowhere for the people to shelter and the army made no move to assist them.

Left to their own devices, the people stood helpless as the sand-dwellers captured them one by one or a dozen at a time, binding their hands and dragging them back to their homes, back to reveal whatever riches they might have buried or hidden, back so the high-desert men could steal the gems that swung from their necks or the golden bangles on their wrists. The outlanders upended the houses of the wealthy, but Mered did little more than idle atop his throne.

What's he doing? thought Sarra. *Why won't he protect the people?* Then she saw it. The army of Harkana had breached the gate and were driving their way through the city. They rode toward the Waset, to the very place where Mered's soldiers waited, spears planted in the earth, archers at the ready. Mered had at last found an opponent, and every fighting man in his host set themselves to receive the Harkan charge. For a moment, all eyes were on the Harkans, and the people were left to fend for themselves.

Sarra stood atop the Shroud Wall, the Empyreal Domain at her back.

There was one place in the city where the people could shelter, but its doors were sealed shut two hundred years ago.

Perhaps it is time to open them, she thought.

⋛ 55 ⋚

"There," said Ferris. He stood at the tip of a rocky outcropping, his outstretched finger indicating an elaborate device set upon the far side of the rift. The siege engine had three large throwing containers, each one arranged so it could be loaded and fired in quick succession. Pits sheathed by linen tarps hid the armaments, and a sentry stood astride each of them.

Ferris hurled a rock at one of the men and struck him on the helm, a high and tinny sound issuing forth as the stone bounced off the iron.

The soldier gave no response, which made the man's presence seem all the more chilling.

"I'm guessing those pits are full of naphtha or something similar. It will burn until there is nothing left of the forest. Each device is similarly armed and they've got hundreds of them. They've been at it without pause, all through the night, digging holes and erecting screens. This army is ready, prepared in ways we cannot comprehend. Mered may have sent soldiers to Harkana, but I don't think his heart was in it. Feren's the real target. There can be no other explanation for such a bold display of force."

Kepi found herself at a loss for words.

"Well, what does my queen say to this? You won the duel, but you're going to lose the war. You gained some support among the lords and you bought us a bit of time, but none of that matters, does it? We have no way to fight against this sort of army," said Ferris. He was practically tearing the hairs from his jaw.

"This would be beautiful to behold were it not the harbinger of my death."

"Maybe you should have . . ."

"What? Killed the boy?"

"They might have let you keep your crown."

"I'd be Mered's slave. A queen in name only, nothing more."

Ferris pursed his lips and spat. "I know. Men such as Mered are fond of their puppets, but only when they're obedient. Adin was left for dead on the dueling ground. They carried him out of the ring, but that was the extent of it. My scouts found him a bit later, when the field was clear."

"What did they do with him?"

"Hauled his sorry ass back to our camp. He's in the physician's tent. Adin will live, but he'll never challenge you. The kite has chosen its lord. Every warlord in Feren watched the match."

"See that he is cared for," she said. "They say he was my brother's friend, and he seemed a decent enough fellow. A liar, perhaps, but I think he was desperate."

"He was a priory boy. That's why I had my men drag him to our camp. He's suffered enough for one lifetime, maybe two."

"Agreed, and that'll be the end of it. We'll give him some farm and a few men so he can make a life for himself."

"You're kind. Personally, and if I hadn't served in the priory, if I were king, I'd have his head parted from his shoulders."

"Treat him kindly."

"Done." Ferris tossed another rock across the rift and snarled as it ricocheted off a catapult. She supposed he was hoping to hit a second sentry on the head. Her men had traded arrows with Mered's all through the day and into the night, striking down any man or woman who came too close to the rift, testing each other's aim and range, shouting insults to break the tension. Ferris even had a man who had walked the forest's edge banging a drum throughout the night and calling out insults to the red army, just to upset their sleep—to keep them from any happy dreams they might desire.

Ferris hurled another rock, daring them to send back an arrow.

There was no retort, so he continued his survey of the rift. "It's terribly quiet out here, isn't it?"

"I don't know, perhaps they are about to come rushing out of the forest," said Kepi.

"Perhaps," said Ferris. "Still, I've tossed arrows and stones, hurled insults too. I've done my best to unnerve the boys in red, but they've gone quiet. All I see are their weapons."

"And there are a great number of them," said Kepi.

"There are," said Ferris quietly. He counted the siege engines as they went.

"One. Two. Three."

They walked.

"Twelve. Thirteen. Fourteen."

"Are you trying to annoy me?" she asked.

"No, just curious really," said Ferris. "Think about the manpower it took to move these machines. It's a wonder there are any men left in Solus. Mered has put all his strength into this fight." Ferris lifted another stone and tossed it across the rift. "It's a risky move."

"Why?" she asked. "Barca?"

"There are rumors that he's within striking distance of Solus, that he's already entered the city, possibly."

"The walls of Solus are impregnable. If Barca attacks, it'll be a siege, and a long one at that. Desert sieges do not end well, not historically. I doubt Barca will fare any better—"

Ferris gripped her arm.

"What is it?" she asked.

"There!"

She looked, but Kepi saw nothing more than a row of tall and spindly catapults.

"Look again. Widen those pretty eyes of yours, girl."

Kepi stared across the rift, resentful at having to search for what Ferris had already discovered. Machine after machine sat in its place, munitions too, but there were fewer guards than she recalled. In fact, one stood directly across from them, but he'd fallen to the ground. The red armor was disheveled, the head removed, dry grass poking from the neckline.

"I hit him with a stone," said Ferris.

"A straw soldier?"

"There're all straw," said Ferris, his eyes widening as he spoke, the realization of what stood before him dawning on the warlord.

Quickly, Kepi glanced up and down the line. There were sentries, but each stood as motionless as a scarecrow.

"Where are the men—the army?" she asked.

"Gone," said Ferris. He started out at a sprint, darting back to the camp, yelling for his men. She was queen, and the least Ferris could do was wait for her, or at least have the courtesy to not leave her alone, but Ferris wasn't the type. Halfway back to the camp they collided with two of Ferris's sworn men and one that belonged to Baen Muire.

"Gone," said the first man they met. Fearghal, she thought.

"All of them?" she asked. "Up and down the rift?"

"Yes," said Fearghal. "The soldiers are all dummies, stuffed with desert grass. Before sunrise, at the farthest edge of the rift, our men caught sight of their retreat. By torchlight, the soldiers in red took orders, scrolls sealed in red. We saw that much. After that, the men gathered their weapons and retreated, leaving the straw men in their place. In fact, they've left everything behind: the machines, the munitions, the stones, and whatever hellish devices they have hidden in the forest."

"Barca," said Kepi.

"He attacked Solus, and Mered ordered his men to retreat. He needs them to defend the city," said Ferris.

"Why else would they leave with such haste? Perhaps those impenetrable walls are not as sturdy as Mered thought. Barca *was* one of their own—maybe he knows some secret, some way to spirit his men into Solus."

"I don't know. In fact, I don't care," said Ferris. "Llyr has smiled upon our miserable asses. This war is done!" he hooted. "By the time they return, we'll have burned every one of their precious machines or cast them into the rift. I might even save a few of those bridges for my own use."

"No, there's no time for that," said Kepi, her words slow and commanding.

"What do you mean?"

"Don't you see it? The tables have turned."

It was time for Ferris to offer up a blank stare. He took a step back when he finally understood Kepi. "No," he said. "You're a fool."

"I don't care. I am queen and Kitelord and you had better start treating me like one. There are bridges here, ones we can use to swiftly move our men across the rift. We are going to follow the red army and the Protector's too. Without their machines, scampering home to save their masters, they will be at our mercy. Gather the men, we're marching on Solus."

⇒ 56 ⇐

When his army had entered the city, Barden's soldiers took up positions around the Rising Gate, occupying the pylons and the winch room, freeing up Ren and the kingsguard to do as they pleased. As the Harkans handed off the gates, the soldiers patted one another on the shoulder. The kingsguard shuffled down the steps and out of the fortifications.

Ren stood with Tye on the south Pylon.

"We're at the gates of Solus," she said. "And we've done our part in this fight." She looked at him, joy coloring her face, warming her pale cheeks. "Don't you get it, Ren? You're free. You can finally get yourself out of here. You did your work. Now Barden will do his. And your sister is here, in Solus. The throne of Harkana sits empty."

Ren gave no reply. He simply watched as the last of the invaders poured into the city. It had taken hours for Barden's force to ride past the gates, so he guessed the sack was well under way. Perhaps a good portion of it was already done. Fires lit the distant skyline, and the clash of metal thundered in far-off streets.

Tye did have a point, and it was a damned good one too. She tempted him. He'd completed the hunt. His father had named him heir, and he had the support of the kingsguard. He could take the crown. It stood within his grasp, but he dared not reach for it.

"It's no way for a king to claim his throne," said Ren, his grin fading, eyes cast toward the city beyond. "The Harkan Army is in Solus. If I run, they'll call me a coward. The King Who Fled."

"Then be a coward, Ren. Be the Coward King. At least you'll be alive. If we go back into that city, into the one place we've been trying to escape, there's no telling what'll happen. The Harkans don't know your face. They don't know *you*. They might fight at your side or they might just cut you down for standing in the wrong place. It's a risk, Ren. There are a dozen different armies in this city. Everyone is fighting. Do you really want to go back into that?"

"No," said Ren, eyes distant. "It's got nothing to do with wanting. I want to get out of here, but I'm not going to do it." Ren faced the desert. The Plague Road lay before him. The way was open, and he was almost tempted to follow it.

"We find Kollen, then we meet up with the Harkan Army. I've got a duty to attend to, but you don't," Ren said, hoping she would stay but wanting to remind his friend that she, too, could find her freedom.

"Oh, I wasn't leaving. I'm going after Kollen."

Ren almost laughed. "Am I the only coward?"

She cocked an eyebrow. "I only thought it should be said."

"Same here," he said as they made their way down the stairs and out into the courtyard where the kingsguard had assembled. A quiet came over the men as Ren threw open the door and stepped out of the pylon. The men looked eager to hear him speak, so he wasted no time and addressed them. "Barden's army will join ranks with the Harkans at the Shroud Wall. At least, that's what Barden said in his notes." Ren held up the parchment Merit had delivered to him. "We're going there, but we need to find Kollen and Edric and all the others we left behind. We'll locate our friends first, then our countrymen. Do any disagree?"

The men gave him a cheer or something like one, and briefly he felt like a leader, a man that men might follow. He'd promised a way out of the city and he'd found it. He had only this one last task to complete.

"We head for the Waset, to the Plaza of Miracles," said Ren.

"And what if we find the Protector? What if the Harkan Army never meets Barden's. What if Mered's soldiers cut down the traitor? What then?" Asher asked. He was standing with the kingsguard. Ott was there, too, and Butcher.

"Then it'll be four thousand versus four hundred," said Ren.

"I only wanted to say it," said Asher. He nodded a bit, a queer smile crossing his face, suggesting that he might actually enjoy those odds. He ordered the men to form a company of scouts and sent them out ahead of the kingsguard. "We'll move slowly," he said. "We need to make certain of what's ahead of us.

"And behind us," said Butcher, who had once more strapped Ott to his back. "This won't be easy. We're strangers here and the sand has made a mess of everything. There's smoke in the air too. Don't be so sure we'll spot the enemy before they're on top of us, and it won't be an easy task to retrace our steps."

"I can do it," said Ott.

"You might, but I can help," said a man who wore the bronze armor of the Alehkar. He'd scraped the decorations off his chest plate and re-placed them with a broken circle. He was one Barden's men. "I was born and raised in the back streets of Solus. I know every quarter of the city. I'll get you to the Waset, if you'll have me."

"What's your name?" said Ren. He eyed him warily. Ren wasn't certain he trusted his uncle's men, not all of them. They hailed from Solus, after all.

"Woser's the name, and you can stop lookin' at me like that, boy," he said. "I swore an oath to your uncle, so I might as well have sworn it to you. I've been waiting the better part of my shitty life to see these well-born bastards get their due, so don't start thinking I'll lead you astray." There was a snarl on his lips, a bit of anger in his voice. "And besides," he said, "the Shroud Wall's as tall as a mountain. Only a fool could miss it."

That was enough for Ren. Woser led them, but Ott confirmed every

turn, checking Barden's map, studying the landmarks. In the haze of
the sandstorm, each street corner looked like the last one, and Ren had
enough trouble just keeping up with the pace of the Harkan charge. He
was unaccustomed to a forced march, to the speed at which a trained
soldier moved. Like Tye, he wore stolen armor and it fit him poorly. His
only consolation was the absence of organized resistance in the outer
districts. He saw only looters, some of them working in large companies
while others roamed about in loose bands. In many places, the houses
were burned down to their foundations, the mud brick scorched and
black. The city smoldered and the storm pelted him with sand. Each ker-
nel stung as it struck his face or any other part of him that was exposed,
and the smoke burned his throat and eyes.

A band of marauders caught sight of his leather-clad companions.
They recognized the black shields as allies and paid them no heed, but
Ren wasn't certain he wanted to leave these men to their business. Hundreds of half-dead soldiers, bodies in red and blue armor, rested in great
heaps, some living, still moving. Meanwhile, all around him, men with
pale faces forced the wellborn to their knees, tying them in packs, robbing them not simply of their jewels but often their clothes as well. They
defaced the city's statues and steles, carving curses into the ancient stone,
leaving destruction wherever they went.

"Ren, it's . . ." Tye came up short, dumbstruck, and unable to speak.

"I know. It's worse than I thought," said Ren, fearful to even lift his
eyes, worried at what new horror they would discover.

"No one deserves this; it's not right," said Tye. "This is Barden's
work," she said, perhaps trying to console herself. "We didn't do this."

No, thought Ren, *but we did let him into the city.* Ren had agreed to his
sister's plan, but she had not revealed the true extent of Barden's agenda.
Ren hadn't known they would plunder the city, not like this, and he hadn't
guessed they would burn every structure to the ground. He'd wanted an
honest fight, but he didn't know if such a thing even existed.

What he saw in the streets was pure barbarity. He wanted none of it,
but he could not deny that he was a part of it. *I opened the door, but I didn't
know who'd come running through it.* Ren was only now beginning to grasp
the scope of what was happening. *This is no war,* he thought. *This is an
annihilation. A Devouring.* Part of him—a selfish, small part of him—felt
a stab of joy at the sight of it. These *were* the people who had imprisoned
him, who'd tortured his every waking moment, and now they were being made to kneel, forced to suffer every conceivable humiliation.

Woser took Ren by the shoulder and pointed to the hazy outlines of a distant wall.

"That's it," said Ott, "the Shroud Wall. This is the Rellian Way."

Ren saw the hazy rim of a massive fortification, a white line against the leaden sky. And he glimpsed the statuary garden. Once again, it shimmered in the sandy air, giving off an unnatural glow. He heard that buzzing at the back of his thoughts, distant but growing louder as they approached the garden. Instinctively, he reached for the eld horn, but let go of it the moment his hand touched it. He turned away from the statues, but they pulled at him, drawing him closer, and that buzzing in his head was a riot.

"Ren!" cried a voice. "I've found them."

"Found—" Ren halted in his tracks. They had come upon the Plaza of Miracles? At least, that's what he thought it was called, but there were no miracles here. The Ray's men had done the promised deed. Edric slouched, a spear in his gut, the head parted from his shoulders. The captured kingsguard kneeled—all dead, all tortured.

"We're too late," said Ren, his voice as soft as a whisper.

"They must have executed them when Barden entered the city," said Asher. "They killed the prisoners and ran."

"Kollen!" Tye cried out. His body was nowhere to be found, but they searched for it anyway, turning over corpses and studying faces.

There were bodies everywhere and the sand was already covering them in a layer of grit.

Ren worried they would never find him.

Tye collapsed in frustration.

"He should be here," said Ren, voice shaking. "Maybe—"

"You can stop your searching," said a familiar voice.

It was nearby.

Ren glimpsed a row of statues. There, he found more soldiers, more dead. But among them, he caught sight of four who lived.

"How?" Ren asked, turning to see his friend. He was in the company of three soldiers Ren did not recognize.

"How did I fucking survive?" asked Kollen. "Three of the guards were Rachins, press-ganged into the army of the Protector. Can you imagine that? When I saw their faces, I knew my fellow countrymen, their gray eyes and long beards. They did nothing at first, but when the orders came down and the soldiers drew daggers, I told them I was the heir of Rachis and they had better defend me. Turns out I've got my own kingsguard and they're as merciless as yours."

The Rachins did look as fierce as the Harkans, thought Ren, with their wild beards and long, slender limbs.

"Would your army of three like to join with my four hundred?" asked Ren. He'd have made a smile if he'd had the strength for it.

"Well, I suppose you bastards could use the help," said Kollen. "So, where are we going?"

"To find the Harkan Army," said Ren. Then he looked to the Rachins. "When your men fled, which way did they go? Where's the battle?"

One of the Rachins, a man who introduced himself as Tarix, took a step forward and spoke. "The Protector's Army entered the city just ahead of the Harkans. We took up positions in the inner city. They've got a formation right here, at the plaza, and a line of soldiers that starts at the Shroud Wall and extends out toward the stairs of the Waset. If you'd gone a bit further you'd have run straight into it."

"Where're the Harkans?" asked Ren.

"There." The soldier pointed, and when the sandstorm momentarily subsided the clearing revealed a long line of bronze shields that stretched from the Shroud Wall out as far as the eye could see. On the far side of that wall, barely visible, the boiled black of the Harkan Army rode through the streets of Solus.

"There's no way to reach them," said Asher. "They're on the far side of our enemy."

"We're cut off," said Tye.

"No, it's worse," said Ren, who was pointing toward the great phalanx of the Protector's Army. As the winds subsided, it was not simply Ren who saw the army of the Protector, but the army who saw him. The black shields were not alone in the plaza. A man in red stood upon a palanquin. He spoke some command and a thousand bronze heels pivoted, a thousand shields were lifted, and just as many spears were set for the charge. A clarion rang out, the answering calls echoing across the lines as the army of the Protector made its slow and inexorable march on the kingsguard.

≋57≋

Merit sat with her ass in the dirt.

She watched as the outlanders carted away the city's treasures. Some were made of gold, others of flesh and bone. Merit guessed she fell into the latter category. She was a prisoner. A future slave, or more likely a ransom of some kind if she were given the chance to reveal her identity. Merit had, as of yet, refrained from any such action. There were gangs of prisoners and former servants running amok in the city, killing anyone who looked wellborn or had the means to dress in anything other than a beggar's rags.

She sat among a dozen or so prisoners, all of them tied in a gang. The knots were hastily fastened. With enough time, Merit was certain she could wriggle free of her bonds, but what then? She was safe for the moment. Her captors were preoccupied, moving from house to house, looting and burning. Whether their plunder was made of flesh or gold hardly seemed to matter to them. Both were treated with the same dispassionate air. They tossed children in one pile, crescents in the other. Centuries of warfare had fostered deep resentments between the outlanders and the people of Solus. She could only guess at the atrocities the Protector's Army committed in the outlander wars. She had no doubt they'd earned this comeuppance.

Harkana had fought its own war with the western clans. In fact, it was her father who sent the outlanders scrambling back to the High Desert, but he had fought with some semblance of honor. She doubted the same could be said for the army of the Protector.

Her head jerked around when one of the outlanders raised his spear, erasing any thoughts she'd had about honor in war. The man's pale white skin was slathered in woad, a symbol of some clan, she guessed. He did not speak the emperor's tongue. None of them did, but he motioned with a sharpened stave and the others knew to stand. The outlanders were moving their caravan to the next great house. Merit did her best to comply with her captors' orders, but she was slower than the others. They were all tied in one long chain, so when she got behind the pace of their march she found she was pulled unexpectedly forward by the man in front of her. She knocked into him and felt something rough. She recognized the distinct outlines of metal folded into lobster-like plates, one overlapping the other. This man, who was dressed in loose layers of rags, wore a coat of armor beneath the torn strips of cloth.

"Who are you?" she whispered. "And why are *you* in chains?" She guessed he belonged to one of the free companies.

"Quiet, woman," said the man.

"You're armored. What are you—a mercenary?"

A brutal thrust to her ribs silenced Merit, but only briefly. "If you've got armor, then you have weapons. What are you waiting for? Get us out of these ropes."

The man spoke beneath his breath. "We're waitin' for the right moment, so just hold tight, lovely. There's only eleven of us. We're a small company, shields for hire and swords too. We were up north in Feren for a while, worked for the king before he fell, but we heard Barca was offering the greatest plunder in the history of the empire. Only we figured we'd go in by ourselves instead of joinin' with the man. Didn't want to split our share, but the outlanders got hold of us."

"What's your plan?"

"My plan is for you to shut up."

For once, Merit listened.

When the outlanders had filled their carts and acquired what she guessed was a manageable group of prisoners, they would haul their plunder back to the Rising Gate. She'd seen it done once or twice, so she could tell when a group was nearly finished with their looting. The carts beside her had been filled to twice their capacity, and the outlanders had taken maybe fifty or sixty men, women, and children. She feared they would all be carted off to the gates at any moment, but the outlanders decided to approach one last house. It was an elaborate affair, the walls edged with gold, gates forged of bronze, the fretwork plated in electrum.

Six or eight of the outlanders hacked at those same gates, hammering the bars with clubs and axes, ramming the bronze with what looked like a column pilfered from some temple. After one or two hits with the pillar, the gates gave way and the outlanders rushed inside. The captives, Merit included, were left unguarded. She felt a sudden release of pressure as the man at her side produced a small knife and severed his bonds. The others in his company did the same, slitting their ropes and freeing themselves from the gang, heading off to do their own plundering.

"Help me!" she cried. "The least you can do is cut my bonds. It'll do you no harm," she implored, but the man who'd sat beside Merit said nothing. His little band of marauders was already arguing over which house they would loot, discussing some plan just out of earshot.

She stood, hands and feet tied.

She was freed from the gang, so she could hobble slowly away, but with her feet bound she could only go so far. Surely the outlanders would find her, and they'd punish her with a quick death or something worse.

Still, perhaps it was better to die here. She took one step, but paused before the second. Something flashed in the dirt beside her feet. It glinted like metal. A knife lay there. Merit guessed the man had pitied her and left the blade for her to discover. Perhaps he had not wanted to show kindness in the company of his brothers. Merit quickly freed herself then tossed the knife to a family that was similarly bound.

Fearing the outlanders might return at any moment, she dashed toward the Shroud Wall, her limbs aching from where they had been bound. The pain didn't bother Merit. She'd been in one form of pain or another since she left Harkana. She wanted to find the Harkans or Barden. Either would do, but she saw only the outlanders and the armies of Mered. She was alone, so once more she gazed up at the great wall. Her mother stood behind the massive fortification, and earlier Merit had thought she'd glimpsed the Ray through one of the windows.

The crowds gathered, and they beat on the doors of the Shroud Wall. The noise was intolerable, but beneath it all Merit heard a slight creak, a sound like something breaking. The doors to the Empyreal Domain were opening.

⇥58⇤

A series of ironwood bars held the doors of the Empyreal Domain in place. The men of the Kiltet had already removed one of them and the doors had parted just slightly, but three stout timbers held them in place, preventing the great panels from opening much more than a hair's width. The work was not yet done, so the men looked to Sarra for instruction, but she gave no command. Outside, the people screamed, and their sandals beat against the cobblestones. There were cries of pain or exhaustion. Some men uttered their last breath while others shouted to the heavens, begging for the gods to appear.

Three bars stood between Sarra and the people of Solus.

If the scrolls were to be believed, these timbers were a recent addition. The doors to the Empyreal Domain were left open when the Soleri ruled over the city. The gods did not fear their enemies. In fact, it had always been the other way around. It was the empire's foes who feared the gods who lived in the domain. Hence, the doors stood open. For thousands of years, for the duration of the Old, Middle, and most of the New Kingdom, these doors had not once been shut. She knew this to be true. These were histories, not stories or myths. The Soleri had lived here once and they'd brought ruin to armies and subdued kingdoms, creating an empire that stretched from the Cressel and the eastern desert to the Shambles and north, through impassable mountain reaches to the highest cliffs of Rachis and back down into the depths of the Gray Wood. They'd taken everything east of the Denna Hills and called it their empire and still the doors remained open. Their enemies quadrupled, but the Soleri showed no fear. The histories said that Reni Nahkt, fifth in his line, stood at this very threshold and subdued an entire army of invading Rachins. Nahkt made soldiers into ash, reducing the army and its armor into nothing more than dust. But that had only been the start of his assault. He shadowed the Rachin Army, following them back to their capital, where he burned and plundered the kingdom's riches. Then he cut down every tree, salted the earth, and killed every strong-backed male in the kingdom. He left nothing. Any man who showed the slightest bit of fight was slaughtered, or so the story went. The tale was a thousand years old, so she guessed the facts had been massaged. Yet the part about the doors was likely true.

It was Ined Anu who sealed the great ironwood panels, hastily fixing those four bars into place. The coarseness of the work looked out of place amid the wonders of the domain, but it had not been the Soleri who'd sealed the two great panels, and it would not be the Soleri who opened them.

Sarra stood before those same doors and watched them quiver. Outside, the people howled, with anger or perhaps fear. They came by the thousands, by the tens of thousands, pressing their bodies to the wood. Through a crack in the timbers, blood dribbled down the face of the door. A finger squeezed into the gap, but the tip was quickly separated from the hand. The two great panels trembled, but the barrier held. The gates would not part unless Sarra gave the order.

"Take down the bars," she said.

The men of the Kiltet had no tongues, but they understood. They were people, after all. They were not immune to the suffering that lay outside of the wall. They, too, wanted to help, or so it seemed.

"As quickly as you can," she said, though Sarra was not certain they could truly understand her words. Perhaps they only understood the gist of what she said, the tone and urgency of her commands.

The blackthorn logs fell, one, two.

A single log now barred the entry to the domain.

She waved her hand and the men halted their work. Sarra climbed to one of the veiled windows. The press of the crowd was worse than she'd imagined. All of Solus was here. The people had fled to the center, to the gods, to the place where Nahkt had once stood and obliterated an army. They knew the stories. Thus, they pleaded for their gods to save them. Mered had made the same request. He'd commanded Sarra to produce the Soleri. He'd given her this one task—a final test to know if she truly wielded power or was simply a farce. Unfortunately, it was the latter.

The Soleri could not speak, but Sarra had a voice. The will to act. The people of Solus were trapped. The outlanders hacked at them from one side, and the wall pressed back at them from the other. One log held the doors closed. The men of the Kiltet looked to Sarra for direction.

Their eyes begged.

The bar twisted a bit, but it held.

That one piece of wood was the last little stitch in a latticework of lies and deception that stretched over two centuries.

Remove the wood and end the lie.

She tried to think of what the world might have been like if the Anu family hadn't taken this empire for their own, how two hundred years of brutal subjugation might have been avoided. She had the power to end all of that.

That ironwood bar contained all the bitterness of her former husband. It held her own lie, the way the priesthood had concealed the death of the amaranth.

She wondered what would happen if that log were removed.

Though she no longer bore the title of Mother, the people outside had been her children once. She could not leave them to the whims of the outlanders, and Mered refused to act. Panic cannot describe what she saw in the people's eyes. Even the Kiltet were stricken with worry, their hands trembling as they held the last bar. The doors rattled on their hinges, and the people cried out to their gods. Sarra faced the doors and made her decision.

≷59≶

A crack like thunder rattled the air.

In a single motion, the great and towering doors—each as tall as a desert palm, hewn from ironwood and glistening white in the sand-filled air—gave way. The doors parted. Thrust inward by the force of a thousand hands, by the weight of a hundred dead bodies, by the desperate people who climbed on top of one another to make their way inside. The doors were flung wide and the sacred precinct was revealed to the people. If Merit hadn't known better, she'd have expected the Soleri themselves to materialize at the gates, to put an end to this business and set things to rights. Unfortunately, no gods stood at the doorway, so the crowd stumbled forward into their sacred realm, and Merit, swept up by the mob, joined them.

It was an untidy affair. Knees and elbows jostled her from every side, sandals beat her toes. She fell. Sand-gray robes blotted out what remained of the sun. There was no light. She was on her hands and knees, crawling frantically, lifting herself up only to have someone slam her back down. A sandal mashed her fingers; she drew both hands close to her chest. Instinctively, she curled herself into the smallest possible area, but countless bodies shoved her to and fro. She was kicked, punched, and clobbered from a hundred different directions. She lost track of the blows and who'd dealt them. She was awash in agony, broken and barely able to move. A sudden kick knocked the wind from her lungs, and she screamed but no sound issued from her lips. A moment later, her chest heaved as the wind flooded back into her lungs, her fist pounding at her collarbone.

She was alive, but trampled. *If I've got some strength in me, Mithra, help me find it.* Still dizzy and confused, Merit stood. She was uncertain of which way to go, but fortunately for her, the crowd did the hard work and carried her toward the doors. They toppled the stylites from their poles. The pilgrims crushed the tents and other makeshift structures they'd erected.

Through the gates of the Empyreal Domain, she saw bright-green palms and gorgeously, almost impossibly well-groomed lawns. That was her destination, and she hobbled toward it until, out of nowhere, a flash of bronze streaked across her vision, then swords appeared, men on horseback charging at the outlanders.

Merit guessed that Mered's army had at last turned their backs to the Harkans. They'd made some attempt to save the people of Solus by arresting the sand-dwellers' push and preventing the marauders from following the people into the Empyreal Domain.

Briefly, the conflict held Merit's attention until, sometime later, a second thunderclap sounded, this one softer than the first. Her head swung around and she caught sight of the great doors of the Empyreal Domain. They moved once more, but this time they were closing. In what had seemed like only a few heartbeats, the greater portion of the populace had fled into the domain. The people had left the city, and someone was closing the doors, sealing the populace inside the domain, where they would be safe from Barden's horde.

A middle-aged man in a fine shawl of muslin cried out to her, "Hurry, you fool, or you'll be locked out."

Locked out? thought Merit. She was still reeling from the stampede, barely able to think. *I certainly don't want to be locked out,* she thought distantly. She was still trying to gather her wits. The army of the Protector swarmed at her back, ushering the last of the people inside the domain.

She eyed the narrowing gap. In a moment, the doors would be shut.

If she entered, she would be safe from the outlanders. She would also be cut off from the Harkans, unable to reach her generals and the army they commanded. This single notion brought sudden clarity to her thoughts. She'd have her life, but her part in this conflict would be ended, her dream of riding at the head of the Harkan Army finished.

She looked for the soldiers in black, for her generals, but saw only sand in the air and Mered's army storming the field. One soldier cried out to Merit, commanding her to retreat, to find safety in the domain.

Is that what I want?

By degrees, the doors were closing. In a heartbeat, they'd be shut.

The gap narrowed to the width of a child.

Merit drew in a breath; she'd made her decision.

60

The kingsguard set their spears against the Protector's furious charge. They waited, sweaty hands clutching worn shafts of wood. Every man gritted his teeth or mumbled some silent prayer. A great gust of wind blew across the plaza and a gray, sand-filled haze descended upon the field of battle. There was no sky, no army, and no city either. And when the cloud dispersed, there still wasn't much to see. The army of the Protector ought to have been right on top of them. Instead, Ren saw the bronze soldiers dash toward that tall white wall, clashing with the outlanders as they went. For once, it appeared, the Protector's Army had earned its namesake: They protected the people of Solus.

For Ren, for the kingsguard, it was nothing short of a miracle.

"We've got to go, to get out of this plaza while the army is occupied with the sand-dwellers." Ren called Asher to his side. "Send orders down through the ranks," he said. "We'll head south, away from the wall and around the Protector's position. If we're quick enough, we can dash through their broken lines and catch up with the Harkans."

"And if we're too slow and they re-form their ranks, we'll be trapped among the Protector's men," said Asher. "None of us know how deep their lines stretch or how many men they left behind when they charged the wall. A seasoned commander would not take his entire force from the field." Asher planted his spear on the ground, punctuating his words.

"It doesn't look like he's left many soldiers," said Ren. Kollen was at his side, nodding. It did appear as if the full force of the Protector's Army had charged the wall. Not far from where they stood, the men in bronze engaged the outlander horde. Well armored and well trained, the Alehkar drove at their foes, pushing them back with ease while a second team of soldiers came around from behind the outlanders and cut off their retreat. After that, it was all chaos, the scream of iron ringing in the air, men grunting, crying out in pain—but only the outlanders were falling. They had come in their loincloths, shirtless and unarmored. Some bore spears, but most had simple clubs, weapons made from logs or sharpened flints.

"This'll be over before it started," said Ren. "We need to march."

In spite of Asher's warnings, Ren led the kingsguard around the battle. The Protector's Army had indeed left behind sentries, and the black shields skirmished with them, but there weren't enough men to block their progress. Ren steered the men past the burnt remains of some great and golden hall, and they ran astride the old well where they'd sheltered. He made certain the tall steps of the Waset were always at his right, so he knew he was circling the Shroud Wall, coming around to the south side of the Waset while still keeping his distance from the battle.

Skirmish after skirmish came and went as they quarreled with some sentry, a house soldier in blue, or a squad from the city guard. Their greatest ally was the sand, which had come again, denser now, impenetrable. It hid them from view, but it slowed their movement. Ren could barely see the tip of his outstretched hand. Even his sword point was swallowed by the storm. He halted the guard, waiting for the gale to subside.

"We should have found the bastards by now," said Kollen, his fellow Rachins at his side. "Where are the Harkans?"

"I don't see your little army of three helping us find them," said Tye.

"Ott, any clue?" Ren asked. "Where are we?" He looked for Woser but was unable to find him.

Ott stuttered his reply, perhaps out of uncertainty or maybe it was just the sand catching in his throat. "I don't know," he said. "We're past the necropolis. Perhaps we're at the ruins of the priory."

"That would be fitting," said Kollen, "back where we damn well started."

"We keep going," said Ren. He guessed the Harkan force had shifted position when the Protector advanced on the wall. They'd moved, but he had no idea where they'd gone.

The only people who seemed to know where they were going were the outlanders. Those who had not gone to the wall were retreating, carts piled high with loot, sacks thrown over their shoulders and stuffed to the point of breaking. Loaded down with the city's riches, the outlanders were making their way out of Solus. They poured over the steps of the Waset, their carts crowding the chariot ramps.

"It looks like they're in a rush to get out," said Tye.

"I'd be too if I had that much loot," said Kollen. "Maybe we should nab a bit for ourselves, so we can stuff the old coffers when we get home."

"Go ahead," said Ren. "I'm more worried about *why* they're in such a rush to get out."

"Maybe they saw what the Protector did at the gates," said Asher.

"Perhaps," said Ren, "but I think it's something else. There's a look of fear in their eyes. Something's happening, but I don't know what it is."

A few steps later, Ren stumbled into the first of the bodies. They were resting on the ground, half-covered in sand, shields rent, swords splintered.

"The Harkans?" Ren asked, his heart sinking in his chest. Had Mered cut them down? It would explain why the outlanders were fleeing. If the Harkans were gone, there was no one else to preoccupy the army of the Protector.

"No," said Tye. "Definitely not your folk." She lifted a shield from the sand.

"Bronze?" asked Kollen.

Still uncertain, Ren bent beside one of the fallen bodies, sweeping away the sand to reveal a chest piece with a broken circle carved into the metal. "Barden," he whispered. "These are Barden's men, cut down—but who? Who did the killing?"

"Over here!" cried a voice Ren did not recognize, but he went to it anyway. There, he found a man of middle years, roughly bearded and somewhat familiar in appearance. "Barden?" asked Ren, and the man nodded his assent. This was his father's brother. His uncle. *He has Arko's eyes,* Ren thought, *and he's in terrible shape.* Blood seeped from his armor, at the gorget and beneath the arm.

"They came upon us so quickly there was no time for talk, and the sand was everywhere. I could hardly see the tip of my sword. They saw only the bronze."

"Who? Who saw the bronze? Who attacked you?" Ren begged.

"The Harkan Army."

Ren bit down hard on his lip.

"In the sand, in the fog of battle, they saw only the color of our shields. The Harkans thought we were an advance force, part of the Protector's Army, so they came at us. They moved with such speed that we had no choice but to defend ourselves. By the time I could explain . . ."

"It was too late," said Ren. "I see it."

"They barely stopped to inspect the corpses," said Barden. "They were moving fast, taking up some new position while the Protector was distracted."

"But your men, your army?" asked Ren. "All dead?"

"It was mainly the outlanders that bolstered my legions, the mercenaries, and the freed servants. They made an immense force, but my own numbers were relatively few."

"The outlanders left you," said Ren.

"I know. That was our agreement. The free companies will be gone by sunset, the others as well. They were here to burn and loot—nothing more."

"The Harkans came to fight, not to plunder and rape."

"Rape." Barden swallowed as he spoke the word. "You judge me harshly—I see it," he said, "but I did what I thought necessary. I didn't know I'd have a man on the inside, someone who could open the door. I had to assume there would be a siege and I would need a great host to combat the Protector."

Ren looked at the man with pity. "You were cut down by your own plot, by the confusion you sowed within the city."

Barden gave no reply. The truth of Ren's words lay all around him, in fallen bodies and cloven shields.

"The battle is not yet over, Ren. You haven't said your name, but I know who you are. I see my eyes in that face of yours. I did this for you, for our family. We will never again suffer beneath the empire. I know what they'll say about me. They'll call me the Butcher of Solus, the man who plundered the city of the gods. I don't care. I'm dead anyway, but your hands are clean. Find Mered and finish what I started. The city is crippled. I made a terrible bargain to get it done, but those choices are in the past. Join the Harkans and take on the army of the Protector. It's an honorable fight, and it's good to see it fall to an honorable man. I never had the luxury of honor. I grew up without name or rank. I was no one, but I raised a great army and did what no one else could accomplish."

"I know," said Ren. He wanted to judge the man, to tell him of the atrocities he'd seen, but he bit his lip. The life was already fading from Barden's eyes.

"Go," Barden said. His grip loosened on Ren's hand and the life fled from him, his skin turning gray, his face drooping, the muscles relaxing as death took hold of him.

Ren's fingers remained enmeshed with the dead man's. *This is my uncle, my blood.* He saw the good and the bad. Then he stood, his hand parting from Barden's lifeless grip. There was not even time to say a word in his name. The battle called.

⇒ 61 ⇐

Sarra stood on the high wall, watching as the Kiltet completed their work. The doors of the Empyreal Domain had closed with an awful crack, rending spears and whatever else was thrust into the breach. In those last few moments, as the doors snapped shut, there'd been a terrible flood of men and metal, soldiers and civilians, people carrying everything they had, jostling one another to slip through that ever-narrowing gap. A bit of wood burst in two when the doors at last met. Splinters showered the lawn and a bronze sword bent sideways. A dozen stout men stood beside each door, sweat on their backs, their hands gripping the massive, wheel-like mechanisms that slowly ratcheted the doors closed. The gears made a click-clicking sound that rang out with each rotation. Click. Turn. Click. Turn. They gave it one last crank, one more deafening click, then shook out their weary hands. The work was finished. The people were saved, or at least most of them were. A small crowd gathered outside the wall, but the better part of Solus was protected by the wall and the army of the Protector. Sarra had seen them in those last moments, rushing to cut off the outlanders' advance, and they'd done it.

The doors of the Empyreal Domain were at rest.

The air was quiet, hushed.

The people stood in awe. This was not Solus, not the Waset, nor was it even the White-Wall district. This was the true city of the gods.

The Empyreal Domain.

No god had trod upon these stones in two centuries, but little had changed since the Soleri walked these paths, or at least it looked as if that were the case. The stone paths were raked thrice daily, every pebble put in order, every stray blossom swept away before it could disturb the order of the place. This was the sacred precinct Sarra had come to know: a place where the walls were so white they did not reflect light, they became it. Every surface was plastered in a lime so fresh, so smoothly polished that it showed no blemish, nor did it give evidence of the worker's hand. Every wall was a mirror to the sun, a reflection of Mithra cast out onto the world, and that reflection brought awe to the masses. They had lived in Solus and known opulence. Some might have witnessed Mered's palace, as Sarra had, and there was beauty there, but the Cloud Garden held none of the domain's splendor. This was the gods' sanctuary.

The people turned in circles, stumbling, trying not to crush the delicate flowers, sidestepping the many-blossomed plants as they attempted to fan out, to give one another some space, room enough to take it all in.

Sarra realized the usefulness of the moment. She stepped out into the crowd, her robe of gold gleaming like the walls of the domain. It glowed like a ray of Mithra's light. *They must know I saved them*, she thought. *I opened the doors and rescued them from the outlanders.* She motioned for the people to approach their Ray, and a crowd gathered around Sarra.

"I am Kantafre of House Ini," said one man.

"I am Sandir of House Teron."

"Tramor of House Illyd."

"Gilia of House Ajor."

They came to Sarra and she comforted them. "We are safe here," she said to the dozen or so who surrounded her, to whomever was in earshot. "No army has ever pierced the Shroud Wall. There is food in the fields. We can shelter here until order is restored." She made no mention of the First Among Equals, or whatever it was Mered had named himself. This was her moment. Though the Protector *had* come to the people's aid, he'd waited too long. Too many were slaughtered while Mered stood idle.

Sarra *had* acted. She had opened the doors and given shelter to the people.

There was an irony in it all.

Mered had locked her in the domain, but in doing so he had put her in the one place where she was safe. In fact, it was also the one place where she could provide aid to the people of Solus. The sacred precinct protected Sarra, just as it protected the citizenry. She had at last earned the goodwill of Solus, of the thousands who had hurried through the gates.

She did her best to accept their thanks, to show her generosity, her kindness. She offered them food and protection, and everyone was glad to accept it, more than glad—they were ecstatic. Some kissed the ground, praising the gods they had so recently scorned. They walked in amazement, gaping at the golden monuments, at the dancing fountains and strange grottos, still shocked by the opening of the doors and the realization that they were alive and well and safe from the marauders. Every last one of them, she guessed, had given themselves up for dead, but they lived. It was almost as if they had entered a second life, for surely the first was lost, and this new life was filled with beauty, with glistening white walls and statues polished to a mirror's radiance. *This must feel like the afterlife to some of them,* she thought, *or something close to it.*

In the distance a small group of men had at last made it to the great doors of the palace, the ones that led down under the ground and into what had once been the true home of the Soleri, the throne room and the grand solar. They stood at the doors but none dared touch them.

Sarra eyed the tower of the Ray.

She raised the hem of her golden robe and took one small step toward it, her eyes cast in the opposite direction, looking as if something in the distance had caught their attention. She did not walk directly to the tower, nor did she allow the slightest bit of concern to show on her face. She patted backs and kissed children. She followed the winding paths of the garden, ever watchful.

I allowed myself to be caught up in the moment, she thought, *but there is still a secret here and I had no time to conceal it.* The doors to the palace were not barred in any way. No sentry stood before them. Beyond the threshold, the people would discover the true domain of the gods. If the stories were true, the light of Tolemy would reduce them to ash, but she very much doubted that would happen. Still, no sane man would cross that threshold, but this had been a day without sanity. The people had lost their fear. Sensing the mood of the crowd, Sarra walked a little more swiftly, patting fewer backs, skipping over a handful of greetings as she made her way to the tower.

One of the doors of the great house swiveled just slightly on its hinges.

Perhaps a breeze had caught it. The movement was nearly imperceptible. Still, Sarra walked a little faster, knowing all too well what someone would find inside and how they would react. She had once felt the shock of seeing the burnt chamber, the Amber Throne smashed. She doubted the commoners would view it with the same sense of calm detachment she'd summoned the day she walked into that room.

A man slipped through the open door of the great house. He quickly retreated, but a boy took his place. Others followed, slowly, cautiously. A girl crossed the threshold then withdrew, body shaking. A woman nearly collapsed with fear when she saw what must have been her husband cross beneath the lintel. Right after that, a young boy passed through the doorway, only to retreat like the others, but he was the last to be cowed. One after another they disappeared into the dark halls of the great house.

For her part, Sarra maintained her composure. She showed no fear, though she felt it, in her bones and in her quivering fingers. *If only I'd had the time or the foresight to block off the palace,* she thought, but quickly banished the notion. If the doors had been barred, the people would have ripped down the barriers. They were an unruly mob. Many had seen members of their family put to the sword—husbands, wives, and children. Their houses were, in all likelihood, looted or burned to the ground, maybe both. They'd been chased by outlanders or robbed by one of the free companies. They were at their wits' end. The people wanted protection; they wanted to see the faces of the gods and know why they'd hidden behind this wall. *They won't like the answer,* thought Sarra.

She made her way as best as she could, eyeing the tower, motioning to the Kiltet, signaling with hand gestures for them to gather at the entry.

A shout rang out from the depths of the palace. She guessed they'd come upon the throne room. A moment later, men hurried through the open doors of the great house. They carried the Amber Throne. A dozen or more held up its burnt remains. Confusion washed over the crowd. The people looked at the wonders around them, at the winding gardens and glistening statues. None of them knew how to make sense of it. Then the bodies of Suten Anu and Amen Saad emerged through the palace doors, carried high above for all to witness.

The people saw the truth.

It lay in the dead body of Sarra's predecessor and in the burnt remains of what had been the gods' throne.

Sarra scissored through the crowd. The people's eyes were still on the chair and they flocked toward it, to the center of the domain, not the periphery where her tower lay. She pushed roughly past the crowd she had formerly embraced, knowing full well what would come next.

The Kiltet were in position. The tower was a kind of spiral, a cone of sorts, larger at the base and smaller at the top. A stone stair wound its way up the interior, doors at every level. There was safety in the spire, but she needed to reach it before the crowd blocked her path. Someone called out to her, to the First Ray of the Sun, the woman who was once the Mother. They cried out for some explanation, for surely Sarra, if anyone, ought to have it.

The crowd wanted answers she could not provide. How could she even attempt to unravel the mystery of the burned throne room? She did not even understand it herself.

The people cried out to Sarra, but she did not run. Only the guilty flee.

When they shouted, she acted as if she could not hear them. When they cried for answers, she gave them no recognition. The tower was close, after all.

Men ran toward her, coming at her with the bodies, the throne, and a thousand different relics they'd unearthed from the great house. The truth of the empire was exposed. Sarra had saved her people, but not herself—not yet, at least.

The Kiltet waited. They opened the tower door for Sarra and she was only a step or two away from it, but the mob had gotten there first.

⇥62⇤

Merit Hark-Wadi wanted to live. She'd stumbled through the gates of the Empyreal Domain, but that was as far as she'd made it. Somewhere just inside those grand doors she'd collapsed on the stony path. Merit was almost certain her right foot was broken, crushed by the mob, and there was something wrong with her knee. She had a stabbing pain in her ribs and in her jaw. Merit had to punch her own chin just to throw it back into place. She thanked the gods that only one of her hands was broken. Her jaw felt better, but every other piece of her ached. The crowd had done more damage to her body than she'd realized.

"I'm going to live through this day," she said aloud, but no one paid her the slightest bit of attention. The people were shouting and running this way and that. It hadn't been like that a moment ago. They had been celebrating. Through the pain, she remembered how the people had rejoiced upon entering this holy place, but for some reason they'd traded those cheers for snarls.

"What's happening?" she asked the man who stood nearest to where she knelt.

He was pulling at his well-groomed beard, at the rings that were threaded into the black hair. He gave no reply.

"What are they doing?" she asked.

He gave her a pitiful look, which told Merit she was in worse shape than she had guessed.

"They've found . . ." The man started, but he didn't seem to know how to finish.

"Found what?" Merit asked.

"The throne of Tolemy," he said, his words coming out slowly, reluctantly.

"Where?"

He pointed with one of his ringed fingers, but Merit had already caught sight of the thing.

The throne room is smashed, destroyed centuries ago. She recalled her father's words. The truth behind the empire had at last seen the light of day, and the people of Solus were not pleased with their discovery. Merit needed to move, lest she be trampled once more. She marshaled her strength and tried to stand, but her foot would not comply. She was forced to crawl instead of walk until she reached the Shroud Wall, where Merit braced one arm against it for balance and righted herself. With only one foot, she would have to follow along the wall if she wanted to move around, and she definitely needed to do that. Merit wanted desperately to find her mother.

"Keep your eyes open." She was talking out loud again. "You're not going to die today."

A man heard her speak, another highborn fellow with a well-groomed beard and silken robe. He looked twice in her direction then moved away. The people were all gathering around some tower, clambering to get inside, but the door was closed.

"Is she inside?" Merit asked, leaning against the wall, pulling at the silken robes of some stranger. "Is she in there? Is the Ray inside that tower?" she asked another.

"No," said a woman, a commoner in a common-looking tunic. The man beside her, a soldier in bronze mail, disagreed. He said the Ray of the Sun *had* gone into the tower. "I seen her robe, the gold one, go right through that door before they shut it."

"And her hair?" Merit asked.

"Red as the bloodiest of sunsets," said the soldier.

The other was still shaking her head. "She escaped. She's among us somewhere. Find the Ray!" she cried, and others did the same, but most were gathering around the tower, besieging its doors as they had once besieged the doors of the Empyreal Domain.

Is there no end to this? she wondered.

Merit wanted to sleep. She wanted to shut her eyes and never wake.

"No," she muttered. "Not today." Then she felt a sudden dizziness. She was moving. Hands wrapped her mouth, covering it so she could not scream. She was lifted from the ground; her feet dangled in the air. She struggled but she lacked the strength to set herself free. In truth, she had almost no strength at all, and the man must have been twice her size, twice her weight as well. Any fight would be futile; she would only harm herself. Merit relented, and the man drew her through the crowd. Merit's vision wavered. There was darkness, a door, then light. A voice. Someone was speaking to Merit.

"Be gentle," said the woman.

Merit knew she ought to recognize who was speaking, but she didn't. "I know you."

"Open your eyes."

Sarra Amunet stood before Merit.

She was dressed in the Ray's livery, a robe woven from threads of gold, a garment so marvelous it did not even look as if it were a piece of clothing. It had the character of a gem-encrusted crown, an ornament, something so precious that it ought to be stored away in some great vault. Instead, it was caked in dust and sand. Sarra stood there, sweat beading on her forehead, hair sodden, dirt on her hands. A dozen men surrounded the Ray, the servants of the Kiltet, or so Merit presumed.

Sarra made some gesture indicating that two men should stand guard at the door while she took the rest of the Kiltet and hurried up the stair. They climbed and a door was shut behind them, a bolt slid into place. Safe.

Sarra went to the window.

"I saved them," she said. "I saw what the outlanders intended and I could not allow it. They were my flock, the followers of Mithra. How could I let them die? I was their Mother . . ."

"And mine," said Merit.

"I know. It's why I opened the doors, I couldn't . . ."

"It's all right," said Merit through the pain. "I know . . . what you did. You gave away the most precious thing in the world."

"The secret of the Soleri?" asked Sarra. "It was my pleasure to reveal it." She rubbed her hands across the golden robe, crinkling the metallic threads. She breathed. "We have some time, not much . . . but a little." They climbed another stair, passed another door, and entered a small and sparsely furnished chamber.

The strong man laid Merit on a low pallet, carefully resting her against the wood. Then he left the chamber and the two were alone—mother and daughter.

"Do you know why I left Harwen?" Sarra asked without preamble. She simply cut to the heart of the matter. Time was in short supply, after all.

"What?" Merit asked, still shuddering, still fighting to stay conscious.

"Why I left Harwen. Did you ever learn the truth?"

"Truth?" Merit asked.

"Yes, the truth. I left to save your brother," said Sarra. "I wanted you to know before"—she was briefly at a loss for words—"before this ends. I need you to know that I didn't give up on my family. I didn't want things to go the way they did. After I left Harwen, I reached out to you. I assumed your father hid my scrolls, but when you were older?"

"I ignored the letters. I never broke the wax. I'm sorry. I knew only what Arko told me. He said that leaving was your idea, and that you had chosen to go. I guessed there was more to it. There were whispers of another woman, one he truly loved."

"Don't," said Sarra. She raised a hand.

Merit was surprised that the near mention of that other woman, her father's mistress, could still bring hurt to her mother. She knew so little of Sarra, so naturally she had questions. She'd heard Ott's explanation of Sarra's leaving, but she hadn't fully accepted it.

"Again, tell me why you left Harwen? I've heard your son's version of it, and a bit of yours, but I don't know if I believe either. Instead of leaving us, why not simply hide your child? Let the butcher's wife raise the boy. Keep him close at your side but stay at your throne, and with your family. Stay and be queen. Why did you leave us? That's what I've always wondered, and what Ott's story did little to explain. Why did you leave? Was it all about Ott? What about your daughters, your husband, and your kingdom too?"

The questions gave Sarra pause. "I couldn't stay," she said at last. "I wore the crown, but I was not queen, not *his* queen. I could not stand the insult. I know that other women accept such things, that Arko's mother had lived with Koren's mistress. I couldn't do it. I could not stand the shame. You cannot understand what it's like to be a girl from a poor and dishonored family, a small house from an even smaller kingdom. We were gnawing on fish bones when the Harkans came to escort me to Harwen, to meet the great king and stand in his mighty hall, to be the arranged wife of the man whose father stood against Tolemy, against a god, if you believe in all that. I wanted his acceptance. I needed it more than anything I had ever desired."

"Yet you were denied?"

"Always. Remember, the emperor arranged our marriage. Your father saw me as Tolemy's proxy, a punishment of sorts—nothing more."

"I guessed at some of this. I was ten and six. Girls of that age are sensitive to such things. I'd heard rumors about the other woman. I just thought . . ."

"You thought . . . what? That it did not matter that my husband loved another, had loved her as a child, and loved her still on the day he died? It mattered to me. I wanted to be his equal, his queen, the one he valued above any other, not some peasant girl from a nowhere island in the Wyrre. But he never treated me as anything else. Our marriage was a burden, an awful edict from an unkind emperor. I was no prize. I was a penance. And to make matters worse, to make the insult complete, the girl—that bitch, Serena—was born in the Wyrre. Her father was bred from slave stock in the southern reach, but he was said to be the best scribe in the city. He was called on to tutor the boy who would one day be king, and he brought his daughter to live with him in the Hornring. Serena. The honey-haired girl who wrecked my kingdom. I never had a chance with the king, and he never gave me one. I was just another casualty in his little war, you see. The man was stuffed full of defiance. He didn't serve in the priory. He did not observe the Devouring. And he certainly would not fuck the woman Tolemy named his wife."

"You've said that twice," said Merit. "I feel for you. I'm sorry, but some admired his determination. They saw strength in it. He was the one man who never bent the knee, never surrendered. If it will offer you any comfort, it was only the commoners who worshipped him. In his own eyes, in my father's estimation, he *was* a failure. He failed to stand against the empire. His father had done that. He failed at his own marriage and he knew it, Sarra. He knew he failed you, that you wanted more. Is that why you sought your own power, your own place beyond Harwen?"

Sarra seemed restless now. She paced, her hands pressed to the golden robe. "Perhaps," she said, her red hair as luminous as the golden robe. *She's beautiful,* thought Merit. *How could any man reject her?*

Sarra spoke softly when she continued, "There was only one place I could go, one place where even a king could not touch me. Mithra shelters all who see His light—or claim to, at least. I saw little of Mithra, but I took full advantage of His protection."

"You found what you wanted?" Merit asked.

"I found what I needed, what I still I need. Ott was only the excuse I had long sought. The last shove that sent me toppling over the edge. I did not want to leave my daughters, but I could not take you with me. You belonged to the king. If I'd left with you and your sister, Arko would have chased after me. It was the only way out, I'm . . ."

"Don't apologize," said Merit. "I've never done it, so I can hardly expect you to do it either. After all, I am your daughter, and I've committed my share of sins. I'm sure you're aware of them."

The distant sound of breaking wood reverberated throughout the room. The mob had entered the tower, and their footsteps beat against the stair. Merit eyed the heavy wooden door. "There must be some way out of this place," she said, voice trembling. "Why else would you bring me here? Why not hide in the limitless depths of the palace?"

Sarra nodded, but her eyes were mournful, her face paler than usual. She did not speak.

The door rattled.

"We should go," said Sarra, almost absently, as if death did not wait beyond that barrier.

They ascended a set of stairs, feet shuffling over sand-covered winders. They entered a chamber and the men of the Kiltet closed the door, the wood sealing shut with a whisper, the bolt sliding home with a thud, the sound of footsteps chasing Sarra, the crowd howling at her back.

⩘63⩗

Solus. In all her ten and six years Kepi had never once seen the empire's capital. She'd heard plenty about it. The city was said to shine like the sun itself. The stories all claimed it was a marvel to the eye, its walls polished like marble and sculpted by men whom the gods themselves had trained, whose skills and talents were lost to time.

However, the Solus she saw didn't look much like the one in the stories. As a matter of fact, it didn't look like much at all. Perhaps it resembled a campfire someone had forgotten to stamp out, but that was the best image she could summon. Smoke obscured most of the city. Only the faint outlines of the ramparts were visible, a pair of pylons, and the last of Mered's soldiers, hurrying as they fled toward the city gates.

Kepi rode near the head of the Feren column, not far behind her scouts, racing with Ferris and his sworn men. They'd followed Mered's army, hounding them through forest and desert, trading arrows while the red soldiers rode back-to-back to fight off the oncoming riders. There were casualties all around, but Mered's forces had refused to slow their retreat and the army of Feren had nipped at their heels. She'd pursued his army, but she had not overtaken them, not until they reached the walls of Solus, where Mered's soldiers were forced to narrow their ranks to pass through the city gates. His army piled up against the wall and the Ferens galloped into their ranks, cutting at them from behind.

Perhaps the retreating soldiers hoped the wall's defenses would protect them. There were archers on the pylons. They cut loose with a great volley, but the shafts struck bronze armor just as often as they hit Feren mail.

As she came upon the gates, a gust of sand swept over the city, blinding her opponents, blinding everyone. In the confusion, the red soldiers struck at their own and the Ferens did the same. They fought amid the sand, the soldiers in red half retreating, half fighting, clashing here, escaping there. The bowmen on the wall had all but given up. The gates were open. Mered needed his men. The doors to the city yawned and Kepi bolted toward them, the kite flying low beside her horse. She felt the air on its wings. Her thoughts wavered and she saw through the kite's eyes, saw herself and Ferris. *Up,* she willed the creature, and it soared above the wall. The archers sent shafts chasing after it. The kite wheeled, carving a great arc in the sky before descending upon the bowmen. It took hold of one, lifted him from the wall, and tossed the man at his own soldiers. Three more followed him in close succession.

"Kepi!" Ferris knocked into her horse.

No, she realized. She had bumped into his mount and nearly sent the two of them tumbling to the ground. He held the reins to her horse. Ferris placed them in her hand. "This is no time for daydreams."

"I . . ." She'd seen through the kite's eyes. There was no way to explain it, so she gave her horse a good kick and rode off. They were at the wall and Mered's men were all around them. In fact, one slipped between Ferris and Kepi, but the kite swept the man from his horse with unearthly speed, making it seem as if he'd vanished from the saddle. Even the horse was confused; it bucked and turned, searching for its master.

An arrow struck her saddle, wedging itself into the heavy leather. There was a shield tied to her mount and she unslung it and held it above her head as they rode beneath the wall. She gripped the horse with her legs and let go of the reins. She needed her sword arm free, and the other held the shield. Ferris had done the same and she saw some of his men copying the move. They would not pass easily through the walls of Solus, even with Mered's men in their company and the sandstorm obscuring the view. The fortifications above and beside them swarmed with soldiers: archers nocking arrows, footmen tossing stones or lobbing them with slings. A jar exploded into flame as she rode through the gates. It burned more soldiers in red than silver, but such was the day. The Ferens had thrown the imperial retreat into complete disarray, and they were determined to keep it up.

"Keep the fight here, at the doors," said Kepi. Though they'd passed into the city, the Feren riders needed to reverse their charge and block the red army's advance. It was the only way to make certain the gates stood open. Sooner or later they'd close those doors and she'd have no way to open them. The mechanism appeared to be hidden within the pylons, and she had no means to breach the towers, and no time to attempt it.

Kepi turned her horse, galloping into the oncoming soldiers, veering left and right, avoiding the men in silver, striking whenever she saw red or bronze. Ferris turned too and his sworn men followed. All in all, a hundred or so Ferens lingered at the gates, making a mess of things and hacking at every foe who passed. They danced between the oncoming riders, allowing the Ferens to pass while they blocked every soldier in red who came within their reach. It didn't take long for their foes to respond. A portion of Mered's army halted their retreat, formed up a squad, and came charging at Kepi and her company. However, this only had the effect of causing more confusion, which made the scuffle at the gate even larger, delaying both sides from passing through it.

If it were not for the kite, the battle might have tipped in favor of the red army, but the mere presence of the creature had caused a stir. Some stood on the wall and simply gawked at the thing. They were the first to be tossed from the walk, but not the last. Though arrows struck the great bird, the creature was undeterred, perhaps even unharmed. It flung soldier after soldier from the ramparts and it did so with deadly aim, hurtling the bronze-armored warriors at the red ones, toppling man and horse in a single strike. It cut through rows of soldiers, sending men fleeing in all directions. Out of sheer exasperation, the gates were at last closed. Perhaps the men who operated them feared the kite would allow only the Ferens to pass, which was exactly what it had done.

The Feren Army had entered Solus.

Kepi steeled herself for a fight.

She assumed Mered's armies would stop this host of invaders from pouring into their city. Any rational man would bar the Ferens at the gates, but the armies of Mered rode off toward their companions, leaving little or no one to thwart the Feren charge.

"Strange," said Ferris. "They must have orders to march straight back to Mered's side. He's let fear overcome his judgment."

"Let's not worry over the reasons," said Kepi, her horse turning this way and that. "We are in Solus and they've closed the doors behind us, if you haven't noticed."

"Aye," said Ferris, "we should ride."

Kepi knew that victory was the only key that would allow them to leave, so they took up their pursuit, galloping into a city that was already packed with invaders. Armies of mercenaries roamed the streets, looting and burning the houses of the wealthy, and the sand-dwellers were everywhere. The city was awash in flame. Men ran this way and that, carrying buckets to douse fires while others lifted spears to chase after the sand-dwellers. There were caravans piled high with stolen loot, packed up and headed out of the city, toward some other gate, she guessed. The outlanders clashed with the soldiers in red and blue and yellow, but there were simply too many intruders in the city and not enough men to protect it. The defenders were split between the battle, the looters, and the fire.

As far as she could tell, they were losing on all three fronts.

The fighting was all around them, but Kepi rode through it. She pursued, and the armies of Mered fled toward what she guessed was the Waset. A tall white wall rose in the distance and there, at its base, stood the main force of the Protector's Army. She knew them by their amber mail, but just beyond that patch of bronze, barely within the grasp of her view, she saw a small force, almost impossible to perceive at such a distance, but she glimpsed them: four or five hundred men, their armor as black as the night.

64

A loud thump announced the mob's arrival. The crack of an ax striking ironwood followed soon afterward, ringing in Sarra's ear, the wood
shattering, voices penetrating the door. The hacking would be slow.
Blackthorn did not easily split, but it could be sundered if enough force
were applied over a long enough period of time, and it did split. Hours
passed and more doors fell, one after another, hitting the ground with what
seemed like the regularity of the bells that chimed in the square. Soon
there would be no more hours, no more doors to break down, and no more
stairs to climb.

The nameless servant of the Kiltet set Merit down on the floor of the
last chamber, the highest room in the tower.

"Rest," said Sarra, then she turned to one of the spy holes in the tower
wall. The flames outside were brighter, the sky darker. Mered would
fight on; he had his army and the Protector's too, but Sarra saw little
point in it. There was hardly any city left to defend.

She pressed her back to the tower wall. The cold stone chilled her
skin, and her heartbeat slowed. She slumped to the floor and sat shoulder
to shoulder with her daughter.

"I have food," she said. The chamber had a chest and she knew there
were provisions in it. Sarra went and opened the box. She set out a cloth
and placed dried meat on it, jars of amber.

"We could have a proper meal," she told her daughter. "Just you and
me, just this once."

Merit opened her eyes. Her lips were dry and cracked. "Yes," she said.
"It's been some time since I've eaten." Sarra put the cup to her daughter's
lips and Merit drank.

"One last meal," said Sarra. She offered Merit a bit of meat, tearing off
a strip for her to chew. Sarra took one and she offered another to the man
from the Kiltet. He gnawed at the meat as he pressed his back to the jit-
tering door. A loud thump rang out as some ax or club struck the wood.
Sarra ignored it. *I just want one moment, one meal with my daughter.*

"You look like shit," said Sarra.

Merit grinned.

"It's nothing that won't heal, but you may want to take some time to rest when this is done."

"When what is done?" asked Merit. She was clearly in pain, barely conscious by all appearances.

"All of this, all of Solus really."

The strike of an ax rattled the door.

"This isn't the first time the rabble has come for me," Sarra said, "though it is the first time they've come after the right person."

"You're talking about the last day of the year?" Merit asked, her voice soft, distant, her eyes fixed on the wall.

"I was supposed to stand on the wall."

"I know."

"But it wasn't me. They tore apart a priestess, a girl who shared my features."

"Are you confessing?" Merit asked. "There's hardly any point in that." She seemed more awake, more aware. Perhaps the amber had done her some good.

Sarra offered her daughter another drink. "I'm not confessing. I'm just pondering the last few weeks. Perhaps I've been living on borrowed time. Maybe the crowds *were* meant to take me that day, but I cheated death, deprived Him of His prize."

"I thought Horu could never be robbed." Merit reached for the dried meat. She could barely chew.

"My point exactly," said Sarra. "Maybe these last few weeks have just been an afterlife of sorts, a chance to make things right."

"To meet your daughter?"

"Yes. I didn't want to leave this world without seeing your face or Kepi's." Her voice went quiet. "I suppose one is more than I could wish for. At least we have this moment. One meal. One hour. Just the two of us, here, at the end of it all. If only . . ."

"Kepi were here?"

"Yes."

"You would have liked her. She has a fierce soul. I saw her in Feren and she had the look of a queen, a true queen. They say she is Kitelord, a rightful ruler of Feren."

"I know. I know it all. I've heard every bit of news there is to hear about the both of you. It was only your faces I missed, and your voices too. I've forgotten Kepi's. She was six when I left, so I see that six-year-old. Is she still that girl? Would I know my own daughter if she stood before me?"

Merit chuckled a bit but came up short. Clearly, it hurt when she laughed. "She's hasn't changed a bit. She has the wrath of a girl half her age and the patience to match it. She is unchanged, though her hair is a bit shorter these days. It was long when she was a child, but she cuts it at the nape, wears it like a boy to match her figure, and her manners. She's Arko's daughter, though she would never admit it. She was the son he never had. Whether he forced her into that role or she did it just to please him, I could never tell, but she made every effort to become the boy that was stolen from him. She fights with the ferocity of a king and it has done her some good, saved her life more than once from what I've heard."

"Keep speaking," said Sarra. "We have time."

The door shook, but Merit went on about Kepi and their childhood. She spoke about her life, about Dagrun, and the wedding in Feren.

"I wanted him, that fool of a boy, that brash young king. I wanted Dagrun, but I never admitted it to myself. I don't even know how such things are possible, but I swear I kept the truth from myself. I said it was a ploy. Shenn and I talked about it like a game of Coin, how we would manipulate the man, forcing him into a marriage he did not want. Then we would marry General Tomen's eldest to Dagrun's warlord, Ferris, and another to Deccan. We had plans to entwine our kingdoms at every level. All for the purpose of doing this"—she gestured toward the window, to the fires and the looting—"the destruction of Solus. None of what I wished for came to pass, save for the last bit, the part I wanted most. Now I wish I had the rest. I wish I had Dagrun and none of this had ever happened."

"Have no regrets, your life is not yet at an end."

"Isn't it? Isn't *this* the end? Our last sup before the door comes crashing down?"

Sarra dipped her head and shook it slowly from side to side. "There is a way out," she said, "a passage that leads into the Hollows."

"Thank heavens," said Merit.

"There is a way out," said Sarra, "but it's not for both of us."

"Those aren't the Harkans," said Ren.

Tye caught sight of the distant army. "No, they're Ferens."

"We can all see them," said Kollen as he climbed to where Ren stood with Tye and Asher. They were perched atop the stairs of the Waset, raised above the inner city, still trying to find the Harkans when they caught sight of this new army. The Ferens chased what appeared to be imperial soldiers, hounding the men in bronze as they retreated toward the main body of the Protector's Army.

"Look, Ren, at the head of the Feren Army. There's a girl and she's got some sort of bird," said Tye. "Do you think?"

"It's my sister? Maybe," said Ren. "I can barely make out her face."

"Too bad she's chasing the ass end of our enemy," Tye lamented.

"Well, that's generally how a chase works," said Kollen, "but I take your meaning. Your sweet sister won't be helping us anytime soon, Ren."

Mered's army stood between the Ferens and the kingsguard.

"Where are the damned Harkans?" Ren asked. He still hadn't set eyes on them.

"There!" Tye said, punching at Ren's shoulder so he'd turn. In the distance, beyond the Protector's Army, past Mered and his palanquin, black spears poked at the sand-infested sky. The army of Harkana had engaged the Protector.

"They must have marched the whole army up and out of the Waset, coming around so they could strike at the Protector's back," said Asher. "That's why we couldn't find them. They left the inner city."

"Yes, but how'd they get all the way over there? They must have run like madmen," said Kollen.

"Like soldiers," said Asher with a scoff. "Those are Tomen's men."

"It might be a brilliant maneuver, but it does us no good," said Ren. "Our allies have surrounded Mered. He's outflanked, but they've left us in a lurch."

"What do we do?" asked Tye, sheepish, exhausted. "They'll slaughter us if we stand here."

Mered was once more standing atop his palanquin, directing his troops, sending more soldiers hurrying toward the kingsguard. He barely took notice of the Harkan Army.

"He's bent on defeating the kingsguard," said Kollen, "or maybe he's just got a grudge against you, Ren."

Ren simply shook his head as a wall of bronze shields approached, the soldiers advancing one step at a time, a drum beating, the now-familiar clarion ringing in the distance. Some unseen commander shouted orders. Signal flags waved. A red one flashed. Arrows dotted the sky. A blue one flapped and rocks pelted the Harkan shields.

"We can't hold this position," said Asher.

"That wasn't my plan," said Ren, his voice nearly swallowed by the relentless din of the approaching army. The clap of their sandals was near deafening, and the drums were even louder.

"Behind us," said Asher. Mered's house army had begun a second advance. Red shields approached from one direction, bronze from the other.

"Trapped," muttered Ren. He looked for a way out, but it was too late to find one. The red army struck with astounding speed, driving the Harkans back toward the bronze soldiers. The kingsguard withdrew, Butcher dragging Ott, the ransoms stumbling, jostled this way and that by the retreating men. The black shields simply did not have enough soldiers to hold back their adversary's charge, so they were flung to and fro as the two armies, the red and bronze, converged on them.

Heels ground against the cobblestones, men shouted, and swords danced in their air. A spear struck the man at Ren's side. A clean shot, in and out. The Harkan hit the earth and no one took up his place. Everywhere, the kingsguard were falling; one by one they hit the stones. Dozens, possibly more, lay dead, and they were dropping faster than he could count. A spear here, an arrow there. A bullet struck one man; an arrow dropped another. A push. A shove. A dozen shouts. Ten men fell. Another twenty dropped to their knees. A cloven shield arced through the sky. A man searched in vain for his dismembered hand. Ren had never seen such carnage. There was no hope here, no mercy. The black shields were overrun. The Harkans fled and they trampled one another. Feet mashed limbs. A man dodged one spear, but collided with another. Soldiers butted heads, knocked shields and armor. There was nowhere to go. There was nowhere to even stand, not unless Ren wanted to step on one of his fallen companions.

He saw the truth of their situation.

Soon there would be no kingsguard, no ransoms, and as if that were not reason enough for Ren to lose his mind, that buzzing sound appeared once more at the back of his head, louder and more distinct. It called to him, and the gnarled eld horn felt heavy in his pack. Tye stood with the last of the kingsguard. If he wanted her to survive, to live, he needed to end this fight.

Some instinct made him run.

He fled the Harkans' ranks, hurrying toward the garden of statues. When the black shields saw him run, some called him a coward, a foolish boy who had shirked his duty. Perhaps they thought he'd lost his nerve, or that he was never meant to be a king.

Ren paid them no attention; he knew what he was doing.

He'd circled those golden effigies since he stepped out of the Hollows. He'd fought among the twelve and beside them. He'd sheltered in the caverns beneath the statues. He'd come and gone and all the while that odd buzzing sound had followed him. At first, he thought he'd knocked his head a bit too hard on that granite pedestal. He told himself the noise was just a good headache, but he knew better. Instinct told him to open his ears, to close his eyes and follow the sound.

Ren stumbled into the garden and fell to his knees, his hand touching the eld horn. He cleared his thoughts and the terrible sound transformed. Slowly, bit by bit, that awful humming, that horror in his head that had sounded like the buzzing of a thousand bees, resolved into something distinct. He heard voices, twelve voices, that spoke in volumes. Each utterance was a thousand words crammed into the space of a heartbeat, and it all sounded like noise to Ren. There were simply too many words crushed into too little space. His mind had no way to parse it. Then something changed, or maybe *he* changed. Perhaps he was at last ready to speak to the twelve.

Ren had spent the better part of his life trying to find out who he was and where he'd come from, but the answer to that question was something older and stranger than anything he could imagine. Noll had told it all to him, but he hadn't embraced it—not fully. He wasn't even certain how to take hold of it. Ren held the blood of Mithra. It coursed through his veins, and there was proof. He'd communed with the eld, and his sister had done something similar. In the air, above her army, the kite circled. He felt its power and knew it was the same strength that flowed through the eld horn. He guessed that Merit and Ott also shared that power. The children of Arko held the blood of Mithra-Sol and his offspring, Re and Pyras.

Ren gripped that gnarled tusk a bit more tightly.

He feared what would come next, but he had little choice. With every heartbeat that passed, a man fell to the ground. The four hundred soldiers became three and soon there would only be two and so on. The black shields would not last the hour.

Ren took up the eld horn staff, and an odd sensation wriggled through his fingers. It washed over him in waves, and each one made him stronger. His blood beat faster, his thoughts raced. He kneeled before the twelve and knew their names. They revealed their true nature and he accepted it. They were the sons of Pyras, the ones who struck at Soleri. Centuries ago, the gods fought one another to a standstill. In that conflict, the Pyraethi sought to destroy the Soleri and their empire. And now it was time for them to complete that task. They spoke . . . but something broke his concentration. Cries of war, the terrible shouts of men, shattered the air. Sandals beat upon the cobblestones. Soldiers in red, a whole pack of them, charged straight at him.

⇟ 66 ⇞

There were no more doors, and nowhere left to flee.

"What now?" Merit asked, her body awash with agony. She could no longer walk or hobble as she'd done in the yard. Her knee and foot were swollen, and even the slightest pressure elicited an unbearable pain. Her jaw throbbed and the amber had done little to quell her thirst.

"Where do we go?" Merit asked, coughing a bit when the pain set in again.

Sarra pursed her lips. "At this level, the tower connects to the Shroud Wall. There is a passage within the wall itself. It will take you down into the Hollows. Beyond that, there is a web of tunnels. These corridors were once used by the Soleri to commune with the priests and priestesses of the royal cults. This place we're in, the Tower of the Ray, was once the royal observatory. The Soleri came here to see the stars, to speak of poetry and philosophy, to talk of Mithra and the home before time. I read this in Ott's notes, my son's notes—"

"Sarra," Merit interrupted.

"I'm sorry. I was just trying to keep my mind off the present." A loud thump echoed through the chamber.

"The ax," Merit muttered. "They're at it once more."

"I'd give it a rest if I were them. I saved their lives. The least they can do is thank me."

"I doubt there'll be much time for talk when that door comes down," said Merit.

"No, there won't be, but I'll give it a try. I've talked my way out of more situations than I can recall. Why not one more?"

"Yes," said Merit. She forced her voice to sound hopeful and high. "But why not escape into this passage you described?"

"They'll follow us, just as they followed us up the tower steps. The mob wants my head. They need someone to blame. They want to find the liar and put their hands around her neck."

"You don't know that. You saved these very same people, you said as much a moment ago."

"Yes. I saved them. And when I did, I hoped fear might keep them out of the palace of the Soleri. If only I'd had time to seal the doors . . ."

"They'd have wanted to see their gods eventually. The people of Solus begged for the Soleri, not Sarra."

"I know. We are curious beings. We seek answers to the questions that cannot be answered. I will do my best to provide the impossible. Perhaps the mob will listen," said Sarra.

"Don't chance it."

"I have to, but you don't," said Sarra. "You're leaving. Now, preferably." She gestured, and the man from the Kiltet lifted Merit.

The pain was exquisite.

Merit motioned for him to set her down, but that only elicited more pain. All movement meant pain. The best thing she could do was sit still in this man's arms.

"You will go and I will stay," said Sarra.

"Why?"

"Don't be foolish. You know how this must end," said Sarra, and indeed Merit did know what was next.

"The people watched me slip through the tower door. They will not rest until they've found me. They want answers. For two centuries, this city lived beneath a lie. They toiled away at their petty lives thinking they were protected by the all-powerful Soleri. They believed they were forever safe, that no army could penetrate these walls, that no one would even dare. In truth, those same gods are absent, gone for centuries. Maybe they've been missing since the Harkan revolt. That's my guess. This mob wants answers, but I have none. Suten must have known a few of them, and maybe he passed that knowledge to Arko. The truth is out there, but the tablets are written in the gods' own script, and we hardly had time to decipher much of it. The mob will demand some explanation from the Mouth of Tolemy. They saw me enter this tower. You, on the other hand . . . you aren't even here. No one saw you enter and no one will see you depart. If I leave, they will follow me. If I stay, they'll have what they want. They won't stop to look too hard for a secret door, a hidden passage that leads into the Hollows."

"Mother."

"Stop. You cannot deny the logic of it. If I am not here, they will tear this chamber apart. The mob will find the concealed door and the pursuit will begin anew. My flight ends here. I will stay, and our friend will carry you to safety."

"I won't go."

"You don't have a choice," Sarra said. "Remember, the oaf works for me."

"I'll refuse. I'll pull myself from his arms. I'll scream until the mob finds the passage."

"Will you?" Sarra asked. "There's no point in both of us dying, and perhaps I can yet talk my way out of this. You will go."

"No."

"Go," Sarra begged. "For once, let me be your mother. Give me this one favor. One good deed to offset a lifetime of bad ones."

"It—" Merit bit her tongue. She could neither leave nor stay. Both were impossible. It was all impossible, and her health was quickly deteriorating. Her wounds might claim her life before she made it out of the Hollows. At least her mother was healthy. Sarra ought to be the one to go. She had the best chance at survival. What possibility did Merit have? *What life will I lead? The boy will take my kingdom and then what will I be?*

Merit had no desire to sit at feasts in the King's Hall and giggle at poorly told jokes. She would not spend her remaining days tying her hair in knots or picking out dresses.

"All is not lost," said Sarra. "You are no doubt wondering where you will go and what you will do. Harkana is not your only option. In fact, it might be your worst. I know what you've done. The boy, Ren, is kind, but he'll never trust you. In truth, you'll never be welcome in Harkana if he takes that throne. You must go where there is power."

"Power? Where? If I cannot go home, will I run to Feren? I've followed a stern course of action. It allowed for no errors and it seems I've made nothing but them. I have few friends."

"You won't need them where you're going. All you'll need is your blood—if I am right. Ott was working on something before he left, trying to put together the history of the Soleri, to find out where they went, who left them for dead, and how it all came to pass. I read his notes, the things he learned from a boy named Noll, the history of your family— our family. His efforts were not without results."

"What are you rambling about?" Merit asked, fearing her mother had lost track of her senses.

"Go to the Temple of Re. There is a passage that leads there, to the inner sanctuary. You know the symbol?"

"The circle and stars."

"Yes, there will be a door carved with that mark and it will take you to the temple. There is power there, though I cannot describe its nature. Go to the house of Re and you will find what you desire. That is all I can offer. Go," said Sarra. "Just this once, do as I've said. Like you did before I left Harwen, when you were but a child and I was still a queen. When I was your mother and you were my daughter." Sarra swallowed bitterly, then she looked like she was trying to put on a smile. "We shared a perfect day. We ate and we drank and I cherished the sound of your voice. Let's leave it at that. I have that one memory. It's enough."

Sarra led Merit and her servant to a place where the wall was uneven. A simple touch made the stones shift, revealing a passage of sorts, a concealed door.

Outside, the mob howled; they pounded at the wood.

"Go, foolish girl." Sarra pressed her lips to Merit's forehead. One kiss and it was done. The hidden door sealed and the other one shattered. There were raised voices, screams, but Merit was already moving away as Sarra's servant carried her blindly through the darkness.

⇥ 67 ⇤

The Feren Army pursued Mered's soldiers with the relentlessness of a hungry pack of dogs. With Ferris and his sworn men at Kepi's side and the kite flying low above her shoulder, they followed close on their heels, forcing a portion of the men to turn and engage the Ferens while the rest of the army rode off toward the white wall. Their rear guard was relatively small, and the kite alone might have won the contest. It ripped through their lines, taking hold of two or sometimes three men and tossing them at their brothers. Each dash through their lines opened a path wide enough for a pair of horses to charge past the red shields. By the fifth or sixth pass, the rear guard had no lines to speak of and the army of the Ferens gained on their foes, charging at the soldiers in red and bronze.

They chased them to the steps of the Waset, where Kepi caught sight of the black shields of Harkana. Two armies had set themselves against the kingsguard, and either seemed large enough to defeat the Harkans.

"They don't have a chance, do they?" she asked as she rode, her sword pointing at the black shields.

"Them?" asked Ferris as he turned his mount. "They're dead men, but we're doing splendidly. Keep that bird in the fight and we might have a chance at reaching Mered."

"I don't care about Mered, it's the black shields I'm worried about. Those were my father's men, the ones he handpicked from the army. He loved each one of them. I won't watch them die." She tugged at her horse's reins.

"You can't reach them," said Ferris, who was still half engaged in the battle, shouting orders and conferring with Baen Muire. "We've got our hands full, if you haven't noticed," he said. "Fight this battle, then we'll worry about the black shields."

"They'll all be dead by then," said Kepi as she sheathed her blade.

"So be it. Your kinfolk can wait." Ferris was trying to draw her back into the battle. He wanted her help, but Kepi would not lend it.

"They're slaughtering them," she said.

Ferris glanced at the black shields. "An army stands between us."

She'd noticed. She just didn't care. Ferris and Muire had the battle well in hand. It was her father's men she cared about. They were his true friends, and hers too. She'd spent months with the guard, ranging about the western lands as Arko strove to hold back the outlander armies. She knew their names, had met their wives and played with their children. *And Ren's with them.* They called him a bastard, but she didn't care.

She recalled the last time she'd seen him. The memory came to her unbidden, so she guessed her mind was just playing tricks on her, but an image formed in her head: a boy crying, two soldiers, one of them holding the child, her father standing tall, expressionless; her mother quiet, indifferent as Kepi ran to one soldier and kicked him with all her might. Had he laughed at her? Yes, that was what she recalled. The day the imperial soldiers took her little brother from the Hornring.

Ren. She looked for him, for the boy who was stolen. She searched, but she did not use her eyes. The kite spied him, and a blurry picture formed in her thoughts. Ren kneeled amid a garden of statues, eyes closed, a white staff raised above his head. He spoke in a language she could not understand. He was alone and defenseless, and the red army had taken notice of him. A pack of soldiers had broken off from the rest and were rushing toward him.

Ren needs help.

The kite's talons bit into Kepi's armor as it lifted her from her horse, carrying her up into the sky. Like a leaf caught in a breeze she tumbled through the air, hands fumbling for her sword, trying to make certain it had not fallen from its scabbard. The kite listed, throwing her to one side as a second weight was added to the first.

"I couldn't let you go alone." Ferris had latched onto the kite's other talon. Both hands gripped the scaly flesh, and he held on for dear life as the two of them swept over the battlefield, dashing through clouds of smoke and wind-blown sand.

Ferris howled and kicked, his eyes wild with excitement.

"I don't care if I die today. I've flown upon the talons of the kite!" he cried, his voice crazed, astonished. The kite shook loose Ferris's grip and released Kepi from its hold, sending both of them hurtling toward the battlefield.

She used the back of a red soldier to break her fall. She clobbered the man with all her weight then drove her blade into his chest while he was still trying to figure out what had happened to him. Ferris hit the ground and tumbled, knocking over a pair of soldiers. He was the first to his feet, the first to raise his blade.

Kepi ran to the place where her brother knelt, alone and unprotected.

I will be your sword, brother. She stood before Ren, and Ferris had his back. Her brother was safe. No spear threatened him.

He had time, and Kepi prayed he did something with it.

⇥68⇤

Ren needed a moment of quiet, a sword at his back, and somehow he'd found it. Protected, shielded from the oncoming soldiers, he tightened his grip on the staff. He sought out the voices of the twelve children of Pyras and found them. Their words filled his thoughts and an almost electric charge wriggled through his fingers. He called to the old foes of the Soleri and asked them to finish what they'd started in the Shambles. He offered them his strength so that they might walk again.

At this, the eld horn trembled in his grip and he nearly lost hold of it.

The world shifted and everything in it changed.

The air was still.

No one cried out.

There were no shouts, nor did he hear the clamor of battle.

The fight had stopped. In fact, the whole world seemed frozen in place.

Nothing moved except the twelve. The statues were alive, or maybe they had always been alive and they'd just been caught in some strange instant. The gods had no notion of time. He knew this; they told it to him. He knew that time had no importance here. He was one of them, a child of Mithra, and the world around him was nothing more than a frozen panorama, a tableau of blood and hatred.

In a flash, the twelve drew glistening blades and set themselves against his foes. Twelve lights flickered amid the gray, creating a surreal vision of men who were not men, of beings made of fire cutting their way through the haze.

It was a world turned upside down, an impossible dreamlike world, and Ren was in it.

He saw every cut and blow.

He beheld the grief on each soldier's face.

The twelve who once stood in the garden had entered the fight, and the soldiers in red were simply dropping, one after another in an ever-widening ring.

The kingsguard stood at the heart of that circle, their faces looking dumbstruck as their foes collapsed to the sandy cobbles. They witnessed the blood, saw it pool amid the dust. To their eyes, the battle must have appeared as a kind of miracle. In a heartbeat, a thousand men had fallen to the earth. A moment later, a thousand more collided with the stones. For the Harkans, Ren guessed the fight looked like nothing more than a flash of light followed by what could only be described as a persistent rain of bodies, one toppling after another.

In a pair of strokes, every man who had set himself against the kingsguard, the two thousand Mered sent to put down the black shields, were vanquished, their bodies cut down, bled out or halfway there. Corpse lay upon corpse, swords poking at the sky, blades notched, armor broken.

Utterly dumbfounded, the kingsguard stood in their kohl-stained rags, wobbly-kneed, faces smeared with dirt, with blood. They were half-starved, half-mad, but alive. Some cried; grown men shed tears. Others fell to their knees. All of them must have thought they were dead. Two great armies had set themselves against the black shields. Surely, they thought they were done for. This must have seemed like the end, but everything had changed and it had happened in an instant. The kingsguard could barely believe their eyes. They had spent weeks in a lightless world. They'd seen friends and companions die. Nearly half their number was depleted, gone, hacked to bits in front of their very eyes. They'd survived, but the wounds remained, the faces of the fallen men filling up their thoughts. It was more than any man ought to bear, and these men had already borne their share of burdens. They had lived beneath the empire's yoke, seen children taken as slaves and crops sent off to feed the wealthy of Solus. They'd lived a bitter life, but they were not bitter folk. Nevertheless, these men were accustomed to a dying world, as was everyone. The desert loomed over all who lived in it. The amaranth was gone. Hope was in short supply. They could hardly even conceive of the otherworldly. Surely this earth was bereft of anything close to what could be described as divinity. They gave tribute to the golden statues, to the temple, but expected nothing in return. As far as they knew, that was the way of the world. The gods neither spoke nor acted. They were characters in a story, creatures of myth, but the twelve had left their pedestals. The gods had returned and they held the Harkans in their favor.

They'd dispatched the immediate threat, the thousands who were sent to vanquish the kingsguard, but the army of the Protector stood in the distance, and the house armies waited at the ready. The fight was not yet over, but the twelve halted their attack. They allowed their foes a bit of time to retreat, to find a place to regroup and address this new and unexpected threat.

The army of the Protector fled, and the Ferens did not pursue.

The Harkans stood idle.

No one understood what they saw, but they knew their part in this conflict was finished. Ren saw it in their faces. Some unearthly force had taken up the fight and there was no sense in getting in its way. The Harkans lowered their spears and the Ferens sheathed their blades. Ren stood alone, the eld horn raised to the sky. They watched him and knew somehow that he commanded this new army—this impossible force.

The soldiers of Mered hurried past the place where Ren's father had once presided over the city. They stumbled about the Golden Hall, where the Soleri had reigned. They trampled through the necropolis. The Well of Horu was not far away. It sat open, mouth gaping like some beast awaiting its prey, and the twelve ushered their foes toward it.

Mered's commanders issued orders, waved flags, and blew horns. They guessed the clearing beside the Mundus was a good enough place to regroup. They thought they'd picked the spot, but they were herded there, collected in this one place, and when they were all in it, the twelve made their push.

They drove at their foes, shepherding them into the well.

With nowhere else to go, the once-proud soldiers plunged into the infinite black, falling by the hundreds, by the thousands, possibly, tumbling one over the next, vanishing into the depthless pit.

Even their cries were lost in the void.

No foe remained, but the twelve were not yet finished.

In the gasping silence that followed, the twelve called to the desert and the winds answered. They came from every direction, rolling across the sands, circling, coming closer, rippling across the scarp wall and the outer districts, tearing through the white-walled towers and the temples of the Soleri. Ren and the kingsguard, the ransoms, and the armies of Harkana and Feren stood in the eye of what appeared to be a limitless maelstrom, watching as the sands devoured everything.

69

The nameless servant of the Kiltet set Merit on the granite floor of the Temple of Re.

They'd passed through the door, the one marked with the circle and stars. She knew this was the place, but she worried she'd arrived too late. The priests in the temple were all dead, cut down by the angry mob, or the sand-dwellers. Someone must have looted the temple. Statues sat with empty eye sockets, plinths lay bare where once some urn or other treasure had stood. In fact, the only thing that hadn't been overturned was a ring of statues, but they'd been set aflame, or so she guessed. The statues had an odd appearance. On second glance, they weren't burnt. They were black, but they glistened, winking like distant stars. A voice within her head told Merit that the twelve statues were the last of the Soleri.

A shuffling sound issued from the darkness. Footsteps. A voice. "You've come," said a man she did not recognize. He wore the white robes of a priest.

"I am Nollin Odine. Call me Noll." He flattened his lips. "I hid when the looters came. The priests gave their lives to protect me. They said someone had to remain behind in case one of you showed up."

"Showed up?" she asked. Merit was so tired she could barely form words.

"Yes, one of the four—the children of Arko Hark-Wadi. They guessed any of you would do."

"Do? Do for what?" she asked. "What're you talking about?" Her voice was a whisper. Merit could not quite tell if she were asleep or awake, alive or dead. Her strength had long since fled, and she could barely hold herself upright. *Sleep!* a voice told her. *Sleep and all your pains will be gone.* She knew it was true. Death tugged at her consciousness, but her curiosity pushed back.

"Explain this to me. Why did my mother send me to this place?" she asked, and this time Nollin produced a glistening white staff. It was not quite straight. It had crooks and bends, as if it had been carved from something long and twisted.

"I'm told this belonged to one of the kings of Harkana." Noll placed it in her hands, pressing the horn to her skin and wrapping her fingers around it. She did not have the strength to do it herself.

"What now?" she said, her voice growing faint. These were her last words. She would not speak again. *Time to sleep. Time to bid farewell to this world.*

No. She gripped the horn and Nollin lifted her chin.

"They are here," he said. "These are the twelve, and they have waited two hundred years for this moment. They need only a bit of your strength to rise once more."

Merit looked at him in bewilderment. Strength was the one thing she lacked.

"Fear not," said Nollin. "They do not seek your body's strength." He told Merit what he'd told Ren, about her blood and the power it held. He said she could bring these statues to life.

"Why?" she asked.

"Because they made this empire. The Soleri made you and they can make you again."

Perhaps, thought Merit.

It was her last thought.

She held the horn and locked eyes with the twelve statues.

Then she was done with this world.

Her head hit the floor. The lights dimmed.

She guessed she saw movement, something shifting in the darkness.

She dreamed the twelve had come alive, but the vision faded as quickly as it had appeared.

Her thoughts dimmed too.

Her heart no longer beat, and her lungs drew no air.

≋70≋

When the storm had come and gone and the winds ceased to blow, the sand settled to the earth and the sky cleared.

At the outermost edge of what had been the city of the gods, the scarp wall was gone. The mud-brick rampart was nothing but dust, and the great circle of stone that once protected Solus was ground down to the earth.

Only pieces of it remained. Here and there a ragged stone poked from the dunes. Where the great pylons had once flanked the city gates, there was nothing left but the foundations. At the periphery, where the buildings were old and not so tall and their walls were made of sunbaked mud, the destruction was complete. Only pale mounds of sand remained, lighter spots among the darker gray of the desert. However, these accumulations, these hills of dust, were made of more than mud. Every piece of every dwelling and everything in them was ground into that dust. The livestock, the hay, and the feed were made into powder. Each pile contained a thousand memories: a home, a family, and the objects they left behind.

The markets were no different.

They twinkled with a soot made from every conceivable substance: fine muslin, rare spice, ivory and silk. The most colorful mounds appeared in the place where the great bazaar once stood. Bright spots flickered among the great waves of sand, the last traces of the brilliant hues that once marked the many stalls and tents.

The devastation was near total and it was not limited to the outer districts. Deeper into the city, where the buildings were made of stone, the dunes grew taller. At the White-Wall district, there was a distinctly lighter shade of sand, and it sparkled with flecks of gold and copper. Beads of electrum danced in the air, the great ornaments of the houses reduced to mere motes, tossed about by the slightest breeze.

Onward, past the steps of the Waset, in the place where the great temples of the Soleri once stood, the winds and sand had worked with unparalleled effort. The Cenotaph was simply gone, as was the Repository at Solus, the Circus of Re, the House of Viziers, and the Hall of Ministers. The Golden Hall was perhaps the richest of the ruins, a great dune blanketed in a dust made of gold. The Temple of Mithra-Sol was intact, but that was the only building to survive the day.

In spots, the sand and wind had worn away at the earth itself, cutting through the streets, delving down into the Hollows beneath the city and exposing the place that had once been the empire of the Pyras. Structures that had not seen the light of Mithra-Sol in three thousand years were left open to the sky. The pyramid in the Night Market stood as it had in the time of Pyras, and the Well of Horu was once more a tower.

The winds settled and a quiet came over the city, but it was not the quiet of the desert. It was another sort of silence, the kind that belonged to the whole of the known world. It was the silence of a great empire and the destruction the sands had wrought upon it. It was a quiet that would live on in the hearts of those who'd witnessed the desolation.

Where towers had once stabbed at the heavens there was nothing but dust. Mounds of sand replaced walls, and hills of gold lay where temples had once stood proud upon the earth.

The desert stretched to infinity, dotted here and there by the invading armies, the scattered survivors.

Everything else was just sand.

≈71≈

Kepi stood with Ferris, back to back, breathing heavily, still trying to comprehend the destruction that surrounded them. In an instant, in that moment when she'd cleared a circle around Ren, the whole world had shifted. Everything around her had turned to light and the statues had moved. She swore it. She'd witnessed a dream, a blurry, light-filled illusion. That was the only way she could describe it. Gold turned to flesh and fire, the twelve walked the earth, and it had all happened in a single protracted instant. In a flash, their enemy was struck down or driven into the Mundus, but that had only been the start of it. The storm followed and the city itself was reduced to sand, a heap of dust and ash punctuated by shattered buildings, dotted here and there with soldiers from the surviving armies. The Ferens were among them, standing in the distance, on the far side of a vast field of corpses. Ferris motioned to his sworn men.

"They're fine," she said.

"You sure about that?" He was still gazing through the smoke, trying to count his men.

"Yes, they struck only Mered's men; you saw it."

"I don't know what I saw."

"Neither do I." Kepi was shaking her head, still out of breath, confused, still wondering if this was all some kind of dream. That was the only reasonable explanation that came to mind, but even her dreams had never held anything like the vision that had flashed before her eyes. It was a delusion, a mirage. She wanted to forget it, but every bit of her was caked in dust and sand, and the stench was already in her nose, reminding her of all she'd witnessed. "What was that . . . ?"

"Don't know. Don't think either of us will ever know," said Ferris. "And I don't think it matters. The war's ended, *this place* is ended." He gestured toward the rolling sands that were once a city. "It's all ash and there's no army, and certainly no one left to fight."

"I know," Kepi said as the reality of their situation slowly took hold of her, as she surveyed the ruined city, the field of bodies, and the men left standing. "This is a dead place." It was true enough. "We're done here."

The army of the Ferens rode to where Kepi stood, the men leaping from their horses. Some collapsed to the ground, others simply bent over double. They had ridden nonstop from the high city to the rift, and onward to Solus. They had not taken a moment to pause or rest. When they did, their bodies gave out and they fell to the ground in exhaustion. They had assailed the city of the gods. Tired and out of strength, they had charged the armies of Mered and somehow survived. Ferris went to Baen Muire and he found his sworn men. He was already slapping backs, poking fun at those who had collapsed, and hugging the ones whose exhaustion had overcome their senses. Grown men shed tears; some simply hid their faces.

Ferris found Kepi and gave her a hard knock on the shoulder. "Join us. Let's find amber and drink till we can't see straight."

His offer *was* tempting. She gripped his shoulder. "A moment, Ferris. There is something I must do first."

≋72≋

The winds left Solus, but the twelve children of Pyras did not.

A man made of flame broke off from the others. His glimmering form entered the Antechamber ruins and the fires swirled around him. Even after the city's destruction, after nearly every structure was reduced to dust, the Antechamber fire raged. The flames burned higher. The sky turned red and a glowing figure emerged from the pyre, the fires chasing him, coalescing around him and into him, swirling into his clutched hands where a golden citrine sparkled with life.

The Antechamber fire vanished.

All that remained of it was that marvelous little stone, the fires still eddying beneath its surface.

Ren had seen the citrine once before, when Suten Anu had taken off his mask on the last day of the year. The stone was called the Eye of the Sun and it hung upon the Ray's forehead, but it had not belonged to Suten. For him, it held no power. He was only a steward. He could not wield its strength. Arko could. Ren saw that, but his father hadn't known it, hadn't even guessed at it. Oren Thrako, the onetime Prior Master, had called Ren's father a drunk, and maybe he was right in some sense. Perhaps his father was too overcome by his own self-pity to sense the power within him.

The stone passed into Ren's hands and he placed it on his brow.

The battle was over and the twelve were gone, vanished into starry dust, gone back to Atum.

Shaking it a bit, Ren sensed some stiffness in his right hand, but he dared not look at it. He knew that if he gave them life, the twelve would take a part of him. Like wood burned by a fire, a part of him would be consumed. His fingers were no longer fingers, and his hand was no longer flesh. The limb was blackened, but it glistened like the stars. He'd paid a price, but he'd also earned himself a boon of sorts.

When he gripped the citrine, memories flooded his mind. They were not his recollections. The figures in them were not familiar, not at first. He saw a younger version of Merit, then Kepi and Sarra, and finally himself, as a three-year-old child. He found Gneuss and Asher too. These were Arko's memories, and they came to Ren in no particular order but they were all there. A whole lifetime of recollections filled his head. He'd wanted more than anything to know his family, his father. Arko Hark-Wadi was dead, but his memories lived. They were with Ren and they would always be with him. In an instant, he knew his father through and through. He saw the good and the bad, the happy and the sorrowful. He witnessed the fire that ended it all.

Ren looked at the twelve empty pedestals and recalled what the twelve had said to him.

"*We are the ones who came before.*

"*We are the Pyraethi, the First and the Last.*

"*We are from the time before the Soleri and after the Soleri we will be.*"

"Give me a moment," Kepi said, her hand leaving Ferris's shoulder.

Not far from where she stood, the kingsguard surrounded Ren, heads going this way and that, men edging past one another, trying to catch a glimpse at the one who saved them. She did the same. She observed the way he talked, his back straight, head high, and how he laughed, shoulders bent and flapping, and the way his lips curled when he grinned. *My brother.*

A whole lifetime separated them, or at least a portion of one. She had gone off to Feren as a child and a bride. She'd seen her first husband die, and spent a year in a Feren prison. Later, she was wed to the king of that same land, and she'd watched him die. She lived each day with that grief, and Ren knew nothing of it. He was her blood, yet he was a stranger. He'd spent the last ten years in a cell, locked deep beneath the earth, somewhere in this ruined place that was once a city.

Kepi saw the chance for a reunion of sorts.

There was hope, or something like it.

This was an opportunity to start again, or to make a start.

She went to Ren, and as she did so her thoughts spiraled backward to the last time she saw him. Kepi was there again, watching the imperial soldiers as they dragged Ren from the Hornring. She was a child once more and angry that someone was taking away her little brother. Years had passed. Long years. Nonetheless, Ren was back and he was changed, but Kepi still held that child's anger. She ached with the pain of their separation, so that part of her, that child, caught hold of Kepi and she ran to him.

⟨74⟩

A girl approached. Ren recognized her as the one who'd held back Mered's soldiers—the girl who'd given him that moment of quiet he'd needed. His sister, he knew.

Ren went to her, reluctant at first, unsure, but she ran to him with open arms and they embraced.

"Brother," she said, "and king."

"Yes, sister," he said, overwhelmed by her unbridled affection, by her blissful grin, her simple beauty. He'd feared she was an enemy, Merit's stooge. He was wrong. She was someone else entirely. The kite settled upon her shoulder, its eyes glistening with the same fire he'd seen in the eyes of the eld. In an instant, he knew again they were the same. They shared the same blood. The eld. The kite. She saw it too. They came together as equals and embraced, holding each other for a moment before parting.

Someone was clearing his throat. Abruptly, Ren realized he was not alone.

Kollen gaped; he had no words.

Tye simply cried, whether out of joy or fear he couldn't tell.

Ott sat on the ground, his head shaking. He caught sight of the blackened fist, but Ren quickly covered it with the tunic he wore beneath his armor.

Seeing that Ren had his own people, his sister took a step or two backward and allowed the black shield to once more encircle Ren. The best warriors in Harkana, men who had seen whole lifetimes of battle, were struck silent by the destruction of the city. Butcher wobbled on his feet. Asher said nothing.

The dead were everywhere, but not everyone had fallen. In the distance, the Harkan Army rode cautiously forward. Unharmed but reluctant, they cantered toward the black shields, carefully picking their way through the bodies. Others had survived as well. A scattering of the red soldiers lived. Whether this was by chance or design Ren did not know, but they were there nonetheless, and Mered was among them. His palanquin had fallen to the ground. The men who'd held it were dead, eviscerated. Mered rose from the field of bodies, his eyes as shocked as any other. A scattering of captains surrounded him, their rank made clear by their royal attire. There were foot soldiers, too, men who'd hidden beneath fallen bodies, or so he guessed.

Ren approached Mered, trying not to step on the bodies or the sundered remains of a thousand different weapons.

Mered stood among his captains. His foot soldiers gathered at his side.

Ren held the horn in one hand, and the golden citrine hung glistening on his forehead. It sat just as it had upon his father's head and on Suten's as well. It stood as it had upon the brow of Re, first of the Soleri.

There were armies at Ren's back, but he didn't need them. He'd vanquished several already. He guessed that was enough to cow any soldier.

Mered's men, the captains and soldiers who'd sworn their lives to the first citizen, turned on him at Ren's approach. One after another they stabbed Mered with their blades, each one taking his shot, sliding home the knife until Mered's pale red robe was torn and dappled with darker spots of red. He fell, a look of disbelief still clinging to his face. Even in the end, he'd trusted his men. He'd thought their loyalty was absolute.

He was wrong.

Mered's body struck the earth, and his robe fell open, revealing that *he* was not actually a man but was instead a woman, her true sex revealed to all in the moment of her passing.

Their master had collapsed, and the generals and foot soldiers fell to their knees, frightened, uncertain. Some dropped their blades, others held up their bloody knives as evidence of their newfound loyalty. There were too few of them to be of any consequence.

"Go. Leave and never return," Ren said to them.

Solus, whatever it had been, whatever it could have been, was ended. The city was no more. There were no more white-walled houses, no temples, no monuments . . . and no walls.

When the soldiers left his company and Ren was at last alone with Tye and Kollen, he spotted the Rachins, marching carefully over the dunes, raising a cloud of ash and sand in their wake.

Upon arrival, a soldier tore off his helmet, revealing long black hair. His beard reached down to his belly. "I'm the lord marshal of the guard. You the boy?" His eyes were on Kollen.

"I'm the son," said Kollen.

The man paled ever so slightly. "The king's dead," he said. "Been that way for a week. Poison. Mered's doing, or so we guessed. Seems he had his eye on our kingdom."

"Dead . . . the king . . . I thought . . ." Kollen stammered, apparently unsure of what to say.

"You're the king, sire, or you soon will be if you ride out with us. We'll be a week on the road, maybe longer if the high passes are blocked."

"Don't care," said Kollen. "I just want to go home." He looked to Ren. "You'll pardon me if I leave, but I think I've spent enough of my life in this city. It's time for the ransoms to go home, time for all of us to go home." He gave Ren a manful hug, surprising him with a quick embrace. "I'll see you again, friend."

"Go," said Ren. "I've been trying to get our asses out of this city since we left the priory. Get out of here. There will be nothing here within a day, a mound of sand and nothing more."

"We'll be the first to leave," said Kollen. "I don't want to sleep another night in this place." It seemed as though he were going to say something else, but the Rachins all gathered around him, wanting to get a good look at their new king. Ren thought he saw the smallest hint of a smile on the boy's face. He let Kollen have his moment.

"Must be nice," said Tye. "Being king and all that and having a royal escort. No one's going to ride out for me. They say Barden killed the lords of the Wyrre, murdered every last one of them."

"Come to Harwen. You'll always be welcome—"

"No, don't you get it Ren? They're all dead, which means I'm the last living bit of Wyrren royalty. When my father dressed me as a boy and sent me off to the priory, he did it to save his son, but the king must be dead and my brother as well. Isn't that the strangest thing? The priory saved me. I'm the last one, the queen of all the Wyrre—assuming anyone is left alive in it."

"There're people. You'll see. Still, I wish you'd stay."

"I can't. Didn't you hear Kollen? It's time for all of us to go home: you to Harwen, Kollen to Zagre, your sister to Rifka. We're all going home."

"I'll send two hundred Harkans. I'm sure the army can spare the men, and you can't just march into the throne room and declare yourself queen. They'll think you're some peasant girl with a delusional mind."

"You do have a point," she said, but then she scrunched up her face as if in thought. "Ren, I see what you're doing. You're still trying to protect me. You won't stop."

"I don't care."

"Ren."

"What?"

"I'll come to Harwen. One day, when I'm queen."

"I'd like that."

"I know, and I'll take the soldiers. For old time's sake, I suppose, I'll let the king of the Harkans lend me a hand."

≩76≨

Kepi rode out with the Feren Army, the ruins of Solus still smoldering in the distance. They'd come here to end a war and they'd seen it done, but not in the way they'd imagined. There'd been no great battle. Ren had done the work of ten thousand men and he'd done it all in an instant. She didn't pretend to fully understand what had happened. He'd been over it all, told her the story of the gods, but she struggled to accept it, to know that her family and her blood held such power. It made her head spin, and she longed for home, but it was not the place of her birth that captured her thoughts. Though she'd spent a good portion of her life dreading the forest kingdom, avoiding a marriage to this lord or that one, she found herself feeling heartsick for the forest. She longed for the cool air, the dampness of the fog.

She was done with the desert; there was no need for them to stay in this place.

The city was gone, the empire finished. Ash remained, and smoke. In fact, that was all that was left of the city.

Kepi rode north toward Feren.

A kingdom of problems awaited her arrival. There were traitors to be found, warlords who had taken coin from Mered. There were laws to change, and customs to end. Good men would be in short supply, but she swore to find them. Kepi would not want for work.

"You're coming to Rifka," she said. It was a command, not a question.

"My queen requires it?" Ferris asked.

"She does." Kepi paused here, feeling suddenly vulnerable. She did not want to admit anything, but she couldn't help herself. "I'm all alone there, and you cannot tear a kingdom apart without an ally."

"Aye, so it's the army at Caerwynt you're after?"

"No, well . . . yes, I do need them on my side. But I need more than just swords. I'll give you some damned title if it means something to you, but in all honesty . . ."

"What?" he asked.

"I just need a friend." The words hung in the air. She felt sheepish, much as she had on the night of her wedding to Dagrun.

"Aye," Ferris said, and he nodded his understanding as they rode northward, the ruined city vanishing into the sand kicked up by their horses.

≋77≋

"Do you hear that?" Ren asked Ott. The pair stood on the ruined stairs of the Waset, the sun setting at their backs. The battle had come and gone. A day had passed. The army had needed time to mend wounds, time to rest and regroup, time enough to bury the dead.

"What?" asked Ott.

"The quiet," said Ren. "When I lived in the priory, all I heard or knew of this city were the calls of the hawkers, the sweet songs of the buskers, the cries of some captain drilling his soldiers in the plaza, the damned bells. I heard every bit of it—sometimes all at once."

"But you never laid eyes on Solus."

"Not until they set me free, but I spent most of my time running this way and that. I don't remember much."

"And now it's gone."

"I suppose," said Ren. He looked out at the dunes, the waves of sand, punctuated here and there by some piece of tower or wall. There was no city to be seen. "Maybe they'll call this the City of Sand in fifty or a hundred years. Perhaps they'll forget all about Solus and what we did here. It'll be the city of ash—not light. There's hardly any trace of it left." Indeed, the only life in the city seemed to come from the tents of the invading armies. On the field below, in the place that had once been the gardens of the Empyreal Domain, the Harkans made camp while they mended their wounds and readied themselves for the march home to Harwen. Ren would lead that charge. He would return, at last, with the horn strapped to his back and his father's blade. A bastard, but a king nonetheless.

Merit could not be found.

"I'm not going to contest your rule," said Ott. "I hope that's not why you called me here. We've been over all that."

"I know, but I don't mind you mentioning it. No, this is the only spot I could find that didn't have a tent on it." Ren tugged at the linen wrappings on his hand. After he put to rest the army of Mered, he wrapped his tunic over the fingers and later he called it a wound. Ren unwrapped the linen and revealed the skin that was not skin. He showed Ott the shimmering yet black thing that stood in place of his hand.

Ott squinted, then sighed just a bit. There was recognition in his eyes, just as Ren had hoped. He seemed to recognize the disfigurement.

"We share more than just our father's blood, don't we?" Ren asked. He was already rewrapping the glistening hand. It glowed faintly beneath the cloth.

Ott appeared to be lost in thought, or possibly at a loss for words. Ren went ahead and prompted him. "Your arm?" he asked. "The shriveled arm you conceal—does it look like this hand?"

Ott shot him a reluctant glance.

"Will you show it to me?" Ren asked.

"I've never really . . . I . . ." Ott stuttered a bit.

"It's all right," said Ren. "I simply want to see it. I need to understand what's become of me."

Reluctantly, Ott pulled back his sleeve. He removed the leather wraps and the padding. The process was slow, but the boy needed only reveal a bit of the arm, and that's what he did. It was all Ren needed to see. For there, on Ott's withered arm, Ren saw the same flesh that was not flesh, the same shining, starlike glimmer.

"How?" asked Ren. "I was told you were born a cripple."

"A cripple?" asked Ott. "What a strange way to describe me. No, I was never a cripple. This arm is a miracle or something like one."

"Can you explain it?"

Ott shrugged. "I'll never know for certain, but I've made guesses. Perhaps, during my birth, my life was in jeopardy. I had not yet been born, but I must have had instincts. Maybe I made use of the power that lay dormant in my blood. I survived death, but I paid a price." He nodded toward his withered limb. "It's all just guesses. The arm was hidden at birth and I've kept it covered ever since."

"Surely some have seen it."

"Why do you think Sarra fled Harwen? When I was younger, I feared the thing. I dreaded what it might do to me. Would it overcome me, would this flesh that was not flesh consume my whole body? What would I become? I still have questions. It moves and grows; it flickers with the same life I saw in the statues of the Soleri. I'm not crippled. There's power within the thing, within me."

"I know. I'm a bastard twice over. Son of Arko, child of the gods. We hold some bit of their blood—but what does that mean? And why did my flesh change? Is it growing or withering? Are we meant to be men or gods? And what does that word, god, mean? I don't know. I wish we hadn't lost Noll in the Hollows."

"He may yet live."

"Then we'll find him."

"Perhaps. The twelve you set free—where did they go?" Ott asked. "I saw them dissolve into light, just as the gods were said to do when they passed. They've returned to Atum?"

"Don't know. They could be anywhere. And what about the twelve in the temple?" Ren asked.

"It's destroyed. My priests spent the day sifting through the ruins, looking for signs of life, pieces of black statues. They found nothing."

"You won't find them," said Ren. "I feel it. You won't set eyes on those statues and you won't find Merit, either, not yet. My sister has found some other calling. I sense it. Her reign is done for now, and I'm going home, leaving at dawn so we can reach Harwen by nightfall."

Ott looked at him askance. Perhaps he wondered how Ren was certain of such things, but he didn't ask and Ren made no effort to provide an answer. In truth, he had none. In that brief span, when he'd made contact with the twelve children of Pyras, he'd seen all sorts of things, the past, the present, and things that had not yet come to pass. It was as if the writing on a thousand scrolls was read to him at once. There was simply too much information in his head, but the memories came to him now and then, in pieces, slowly providing answers when he least expected them.

Ott cleared his throat. "Off to Harwen?"

"Posthaste."

"Well, at least you have somewhere to go. This place is destroyed and I'm finished with Desouk. Too many memories."

"Of your mother?"

Ott bowed his head. "They never found her body, but more than one man said they saw her torn to pieces. Others claim she survived. They once called her Twice Blessed, and I fear she's done it again, blessed once more by the gods. They found no body."

"She's alive?" Ren asked.

"Sarra once told me that she never entered a room unless she knew two ways to get out of it, preferably three. I doubt she met her end in that tower. She escaped Mered. It's hard to believe that some pesky mob put an end to my mother. Every priest in Solus is searching for her, but we've found no trace."

"Never met the woman—not my mother, and you know my thoughts on the subject. It's no time to repeat them."

"Fear not, I'm done being a priest."

"Good. They're a boring lot." Ren moved to pat Ott on the back, but he recalled that Ott did not like to be touched. Words would have to suffice.

"Come with me to Harwen. While the world is at peace, for as long as it lasts, I want to eat and drink. I want my freedom and the kingdom I fought to rule. Come. We're both strangers in Harkana. Let's ride there together and see the King's Hall. Let the sons of Arko share in the joy of our return. You fled the kingdom and I was stolen from it.

"I was a stranger when you met me, but you showed me more kindness than any soul I've met. I claim the title you own, but you've given it to me and granted me your friendship as well. I cannot know your mind or even understand it, but the crown is yours as much as it is mine. Let us walk jointly into the Great Hall and stand before the Horned Throne. I will be king and you will be my counsel in all matters, but we will be brothers first." He moved to embrace Ott, and for once the boy allowed it. Ott reached out with his good arm and gripped Ren's back, eyes stinging.

⇥78⇤

There was darkness, but there was no longer death.

Merit had died. She knew that. She'd passed from this world and into some other one, but the gods had brought her here. It was a gift, an exchange.

One life for twelve. A good enough bargain.

The polished walls of the chamber revealed her face and arms. She was whole again and beautiful, voluptuous even.

The white priest's eyes widened in astonishment. "You rise at last," he said.

"At last?"

"Yes, you've been out for a week," said Noll. "I nursed you as best I could."

"'Out'? What do you mean, and where is the temple, the statues?"

"We're in the catacomb beneath the temple. We sheltered here when the storm took Solus. I'm afraid those statues are gone, stolen by looters or destroyed like everything else in this city."

"Destroyed? Stolen? How could they be stolen? The Soleri moved . . . they walked. I saw it."

"If only," said Noll. "No, you tried but failed. They're gone."

"Yes, you've said that," said Merit. She was still looking herself up and down in the brightly polished stone, still moving her chin this way and that, searching for scars. There were none. No scrapes. No bruises. No broken bones. All the damage she'd suffered—from the beating in Harwen to the ravages of the mob—was gone. She was whole again. In fact, she was better than whole, she was renewed. She had the body of a girl half her age and twice her strength.

And the priest lied.

The Soleri had restored Merit; there could be no other explanation.

This boy was a terrible liar. She'd seen the statues walk. She'd held the horn and called the twelve Soleri back to this world just as they had in turn called to her after she'd left it. Merit had seen them walk. For better or worse, the Soleri had returned, and so had the firstborn of Mithra, the Pyraethi. The gods walked the earth once more. Whether they would find their peace and return to Atum or build some new empire she knew not, she cared not.

Merit lifted herself up from the pallet. She saw a stair, a distant shaft of sunlight shining from the top of it.

"Where're you going?" asked Noll.

She guessed there was no harm in giving the boy an answer. He'd lied to Merit. He'd used her to bring back his gods and then deceived her about it. Clearly, he had his reasons. Merit simply shrugged. She wanted no part of his gods, not today. She'd lost her life, her family, and her husband. She'd even lost her kingdom. She knew that. She'd lost it all. Yet she was not bothered. In fact, she felt nothing but joy. She was born again, and young. A maiden, too. All her burdens were lifted.

"In case you haven't noticed, I've just come back from the dead," she said. "Since I don't recall anyone ever pulling that one off, I think I ought to take advantage of my position." She grinned faintly. "I'm going to start all over again."

⊰ THE SUN'S FATE ⊱

High in the Denna Hills, Noll stood atop a barren and rocky outcropping, the ruins of Solus still smoldering in the distance. He was not certain how he had come to this place or when he had arrived. The hour was indeterminate, the sky gray.

The twelve Soleri gathered around him in their shimmering robes of gold.

"What now?" he asked, plain-faced and curious. "I did what you asked." Noll looked to the twelve for some answer, but was instead distracted by the absence of two of the children. In fact, when he counted there were only eight Soleri, and a moment later he was almost certain that only six remained.

Then there were four.

The Soleri were vanishing all around him.

Four, then two.

Sekhem Den and his wife, Sakkara, stood before Noll, faces concealed by eyeless masks of gold, cowls drawn low, golden robes shimmering despite the gloom. Den lifted a gloved hand and removed his mask. Golden eyes stared at Noll, but no light shone from them.

To stand before the Soleri is to stand before the sun, and no man can survive that light. Those were the words written in the *Book of the Last Day of the Year*, the sacred mantra of the Soleri, words inked before time itself, an image that had struck fear into the hearts of endless foes.

"Lies." Noll blurted out the word. "If all those stories, if every word in the book is as false as the ones I've just recited in my head, it's all just . . . lies. So . . . what are you? Don't you owe me that? Just one answer. If not gods, then . . . what?"

Noll shivered as he held the gaze of Sekhem Den, but he was not reduced to ash, nor was he changed in any way. The book had lied, but it was not a complete falsehood. Noll had seen the destruction of Solus; the power of Mithra's children was undeniable.

"Please, tell me this . . . what are you?" he asked again, his mind awash in curiosity.

Were these creatures possessed of some as-yet-undiscovered knowledge, some discipline that enabled them to accomplish what could only be described as divinity, or did they hail from some other place, some uncharted realm? He lusted for answers, but Sekhem Den gave no reply. His wife had vanished, and when Noll glanced back to meet the gaze of the last emperor, he was gone as well.

GLOSSARY

Adad, Enger: a young Harkan general, commander of the outer legion of the Harkan Army.

Alehkar, the: the elite soldiers of the Protector's Army of Solus.

amaranth, the: the sacred crop, raised in the highland Oasis of Desouk and tended only by the Mithra cult, a gift from the gods themselves, the leaves of the plant form a thick paste that makes the dry soil of Solus fertile. The amaranth supply is exhausted, and the existing plants no longer bear seeds.

amber: ale, made from ground millet and emmer.

Amber Throne, the: the throne of the Soleri emperor, located behind the Shroud Wall of the Empyreal Domain in a palace hidden beneath the ground.

Amunet, Sarra: the onetime wife of Arko Hark-Wadi who fled the Harkan kingdom with her son, Ott, and joined the Mithra cult. She is the former ceremonial wife of Mithra-Sol and Mother Priestess of the cult and current First Ray of the Sun.

Antechamber, the: the seat of office of the First Ray of the Sun, destroyed by fire.

Anu, Ined: Father Protector of the armies of Solus at the time of the War of the Four, the man who drove the Harkans out of Solus, the first to call himself the First Ray of the Sun.

Anu, Suten: former First Ray of the Sun, deceased.

Asar: an island in the Wyrre, birthplace of Sarra Amunet.

Ata'Sol: located beneath the Temple of Mithra at Solus, home of the Mithra cult in the capital of Sola.

Atourin: sister of Arko Hark-Wadi, married to a Rachin lord.

Atum: home of Mithra-Sol and his children, from the time before the making of the world.

badgir: a windcatcher, used to cool Harkan homes.

Barca, Haren: former captain of the Outer Guard of Sola who led a revolt and murdered the commander of the guard. He commands a vast army of outlanders, mercenaries, and former Soleri soldiers.

Basin of Amen: the low desert flatland that separates the kingdoms of Harkana and Sola.

Battered Wall, the: also the Ruined Wall, a section of Harwen's fortifications, damaged during the War of the Four and preserved as a war memorial.

Book of the Last Day of the Year: one of several holy texts used by the Mithra cult, the tome that contains the prayers read during the Devouring.

Caer Rifka: located in Rifka, capital of the kingdom of Feren, it is the Feren citadel and high seat of Feren power, home to the Chathair.

Cannet, Tomen: a Harkan general.

Catal: a desert stronghold, the ancient seat of Feren power.

Chathair, the: an ancient ironwood stool, the throne of the Feren king or queen, also refers to the room in which the throne resides.

Children's War: the war led by Koren Hark-Wadi, the father of Arko, fought against the empire of the Soleri to prevent Arko from serving in the priory. After two days of conflict, the fight was settled by mutual agreement of the Father Protector Raden Saad and Koren, the king of the Harkans. The treaty allowed Arko Hark-Wadi to be raised in Harwen, the Harkan capital, forestalling but not removing Arko's obligatory service to the empire as agreed upon after the War of the Four.

Chime Gate, the: the gate at Caer Rifka, made from suspended wooden logs.

Coin: a common board game.

crescent: a coin carved from the ancient metals of the Soleri Middle Kingdom, resembles a crescent moon, the common coin of the Soleri Empire.

Cressel Sea, the: a large sea located along southern borders of both Sola and Harkana, home to the Wyrre.

Dawn Chorus, the: the singing of birds before dawn; in Feren, the hymn of the kite, sung in the Blackthorn Chathair for the crowning of the Kitelord.

Den: in the time of the Children's War, the surname of the emperors of the Soleri.

Den, Sekhem: last in the line of Den, former emperor of the Soleri during the War of the Four, two hundred years ago.

Denna Hills: the highlands, south of Solus, home to the Desouk priesthood and the Amaranth fields.

Desouk: in the Denna Hills, the city of priests and scholars, home to the Mithra cult, the fallow fields of amaranth, and Repository at Desouk.

Devouring, the: the high festival of the Mithra cult, the solemn rite of the Soleri, the time each year when the moon eclipses the sun and Mithra-Sol blesses the emperor and his servants.

Dromus, the: built during the Middle Kingdom, a high circular wall, running astride the border of the kingdom of Sola, separating Sola from the lower kingdoms.

Eilina: sister of Arko, married to a Rachin lord.

eld: a many-horned, four-legged species, similar in appearance to a deer, but larger, and some say, a god.

Elden Hunt, the: Harkana's sacred rite, the right of kings, every king of the Harkans since Ulfer has taken an eld horn and fashioned a sword from it as a symbol of his kinghood.

Empyreal Domain, the: guarded by the Shroud Wall, the sacred precinct of the Soleri, home to the gardens, temples, and the underground palace of the Soleri. Only the First Ray of the Sun may pass in and out of the ward. The grounds are maintained by a service cult known as the Kiltet.

Eye of the Sun, the: a golden citrine worn by the First Ray of the Sun, a signifier of his power and position. A relic forged by the first of the Soleri, Re.

Fahran, Adin: the son and only heir of Barrin Fahran, a friend of Ren.

Fahran, Barrin: Barrin the Black, the Worm King of the Gray Wood, the former king of Feren, father of Adin, deposed by Dagrun Finner, deceased.

Feren: a woodland kingdom, north of Sola, ruled by the new queen, Kepi Hark-Wadi, and known for its plentiful resources. One of the four lower kingdoms of the Soleri Empire.

Feren Rift valley: a steep-sided gorge that runs along the southern border of Feren, protecting the kingdom from its neighbors to the south.

Finner, Dagrun: the former king of the Ferens and husband of Kepi Hark-Wadi, a merchant who purchased a mercenary army and took the Feren throne by force, deceased.

First Ray of the Sun, the: the right hand of the emperor, the eyes and ears of the Soleri, the only man or woman permitted to pass through the Shroud Wall and into the Empyreal Domain.

Garah, Seth: Kepi's former lover, a former servant of the Hark-Wadi family, and a rebel and traitor who murdered the king of the Ferens, Dagrun Finner.

Gate of Coronel: The southern gate of the Dromus, the sea gate, located along the southern coast of Sola, on the black-sand beach, three days' ride from Solus.

Golden Hall, the: built during the Middle Kingdom of the Soleri, the formal and public seat of Soleri power, the place where the First Ray of the Sun observes the Devouring each year.

Gray Wood, the: the blackthorn forest of Feren.

Hacal, Asher: the captain of the Harkan kingsguard.

Hall of Histories, the: located beyond the Shadow Gate, along the path that leads to the Empyreal Domain, this corridor contains large-scale carvings depicting the history of the Soleri Empire.

Harkana: a desert kingdom, founded by Ulfer, ruled by the Hark-Wadi family, one of the four lower kingdoms of the Soleri Empire.

Hark-Wadi, Arko: the Bartered King, the former king of Harkana, the only king of the Harkans to avoid serving time in the priory, deceased.

Hark-Wadi, Kepi: youngest daughter of Arko. Kepi is the Kitelord and queen of the Ferens.

Hark-Wadi, Koren: father of Arko, former king of Harkana and leader of the second revolt, the Children's War, deceased.

Hark-Wadi, Merit: older daughter of Arko, queen regent of Harkana.

Hark-Wadi, Rennon: bastard son of Arko, a former ransom who was set free from the priory and named the heir of Harkana by his father, the deceased king of the Harkans, Arko Hark-Wadi.

Harwen: capital city of Harkana, seat of Harkan power, home to the Hornring and the Horned Throne of Harkana.

High Desert: west of Sola, an arid region occupied by nomadic peoples, often referred to as outlanders or sand-dwellers.

Horned Throne, the: the Harkan seat of power, located in the King's Hall of the Hornring.

Hornring: Harwen's keep, home of the Hark-Wadi family and the Horned Throne of Harkana.

Horu: brother of Mithra-Sol, the Soleri god of death and war.

House of Ministers: the administrative center of the empire, the chief clearinghouse for all messages coming in and out of the empire's capital.

House of Viziers: refers to the structure that stands along the Rellian Way as well as the actual body of viziers. In the time before the empire, the viziers ruled Solus as a collective body. After the formation of the empire, this legislative body's powers became largely symbolic.

Hykso: a nomadic High Desert clan common to the southern regions of the High Desert, as well as the borderlands between Harkana and Sola.

Jundi: the foot soldiers of the Protector's Army.

Kiltet: a service cult dedicated to the maintenance and protection of the grounds of the Empyreal Domain.

kingsguard: also the black shields, the sworn soldiers of the king of the Harkans.

kite: a large, black-feathered bird, a sacred animal, worshipped in parts of Feren, the symbol of the Feren king or queen's divine rite of rule.

Kitelord: a Feren king or queen who has endured the Waking Rite, a divine ruler.

Llyr: the *Kitefaethir,* mud god, the ancient god of Feren, god of the blackthorn trees.

Lower Kingdoms, the: the four kingdoms that serve beneath the Soleri Empire: Harkana, Rachis, Feren, and the Wyrre.

Middle Kingdom of the Soleri: the Amber Age, the Age of Marvels, the time when the Soleri built the miracles of Solus: the Dromus, the Golden Hall, the Cenotaph, and the Great Circus of Re.

Mithra's Door: a passage reserved for the Mother Priestess, used in the Middle and New Kingdoms, blocked after the War of the Four but opened again by Sarra Amunet, this corridor connects the Ata'Sol to the Empyreal Domain.

Mithra's Flame: a literal trial by fire, if the accused live they are innocent, if they die they are found guilty by the sun god.

Mithra-Sol: the sun god and father of the gods, father of Re and Pyras.

Mosi, Sevin: captain of Merit's guard, a man from the Wadi clan, one of Merit's sworn soldiers.

Mundus of Ceres, the: a large dome located in the Waset, the seal that covers the Well of Horu. As part of the annual schedule of feasts in the city of Solus, the Mundus is opened each year for a two-day festival. The lower portion of the structure predates the founding of the Old Kingdom.

New Kingdom of the Soleri, the: the present age, also known as the Imperial Age, includes the time of the Soleri's sequester behind the Shroud Wall.

Odine, Nollin: a boy from the Wyrre, a scribe of the hierophantic order of the Desouk cult, who journeyed with Sarra Amunet and discovered the remains of the Soleri in a solar in the Shambles of Harkana.

Old Kingdom of the Soleri: the first age of the Soleri, ends with the unification of Sola and the lower kingdoms.

Ott: Sarra Amunet's personal scribe and son, the trueborn son of Arko and Sarra, rightful heir to the Harkan throne.

Plague Road, the: the road that connects Solus to Harwen.

Plaza of Miracles, the: renamed as such by Ined Anu during the construction of the adjacent statuary garden, this square is the largest public space in Sola. It faces the Shroud Wall on one side and the Statuary Garden of Den on the other.

Priory of Tolemy, the: also the House of Tolemy, a prison-like school where the noble-born sons of the lower kingdoms are held until their fathers are dead.

Protector's Tower: also the Citadel of Solus, the seat of power of the commander of the armies, the Father Protector.

Pyraethi, the: a family of gods, founded by Pyras and descended from Mithra-Sol, twelve in all—a father, a mother, and ten children—and rulers of the first empire in the time before the Soleri.

Pyras: the first of the Pyraethi and founder of their empire, the first child of Mithra-Sol.

Rachis: a mountain kingdom, north of Harkana, east of Feren, home to the mountain lords, one of the four lower kingdoms of the Soleri Empire.

Re: the first emperor of the Soleri and the founder of their empire, the second child of Mithra-Sol.

Rellian Way, the: the largest and most prominent street in the Waset, home to the house of Ministers, the Circus of Re, the House of Viziers, and the Plaza of Miracles.

Repository at Desouk: the largest library of scrolls in the Soleri Empire.

Rifka: the High City, seat of power of the Feren king or queen, home to the Blackthorn Chathair.

Saad, Amen: the former Sword of Mithra, the Father Protector and commander of Sola's armies, deceased.

Saad, Mered: uncle of Amen, brother of Raden, a wealthy, highborn citizen of Solus, figurehead of the prominent military family.

Saad, Raden: Father of Amen, deceased.

scribe: a priest of any faith who dedicates his life to scrollwork.

second death, the: a body must be whole to pass into the afterlife; if a corpse is dismembered it dies a second death and is denied entrance in to the world of the deceased.

Shadow Gate, the: an archway in the Shroud Wall, the ceremonial entry to the Empyreal Domain of the Soleri.

Shambles, the: in Harkana, south of the Feren Rift valley, a desolate stretch of land, home to the sacred rite of the king of Harkans, the Elden Hunt, and the hidden palace of the Soleri.

Shroud Wall, the: at the center of the empire's capital, the barrier that separates the Empyreal Domain of the Soleri from the city of Solus.

Sirra, Tye: the only girl in the priory, the daughter of a prominent lord of the Wyrre, friend of Rennon Hark-Wadi, freed from the priory by Ren.

Sola: the kingdom ruled by the Soleri.

Soleri, the: a family of gods, founded by Re and descended from Mithra-Sol, twelve in all—a father, a mother, and ten children—and rulers of the Soleri Empire.

Solus: capital city of the kingdom of Sola and the Soleri Empire.

Statuary Garden of Den, the: constructed after the reign of Den by Ined Anu, the sculpture garden sits adjacent to the Plaza of Miracles and contains twelve golden statues set among winding garden paths.

Stone Forest, the: also the Cragwood, the site of the Waking Rite, the Feren ruler's sacred rite of passage.

Temple of Mithra at Desouk: the first temple of the Mithra cult, an ancient open-air structure in the city of priests.

Temple of Mithra at Solus: in Sola, the temple of the sun god, and home to the Ata'Sol.

Ulfer: the first king of Harkana, the first to take the eld horns as his symbol.

Wadi, Nirus: deceased, former king of the Harkans, and later the Harkan emperor, the man who held the Amber Throne during the War of the Four, two hundred years prior to the present day.

Wadi, Shenn: husband of Merit Hark-Wadi, a tribal lord of the Wadi clan.

Waking Rite, the: also the Night Vigil, the Feren ruler's sacred rite of passage. The time when the kite chooses to support the rule of a would-be king or queen, elevating them to the status of Kitelord, divine ruler of Feren.

War of the Four, the: during the rule of Sekhem Den, the revolt of the four lower kingdoms against Sola. Led by Nirus Wadi, the lower kingdoms joined their armies and rebelled against the armies of the Soleri. The Harkan emperor held the Soleri throne in Solus for twenty years before the Protector, Ined Anu, routed the Harkans, taking back the capital city of Solus and defeating Nirus. After the war, the Soleri instituted a system of tributes to admonish the four lower kingdoms. The noble-born daughters of each kingdom were forced into politically inconvenient marriages, while the noble-born sons were kept in Tolemy's House, the priory, until their fathers died, thus weakening the royal lines of the lower kingdoms.

Waset, the: in Solus, the old city, the most ancient precinct of the holy city of the Soleri, home to the Golden Hall, the Cenotaph, the Shroud Wall, the Hall of Ministers, the House of Viziers, the Statuary Garden of Den, the ruins of the Antechamber and the priory, the necropolis, the Plaza of Miracles, and the Empyreal Domain.

Wat, Khalden: chief adviser and first servant of the Ray of the Sun.

Well of Horu: an ancient structure that predates the Old Kingdom of the Soleri, a deep well with a spiral ramp at its midpoint. The ramp is accessed by way of tunnels in the Hollows. The Mundus of Ceres covers the well.

White-Wall district, the: home to the highborn families of Solus, this district sits just outside the Waset and is known for its famously tall and well-polished white walls.

Wyrre, the: also the Southern Islands, a vast archipelago composed of more than a thousand islands, one of the four lower kingdoms of the Soleri Empire.

Zagre: city of birds, capital of Rachis, seat of Rachin power.

ACKNOWLEDGMENTS

My wife, Melissa, and daughter, Mattea, deserve more thanks than I could ever hope to offer them. Also, Richard Abate, my agent, cannot be thanked enough. Thanks are also due to Chris, Loni, and Samantha at Zoic. And at Tor, credit is owed to Bob Gleason, Elayne Becker, and Robert Davis.

ABOUT THE AUTHOR

MICHAEL JOHNSTON has always been an avid reader of science fiction and fantasy. He studied architecture and ancient history at Lehigh University and earned a master's degree in architecture from Columbia University. Johnston worked as an architect in New York City before switching to writing full time. He lives in Los Angeles with his wife and daughter.